CHEROKEE ROSE

A NOVEL INSPIRED BY THE WEST'S FIRST COWGIRL

JUDY ALTER

TWODOT®

ESSEX, CONNECTICUT
HELENA, MONTANA

For Uncle Bob,
who made riders of
my children and, sometimes,
a better person of me,
in grateful memory.

A · TWODOT® · BOOK

An imprint of Globe Pequot, the trade division of
The Rowman & Littlefield Publishing Group, Inc.
4501 Forbes Blvd., Ste. 200
Lanham, MD 20706
www.rowman.com

Distributed by NATIONAL BOOK NETWORK

Copyright © 2022 by Judy Alter
First published by Bantam Books, New York, 1996
ePublishing Works!, 2013
First TwoDot edition published 2022

British Library Cataloguing in Publication Information available

Library of Congress Cataloging-in-Publication Data available
ISBN 978-1-4930-5271-4 (paper : alk paper)
ISBN 978-1-4930-5272-1 (electronic)

∞™ The paper used in this publication meets the minimum requirements of American
National Standard for Information Sciences—Permanence of Paper for Printed Library
Materials, ANSI/NISO Z39.48-1992.

PART ONE

CHAPTER 1

Men and horses—I've known a lot of both in my time, but the horses never caused me any trouble, only the men. Whether I was roping or riding or both, I could always make a horse go the way I wanted. But men, from cowboys and presidents to husbands and lovers, baffled me—and still do to this day. But I wouldn't have traded a minute of my life as a cowgirl for anything, especially not a life that some would think more "respectable." I've ridden with Wild West shows from Oklahoma to New York to London, and along the way there've been exciting times, a few romances, and a few women I called sister and meant it—not that silly feminist business they talk about today.

Everyone thought President Theodore Roosevelt first called me a cowgirl, but in truth, some snobbish girls in a St. Louis convent had christened me that earlier. Still, when Roosevelt made the name public, it stuck. For a time there, when people heard the word *cowgirl,* they thought of me. Sometimes folks would say, "You mean like Annie Oakley?" but the question made me furious. Annie was a lot older than me, for one thing—she'd been in Wild West shows since about 1886, before I was born, for goodness' sake! And she wasn't a westerner, she hadn't grown up roping and riding like I had. She was from Ohio, of all places, and she told me once she never rode a horse until two or three years after she joined Buffalo Bill's show.

And Annie, she was flat dull. They used to talk about how she "tripped" onto the stage, smiling and bowing like everybody's little sister. She spent her free time sitting in a tent sewing a fine seam. That's what she was like off the stage and out of the arena—everybody's little sister. She married Frank Butler before she was old enough to know what men were about. I made that early marriage mistake myself, but I didn't stay with it.

The big thing about me and Annie, of course, was that neither one of us was a trick rider. Somehow people got the notion that any woman in a Wild West show was a trick rider. But Annie was a shootist, the best there ever was, and I was a roper, and I'll be bold to say it—the best there ever was. Oh, I rode my share of broncs—wasn't afraid of the wildest horse you could show me, and I had a horse that could do some tricks—but I never had the stomach for the Roman ride, where you stand with each foot on a different horse, or all those fancy tricks that call for you to crawl under the belly of a galloping horse. The best I could do was to stand in the saddle, and by the time I'd learned to do that, it seemed to me every fourth girl I met could do the Roman stand. And then something happened that made me never want to trick ride again, but that's further on in my story.

Early on, some folks thought I was a man, 'cause everyone called me Tommy Jo. It was an unfortunate set of circumstances, all due to my mama, who named me Thomasina after her father, long departed this earth when I was born. My own father, a determined but eternally poor cattleman, short-ened it to Tommy and added the Jo because, as he said, "it fits." Fight though Mama would, nothing else ever stuck on me. I was Tommy Jo "Cowgirl" Burns in the show ring and out—until I changed it to Cherokee Rose. And I had a good reason for making that change.

Once some folks set out to prove I was a boy—wanted to undress me, I suspect because I was tall and thin and built like a boy till I was nearly grown. My hair was sandy-blond, like Papa's, and I wore it pulled back till I was eighteen, so that maybe from the front I did look like Papa's son, not his daughter. Papa thundered those folks off in no uncertain terms, let them know that I was a girl—and then added that I could ride better than any of their sons.

The Wild West shows are long gone, and few folks realize the truth of what women did in those shows—riding broncs, roping steers, all the things the men did. Some married cowboys and raised families; some greeted queens and rode for royalty in Europe; a few were hurt bad, like Fox Hastings, whose horse fell over on her, or Florence Randolph, who was carried out for dead several times. But up or down, we were bound together in a world no one understands—and we had more fun, more pure excitement than any movie star today could know or dream about.

There's one more thing—or maybe one more misconception: it's easy, all these years later, to think that all the cowgirls who rode in Wild West shows were cowboys in feminine garb, women who would rather be men. Nothing could be further from the truth, and I guess I'm the living proof. Oh, sure, I was a tomboy, but my mama sent me to a convent where I learned to talk properly, to mind my manners, and then I mixed with some swell folk because of the shows . . . at my best, I could have drunk tea with the Queen of England and never slurped a sip. But that was a long time ago, a different life it seems, now that I'm growing old back on an Oklahoma ranch, actin' just like the plain folks that I come from.

So this is a story of a special band of women, the times they shared, the men they loved—and the horses they rode.

Like lots of ranch-bred girls, I was more boy than girl as a youngster, mostly because Papa didn't have a son to teach everything he knew about horses and cattle. Papa was a born cowboy from down in Texas. He'd ridden up the Chisholm Trail behind great herds of cattle with his own father, just after the Civil War, and he'd never known any other life but being a cowboy, never had much schooling beyond a few years in Texas while his father was off fighting for the Confederacy. When my grandpa—whom I never knew—came back from the war, he pulled Papa out of school and put him to work herding cattle. After Grandpa Burns died—thrown off a cantakerous horse—Papa drifted a few years from this ranch to that and finally settled in the Cherokee Strip, only because Mr. Luckett offered him a job. Mr. Luckett lived in Guthrie and didn't have much to do with the ranch, other than to check the books, so Papa got to act like he owned it, and that suited him fine. I suspect sometimes he even passed himself off as a ranch owner, when he was sure it was someone who'd never find out the truth—like a city slicker in St. Louis.

His years in the saddle had made Papa tall, lean, bowlegged, and permanently sunburned, though his forehead above his hat line was startlingly white. Papa was a man who, as some folks said, "cut a wide swath." Everybody else in the world called him Sandy—yes, it was a corny name and sounded like every third cowboy you met, but it really fit Papa because his hair was a reddish-gold color and even his mustache matched. His face was generally burned the same shade. The whole effect when you looked at him was like looking at a man who was all one color—sand color, with lots of red highlights like our Oklahoma mud.

But Mama always called him James.

We lived on the Luckett spread, some fifteen miles north of Guthrie, which was a city full of red brick buildings, lots of history, and as far as I was concerned, all the things interesting in the world, from Miss Lizzie's boardinghouse—Papa always rushed me by it, though I asked about the music coming from upstairs, and he once turned red when a pretty lady stuck her head out the window and hailed him by name—to the printing company where great presses clacked and rolled. I used to peek in the basement windows to watch them, and then Papa let me read the newspapers they printed.

" 'Course," he said, "the St. Louis paper is better."

Papa always took the St. Louis paper and read it like he had a fortune invested in that city. "Man needs to know what's going on in the world," he'd say pompously. I always thought he subscribed to the St. Louis paper, way out there in the Cherokee Strip, because he wanted to impress Mama.

Mama was as dark as Papa was fair and far prettier than I could ever hope to be. She was tall like Papa—I got my height from both of them—and as graceful when she walked as Papa was on a horse. They'd met in St. Louis, where Mama was teaching school and going to afternoon tea dances—she could dance like the angels had taught her—and thoroughly enjoying the life of a young woman in the city.

Papa rode in with some cattle and met Mama in the city park—she always swore that someone introduced them because she never would have spoken to a stranger—and fell right in love with her, or so he said. I suspect he saw her as a challenge. Anyway, when she allowed him to walk her home, he asked her to marry him, and she was indignant.

"I will not follow a cowboy around from pillar to post," Mama told him, in a story that she often repeated. In the telling, she would be seated placidly in a rocking chair in our house in Oklahoma, but her description conveyed the splendor of a fine home in St. Louis where she'd boarded as a teacher. Behind her words though, I heard the angry frustration of a woman who now had little control over where and how she lived.

"You'll have a house and we'll raise babies—and, oh, it will be fine," he told her.

Now Mama never confessed it, but I suspect she had been a little bit lonely in St. Louis. She had no family except an aunt who had raised her with propriety but little love, and she probably didn't see much future for herself beyond teaching and boarding in that fine house for years and years and growing old alone, though Papa always said he had to steal her before all those "city swells" turned her head.

But I think there was more than that. He was handsome, very masculine, determined, and very different from the men she met—and probably she thought him irresistible. Mama left that house in St. Louis with its polished wood floors and velvet drapes, its gas chandeliers and fine oak furniture, and moved to a one-room dugout in the Indian Territory where the floor and walls were dirt, the nearest neighbors were six miles away by horseback, and Papa sometimes left her alone for long spells of time.

"We lived in that dugout two years," Mama would tell me, smoothing back a strand of gray-black hair that had escaped its pinning at the back of her neck, "and I hated every minute of it. I got so mad at your father that I barely spoke to him, but he never seemed to notice. He was hell-bent on raising cattle and horses, and that was all he thought about."

And whether she talked to him or not, the babies came along—two little boys were born before me, but neither lived over a few hours. There were two tiny graves on a hillside not far from the dugout. Mama never spoke of them—and she sure never hinted that they might have lived had she not borne them in a dugout far from anybody—but those graves must have silently accused Papa each time he looked in that direction. And I suspect he gave up on having sons—I always thought that was why he was so ready to give up his dream of being a big rancher himself and go to work for Mr. Luckett.

Papa was gone a lot—"ranch business," he would tell me—for days at a time, just long enough for Mama and me to settle into a routine and for her to think she could civilize me, and then Papa would come home, and I'd be out on the range again.

Mama and Papa loved each other—I never doubted that—but I never understood how they could love each other and yet be so angry so much of the time. She should have loved a banker in St. Louis, not a rancher in Oklahoma, and he should have had a wife who could ride and rope, the kind of woman he was training me to be. I used to think God had gotten his signals crossed when he let those two fall in love. I had no idea then how often those signals get crossed.

My first memory is of horses, of being held in the saddle in front of Papa while he rode across the prairie. The land was rolling prairie—not as flat as Kansas to the north nor as barren as eastern Colorado beyond us. Bluestem grass was horse-high in some places, and there were streams aplenty for horses and cattle to water. Sometimes the banks of a stream, hidden in a shallow valley, would be tangled with wild plum thickets and shadowed by tall pecan trees. Wild turkey and prairie chickens flew up when you rode through, and deer were plentiful. "No wonder the Indians wanted to keep this land," Papa said more than once. "But God made it for horses and cattle and ranchers."

So much for the Indians' right to the land.

When he spurred his horse to a gallop or turned it quickly to rope a balky steer, Papa would say, "Hang on to the horn, Tommy Jo!"

And my hands would grab tight to the horn while the world tilted crazily as the horse wheeled and turned, the wind flew at me, and the earth rushed by as we galloped. Papa, his hands busy with a rope and his attention on his cattle, never held on to me.

"She'll fall and be killed by the horses' hooves, James," Mama would say with a frantic tone edging into her voice, as Papa recounted our latest adventure. He and I would still be sitting ahorseback, and Mama, her long skirts blowing around her, would shade her eyes with her hand and stare up at Papa, anger in her clear blue eyes. Mama had ridden with Papa a time or two—at his insistence—but she was much more comfortable on the ground. She'd never in all her life understand the way Papa and I felt about sitting ahorseback.

Papa, mounted, towered over her, and maybe that was why he stayed mounted. On a horse, Papa was impressive, even commanding—and Mama knew it.

"Tommy Jo will learn the feel of a horse, Jess," he'd say when Mama met him in the corral, and I, young and not knowing any better, would echo, "I'll learn about horses, Mama. I'm safe, I really am."

Mama would turn away in defeat, and I was too young to understand her fears and her resentment of Papa. Her name was Jessica, but he always shortened it to Jess, just like he called me Tommy. Mama didn't look like a Jess to me—she was far too ladylike.

By six or seven, I was riding a big horse alongside Papa when he worked his cattle. He had given me a bay horse named Sam. Riding a horse instead of a pony meant that I could keep up with Papa, and to me riding Sam was the most wonderful thing in the world. Sitting on the back of that big horse, I was queen of all I surveyed.

Sometimes in the mornings, Sam was hard to ride. He'd pitch and toss, as though daring me to stay on his back, but stay I did. The few times he threw me off, I got right back on. Papa had taught me well that whenever you were thrown, you got right back on. Sam was never the boss—I was.

But then, that's what I say about horses—they never gave me any real trouble, and I could always get them to do what I wanted.

"Pretty soon we'll be letting you break the green horses," Papa laughed one morning, after he watched me disagree with Sam and win the disagreement.

"Could I, Papa?"

"No."

But he had planted the idea, and riding rough horses became a goal tucked in the back of my mind. Sometimes I goaded Sam into his pitch-and-buck performances just so I could ride out the storm on his back. By the time I was ten or twelve, I was sneaking rides on the green horses without Papa knowing. One time it got me in real trouble.

"Bet you can't ride that gray," teased Casey, one of the cowboys who worked for Papa on the Luckett spread. The gray—a strong horse, just a shade taller than the others, with a fine head and strong neck—was really midnight black with a dusting of light gray, as though river dust had drifted down over him. The animal reared back and lashed out with his hooves when Casey and his helper, Wilks, tried to blindfold him and put a hacka-more on. They cursed and yelled and held tight to the rope, and eventually the horse was snubbed to a post in the middle of the corral.

"Bet I can," I answered.

"Just teasin', Miss Tommy Jo, just teasin'. Your pa'd skin me alive if I let you on this horse."

"He'll never know till it's over—and then he'll have to give me the horse."

"You've got Sam," muttered Wilks, who rode a horse clearly inferior to Sam.

"Just hold him," I ordered in a commanding tone of voice. I'd learned early that if I gave commands instead of asking favors, I usually got what I wanted—later I'd get into disastrous trouble with that philosophy, but this time it worked.

I looked at the horse again—there was probably just a little mustang in him, but he wasn't too far from pure quarterhorse, with powerful hind quarters and a strongly muscled chest. But it was that dusted black coat that set him apart from any other horse I'd ever seen. "Devildust!" I breathed.

"What kind of nonsense are you talking now?" Casey demanded.

"Devildust," I said. "That's his name."

"You don't go namin' some range horse that'll go to the show ring," he said.

"The show ring?" I asked.

"Yeah. Your pa's got him a contract to provide bucking stock for the Buffalo Bill Wild West, no less!"

Now, everyone knew about Buffalo Bill's show. I'd even read about it in that St. Louis paper that Papa took. In the Wild West show Annie Oakley shot glass balls or playing cards, hitting 950 out of 1,000, and Indians massacred settlers every day for spellbound audiences; brass bands played, beautiful women rode rough and trick horses, and Sitting Bull, the infamous Indian chief, signed autographs. The show traveled all over the country, drawing thousands of people to its performances and filling them with wild and woolly images of life on the frontier. I hungered to see Buffalo Bill and Annie, though Papa scoffed at it and said, "It's all made up. None of that is the way life really was with horses and Indians."

For Papa, realism was essential, but I lived on dreams.

And now this horse—Devildust—would go to the show that I longed to see. If I could just ride him, I thought, I'd somehow have a link to Buffalo Bill and his show. Perhaps someday, five years hence, I could present myself to him and say, "I broke a horse that's in your show." And then, in my fantasy, Devildust would nicker and break loose from the herd, coming to nuzzle me affectionately.

"You can't ride this horse, Tommy Jo." Casey broke into my reverie. "It's too dangerous."

"Just hold him," I said, and without giving Casey a chance to refuse, I put one foot in the stirrup and jumped onto the back of that quivering mass of muscle. That sudden mount was, of course, a mistake—even I knew I should have quieted the horse, let him get the sense of me, before I jumped on his back. But I was afraid Casey would win out, and so I learned that old lesson about mistakes made in haste.

Wilks was the one who removed the blindfold and turned the horse loose. I always thought Wilks resented me—the foreman's daughter who had a finer horse than he did and rode it better too—I think he was ready to see me get into trouble this time.

I never could recall the fraction of time between Wilks's turning the horse loose and my landing on the ground so hard, it took a minute for me to get my senses. As I shook my head, I saw Devildust across the corral, still pitching as though to shake the memory of me off his back.

"Catch him," I said, getting shakily to my feet. "I got to get back on."

"Now, Miss Tommy Jo . . ." Casey was clearly upset.

Wilks caught the horse and got him snubbed again, without ever saying a word to me.

The horse had learned something the first time. He stood quietly now for a minute, just long enough to give me a false sense of security, and then he was off—whirling, jumping, arching his back, and finally flinging me off his back like a gnat. I landed ingloriously in a heap, almost on top of a fencepost.

"Put the horse up, Casey." Papa's voice cut through my fog clearly. "I'll see to Tommy Jo." He hunkered down next to me. "You all right?"

"Yessir. I think so." I wouldn't admit to the light-headedness I felt, nor the sharp pain in the elbow on which I'd landed.

"Good, 'cause I'm gonna tan your hide, and neither one of us is gonna mention any of this to your mama. You'll simply tell her you fell off Sam, and that'll cause enough anger in her for you to deal with. No need for her to know you were fool enough to jump on that horse without doin' it the right way."

And that's just what happened. Papa took a strap to my bottom, as though I were five years old, but the indignation hurt much worse than the blows. And then we explained my appearance to Mama by saying I'd parted company with Sam when a snake spooked him.

"I told you, James, that she shouldn't be out riding alone," Mama said. "You should be in school in St. Louis," she threatened, a specter that haunted me from that day. But Mama never forbade me to ride alone on the prairie—she knew better than to issue an order she couldn't enforce.

After that, I waited until Papa was around to ride the rough stock, because more than jumping on Devildust, that was really what I'd done wrong. Papa would have approved if he'd been there to authorize the ride first.

Devildust went off to the shows when Papa shipped a load of horses a month or so later, and I never saw that horse again—by the time I got to the Buffalo Bill show, he'd probably long been put out to pasture. But he stayed in my mind always.

By the time of the Devildust incident, we were living in the house on the Luckett place. Of white-painted wood, it sat on a rise in the land, its wide front veranda facing west so Mama could watch the sunsets and wouldn't, as Papa said, "be looking over her shoulder toward St. Louis." It was a long, low, one-room-deep house with a sitting room, a kitchen, and two bedrooms. Even the sitting room had linoleum and painted boards, though Mama longed for carpet and wallpaper. Papa had a desk in the corner of the sitting room, since his chores as foreman included paperwork. The desk was always strewn with papers and ledgers, and a pair of longhorns was mounted over it, giving a decidedly masculine air to the room. Mama bemoaned the fact that she had no real parlor for sitting in, but then, she had no guests to entertain in a parlor, either.

There were two objects in that house of which Mama was inordinately proud. One was her stove. Papa had sent to St. Louis for a Home Comfort Stove from the Wrought Iron Range Company. The stove boasted the company's motto, "Economy. Strength. Durability. Good Cooking. Good Eating." Papa always said the eating in our house improved ten times when he bought that stove, and Mama would look offended, as though her cooking hadn't been good enough beforehand. But those were not looks of anger—more of a joke shared tenderly between them. When they looked at each other like that, I felt an outsider.

Mama's other prize possession was the baby grand piano that Papa had also shipped from St. Louis. In Mama's mind, pianos stood for culture and refinement, and having that piano made all the difference to her, out on the prairie in that lonely little house. Often when I came in from riding, Mama would be playing her piano, lost to the music and not, in her mind, anywhere near the Cherokee Strip.

She did not allow me to touch the piano. "No, you must not," she'd say. "When you don't know what you're doing, you might damage it." Her psychology worked wonderfully. Even though Papa once said loudly, "Only girls play the piano"—implying that it wasn't an activity for me—I was desperate to learn because it was forbidden. My desperation soon wore off after a few lessons from Mama, but to this day I can pick out the old familiar hymns and it is sometimes a comfort to me to play "Nearer My God to Thee" and "What A Friend We Have in Jesus."

When Papa and the cowboys branded cattle, I always stayed in the corral, though Mama said it wasn't a proper place for a young lady. "I'm a cowhand," I replied in a boasting tone.

"That so?" Papa asked one day. "Then you best get to work. You can help hold these calves while we brand 'em."

And so, dressed in a calico wrapper because I had only come to watch, I knelt in the dirt, clinging for dear life to the rear legs of one squirming, bawling calf after another, while Papa and the cowboys held the other end, branded the flank, notched the ears, and treated for screwworms. Dirt and slobber and sometimes even a little blood flew at me, and I went home that first night so dirty, Mama made me undress on the porch—to my everlasting embarrassment—and bathe in a washtub before I could set foot inside.

"Papa eats in his dirty clothes!" I complained.

"Papa is Papa," she said, "and you are a young lady." Then she rolled her eyes heavenward as though seeking help to bear all her tribulations.

The calico wrapper was ruined and, once washed, became rags. Mama swore she thought about that day every time she dusted with a piece of that wrapper—and I thought those rags never would wear out.

The next day, though, Mama never said a word when I put on overalls and boots and headed for the corral. Silently she watched me go, with such a long look that I felt it behind me all the way to the barn. I guess Papa had persuaded her again, but she was rarely happy about Papa's "persuadings."

After my hard-earned lesson in branding, I wanted to be able to do everything Papa could do, including rope. With an extra rope of his that I found, I practiced secretly when he and the cowboys were away, building a loop as I'd seen Papa do it, then tossing it at the snubbing post in the corral. Time after time, it sailed through the air, only to fall limply alongside the post. I coiled it in and built a loop again, but I knew that I was doing something wrong. Only I didn't know who—except Papa—to ask, and I wanted badly to surprise him with a sudden great feat of roping.

Papa saw me one day, much to my mortification, and took the rope from me. "This way," he said, showing me how to build up the speed of the loop before I threw it. "Now try."

On my fifth try, I snagged the post.

"It'll be a while before you can try that on cattle," Papa said dryly.

One morning when I was ten—I remember the age distinctly—Papa announced at breakfast that we had calves scattered in the valleys to the west of us. "Wilks and Casey are away," he said, "and I need Tommy to ride with me."

"I need her to help me make preserves out of the plums she brought home yesterday," Mama said firmly.

"Plums," Papa answered, "can wait. Calves cannot. She'll ride with me today." He got up and strode for the door, pulling his hat off the rack as he went by. "We'll be home for dinner, Jess."

"Of course, James," Mama muttered as she watched us go. I knew that by midday, there'd be a dinner of beef and potatoes or chicken and dumplings—Papa liked a satisfying midday meal. I suppose I believed that Mama was never lonely when we were gone—after all, she had her stove and her piano, didn't she?

We rode west until we came to a small stream, its banks so thick with vines that no one could ride through them—a perfect hiding place for calves. Getting them out would be a dickens of a job unless the calves were spooked by commotion and came running out of their own accord—and then they'd have to be herded or they'd just run wild for the next thicket.

Papa and I spent four long hot hours riding through those thickets, yelling "Hee-yah!" at the top of our lungs. When a calf came bawling out, Papa's loop sailed through the air, and the calf was caught before it knew what had happened and was dragged to the branding fire before it could resist.

"Papa, you don't have any branding irons with you," I'd said when he first told me we were going to brand the calves before we turned them loose in the far pasture.

"Gonna use my saddle ring," he said. "You watch and learn something."

I gathered sticks and dried brush, and Papa built a small fire, fanning it until the flame took hold.

Papa threw each calf, but I watched how he did it carefully, so that I could do it next time. The only problem was that Papa hoisted the calf into the air, a feat far beyond my strength. But I was strong enough to hold the heads and front legs, except for one calf who managed a sharp kick on my shin. It startled me so that the calf near got away and Papa said sharply, "Don't be spooking these calves!"

I bit my lip to keep back tears of real pain and never mentioned my leg. Years later I realized it could well have been broken, and Papa would never have known.

Papa used his saddle ring to make marks that looked roughly like a T—an upward stroke and a shorter sidewise one, almost connected.

"Papa, that's not the Luckett brand," I said.

"No, it's your brand. These are your calves, for you to practice roping on. I talked to Mr. Luckett about it, and he agreed to give you ten calves. Otherwise, you and I wouldn't be out here bustin' calves out of thickets where they could just as well stay till we gather."

So that was why we were scratching ourselves on plum thickets and turning to puddles of sweat in the August heat—to give me a herd. 'Course, legend grew up that Papa had told me I could have any calves I roped, and pretty soon I had a herd of fifty, but that's not the truth. The way I told it here is the truth.

When it was real important to her, Mama could stand up to Papa with a ferocity that surprised all of us, mostly him. And if she dug in like a calf at the end of a rope, Mama generally got her way. Usually it had to do with me.

Every time Papa would say that I was a cowhand, Mama was quick to reply, "She's a lady, too. And she'll learn to act like one, if it's the last thing I see to." Mama was firm enough about the ladylike business that Papa never raised an objection when she taught me to cook on that prized Home Comfort Stove, though I grumbled from time to time that it wouldn't do me any good.

"I don't intend to spend my life over a range," I said haughtily.

"That's fine," Mama replied calmly, "but you will know what to do if you find yourself in front of one—or in front of a bunch of hungry men."

And so I learned to make mayonnaise dressing, to cook the wild plums into jelly, to wring a chicken's neck, to pluck and roast a turkey; even Papa admitted that I could put a fair meal on the table. "Mama's turkey dressing is a little more moist," he'd say, or "this piecrust isn't as flaky as I'd like." And then he'd add, "But Mama can't ride like you can, Tommy Jo," as though that made it all right.

Mama didn't have to get stubborn about lessons, for Papa agreed with her completely. She set the dates of the school year for me—from September to May—and the hours of the school day—mornings, from seven-thirty, when breakfast dishes were done, until noon. And then she became my teacher. There was no school close enough for me, and I studied at home until I had to spend that miserable year at a convent in St. Louis.

It was all my fault that I was sent to St. Louis when I was thirteen. One fine fall day, out riding Sam through the pastures, I found a bull that needed doctoring—or so I told myself. In truth, I probably just wanted to practice roping on something more challenging than the steers in my herd, who had by now been roped so often, they were fairly docile about it. Papa had gone off chasing strays, and I was angry that I'd been left behind, but Papa had said sternly he was leaving before school was out, and I was to stay and do lessons. Now that afternoon I had ridden out on the range and sat staring at a reddish-brown bull who lowered his head and stared back.

The bull, sensing my intentions, began to amble away from me, and I spurred Sam after him, building my loop as we went. Then, standing in my stirrups and leaning into the rope, I yelled "Yee-hah!" and let sail the most perfect loop I'd ever made. It settled over the bull's neck, and Sam began to back up, drawing the rope taut.

The bull had other ideas. Snorting, he stomped once and then put all his weight into pulling against the rope. Before I really knew what had happened, the bull was off and running, and Sam broke into a fast gallop out of the necessity to keep up. The rope was dallied around my saddle horn, and Sam was obliged to follow the bull.

We were headed for a creekbed. At that point, if I could have stopped, believe me, I would. Ahead of us, the ground rose to the embankment, then dropped fairly sharply to the banks of a small stream. At the speed we were going, there was no way I could ride down that embankment, and I doubted that Sam would make it in one piece. With a quick prayer that was half apology to Sam for getting him into this, I flew off the horse, instinctively tucking myself into a ball as much as I could so that I would roll instead of landing "Splat!" flat on the ground.

Everything went quiet and dark for just a second when I landed, and then I was aware of Sam whinnying, which told me he hadn't been killed, and a loud thud heard in the back of my mind but not registered.

Shakily, I got to my feet. Once up, I was unsteady, but nothing was broken as far as I could tell.

"Sam?" I could hear him still whinnying, as though trying to tell me something. Looking ahead, I saw him standing motionless at the top of the embankment, the rope still around the saddle horn but now strangely slack. Forgetting my aches and pains, I raced toward my horse.

It took a minute to calm Sam—he skittered and half reared in fright, but I talked to him real quiet, like Papa had taught me, and he calmed down enough for me to hold the reins and look down the embankment.

There, motionless, lay the red bull, his neck at an odd angle. He was as dead as he could be.

"Broke his neck," I said to Sam, sure that he could understand me. "Papa's gonna be furious."

Papa's anger was less fearsome than Mama's. "I thought I'd taught you better than that," he said quietly.

"You taught me to rope," I said, "and I roped the bull. I just didn't know he'd run like that."

"Didn't know . . . You do know that a bull is too strong for you to handle," Papa said. "And when you don't know, you don't act. I thought I'd taught you caution, along with roping."

"I wasn't afraid of that bull," I muttered defiantly.

"Caution and fear are two different things. You could have killed Sam."

That I knew to be true, and it shamed me. I wished Papa would yell, even take a strap to me—which he hadn't done since I rode Devildust—anything but this calm talk.

"You could have killed yourself, too," Mama echoed, her voice louder than usual, and then I knew I was in for anger. Papa left the room, and Mama spoke to me in no uncertain terms about dangerous behavior and, even more important, being ladylike.

"You can be a cowhand if you want," she said firmly, "but you will also be a lady. If you don't, you'll bring yourself a load of grief you never expected. Men won't work with a woman who tries to be like them. If you can learn to be as much a lady as you are a cowhand, you might be all right." Her tone indicated some doubt about the latter.

I heard Mama's words, but I didn't *really* hear them. What did I know about men and their attitudes toward women? How could I understand, at thirteen, what she meant about being ladylike so that men wouldn't resent me? Those were hard lessons, to be learned over years, but never to be believed just because your mother told you so when you were young and green. "I know about ladylike," I said, struggling to hold on to the defiance that had given me courage.

"Good, then you'll get along well in the convent," Mama said calmly.

The convent! I heard the words as one would hear a death sentence. "I won't . . ." I began.

"Yes," she said with a voice of iron that I'd almost never heard from her before, "you will. And don't think about running away so far that we can't find you. Your papa would find you no matter where. And he's agreed with me *this time*." The emphasis was on the last two words.

I fled from the room to fling myself on my bed and melodramatically sob out my fears and anger. I'd never have admitted that I was as afraid as I was angry—but St. Louis was another world, miles away and different from the only place I'd ever known. The very word *city* had a certain terror about it, and I took no comfort from Mama's rose-colored recollections of the place.

Mama let me cry a good long time, and then she came to sit on the edge of the bed. "It won't be so bad," she said softly, smoothing my hair with one hand. "You'll learn manners and to sew fine stitches and—maybe a little French."

"You taught me all those things, 'cept the French," I said, my voice still quavery with tears, "and I don't need to know French. There's no one out here to talk it to, and we aren't likely to go to France anytime." I knew where France was because of Mama's insistence on geography, but nothing in my wildest imagination would ever suggest to me that I'd go to France. Shows how wrong you can be.

"I'll miss you," she went on, as though I hadn't spoken, "almost as much as your papa will—that's hard for you to believe, but it's true. I'm not sending you to the convent for punishment, Thomasina, and it's important that you understand that. I'm sending you, even though I'd rather have you here, because I love you."

It took me years to understand that and to figure out how lonely she was out there in that house, married to a man who intrigued her but with whom she had nothing in common and little to talk about. Her alternative was a tomboy daughter—better than no company—and yet with the best of intentions, she sent that daughter away.

Papa was to deliver me to the convent, though he wasn't any happier about it than I was. He stood by impassively as Mama hugged me.

"I'll miss you," she said, when she could have said a lot of things like "This is for your own good" and "Someday you'll thank me," but bless Mama, she didn't. She'd said it once, and she never repeated it her whole long life. That day she simply hugged me tight and then stepped back, but not quick enough to hide the tears in her eyes.

I'll come back ladylike, Mama, I vowed silently.

For a long time, I didn't understand why Mama didn't take me to St. Louis or even come with us. She was the one who loved the city, knew the convent, had aspirations for her daughter. This was, as it were, her project—and yet she made it Papa's responsibility to take me to St. Louis and deposit me at the convent while she stayed behind, alone, at the ranch.

Papa rode silently in the wagon for a long time, his eyes fixed straight ahead, never glancing at me. Finally, as though Mama had just spoken, he said, "I 'spect I'll miss you more than your mama, Tommy Jo. But I—well, I had to go along with your mama on this."

Why? I wanted to ask. *Why couldn't you tell her that I could be ladylike at home, without ever going to the convent?*

As if he'd read my mind, Papa said, "I tried for several years now to tell myself that you were growing up a lady, in spite of all the time you spent with me. That your mama's influence would win out—but I see that I was wrong. And I guess if I had to choose between having you a lady and having you a cowhand, I'd have to put ladylike first." It was an unusual speech for Papa.

"Mama says I'll be a better cowhand if I'm a lady," I said. "No, what she really said was that I'd get along better with the cowhands if I didn't try to be one of them." I thought about that a minute. "But Papa, I never cuss like they do, or sit around when they talk. I don't try to be one of them."

"There's more to it than that," Papa said, almost chuckling. "And I guess it's the convent's duty to teach you the difference."

We talked no more about it.

Now I have only vague memories of our arrival by wagon in Oklahoma City and the train ride from there to St. Louis. In St. Louis, Papa borrowed a carriage from a friend of Mr. Luckett, and we arrived at the convent in fine style but both as glum as calves on the end of a rope.

"This is it?" I asked, looking at a red brick building, three stories high, with a wrought-iron fence around it. Except that it was bigger than most, it could have passed for just another house in a neighborhood of fine homes. To me, they all looked like fortresses, for my idea of a house was long, low, and made of wood. There were bay windows at the corners of the second and third floors, fireplace chimneys—more than one—sprouting from the roof, and neatly trimmed hedges along the front of the building.

"This is it," Papa said.

Papa left me, and I had no way of knowing, for years, that it would be a full long week before he left St. Louis for the territory. But Mama knew—and that was why she hadn't come with us.

The convent taught me what Papa wanted me to learn—a sense of self-possession, if you will, and a certain kind of pride in myself. But not, I think, in the way that Papa meant.

"Thomasina," Mama had said tactfully before I left, "you might try not to talk about horses and cattle all the time. The girls at the convent—they won't understand."

"They're city girls?" I suggested.

"Yes, and they probably think the Indian Territory is the Wild West."

Mama's warning was prophetic. The girls treated me as a curiosity and an outcast. They called me Cowgirl.

"If men who work with cattle are cowboys," sang Abigail with the blond curls, "then you must be a cowgirl, because you work with cattle. Ugh! I think it's disgusting."

"It is not disgusting," I flared, never one to keep quiet. "It's good honest work, and it keeps you outdoors—and," I added boastfully, "I'm good at it."

"I'm sure I wouldn't want to be good at it," laughed Marcelline, daughter of a rich St. Louis banker. "I'd rather be good at the things ladies are supposed to do."

"Like what?" I challenged.

"Oh, cooking and sewing and keeping house," Marcelline said airily.

"I can do those things, too," I retorted. "I can cook and play the piano—and I know where France is."

This earned me howls of laughter that I didn't understand. But I did understand that arguing with them was a losing battle. Cowgirl I was, for the whole long year that I was at the school.

"Cowgirl, show us how you throw a rope!"

"Cowgirl, do the buffalo roam near your home?"

"Cowgirl, can you outride an Indian?"

If they'd known the truth about the Cherokee Strip, with its history of Indians, outlaws, and trail drives, they'd probably have been even more horrified. But none of them would have listened had I tried to tell them.

If they felt superior to me, perhaps I encouraged them, for I envied Abigail and Marcelline and the others who came from big homes in St. Louis and elsewhere—one girl was from Texas!—and whose fathers were bankers, lawyers, and merchants, while their mothers kept house and gave teas and lived the life that Mama always wanted. Sometimes jealousy ate away at me, and I had to hide tears of anger from the girls, who would have used those tears as another occasion to jibe at me.

Sister Maria Theresa, a diminutive nun who'd probably never seen a horse, saved the year, and me. "To ride a horse," she said, "is a fine skill. Not everyone can do it. If you are good at it, you should be very proud."

"I am good at it, Sister," I said.

"There is," she went on, "a fine line between justifiable pride in our accomplishments and appropriate humility. I hope that you will remember that always."

"Yes, Sister."

The more Sister Maria Theresa talked to me, the more determined I became to learn everything I could during that year—Papa had promised I had to stay no more than one school year—and then get back to what I loved doing. I began to take pride in what I learned at the school, from reading Shakespeare to speaking French—well, with an awkward accent, but I could read it. And I also began to stand tall when the girls teased me and called me Cowgirl. There wasn't, I decided, a name I'd like better.

The religious part of our instruction baffled me and left me feeling awkward. Mama had taught me prayers—"The Lord's Prayer" and "Now I Lay Me Down to Sleep"—but I'd never been to church. The rich pageantry of the Catholic service was a sudden shock to the sensibilities of a prairie girl, and no instruction was offered beforehand. The nuns assumed that everyone knew what to do. I found myself watching the girl in front of me carefully, kneeling when she did, bowing my head at her signal, wishing I could repeat the words that meant nothing to me.

"You did *not*," I wrote accusingly to Mama, "tell me about church. I feel like a fool."

Sister Maria Theresa rescued me again. "You are not comfortable in chapel, are you, child?"

"No, Sister, I never know what's going on. We had no church at home."

"And there's no guarantee you would have gone to the Catholic church if there were one," she said. "I believe your parents are"—she ruffled papers on her desk—"well, your mother lists herself as Methodist and your father put nothing." She could have said something about Papa finding religion in the sky and the prairie and the great outdoors—Papa himself would have made that trite claim—but she simply said, "The Lord does not require church attendance, I'm sure, but he would like you to have some familiarity with worship. We can do that for you."

And she led me through a typical service, giving me much-needed clues as to when I should sit, stand, or kneel, what the various symbols meant, and who the men in front of the church were. It was too much in one lesson, but by the end of the year I had a grounding in the Catholic faith—and a yearning for spiritual certainties that even Catholicism didn't offer.

There was one more lesson I took away from the convent, though it surely was not what Mama intended. Late at night when the lights were out in the dormitory room in which all the first-form girls slept, there was hushed whispering and giggling about boys.

"Eddie McAdams is soooo cute—I wish he'd kiss me!"

"Lem Samuels says he'll take me to the Christmas dance. What will I wear?"

"How many boys have you kissed, Sheila? Tell the truth!"

"Only ten," came the giggling answer, "and your brother was the best kisser of all!" A pillow sailed through the air at the heartless Sheila.

I listened to it all with amazement.

"Cowgirl, what are the boys like where you live?"

"Uh . . . ah, . . . there aren't any," I said truthfully.

"There are cowboys!" came in chorus from several girls.

"Oh, but they're all older, at least eighteen," I said, sure that they would understand.

"Older is better," said the knowledgeable Sheila. "They know things you don't. And when an experienced man kisses you . . ."

"Yes?" breathed an anxious voice to my right.

"Girls! Girls! Do I hear talking? Surely not. You must sleep now." Sister was making her rounds, and a hush fell over the long room with its double rows of metal cots. When Sister had had plenty of time to move on, the whispers began again.

"Tell us, Sheila—what happens when you kiss someone who knows how to kiss?"

Puffed up with superiority, Sheila sat up in the bed and shook her long red hair, now loosed from its proper daytime bun. "Well . . . there's kind of a tingle, kind of all over, and you feel—well, weak."

Choruses of "Oh" and "Aah" resounded around me. I couldn't imagine what she was talking about.

"That's when you have to be careful," she said, sounding as didactic as Sister Maria Theresa did in mathematics class. "If you don't watch, a boy can take advantage—touch you where he shouldn't, all kinds of things. You can't let that weak feeling take over. But oh, it's nice!"

Silence fell, soon broken by a few gentle snores, but I'm sure there were girls who lay awake for hours daydreaming about Eddie McAdams or Lem Samuels touching them in forbidden places—where, for heaven's sake? I was left to realize that I had no one, no young boy, to fantasize about. I soon invented one.

His name was James, just like Papa, though I never examined the importance of that coincidence, and he could ride like the wind. I forget—truly—what he looked like, but I know that he could ride and rope better than I, and that he liked me better than all other girls because I could keep up with him on horseback. When we rode back to the ranch at night after a long day on the prairie, he kissed me tenderly—but there my fantasy grew sparse, for I didn't know what to imagine, what forbidden places Sheila talked of in hushed tones.

Papa came for me in the spring. I thought he had dressed for the occasion, for he was resplendent in a pinstripe suit with matching vest, its wide lapels very current, and a black derby on his head, his shirt collar stiff, and below it a paisley tie carefully knotted. Years later, I realized he had probably been in St. Louis, dressed like that, for days before I saw him.

"Papa!" I exclaimed too fast, putting my mouth into action before my brain. "You have new clothes!"

"Uh, no, not really."

"Mama will be so impressed," I said, knowing that Mama would probably ask some pointed question about where he intended to wear such clothes once he got me home from St. Louis.

"I—I better buy her something wonderful to make up for all this," he said, sweeping a hand down his body as though to point to the clothes. "I wanted to look like the other fathers, Tommy Jo, when I came to pick you up. You know, make you proud."

"Like a St. Louis banker?" I asked, and then rushed on, "Oh, Papa, you look just fine—and I'd have been proud of you in high-heeled boots and a Stetson!" And I meant it—that was part of the self-possession I'd learned. My papa was who he was, not a St. Louis banker, and I wouldn't have traded. But I didn't really know much about my papa.

I said my good-byes to Sister Maria Theresa and paid the required formal visit to the Mother Superior, but when Papa asked if I didn't have friends to take leave of, I lied and said I'd already done that. Poor Papa—all dressed up and the only people who saw him were two nuns!

We didn't talk about school until we were settled on the train.

"You look different, Tommy Jo—older. I hope I—we—haven't done the wrong thing sending you there."

"I was bound to get older someday, Papa."

He turned his head toward the window, almost avoiding me. "Yes, I guess you were. But"—and then he whirled to face me—"can you still ride?"

"I hope so," I said fervently. "I really hope so."

"That's my girl!" he said, so loudly that others in the car turned to look at us.

It was left for Mama to ask the questions about French and decorum and all those things, and she was apparently satisfied with the answers.

"I—I see a difference in you," she said, having come into my bedroom late my first night back home. "You're . . . you know who you are."

"I had to learn," I laughed, "or else feel that a cowgirl was the worst possible thing I could be. That's what they called me, the girls."

"Did you make friends?"

"No."

"Were you lonely?" Her voice caught, as though she were sharing my misery of those past months.

"Yes."

"Oh, my child!" She wrapped me in her arms, and I could feel her tears on my face. "The things we do to fit into the world!"

I should have soothed her and told her I knew she had sent me away for all the best reasons. Now that I was home, I should have lessened her guilt, but the year had been too long, and I said nothing. Mama had not learned, any more than Papa, to be who she was. Out on a ranch in the Cherokee Strip, she was still trying to be a St. Louis society lady—and to mold me in that image.

The next morning, after breakfast, I rode with Papa. Mama stayed behind with her Home Comfort Stove and her piano.

CHAPTER 2

My career as a Wild West star really began with a wolf hunt staged for Theodore Roosevelt.

"Tommy Jo, you want to meet the President of the United States?" Papa stood before me, grinning fit to beat all.

"Meet him?" I asked in amazement.

"Jack Abernathy, the marshal who catches wolves by hand, is supposed to put on a wolf hunt for him next month. Some Texas cattlemen have invited Roosevelt to visit, and they've set this thing up. Luckett knows these men, and he's got us an invitation, says I ought to take you. TR would really be tickled by a girl who can outride any of the cowboys."

"TR?" Mama asked, with a sort of half-smile. "Do you know him that well, James?" Without waiting for him to reply, she went on archly, "Thomasina is *not* a cowboy."

"No," Papa grinned, "but she rides better than most of 'em, and Roosevelt admires skill with a horse. She'll do it, Mrs. Burns." He left no room for argument. Papa could almost always do that with Mama, charm her into agreeing with him. But sometimes charm didn't work, and if it was something that he felt real strong about, Papa would quit smiling and just tell Mama how it was gonna be. And she generally went along, though I often saw her clench her teeth as she turned away from him. When he called her Mrs. Burns, both Mama and I knew it was one of those times when Papa was going to ride roughshod over whatever she said or wanted.

Mama sputtered and fussed and warned, "She'll end up a cowboy, no matter what you say, unless you start treating her like a lady, James."

"But that's the whole point," he protested. "It's just because she *is* a lady that Luckett wants her to ride."

"Will she ride sidesaddle in a proper dress?"

I shuddered at the thought.

"Well, no . . . I don't think she could ride a bronc that way. She'll wear that split skirt you made for her." He smiled, back to using charm to coax Mama out of her unhappiness.

Mama had taken heavy cotton corduroy and made me a wide, full skirt that was really split into pants. It was so full that you almost couldn't tell it wasn't a dress when I walked—but I could ride astride in it. Mama had done that under duress, and she still had second thoughts about it.

"You ought to be riding sidesaddle like a proper lady," she said not once but a hundred times, "and you need to stay off those broncs. It's not ladylike."

"Mama? You're not worried about my breaking my neck?" I teased, giving her a hug.

"No," she said slowly, "I'm just worried about your being more boy than girl."

At fourteen, I was the youngest person on the wolf hunt, and almost the only girl. But I wasn't youngest by much—some of the cowmen had brought their sons, boys not much older than I. No, it wasn't my age that made me stick out like a sore thumb—it was my sex, though Papa seemed fairly oblivious to my distinction in the company that was gathered. Theodore Roosevelt was neither oblivious nor aloof—but that's later on in the telling.

The only other female was one of the wives of Chief Quanah Parker of the Comanches, and she slept in the only other tent, provided not by Parker but by the Texas cattlemen who leased lands from him. But that lady—I never learned her name—didn't venture outside the tent, and I think I saw her only once the entire five days we were in that camp.

The Texas cattlemen who invited Roosevelt on the hunt leased lands in the Indian Territory to graze their cattle, and they dealt with Quanah Parker on the leasing. I thought he was the most interesting Indian in the whole territory—son of the white captive Cynthia Ann Parker and her Comanche husband, Peta Nocona, he had been the fiercest of warriors until

Colonel Ranald Mackenzie whipped the Indians good at Palo Duro Canyon in the Texas Panhandle. After that, Quanah saw the inevitability of the Indians' defeat and was the most important chief to lead his men on the "white man's road." But he still had many wives, and he still wore funny clothes, including an out-of-place derby hat. I was intrigued by him, but I never got to talk to him—and I never got to talk to his wife. I wanted to ask her what it was like to be one of several wives. Papa and Mama sometimes had so much trouble getting along that I couldn't imagine multiplying it.

Papa brought me a small tent, having listened to Mama say that I absolutely could not sleep around the campfire with the men. I slept in my tent and wished I were around the campfire with the men.

"Burns, why'd you bring that girl? I mean, she's a nice enough young-ster, but a *girl* on a wolf hunt?" The voice, unidentifiable, drifted back to me as I lay in the tent, wrapped in blankets against the chill of an April evening. Embarrassed even though no one could see me, I burrowed down into those covers, but the voices followed me.

"Wha'dya mean, a girl?" Papa asked belligerently. "You brought your son, didn't you?"

"Well, of course," came the crisp answer. "Boys belong on hunts. But not girls. They need to stay home and tend to—well, you know, cooking and the like."

"Tommy Jo can outride any of 'em," Papa said, "any of them boys. And . . . well, I wanted her to have the experience."

"It's putting a damper on it for the rest of us," the voice continued. "Got to watch what we say, be careful how we act, where we pee, for God's sake."

"You don't got to watch nothin' for Tommy Jo," Papa said with a certain lack of chivalry. "She's just like your sons."

I cringed. I didn't want to be like anyone's sons, even though I didn't want to be like most people's daughters either.

"I think you ought to take her home," said another voice, this one more determined and angrier than the first. "She don't belong here."

"You want to make me?" Papa asked.

I slid to the opening of the tent and looked out. Papa, silhouetted by the firelight, stood with his legs apart, his fists clenched, staring almost nose to nose with a man no bigger than he, but no smaller either.

The other man stood firm and put his palm up, facing Papa. "I don't want to fight with you, Burns."

"Then quit talking about my daughter!" Papa's clenched fists came up, as though he were ready to strike.

I'd never before seen my papa so near out of control, though Lord knows I've seen many men since rush into a fight with less cause. But Papa—he was always in charge in my mind, and it terrified me that I could be the reason he'd fight. Many a woman is thrilled to have a man go to battle for her, but rarely when it's her father.

Just before I could scream, Papa said flatly, "She stays," in the same tone he sometimes used on Mama. And then he turned his back on the other man, as though daring him to hit a man from behind.

I held my breath as the other man wilted as though someone had let the air out of him. By then, I was sure Papa would have won in a fair fight. It was the closest I ever saw Papa come to a fight. And it was over me.

After that, the men kind of accepted but ignored me, though I could always feel them watching. One who watched me with a different kind of curiosity was Walt Denison, the nineteen-year-old son of a North Texas rancher who owned thousands and thousands of acres in the southeastern part of the state. At least, that was my estimate of his wealth.

"You sure do ride better than any girl I ever knew," he said once, sidling his horse right up next to mine.

Flustered, I said, "Thanks," and spurred Sam away.

"Hey," he called, "don't be leaving so fast. You and I could be good friends." He loped after me.

He was dark-headed, with curls that escaped under his Stetson and plastered themselves on the back of his neck, around his ears, even on his sideburns. His eyes were blue, though, and always laughing. When he looked at me, I thought of Sheila at the convent and Eddie McAdams who kissed so well and all those secret dreams about boys.

"What's your name?" he asked, his horse again almost on top of mine, so that between the animals our legs brushed.

"Tommy Jo," I faltered, "Tommy Jo Burns."

"I knew that," he said, grinning, "but I wanted to ask. All the men are talking about you being on this hunt 'cause your father treats you like a son."

"He does not!" I said indignantly, but then could say no more in defense of myself or Papa. "I got to look for my father," I said nervously, and stood in my stirrups searching for Papa, who was nowhere to be seen.

"How old are you?" he asked, almost angry.

"Fifteen," I lied.

"Fifteen!" he hooted. "Call me when you're seventeen, promise?

Name's Denison—Walt Denison." And with that he trotted after a group of men ahead of us.

I was left to ride alone and look for Papa.

Theodore Roosevelt was the first president the country ever had who appreciated what life on the frontier—or what was left of it—was like. A sickly and spindly young man, Roosevelt had gone to the Dakota Territory in his mid-twenties, stayed to ranch, and literally turned into a new person—he filled out physically to the figure now familiar from history books, not fat but certainly stocky. While he was a rancher, he welcomed every adventure that came his way—from hunting to a barroom brawl in which he decked an obnoxious drunk—and thereby earned the respect of cowboys. Once he was heard to say that it was in the West that "the romance of my life began."

Tom Waggoner of the Waggoner DDD Ranch and Burk Burnett of the Four Sixes, two of Texas's biggest and best-known ranches, had invited Roosevelt on this wolf hunt, hoping that he'd be so intrigued by the Big Pasture—lands granted to the Indians but leased annually by the Indians and the federal government to the ranchers for grazing—that he'd extend the right to graze in the territory. The government had declared an end to the leasing.

To lure the president to the Big Pasture, Waggoner and Burnett arranged to have Jack "Catch-'em-Alive" Abernathy hunt wolves with the president and show how he caught the wild animals by hand. Story was that Abernathy was once attacked by a wolf and had saved himself by thrusting his right hand into the wolf's mouth, grasping him under the jaw, and making it impossible for the animal to bite. He'd become so successful at this that he caught animals for zoos and exhibitions, making almost more money that way than from his salary as a United States marshal. Now the stakes were high—impress the President of the United States.

Besides Abernathy and Quanah Parker and Waggoner and Burnett, who'd arranged the hunt, there were Mr. Luckett, Papa, me, Walt Denison, Sr., his son, and several other ranchers from both Texas and Oklahoma that I never really met. Three of them had their young sons with them, so it was quite a crowd after those poor wolves. Then Waggoner and Burnett had brought the cooks and the foremen from their ranches, along with several cow ponies—there was great competition about whose ponies were the fastest and whose the president liked best.

The first morning, we all rode out in a knot, though I trailed behind some out of self-consciousness. Papa, pleased to be with the men, seemed to forget me and rode on ahead, almost right next to the president. I wouldn't have traded spots with him, for I knew being next to greatness would have made me tongue-tied.

Waggoner and Burnett had each brought a pack of greyhounds, and the dogs flew ahead of us to find the wolves. We followed on horseback—except for Mr. Luckett, who never rode horseback because of an injury and even herded cattle from a carriage. When the hounds flushed out a wolf, they held it at bay until the riders caught up. Then Abernathy jumped off his horse and grabbed the snarling animal by the jaw, and before you knew it the wolf was conquered.

The first time I saw Abernathy do this, I stared openmouthed in amazement. Wolves were one of the few things that scared me on the prairie, for I'd seen what they could do to calves and I thought of them as evil, our natural enemy. My idea of the way to deal with a wolf involved a rifle, and I couldn't imagine anyone pitting his own strength and cleverness against the wily animals without that advantage. Yet this Abernathy—a big, clean-shaven man who always wore a grin—seemed to like hunting wolves. Evidently, he also liked showing off for presidents.

"Another one for you, sir!" he called, holding up a struggling wolf that pawed the air helplessly.

"Bully!" Roosevelt cried. "I wish I could try it."

"Best not," Abernathy said modestly. "It'd be a shame for the President of the United States to lose a hand." And then he laughed as though to show that he had just been joking.

"Right, right," the president agreed, laughing with him. But he was not afraid to walk right up to the wolf that Abernathy held and examine him closely. "Remarkable!"

That was kind of how the first three days of the hunt went. We rode, Abernathy caught wolves, and we watched. The wolves were caged and sent to various zoos back east, though I knew the cattlemen would rather have killed their longtime enemies. Roosevelt prevailed on that point.

I began to think the hunt kind of boring, but Roosevelt seemed to enjoy himself thoroughly. If I'd thought a president would be dignified and distant, this one proved me wrong—he was always laughing, joking with the men, praising the coosie for the chuck, even talking to the horses. He called me "Little Lady" and, contrary to some others, didn't seem at all offended that I was part of the group.

When Sam was feisty in the morning and I had to hold on tight to prove I was the boss, the president praised my riding, saying he'd never seen a girl ride like that. He seemed impressed and even mentioned to Papa how proud he ought to be of my horsemanship. Papa, of course, puffed up with pleasure.

By the fourth day, I was tired of the monotony and ready to go home. But that morning, Papa insisted I ride near him.

"Tommy Jo, come right on up here," he kept urging.

I suspect he was by then feeling comfortable with the president and less reticent about pushing his daughter forward, since the president had bragged on me so. To keep Papa from talking louder, I rode forward as he told me, and next thing I knew I was between the president and Jack Abernathy.

Abernathy asked my age and allowed as how he had two sons right about the same age and that they'd ridden to New Mexico by themselves. I couldn't imagine any kind of a father letting two boys ride alone that far, but it wasn't my place to say so. After telling me that story, he ignored me, his concentration on the hounds ahead.

We rode for a long while that morning, the April sun turning warm enough to cause some discomfort. The hounds leaped and bounded and bayed, but they seemed unable to flush a wolf. Even Roosevelt wondered aloud if we should call it a day.

Then a change in the noise from the hounds, far enough ahead to be out of sight, alerted us. Frantic baying was followed by the ferocious growls of a fight, and everyone—myself included—put spurs to their horses. A large wolf, less easily cowed than the others the hounds had flushed, had turned on the dogs. By the time we got there, blood was dripping from two or three dogs—and probably the wolf—and a fierce battle was under way. All my fear and hatred of wolves vanished in admiration for this lone strong animal who took on a pack of hounds.

"I'll shoot the wolf!" Roosevelt cried excitedly.

"No! You'll hit my dogs!" That was Waggoner, whose pack was running that morning. "I can call 'em off."

"I'll get the wolf," Abernathy said with a kind of quiet confidence. "Call your dogs, Waggoner."

Waggoner called, and the hounds reluctantly backed off. With a firm hand on the reins, Abernathy rode his nervous horse almost up to the cornered wolf, who stood panting, too exhausted to growl. Abernathy jumped off his horse toward the wolf, but the wolf, perhaps more clever than we gave him credit for, chose that moment to back off further.

Without the wolf to land on, Jack Abernathy landed flat on the ground, the wind almost knocked clean out of him.

It was instinct, I guess. My rope was coiled—ever since Papa had taught me to rope, I kept a ready loop on my saddle—and I threw it. It sailed home, right over the head of the wolf. Without a command from me, Sam began backing, drawing the rope taut and pulling the wolf away from the hounds.

For a moment, there was complete silence. The men stared at me, openmouthed.

The wolf, on the end of a line, fought and kicked but could go nowhere.

"I'll take over, Little Lady," Abernathy said, pulling himself upright. "You've done a mighty piece of work." He grabbed the wolf in his usual manner, held it up in the air, and motioned to someone to slip my loop down over its body.

As I sat on my horse, coiling the loop, Roosevelt found his voice. "I—I've seen few men rope like that, Little Lady, but no women. Where'd you learn?"

"My papa," I answered, now tongue-tied and somewhat alarmed at what I'd been bold enough to do.

"She's a natural," Papa said with false modesty. "I only showed her a thing or two, and she practiced. Sometimes I wish I could rope like Tommy Jo."

The president repeated my name, as though memorizing it. "Tommy Jo," he said, "the cowgirl. You wait till I tell folks back east about this. Have you ever thought about Buffalo Bill's show? I bet you'd draw as many people as Annie Oakley!"

I simply blushed and looked down. That year, the Buffalo Bill was barnstorming the country with a new act especially in honor of the president. "The Battle of San Juan Hill" had replaced "Custer's Last Stand" as the battle for folks to see reenacted. I'd read about it in Papa's St. Louis newspaper. But I couldn't confess to the President of the United States that I dreamed of joining the show, of riding in the arena, of showing off for royalty. To think that Theodore Roosevelt himself thought I should do just that! I very nearly felt like I was going to fall off Sam from sheer dizziness.

Around the campfire that night, as we ate our beef and beans, I was the center of attention. Papa made much over me, putting his pride into words time and again, though trying hard to be tactful and modest about it, and Mr. Luckett acted like I was his daughter instead of his foreman's. The other men, one by one, congratulated me, offered their praise, and suggested my future lay in exhibitions. One even allowed as how he wished his son could rope as well as I could, but then he seemed embarrassed that he'd said that and turned away. The young boys mostly sat glowering at me—and I didn't blame them for being resentful.

Later in the evening, while the men sat around smoking, I wandered out a ways from the fire to stand staring at the sunset, thinking about wolves and their place on the prairie. A voice broke into my thoughts.

"Pretty proud of yourself, aren't you?"

I turned to see Walt Denison standing behind me, arms folded across his chest in a belligerent pose.

"No," I said slowly. "I just acted before I thought. I suspect I should have let someone else rope the wolf."

Then he laughed loudly. "Who?" he asked. "No one thought as fast as you did. You should be proud of yourself. But you may also have bought some trouble."

"What do you mean?" I asked, my heart thudding just from the uncertainty of talking to this young man, who was better looking than any of the boys the girls at the convent had dreamed about.

"Most men resent a woman who can do their work better than they can." He moved closer to me and spoke softly.

"Do you?" I asked, backing away nervously.

"No," he said, "not at all. I admire what you did." In one quick—and, I'm sure, practiced—movement, his arm was around my shoulders, and he leaned his face close to mine. "You're older than fifteen," he said, "at least in spirit."

Almost frantically, I put my hands up against his chest to push him away. If instinct guided me, as it had that morning, I would have hollered for Papa, but that somehow didn't enter my mind. And when he kissed me—gently, almost but not quite like a big brother—I did nothing.

He drew back and looked at me. "Someday—soon—you'll act different. I wish I could be there," he said. And then he was gone.

Papa packed us up for home the next morning, and it would be ten long years before I saw Walt Denison again.

But that last night on the hunt ended badly for me. The voices came again in the night as I lay in my tent, angry voices of men who accused Papa. They were not near as admiring of my roping as Walt had been nor as they themselves had been to my face.

"Ain't natural to have a girl rope and ride like that," said one, "and it makes boys look bad. Men are gonna resent her. You've got an old maid on your hands, Burns."

"Sure made my son mad," said another. "If it were my daughter—"

Suddenly Papa's voice—a little too loud—cut through the talk. "Well, it ain't your daughter. Tommy Jo's my daughter, and I'm proud of her. She'll be no old maid, and she'll probably always make your sons look second rate. But she ain't gonna change for their sake."

It took me some time to realize that Papa had really said what Walt Denison had. They both gave me something to live up to.

Next morning, when I was mounted and ready to go, the president walked over to stand by Sam. "Little Lady, we're going to have a bang-up parade in Washington for the Fourth of July, and I sure want to show those folks in the East what westerners are like. Suppose you could come ride with us?"

My heart did a flip-flop! All the way to Washington, D.C., to ride in a parade. As soon as my excitement rose, it died. It was too far, too expensive, impossible!

" 'Course she'll be there," Papa said heartily. "I'll bring her myself."

"I'll count on it," Roosevelt said. "We'll be in touch about the ar-rangements."

I don't remember a thing about the long ride back to Luckett's ranch, for my mind was far from the prairies and hills we crossed. Mentally I was riding down a broad street lined with cheering people.

"Ride in a parade!" Mama said. "Of course she won't, James."

"Oh yes she will, Jess. I gave my word to the President of the United States."

"Please, Mama," I begged, "it's a chance—"

"A chance for what?" she demanded, turning to busy herself at the stove so that we couldn't see the tears of anger in her eyes.

How could I tell her that it was a chance for me to someday ride in a Wild West show? I had figured it out that if I rode in that parade, someone might see me. In my wildest dreams Buffalo Bill stood next to the president and kept asking, "Who is that girl?"

"Name's Tommy Jo," the president would reply expansively. "I found her in Oklahoma. Rides like the wind, but you ought to see her rope."

"I must have her in my show," Buffalo Bill would say loudly. "I must!"

And the fantasy would end with me walking off toward a big circus tent, Buffalo Bill's arm around my shoulder as he offered me a starring position with the show. Of course, Papa was there, too.

But I couldn't tell any of that fantasy to Mama.

"A chance to see the capital, Mama. Won't you come too?"

"I will not!" she said. "I will not see my dreams and hopes for you turned into a joke, while you act like a boy and ride like a wild Indian." She stormed from the room, leaving me behind, stunned.

I stared at Papa a minute, but he was too shocked to say anything. Then, heartbroken because my mother was ashamed of me—for that was how I interpreted it—I ran outside, running blindly until I found myself on a rise where I could look out over the prairie. Only now my eyes were so filled with tears that I couldn't see the land I loved. I sobbed until I had no tears left.

Hours later I found Mama sitting on the veranda, staring at the sunset, the rocker barely moving. Papa was nowhere in sight.

"You've been crying," she said. When she stood up and held out her arms, the tears began again.

"What are your hopes and dreams for me, Mama?" My head was buried in her shoulder, so I couldn't see the look on her face.

"That you not live on a ranch," she said slowly, "and that you have a husband you love and children, and perhaps a maid. . . ."

"Mama, you're describing your hopes and dreams for yourself," I said, pulling back to look at her, though the sadness in her eyes was awful.

She thought about that a minute. "Maybe," she agreed. "I'm lonely, but I'm happy here. I have you, and I love your father, even if it doesn't seem like it some of the time. But there are things I miss, things I don't want you to miss."

"But Mama, I tasted them, or some of them, at the convent, and I missed you and Papa and the ranch and Sam something fierce. If I lived in a city, I'd miss riding—as much as you miss those other things. I'm not you."

She drew me tight to her again. "No, you're not, Thomasina. You're a very special person."

We sat next to each other on that veranda until dark, neither of us saying anything more. But when Papa came out of the barn—slowly, as though feeling things out before he came all the way up on the porch—I greeted him with, "Mama's going to Washington with us."

She didn't contradict me.

The three of us—Papa, Mama, and me—rode the train from Oklahoma City to the capital two days before the parade, with Sam and Papa's horse behind us in the boxcars. Mama was nervous at first, farther from home than she'd ever been—after all, Mama's knowledge of the world was limited to the ranch and St. Louis. Of course, it was farther from home than either Papa or I had ever been, too, but it didn't bother us. Mama was worried every minute—about the food on the train, about the man who carried our bags, about the locks on the hotel room door.

"Jess," Papa said affectionately, "that's why we wanted you to come with us—so you'd do the worrying, and Tommy Jo and I could have a good time."

"I'm having a good time, too," she protested. "I just think it's right to be cautious. Now in the parade—who will ride with Tommy Jo? And where will I be?"

We worked out all those details to her satisfaction, and after the first day, Mama seemed to relax and enjoy the city. It was busier than St. Louis—or so it seemed to me—and different, with more green areas and broader streets, all laid out like spokes in a wheel so that everything brought you to the center of our country's government. We toured the official buildings and monuments, marveling at the walls of marble and feeling a little intimidated to be in the halls of Congress, where they made our laws.

Mama had never ever seen an automobile—after all, it had been over ten years since she'd been to St. Louis, and they had only begun to appear on the streets of big cities within the last two or three years. I'd seen one or two, from a distance, when I was at the convent.

When one whizzed by us as we walked down a Washington street, Mama stared at it as though she'd seen a monster.

"Someday, they're gonna replace the horse," Papa told her. "Lots of people will have them."

"Not me," she declared emphatically. "Too dangerous! I'll stick to buggies." But she was grinning as she said it.

Papa laughed. "I don't think Luckett will buy an automobile for the ranch soon, so you don't have to worry."

"Why won't he, Papa?" I asked. I had absolutely fallen in love with automobiles and was crushed when I learned they cost upward of two thousand dollars—a fortune far beyond Papa's reach, I knew. I thought if Mr. Luckett bought one, I'd at least have a chance to try it.

"They wouldn't be practical on those old rutted roads around the ranch. Before automobiles can be used much, someone's gonna have to improve the roads."

Riding in that parade was the most wonderful thing that ever happened to me—at least up to that point.

The parade was a mile long. At the front was Buffalo Bill's Cowboy Band. Men in cowboy outfits, tan pants, tan hats, and dark shirts with black kerchiefs at their necks—matching like nothing ever worn by a real cowboy—played all the brass instruments while one man beat a huge drum that read "Buffalo Bill's Wild West Show and Congress of Rough Riders of the World." When they were in front of the president, they blasted out a rendition of "Home on the Range." Roosevelt's own Rough Riders marched in formation and paused in front of the grandstand to salute their leader, who stood there with his wife beside him and four of their children on either side; units of cavalry rode in intricate patterns, always letting their horses prance enough to show off the skill of the riders, and there were two military bands who played John Philip Sousa marches. To my everlasting disappointment, Buffalo Bill was nowhere to be seen.

Papa and I rode together, just in front of the Rough Riders, and I built a lot of loops with my rope, because that was what Roosevelt wanted me to do. When we passed the reviewing stand, a man with a megaphone called out, "Miss Tommy Jo Burns, the Oklahoma Cowgirl!" and people cheered. The president waved at me, and I waved back, feeling important for having been singled out.

Sitting on Sam—who'd ridden all the way from Oklahoma in a boxcar—I felt like queen of the world. The streets were lined with people—men held small children on their shoulders, and youngsters of six or seven clutched parents' legs and arms with one hand while waving tiny American flags with the other. Men called and women clapped. When someone in the crowd called my name, I smiled and waved, and if Sam pranced a little and they clapped harder, I made sort of a mock-bow from my saddle. I was, in fact, somewhat of a ham. Papa rode beside me, stiff and straight but a big grin on his face. He left it to me to charm the crowd.

I decided I wanted to be in a parade at least once a week.

Mama said later, with a kind of exasperated weariness, that she'd never expected to hear her daughter's name called aloud on the streets of the capital city. The trip to Washington saw a change in Mama, though later I'd find that it was only temporary. Still, having agreed to come with us, she never said another thing about her hopes and dreams, never let the word *ladylike* pass her lips, and finally she even enjoyed herself. Even Mama was proud and pleased.

A visit to the White House, at the president's invitation, was the highlight of our trip. The handwritten note asking us to come to tea was delivered to our hotel room by a messenger.

Mama was thrilled. "Now, Thomasina, you remember all the things you learned in the convent. You know about serving tea and—" She stopped and looked at Papa, who'd probably never had a cup of tea in his life. "James?"

"I'll drink tea, Jess, with one finger in the air." He crooked his little finger in imitation of what he supposed was the proper tea-drinking manner.

Mama was back to worrying—about our clothes, our manners, our conversation—but Papa quieted her. "Jess, you forget that Tommy Jo and I know this man. We rode with him. He's just folks. It'll be fine."

The president and Mrs. Roosevelt greeted us in their private parlor. "It's the cowgirl!" Roosevelt boomed, rushing to take my hand. "Come, my dear, you must meet Mrs. Roosevelt."

"Theodore," said a dignified lady standing behind him, "don't embarrass the child. She's a young lady, not a cowgirl." She held her hand out to take mine and said, "It was so good of you to come ride in our parade."

"She rides like a cowgirl," her husband insisted, turning to greet Mama and Papa.

"Do you ride any differently than anyone else?" Mrs. Roosevelt asked, her eyes twinkling. "How does a cowgirl ride?"

"With a western saddle, ma'am" was all I could think of.

"Ah, I see. Well, I ride with an English saddle—but we could ride together while you're here, couldn't we? I do ride often."

"Of course," I murmured. "I'd like that." Actually I thought it would probably be a pretty tame ride—a walk around the White House grounds—and I wasn't too excited. But if the president's wife asked you to ride . . . The arrangements were made for us to ride early the next morning, before it got too hot.

"I'll take Jess on a walking tour while you have your ride," Papa said, while Mama gave him a sharp look for calling her Jess in front of the Roosevelts. She'd have preferred Mrs. Burns, just like the president addressed his wife, so distantly and properly.

"Tommy Jo plays the piano real good," Papa boasted, eyeing the grand piano in the corner of the room, while I cringed.

Mrs. Roosevelt looked a question at me, while Mama murmured, "Yes, she does. I taught her."

Out of politeness then, Mrs. Roosevelt asked me to play—what choice did she have? And because I wasn't smart enough yet in the way of adults, I knew nothing to do but move to the piano and struggle through our national anthem. It was the best choice at the last minute, I thought, instinct telling me that "Nearer My God to Thee" wasn't appropriate.

The Roosevelts clapped politely, and I hurried back to my chair. The rest of teatime was given over to reminiscences about the wolf hunt. Mrs. Roosevelt, her eyes always sparkling with laughter, asked many questions about Jack Abernathy and the time I'd roped the wolf, though I'm sure she must have heard these stories all before. Mama sat quietly without saying a word—I think she was surprised that so dignified a lady would take an interest in such barbaric activities.

When Mrs. Roosevelt sighed, "I wish I'd been there," I thought Mama would faint.

But for days after—years, really—Mama talked in hushed tones about the time we had tea in the White House. It was surely one of the highlights of her life—just as the parade had been of mine. But whenever she mentioned it, Papa would say, "If Tommy Jo didn't rope and ride like she does, we'd have never gotten there, Jess."

My ride with Mrs. Roosevelt started out smoothly enough for a jaunt that nearly turned to disaster. We rode not on the White House lawn, as I'd anticipated, but on trails through a city park, and she turned out to be a much better horsewoman than I'd expected, riding at a trot. Of course, she rode a superbly trained horse with fancy gaits while Sam and I just loped along—if Sam had thoughts, I know he'd have been feeling a little awkward and clumsy at that point.

I patted his neck and whispered low in his ear, "Bet her horse can't rope, Sam!"

"You ride well, my dear," my hostess said. "Tell me about yourself."

So I told her about the Luckett Ranch, my year in school in St. Louis, and how glad I was to be back at the ranch.

"And now what?" she asked. "What will you do on the ranch?"

"Ride and help Mama," I said, my heart sinking at the words. I didn't know then the old saying about you can't keep them on the farm once they've seen the city, but that was pretty much how I was feeling.

"Do you have a special beau?" she asked.

Surprised, I said, "No, ma'am. I'm only fifteen."

"And I suppose there aren't many boys around your ranch?"

She sure could hit things on the nose. "No, ma'am, just cowboys, and they're a lot older than me. And Mama wouldn't like me to look at them wrong." Or them to look at me, I thought.

"I can imagine," she said. We'd come to a point where the path crossed a major street, and she held up a hand as though to signal me to stop.

Sam obediently halted, and I waited for her to decide we could go ahead. Two buggies went by, and then, still some distance away, I saw an automobile, the sun glistening off its black paint.

"We can cross before it gets here," Mrs. Roosevelt said, and off we went at a walk.

But the automobile's driver had other ideas—though he was still several hundred yards away, it seemed to anger him that we had not waited, and he gave a great *oompah* on his horn. Mrs. Roosevelt's horse, perhaps a little more used to city ways, skittered but was soon brought under control by a firm hand.

Sam went wild with fright, rearing backward while I held tight to the reins and tried to calm him with my voice. Once his four feet were firmly back on the ground, Sam snorted and took off at a gallop. My hat—a Stetson bought for the trip and very dear to me—flew off as we tore past Mrs. Roosevelt and the offending automobile, headed for I don't know where. It took me forever to get Sam stopped and calmed down. He was so unnerved that I walked him back to where Mrs. Roosevelt waited. We'd probably gone at least half a mile beyond her.

"Oh, my dear, are you all right? Such a ride!" She handed me the hat, which she'd retrieved.

I assured her that I was fine, but she insisted that we walk our horses back to the White House.

"Now I know why the president calls you a cowgirl," she said as we slowly retraced the way we'd come. Then, more practically, she announced, "I gave that driver a piece of my mind. He'll not do that again."

Later, when Mrs. Roosevelt explained to Papa how frightened she'd been for me, he just smiled and said, "Tommy Jo can handle that horse. She's a cowgirl."

"Yes, she is," Mrs. Roosevelt agreed.

After a week in Washington, we left for home. I was both relieved and disappointed. I'd loved the excitement, but I still didn't really like cities, though I wasn't nearly as opposed to them as I'd been in St. Louis when I was at the convent. That was a whole different way of viewing cities. Still, I wanted to ride when I wanted, not have to wait to have my horse brought from the stables, and I wanted to ride on open land, not paths or city streets. But when I thought about going back to the ranch, I realized that the freedom was the only thing I liked. Aside from Mama and Papa, I seldom saw anyone at the ranch, and there surely were no crowds cheering and clapping for me. Even with riding Sam every day and practicing my roping, the days loomed long ahead of me. The worst of it was that I knew, even then, that staying on the ranch limited my chances of ever leaving it. No one, I thought, was going to come to Guthrie, Oklahoma, to look for me. If opportunity—as in a Wild West show—was ever going to knock for me, I'd have to go out and look for it.

Mama was glad to be going home. "I'll remember this trip all my life," she told me, "and it's because you made me come with you. Thank you, Thomasina. But now I'm ready to go home."

"No stop in St. Louis?" Papa asked.

"No," she said firmly. "No more cities."

Papa had not left Mama alone in Washington at all—none of his disappearing for days, like he sometimes did at the ranch or when he took me to St. Louis and later picked me up. And yet I suppose Mama didn't want to test his devotion or expose him to temptation, which must have been how she saw cities and Papa.

Back in Oklahoma, the days dragged one after the other. I rode with Papa, I practiced my roping, I helped Mama put up plum preserves and pickles, I even played the piano and practiced my French for Mama. The Roosevelts had shown me something I'd never known—that families played and pic-nicked together. But Mama and Papa and I never did that. I was either with Mama or with Papa, but we were never together as a family. I was bored and saw before me an endless future, torn between loving my parents and being lonely because there were no other people at the ranch.

Often I went back to the hillside near the house to look out at the prairie and daydream. Some days my dreams were of Walt Denison, and when I recalled his hands on my shoulders and his lips on mine, queer tinglings would start in the pit of my stomach. I wished—oh, how I wished!—that I had done something differently in that brief time, maybe kissed him back—though I wasn't sure how to do that. *If,* I told myself, *you'd encouraged him, he might not want to wait until you're seventeen to see you again.* Seventeen seemed a lifetime away, not just two years.

But more often my fantasies were of the Buffalo Bill Wild West: Sometimes it would tour to Kansas City and Papa would take me there.

There'd be a catastrophe of some kind so that one of their riders was out of the show, and Papa would volunteer me. Buffalo Bill would say, "Oh, yes, I've heard the president speak of her," and I'd ride in the grand parade, rope a wild steer, bow to the audience. Other times Annie Oakley would seek me out to tell me how wonderful life was in the show arena. "But you're married," I would always say, and she'd reply, "Sometimes I wish I weren't. There are so many handsome men in the show." And then, at her urging, I'd see Buffalo Bill about a job, and soon I'd be riding in the show, with handsome laughing men beside me, all of them looking like Walt Denison.

And then reality would set in, and I'd find myself sitting on a hillside, staring at the prairie, and I'd hear the bell clanging, which meant that Mama wanted me to help start supper, or Papa wanted me for some chore in the barn.

The sameness of my days stretched before me unbearably, and I longed for excitement.

# CHAPTER 3

Papa hired a new hand. His name was Billy Rogers, he was part Cherokee, nineteen years old, with a big bashful grin and a shock of hair that fell into his eyes no matter what he did.

I discovered him on one of those evenings after supper when I'd gone to sit on the corral fence and watch the horses while I thought about the world and my place in it. I'd spent the summer reading all of Mama's books—*Tale of Two Cities,* which I thought bloody and awful and could barely finish, Hawthorne's *Scarlet Letter,* which made me furious, and Stendahl's *Red and the Black,* which I loved. I'd heard there was a new novel about the West—*The Virginian*—and I pestered Papa to get it for me, but he hadn't yet, and anyway, I was about read out for a while.

I sat on the top rail and hooked my feet over the next rail down, even though I was wearing a calico skirt and white shirtwaist—Mama insisted I get out of my split skirt and into a proper dress for dinner every night, though Papa didn't give a hoot'n a holler what I wore. Anyway, I folded the skirt around my knees and sat, my back to the corral, looking out over the prairie.

Suddenly I heard a shout: "Bring 'er on!"

A galloping horse appeared, headed toward Billy, who stood at the far end of the corral, out from the fence a bit. When the horse was almost up to him, he threw a huge loop. The rider spurred his horse on, through the loop, before it settled gently around both horse and man. I'd never even imagined that anything like that was possible.

"Wow!" I said, not even realizing I was talking aloud.

·   Billy whirled to look at me, the rope now slack in his hand. "I didn't know you were watching," he said, walking toward me with the most bowlegged gait I'd ever seen. His legs made Papa's look stick straight. Up close, I could see that he wasn't really handsome, not like Walt Denison, but there was something warm and wonderful about his face.

"I didn't mean to bother you. I just came out to sit."

He looked at me a minute, and then said softly, "Good place for that. Jake and me, we were practicin'." He nodded his head toward the mounted cowboy, whose horse now stood quietly a few feet away.

"How'd you learn to do that?" I asked.

"Practice," he said. "Lots of practice."

I wondered what Sam would do if I tried to make him run through a loop. "Did you have to train the horse?"

He grinned again. "It's my horse. But no, a horse will just generally keep going if you spur him." He turned away, then looked back at me. "Come on," he said.

Without a moment's hesitation, I jumped down from the fence and stood watching while he built his loop again and then laid it out behind him in a great circle. When he threw it, I could see from the motion of his arm that the rope was very heavy. But it sailed through the air to form an up-and-down loop a few feet in front of me.

"Go on. Walk through it."

I hesitated, looked at the rope, then at him again.

"The horse did it," he laughed. "You can, too."

Well, I wasn't about to be outdone by a horse! Head up, I marched toward the loop—afterward I thought I must have looked like someone marching to an execution, but I wasn't sure that old rope wouldn't whack into me. It didn't. I walked through it just like I was out for a Sunday stroll. In fact, I liked the idea so much, I walked through it again.

"You should be in the show ring," I told him.

"I aim to," he answered, and let his rope fall.

It was pure dark now, and I could barely see him. Still, I was awkwardly aware that I was standing in front of him, and that he was still holding the rope but looking at me.

"I can rope some," I said softly. "Papa taught me."

"Papa is Burns," he said matter-of-factly, as though wanting to be sure he had it right. "Not many gals rope." It was another statement of fact.

"No," I said, "not many." Then, though I don't know what possessed me to say it, I went on, "I roped a wolf for Theodore Roosevelt once."

"Roosevelt? The president?"

"Uh-huh. On a wolf hunt with Catch-'em-Alive Abernathy."

"Must've been some loop," he said, and a grin split his face.

"I was lucky, I guess." Why was I bragging to this hired hand who could rope circles around me, literally? "I have to go in now. But thanks for the demonstration." I turned to leave.

"Anytime," he called after me. "Maybe we can get us a contest or something. I might learn something from you."

"Sure," I called. "Anytime." I floated back to the house. Suddenly life on the ranch didn't seem near so hopeless or dull.

"Thomasina, what have you been doing outside so late? It's been dark thirty minutes, and I've worried about you." Mama stood at the door waiting, and I had the feeling she'd been pacing, maybe even pestering Papa to go look for me.

"It's all right, Mama. I've been talking to the new hand Papa hired."

"Rogers?" Papa asked. "Seems to be a good man. Works hard, always in good spirits. I like him."

"So do I," I said softly.

"Thomasina, don't be looking at cowboys," Mama said in a half-joking tone. "They'll break your heart." Then she looked at Papa, but he pretended not to see.

If Mama had already gone to bed, I probably would have told Papa about Billy and the loop he threw and how I'd stepped in and out of it. But I didn't—and when Papa found me stepping in and out of loops a couple of days later, it was almost a disaster.

I was standing a few feet from Sam, having just brushed him down after a long ride, when I heard a quiet command:

"Stand still."

"What?"

"Stand still," Billy repeated. He had come silently up just inches behind me, his rope whirling and whirling.

And then his loop settled down over both of us and danced in a circle. This was different from the up-and-down loop he'd thrown the other night. This time the rope went over our heads, more like it did when I roped a steer. But when I roped, the object was always to pull the rope taut around the animal, and for just a moment there I panicked—expecting a good rope burn when the loop tightened around me and, even more embarrassing, expecting to be pulled up tight next to Billy. But the loop stayed at least a foot from me. Circling and circling, it had a vitality that seemed to give it a life of its own. Sometimes it rose to shoulder height, and then again it dropped to our knees. Slowly I turned my head to look at him and saw that his arm, waving that loop, was barely moving so that it did indeed appear that the rope was circling of its own volition. The only giveaway about Billy was the grin on his face.

"I'll put it real low," he said, "and you can step out of it."

The rope fell to my ankles in a constant circle that never wavered, and I stepped over it. Billy kept it spinning and in a second asked, "Want to step back in?"

"Of course," I answered, and once again stepped over the spinning circle. "Billy, that's amazing. How do you do it?" And then the most important question: "Can you teach me to do it?"

"I reckon," he said.

We stood there a long minute, grinning at each other, the rope still doing its sensuous circle, and we might have stood longer if the spell hadn't been broken by a command given much louder than Billy's "Stand still."

"Rogers! You let my daughter go!"

Like an animal that had been shot, the rope fell lifeless to the ground at my feet. I stepped over it, and Billy began to coil his rope as Papa stormed toward us.

"You had her prisoner!" Papa's face was red, his features contorted into a scowl, his fists clenched. Clearly, he wanted to hit Billy, but he was restraining himself. "Pack your gear. Your pay'll be waiting for you."

Without a word, Billy shook the stray lock from his forehead and turned to go. Later he told me he would have left the ranch without ever explaining, ever defending himself. "I won't plead for a job," he said.

"Papa," I cried, "wait a minute! Billy was showing me a trick. I stepped into that loop of my own free will."

"A trick?" Papa's voice was faint as he echoed my words. "That was a trick?" Then his voice grew a little firmer and he said suspiciously, "Where'd you learn to do that?"

"Just learned," Billy said. "Fooled with a rope since I was knee-high to a grasshopper." As he talked, he uncoiled a small rope from his belt and built it into a tiny loop that twirled and danced in front of him.

Papa watched mesmerized. "You really are good!" he finally said.

"Thanks." Billy never looked up, his eyes intent on that circle in front of him, though I knew he looked down not from a need to watch the rope but from shyness.

"Billy's going to teach me," I said.

"Fine, fine," Papa blustered. Then, with words that came hard for him, "Sorry about the misunderstanding. You understand . . . my daughter and all."

"Sure," Billy replied. "I understand."

And I think he did.

My lessons began that day and lasted all winter, whenever the weather was good enough to be out in the corral.

Spinning a loop took a different kind of a rope than we used just catching an old steer out on the prairie.

Billy showed me a cotton rope, about a half inch in diameter, with a whipped end. "The other end is the eye, the honda," he said. "And what goes from the hand to the honda is the spoke."

Hand, honda, spoke—the new terms danced in my brain. I learned that you could spin a rope clockwise or counterclockwise, and that tricks came from combining flat and vertical loops at various angles. I liked being the object of Billy's spinning tricks as much as I did building my own loops.

My first attempts were pitiful. I began with a short rope for a small loop that I could whirl in front of me, like the ones Billy always spun while he talked to someone. I accused Billy of giving me different ropes, because my loops had none of the life his did. They hung in the air a minute and then fell limp.

"It's in the wrist," he said, but he could explain no further. Spinning a rope was instinct for him—and hard work for me. But gradually my loops stayed alive longer and longer, and before I knew it, I was spinning and talking at the same time.

Mama didn't take kindly to my practice, for I had a rope in my hands almost every minute—even sitting around the stove on a winter night. "I don't see you read much," she said. "You're consumed by this roping business." There was a frown, ever so slight, on her brow, and it came from more than concentrating to see her needlework.

Papa looked up from the St. Louis paper. "Leave her be, Jess. She's learning something I bet no other girl can do."

"I see," Mama muttered, and I knew that unlike Papa, she didn't think much of this distinction. But I was determined.

I graduated to spinning a loop around the snubbing post in the corral—or trying.

"You have to throw it wider," Billy said. He rarely wasted words, and I was getting used to his taciturn ways, but I wanted to shout, "How wide? How do I throw it wider?" I threw and threw, and one day, my rope danced around the post for just a minute before it dropped. And the next day it danced longer, and pretty soon I could keep it up for a minute, even while shouting to Billy, "Look! Look! It's doing it!"

"Yeah," he said.

When I really could spin a loop around me and the post, Billy volunteered to let me throw one around him, but he cautioned that it had to be still wider. The first time I tried, the rope whacked him hard on the head, but all he said was, "Wider."

Papa was watching one day when the rope really did circle Billy for more than a minute, putting us both inside that magic circle. Trying to make a joke out of his earlier mistake, he shouted, "Tommy Jo! You let Rogers go!" We all laughed, at which point my loop fell apart.

"What," Mama asked, "good will it do you to know all this rope business?"

I knew she was thinking that spinning a rope was hardly one of the talents a man looked for in a wife, but I just said, "I like to do it, Mama. I really like to do it."

Trick roping, Billy taught me, was different from spinning. For one thing, you had to have something to rope, not just spin it around yourself. And it took a different rope, a rope made from the maguey plant. It was a stiff, hard brown rope, not at all like the soft cotton we used for spinning. The first time Billy gave me a trick rope, I felt like I had a reluctant snake in my hands. "It won't *give*," I complained. "I can't throw it."

"Real trick ropes are expensive, twenty dollars or so," he said, " 'cause they're made by hand under water." Billy had a good trick rope that I was forbidden to touch, and one he was less special about that he allowed as how he could use to teach me some things.

The first thing he taught me was care. "Never plunge a good rope into water. You'll ruin it. Need to bring it back to life, you spray a little water on it, real light, just kind of shake it on."

The life of a rope was becoming very real to me. There *was* a vitality about a rope that went beyond its inanimate nature, even maybe beyond the relationship between rope and roper.

Billy let out one of his longest sentences. "In trick ropin', you got to have something to rope. You ain't quite ready for a horse, and I ain't volunteerin'."

Back to the snubbing post.

Papa was on one of his two- or three-day trips away from the ranch. "Business for Mr. Luckett," he always told us, while Mama turned away from him with a frozen look on her face. Mama was withdrawn when Papa was away, and once or twice I caught her crying into her pillow. But then when he came home, just when I would have thought her mood would improve greatly, she was usually angry with him, cross about everything from the mud he tracked into the house to the way he held his knife and fork. If she wanted him at home, why was she angry when she got what she wanted?

I wasn't too old before I figured it out, though I'm not sure how I first knew that Papa went to see another woman in Guthrie. Now that I look back on it, it must have been common knowledge, even among the cowboys, for Guthrie was small and close to home. And it must have embarrassed Mama even more than it angered her—for everyone knew that her husband wasn't satisfied with her alone.

"Mama," I asked once when I was about ten, "why does Papa go see that lady in Guthrie?"

"I don't know what you're talking about," she said without looking at me.

After that, I didn't ask for a long time, and Mama and I kept up the pretense that Papa was off doing business for Mr. Luckett.

Once when Billy and I were practicing our rope tricks, I said, "Papa's gone to Guthrie on business."

Billy just grinned and said, "Yeah."

"Billy Rogers, do you know where my papa went?"

"Everybody knows," he said, "but it ain't none of my business."

Suddenly angered, I retorted, "Well, it's my business!"

"I s'pose it is," he said. "I s'pose it is. But I doubt you can do much about it."

Papa came home two days later, bringing a silk scarf for Mama and a new white shirtwaist for me. "Fine trip," he said. "Made a deal to buy some Texas cattle for Luckett."

Papa, I wanted to shout, *stop pretending! We know where you've been.*

Mama said, "That's fine, James," as though she truly believed him. But she stared out the window as she said it. Late that night I heard talk that made me know she didn't believe him.

"I will not stand for it," she said to him. They were in their bedroom with the door closed, but Mama's voice was angry enough to carry through the wall to my room next door—and that was unusual for Mama, who was always soft-spoken, usually more so in anger. "Thomasina is getting older, and—well, it's not a good thing for her to know about."

Papa chuckled, as though unconcerned about her anger. "Is that what really bothers you, Jess?"

"Yes, it is" came the frosty reply.

By now I was wide awake and straining to hear every word, though a pang of guilt assailed me for eavesdropping. It was one of the things that Papa said was not to be tolerated.

"I think you're jealous," Papa said, "and you know there's no need. What you and I have is special."

"Not special enough to keep you away from Guthrie," Mama said. Somehow I could imagine her sitting at her dressing table in her old faded wrapper, her hair let down, her hands busy applying a hundred brushstrokes.

"I have business in Guthrie," Papa said, and I could tell by his voice that he had risen from the bed and moved toward the dressing table, which was on the side of their bedroom closest to my room. "Jess, I'd rather be with you any day. You come first," he said more softly but still loud enough for me to hear.

With a gasp that startled me, Mama said, "Oh, James," and then there was silence.

I lay a long time and thought about it. I knew, at fifteen, why they had stopped talking. But I couldn't understand how Mama could be so angry at Papa—and with reason, I thought—and then forgive him so quickly. She couldn't have gotten over her anger—and she'd be just as angry the next time.

I fell asleep, every once in a while hearing a low sound from the room next door. But there was no more talking.

The Buffalo Bill Wild West Show was on what proved to be its last European tour that spring. I read in the St. Louis paper about a new scene, "The Great Train Hold-Up and Bandit Hunters of the Union Pacific." There was a locomotive—well, what looked like a locomotive—mounted on an automobile, but it had one bright headlight and it puffed black smoke, just like a real locomotive. And there were the standard acts—the attack on the wagon train, the Pony Express riders, an Indian dance. I read it and wept, I wanted so badly to be part of the show.

But in another edition of the paper one day, I read something else that caught my eye. A girl named Prairie Rose Henson had ridden a bronc at the Cheyenne Frontier Days. When she first entered the contest, the judges had told her no women were allowed, but she demanded to see the rules, and of course they didn't say anything about women. So Prairie Rose—what a wonderful name!—got her ride. And then I read further and found out she wasn't but two years older than me.

I told Papa about it. "If a woman can ride a bronc like Prairie Rose and a woman can shoot like Annie Oakley, I bet a woman could rope in a show."

"Women," Mama interrupted, "have no business trying to act like men."

Papa acted as though he didn't hear her. "Probably you could," he said. The way he said *you* was clear. He didn't mean the generalized *you* the way some people did when they talked. He meant me, Tommy Jo Burns, roping in a Wild West show. I was smart enough not to ask any more about it in front of Mama.

"Just think," I told Billy. "Me—riding a bronc in a Wild West show, roping—there's no end to the things I could do."

"Better practice your trick roping," he said.

I still couldn't throw a loop that Billy was willing to walk through.

"Yes, you can," he said softly, taking the rope from me for the third time and throwing it into a perfect loop. "Just practice."

Years later, when I saw a picture of a man teaching a woman to play golf, his arms wrapped around hers, his hands on top of hers on the club, I thought of Billy and those roping lessons. He never put his arms around me—Billy was far too shy!—but sometimes, when he showed me how to hold the rope, his hands brushed mine, and I remembered the girls in the convent and the talk about tingly feelings.

One evening our hands brushed, out there behind the corral.

"Sorry," Billy said abruptly, pulling his hand away as though it were burned.

"It's all right," I said, dropping the rope and reaching after his hand with my own, as though to pull it back. Something made me bold, and I took his arm and pulled so that he turned to face me.

"Billy Rogers—" I began, and then, as much to my own surprise as his, I reached up and kissed him full on the mouth. It wasn't much of a kiss—I had to aim quickly, and I wasn't practiced at kissing—but it took him by surprise, and he would have backed away again except that I held on to his arm.

We stood like that a long minute, staring at each other. Billy wasn't all that much taller than me, so our eyes were pretty level, and neither one of us blinked. Then ever so slowly and gently, Billy Rogers put his arm around me and kissed me, softly at first, and then, his mouth moving on mine, with more fire. Walt Denison was wrong—I didn't wait until I was seventeen to respond to a kiss. But Walt Denison was far from my mind right then—as far as the girls in the convent and their tingly feelings.

As though he suddenly remembered himself, he pulled away, and this time I didn't reach to pull him back. With a crooked smile at me, Billy walked away.

I didn't see him for three long days. They were days filled with fantasies on my part—Buffalo Bill was replaced by Billy Rogers, who confessed his love for me, wrapped his arms around me as we threw a rope together—probably a physical impossibility!—brushed his lips against my ear as he whispered that I was the best girl roper he'd ever seen. At night I was restless, tossing and turning sleeplessly in my bed; by day I was cross, irritable, and frantic to know where he was. When I wasn't hanging out at the corral, I was pounding the piano so hard, even Mama begged me to go outside. And the two times I tried to pick up a book, I threw it down in disgust, unable to concentrate.

"Papa, did you send Billy off to some far pasture?" I ventured the second evening at supper.

"Miss him, do you?" Papa asked with a grin. "Is it the roping lessons—or the man you miss?"

"James!" Mama's voice cut through Papa's jocular mood before I could mutter, "Both."

"Thomasina is not interested in that Rogers boy," Mama said, as though to convince herself. "I'll be glad when he moves on." Since most cowboys drifted on after a season or two, this wasn't an unrealistic hope on Mama's part.

"I am interested in him, Mama," I said calmly. In the back of my mind, I'm sure I had figured out that I couldn't go through life doing what would make Mama happy, from going to convent to avoiding cowboys, because eventually that same course of action would make me miserable. And I was, at that moment, miserable in my desperation to see Billy.

"Hush," she said. "You don't know what you're saying."

Maybe not, I wanted to say, *but I'd like to find out for myself.*

"Where you been?" I asked when he finally sauntered into the corral, looking everywhere but at me.

"Riding fence," he mumbled, stooping to pick up something, probably nothing, from the dirt.

"I looked for you."

"I'm sure you did," he said. Then, after a long minute, "I thought about you."

I blushed, pleased but uncertain. But before I could say anything, he went on in that slow drawl, "What I thought is that it's time I be movin' on."

"Moving on?" I slipped off the corral post and started toward him. He moved back, one step on his part for every step I took toward him. I thought maybe I should promise not to grab him again, so that he'd stand still.

"I—yeah, movin' on. Actually, I got a chance to go to Australia."

"Australia?" My voice squeaked. Papa went to Guthrie and sometimes even St. Louis, which was bad enough, but here was the only boy my age—well, almost—for miles around, and he was talking about going to the other side of the world.

"Yeah. They got ranches down there, and they rope. . . ." His voice fell off as though he didn't know what to say.

"How will I learn to trick rope?"

"You half know. Just keep practicin'." He grinned, that slightly cock-eyed smile splitting his face. "I know you'll get to the Wild West shows 'fore long."

"Not without you," I said suddenly, too loudly.

Turning away, Billy pulled that ever-present rope from his pocket and began to spin it. "Tommy Jo," he said, "I'm near twenty years old, been driftin' now for four years. You're not quite sixteen—and you ain't got no business with me." He spun the rope furiously, holding it as a barrier between us.

He left the next day.

"Well, I'm glad to see that Rogers person gone," Mama said next evening as we sat on the veranda shelling peas. It was a chore I hated, but my mood was black that evening anyway, and I thought I might as well be shelling peas as making myself miserable sitting at the corral and waiting for Billy to come along. He was probably clear to Oklahoma City by now.

Papa was down at the barn, supposedly working on some harness but in reality avoiding me. "Rogers drew his time," he had said at dinner.

"I knew he was going to."

"So did I," Papa had said, looking long and hard at me.

I thought maybe Papa understood how I felt, knew that a girl's first crush was important. Those are feelings that a girl's mother usually understands, not her philandering father. But my crush on Billy had frightened Mama.

"I'm not glad he's gone," I said belligerently, mangling a pea in my anger. "Maybe I should follow him to Australia."

"Thomasina!"

"I won't follow him," I said in exasperation. "But when he comes back, I'll be the best girl trick roper in the country." Then I wondered how long Billy would stay—and how long it would take me to fulfill that vow.

Mama's fingers flew over the peas, but she didn't say anything. We worked in silence for several minutes, and then, maybe because I was feeling contrary, I asked,

"Mama, who's the woman in Guthrie that Papa goes to see?"

Mama lifted her chin a little and stared out over the prairie. "I don't know what you're talking about," she said in her usual tone.

"Yes, you do, Mama. I know that Papa goes to see another lady in Guthrie, and that you get really mad at him, but when he comes back, you always make up with him. Why?"

She crumpled in her chair, and the peas fell out of her hands into the bowl. "I—I can't explain it to you. I don't think I can explain it to myself."

It was more honesty than I'd ever heard from her. "Mama, are you sorry you married Papa?" I wasn't sure what kind of an answer I was prepared for.

"Sometimes," she said slowly, "I try to imagine 'what if?' What if I hadn't married him, or what if something happened to him—an accident or something. Or what if he chose Louise—that's her name in Guthrie. But it's never right. I can't imagine not being with your father. He's a good man, Thomasina."

I chewed on that in my mind for a while.

At first after Billy left, my practice went well. As fall turned into winter, I was still working with Papa, doing the daily things that had to be done on the Luckett Ranch. "Can't have you so busy with fancy stuff that you forget how to work a calf," he said. By then I could rope and tie a calf in pretty good time. These days Papa had only Casey and Wilks as hands on the ranch, and I spent many days helping him with branding and doctoring. But Papa, self-appointed, also became my tutor, and he determined that I was proficient enough at spinning a rope.

"You got to learn to throw that heavy trick rope, Tommy Jo. You do, and I'll walk through it—that's a bargain."

Patiently, time after time, I laid the rope out in a circle, just like Billy did, and then I threw it—or tried to. The rope was enormously heavy, and for what seemed like forever, I couldn't get it to do more than sail over my head to plop on the ground in front of me. But then, one day, it stayed alive for just a second before collapsing. And the next day it was longer. Cheered by this small success, I practiced for hours a day.

Finally, one day I was able to hold a vertical loop for thirty seconds. "I'll walk through that next time," Papa said. And he did. Walked through my loop and back again. Then I dropped the rope and exploded into the air in high-jumping happiness.

"Tommy Jo, you're gonna do it!" Papa said, hugging me. "You're gonna take us to the Wild West show."

Us? Was Papa going too? In the back of my mind, whether I held a trick rope or a working one, the Buffalo Bill show was always there. I saw myself approaching Cody himself, telling him that he ought to see me rope, then roping and tying a steer so fast that I beat three men on his regular team. Buffalo Bill, courtly as always, bowed low and said, "Tommy Jo, you *must* join my show." And I graciously accepted. But always in that dream I finally rode off to the show alone, waving good-bye to Mama and Papa, who stood, arms around each other, on the veranda of our house. I hadn't envisioned riding off with Papa, leaving Mama alone on that veranda, and the thought disquieted me.

A day or two later Papa read in the paper that the Buffalo Bill show planned to stay in Europe for a full year. Papa was philosophical when he told me about it, and I knew it wasn't near the disappointment to him that it was to me. A year! Billy would probably be back from Australia long before then, and I'd never make my goal of being in a show by the time he came home. My next thought was that there was no sense practicing if I was never going to be in a show. One didn't throw trick ropes for the amusement of the cattle on a middling ranch in the Cherokee Strip.

It was a nasty evening—the kind when winter teases with an unpleasant taste of what's to come—and I bundled myself into a coat before slamming out of the house, followed by Mama's tentative question, "Where are you going, Thomasina?"

I heard Papa say something to her, but the words went past me, for by then I was running as hard as I could, in spite of my skirts and bulky coat, running as though I could catch Buffalo Bill's show and make it return from Europe and perform in St. Louis by sheer willpower, running in spite of the cold light rain blown into my eyes by a north wind.

Finally, I found myself, winded, at the fence of the corral where Sam was. Nickering gently, he came over to nuzzle me, searching for an apple. Climbing over the fence—an awkward business with my skirts—I stood with my arms around his neck, sobbing and telling him that we'd never ride in a Wild West show. That was how Papa found me. My papa had so often made the world right for me, in spite of his stern manner and wayward ways, that I was glad to see him, thinking he would find the way out of my misery. But the first thing he said made me cautious.

"Foolish to cry over something you can't change," he said. "What's the matter with you, girl?"

"I can't spend my life on this ranch with you and Mama," I said. "There's no—no one my age."

"No young men?" he asked, grinning.

"That's part of it," I admitted, wishing he wouldn't find that amusing.

"Where you want to go? You can go to St. Louis, even if there isn't a show."

"I don't want to go to St. Louis, or Kansas City, or even Oklahoma City. I don't like cities!"

"Appears to me you don't like cities and you don't like ranches. Not much left." Papa spoke in a drawl, slower than usual for him, which told me he was still finding this amusing, the whim of a flighty young girl, I suspected.

"I don't know what I want," I said peevishly, wishing now he'd just go and let me alone.

"Well," he said, "I think you're goin' on a trip. Come on, let's go tell your mother."

"I don't want to go anywhere," I repeated, as he took my arm and pulled me toward the house.

When we walked into the house, its heat hitting us like a blast, Papa did an unforgivable thing. "Jess," he said, "Tommy Jo's gonna spend a week in Guthrie. She's not happy on the ranch, doesn't know where she wants to go, and I think she needs a change."

"Guthrie!" I said. "You didn't say that!"

"I'm saying it now," he said in the tone that brooked no disagreement.

"Guthrie?" Mama echoed, her face turning pale. "Where would she stay in Guthrie?"

"Mrs. Turner's boardinghouse," he said calmly. "She can always use help."

"I don't want to help in a boardinghouse!" I said, feeling just as I had when I was sent to the convent. "And who's Mrs. Turner?"

Mama spoke very clearly, her eyes fixed on Papa. "Louise Turner. She's a friend of your father's."

I whirled to look at Papa, but nothing showed on his face.

"You may not want to work in a boardinghouse," he said, "but you need to see what other possibilities are open to you. What else can you do if . . . well, if you don't want to stay here?"

"Thomasina will marry one day and move from this ranch," Mama said, "but she's too young now."

"And she has no likely candidates," Papa said dryly. "She tells me she wants to get off this ranch, and that's what I'm gonna see happens. She can go to church in Guthrie, meet some people her age. It'll do her good."

The idea of meeting people, of being in a community instead of alone with Papa, Mama, and a couple of old cowboys who resented me, was tempting. But to stay with Papa's lady friend! It was unthinkable. I looked at Mama, but she was staring at the flames in the fireplace, with that faraway look that she always got when the subject under discussion was painful to her. Bless Mama, I knew that she was almost desperate to keep me from Mrs. Turner's boardinghouse, but I also knew that she wouldn't cross Papa. And she wouldn't help me.

"Papa, I didn't really mean—I'm happy here. I was just disappointed about the Wild West show."

"If you were pinning all your hopes on one Wild West show . . ." He didn't need to finish the sentence.

Ah, Papa, you must have known about my fantasies.

I left for Guthrie the next morning. The spitting rain that had kept up all night had turned to a steady dismal downpour by the time Papa brought the covered buggy to the door. Mama hugged me once, quickly, but neither of us said anything. There was nothing to be said.

"I'll be back tonight, Jess," Papa said, and when Mama looked at him skeptically, he added, "I really will."

Mama stood on the veranda, wrapped in a shawl, and watched until we were out of sight.

I was damp and thoroughly miserable by the time we reached Mrs. Turner's boardinghouse. Papa pulled the buggy behind the house, lifted me out, and led the way in through the back door, not bothering to knock. Obviously, he felt at home here.

"Louise!" he called.

A small woman, as tiny as Mama was tall and as blond as Mama was dark, bustled around the corner. She wore a fashionable dress of soft challis, with a dainty lace collar framing her face, and her hair was piled high on her head. This was a lady who took some time with her appearance, and I felt awkward and gangly in my wet woolen skirt and wrinkled shirtwaist, my hair straggly under the Stetson that had sort of protected me from the rain.

"Sandy!" she exclaimed in surprise, using the name that everyone but Mama called him. Then her eyes rested on me, and she stood speechless, looking at him.

"This is Tommy Jo, my daughter. She's goin' to stay with you a week," he said. There was no asking in his statement; it was foregone that she would do as he wished.

"Of course. Tommy Jo, I'm glad to know you. I'm Louise Turner." She never lost her composure, after that first minute of surprise.

"She needs to go to church, meet some people, see how she likes life in town," Papa said. "And she'll help you around here."

Through all this, I'd not said a word. Louise looked at me curiously, and I felt an obligation to say something, anything. "It's nice of you to have me," I said. "I'll try not to be any trouble."

"I'll be glad for your company," she said, and seemed to mean it.

We three sat at the kitchen table and made small talk about the weather, and then Papa said he had to get back to the ranch. With a quick hug for me and a bare nod at Louise, he was gone.

Once he was out the door, she surprised me mightily by sinking back into her chair and bursting into long laughter, laughter almost too loud to come from so small a person. Finally, her chuckles subsided enough for her to say, "Your father is one strong-minded man, isn't he? Now tell me the truth about this story." She propped her elbows on the table, chin in her hands, and looked directly at me, waiting.

I began hesitantly, but she was so open, so interested that words were soon tumbling out of my mouth: about my roping, about Billy, the convent, even my dreams of the Buffalo Bill Wild West Show. Louise sometimes said, "Oh," and sometimes, when I talked about my dreams, "Good for you," but mostly she just looked directly at me with a kind of soft smile playing on her face.

"But I don't understand why you're here," she said, when I finally stopped for breath.

"I think," I said slowly, "for punishment. When I told Papa I wanted to be off the ranch, it angered him—and I guess he thought he'd show me that I wouldn't like being in town any better than I liked St. Louis."

"And he brought you to me," she mused. "It's logical in a way—he knows me better than anyone else here—but it was wrong of him. Wrong to do that to your mother."

"You know my mother?"

"I've met her," she said.

I could tell she wasn't going to explain. Nor would she answer questions about my father. Instinct told me not to ask right then, and later I was glad I hadn't.

"Let's get you settled," she said, "and then we can think about this some more and figure a way to get you to that Wild West show." She led the way through string portières to a parlor chaotically papered with several patterns of ferns and roses, including a rose paper on the ceiling. A player piano stood catercorner at one end of the room, with player rolls on the shelf of a nearby music stand, and across the room a Victrola sat on a center table. Louise was apparently bound and determined to provide her boarders with music. There was a brass spittoon, for those who must chew—something Mama never allowed—and stacks of books on several small tables, for those who would read. Rugs were of Mexican design, pillows sported native American motifs, and the carpeting smacked faintly of Oriental patterns, so that the whole was a wild cacophony of movement. I loved it.

The room I was to occupy was in the northwest corner of the second floor, with windows looking out over the prairie on two sides. I could almost, I thought, look toward home. Determinedly, I pulled the roller blind on the northern window and stared west. Obviously, it was a room meant to rent to a woman, for it was papered with a pale medallion-patterned wallpaper, and a rose-pattern rug covered most of the floor. There was a brass bed with a comforter on it—rose-patterned, of course—and a wicker rocker beside a side table that was covered with a drawnwork scarf. A landscape painting hung on one wall, and on the other, a ribbon-hung series of portrait photos. I deliberately ignored them, fearing that if I looked too closely, I would find my papa among the faces.

But it was a sumptuous room, overflowing with pattern and warmth. I felt disloyal to Mama for even thinking that this room was far grander than mine at home, but it was. When that thought struck me, tears suddenly started down my cheeks, and before I knew it, I was sobbing into the pillows. I think I was crying for Mama, whom I really did love, and who I wished understood me, and who I wished was happier. My disloyalty deepened when I thought about the differences between Mama and Louise, who gave off a kind of happiness and who was already my ally. I had the feeling she liked me. I wasn't always sure about Mama in that regard.

After a while I slept so soundly that I woke with great puffy red eyes and a throbbing head. There was water, tepid but wet, in the pitcher on the bedside stand, and I splashed it on my face, made a pass at my hair, tried to smooth the wrinkles out of my clothes, and went downstairs.

Louise, a white apron over her dress, was cooking supper, large quantities of food that suggested she had several boarders.

"I—I'm supposed to help you," I said tentatively, realizing that concentrated exposure to housework was supposed to be part of my punishment.

Turning from the stove, she looked at me but never said a word about my red eyes. "And so you shall. Here, take this flatware and set the dining table for ten." She motioned with her head toward the dining room, and I obediently did as she said. Flatware was followed by fine china, in a blue willow pattern, and crystal goblets. We'd never had such service pieces at home, and I was surprised to find them in a boardinghouse.

"Remnants of my marriage," Louise said, seeing me look at the table. "My late husband inherited them, and he would have wanted me to use these things, not let them collect dust. Besides, my boarders deserve the best."

My curiosity about her grew.

"Do you cook?" she asked.

"Yes. Mama taught me. I can make bread and pies and pretty good mayonnaise."

This time her laughter burbled gently. "Good. When we need mayonnaise in the middle of winter, I'll let you know. Meantime, you can stir this stew, and I'll see about the bread. It's already rising, or I'd let you show me what you can do."

Dinner was delicious—hearty stew filled with chunks of beef, potatoes, carrots, and onions, bread fresh from the oven and as light as any I'd ever tasted, and an apple cobbler for dessert. Even the coffee smelled so good that I was tempted to taste it—Mama never allowed me to at home, saying it would stunt my growth. One bitter sip convinced me that Mama was right.

There were eight boarders besides me—three men who looked like traveling salesmen and ate their dinner silently and quickly, a schoolteacher who asked me pointedly about my education and frowned when I said that I had mostly been educated at home, a lawyer who had the bad manners to read some papers at the dinner table, the man who owned the printing company and was delighted when I told him how it fascinated me—"You must come for a tour, my dear"—and two ladies who were milliners, so Louise had told me before.

"We will make you a beautiful hat," one said, "in time for church on Sunday."

"Thank you," I said nervously. "The only hat I've ever worn—"

"We know," interrupted her companion. "We saw it on the hatrack and asked Louise who the cowboy was." This struck her as funny enough to send her off into giggles that lasted long enough for me to wish she'd choke.

"We'll make you a hat with feathers on it," the first one said. "Show me your church dress so I'll know the colors."

Seeing that I looked helpless, Louise said, "Tan and gold will do fine." Later she said, "I figured tan and gold went with almost any winter dress."

Later she was taken back to find my one good challis dress was navy blue. At least it had gold trim. "I could find something of mine for you in brown," she said thoughtfully, then giggled when I pointed out that a dress of hers would hit me midcalf and probably not fasten around the middle.

"You're good-sized, like your mother," she said, and her tone made it a compliment.

The boarders all disappeared as soon as they were through eating, and Louise and I cleared the table and did the dishes. "It's a great blessing to have company while I do this," she said. "I'd be grateful, even if you didn't help."

"Papa expected me to help, and I want to," I said, balancing a stack of dirty plates.

"We're going to have a good week," she said confidently.

We did have a good week. The best part was that Louise and I became fast friends. Bit by bit, she told me about herself. She, like Mama, grew up in St. Louis and followed a cowboy west—I thought that was a remarkable coincidence, but I didn't realize that St. Louis was a popular big city with cowboys, and cowboys appealed to lots of women. Unlike Papa, Louise's cowboy was rich, the son of an English lord. They'd ranched in Texas briefly, but he was killed in a barroom fight in Guthrie, where he'd come to buy cattle.

"Poor Billy," she said, wiping a real tear, "I never could convince him to stay out of the saloons and out of the fights. I came up here to collect his body and decided I'd as well stay here as anywhere. Billy'd left me enough money to build this house and take care of myself—and so that's what I do."

"And that's what you'll do for the next forty years?" I asked. The prospect seemed as confining to me as endless years on the ranch.

"I don't think you can look at life like that," she replied. "Something comes along, and your life changes directions. That may happen. Maybe a handsome prince will come along and sweep me away. But if he doesn't, I'm happy here." She looked away for a moment, and then said, "There's an old Chinese proverb that says if you keep a green bough in your heart, the singing bird will surely come. I believe that."

I thought for a minute, fully convinced that a prince would sweep her away but less sure that a Wild West show would adopt me, green bough or not. "Papa?" I said timidly, daring to ask.

"Your papa is a bit of spice in my life once in a while, nothing to be taken seriously. He loves your mama, and she loves him. I'm just a diversion. And he's the same for me."

How could I ask if that was right or wrong? Who made the rules? I said nothing.

When Papa dragged me to Guthrie, I thought I was going into exile where time would drag, but I couldn't have been more wrong. I couldn't exactly play the piano like I did at home, but I wound endless rolls into the player piano and listened to all kinds of new music—waltzes and marches that I'd never heard before. Louise had a wonderful glass-front bookcase in the parlor, filled with books new to me. I dutifully read something called *Self-Effort,* which she treasured because her father had given it to her, but then I plunged into Walt Whitman's poetry, Cooper's *The Last of the Mohicans,* a volume of Poe short stories, and finally *The Virginian,* which Louise ordered specially after I mentioned it. That novel carried me away like no other, and the Virginian soon replaced Billy in my fantasies.

Louise and I cooked together every night, and almost every day she took me shopping, introducing me to curious shopkeepers as Sandy Burns's daughter without batting an eye. We went to the butcher's for meat, to the newspaper to withdraw her boardinghouse ad—"I'm temporarily filled up"—to a ribbon store where she bought grosgrain for her new hat and a hair ribbon for me—"I'll show you what you can do with it"—and we went to church on Sunday.

"I always sit in the second pew from the front," she said lightly. "It's best for a single woman to be visible in church in a town like this."

So I sat with her through the Methodist service—my only earlier exposure to religion had been that abrupt immersion in Catholicism—and I quailed before the preacher who spoke thunderously of heaven and hell, mostly the latter. I watched admiringly as Louise sang all four verses of "Oh for a Thousand Tongues to Sing" without ever looking at the hymnal. That, I thought, was true devotion.

"What are you doing with that cup towel?" she asked one night from the dishpan where her hands were hidden in boiling-hot soapy water.

I looked down, as though the towel and the hand that held it belonged to someone else. The towel, twisted like a rope, was spinning in a circle. "Uh . . . spinning it, I guess," I said sheepishly.

"You miss the feel of a rope in your hands, don't you?" She scrubbed at a skillet and shot her question over her shoulder.

"I suppose so. I haven't thought about it—but yes, I do." Longing hit me with a force, as though it had been hidden inside me until she unlocked it with her words. I missed Sam and riding and practicing my roping and all the things I did at the ranch. I even missed Papa and Mama.

"It's time for you to go home," she said. "I'll send word to your father that he's to come get you."

Mama never gave Papa orders like that, and I asked softly, "Will he do it?"

"He best," she laughed, "if he knows what's good for him."

Later that night as I modeled a new split skirt Louise had made for me, I reminded her, "We never did talk about getting me to a Wild West show."

"Of course," she said. "We were having such a good time, and you never mentioned it." It was a slight accusation given with a smile but nonetheless a hint that I take responsibility for my own problems.

"All right," I said boldly, "I'm mentioning it now. What should I do?" I emphasized that pronoun.

"I have a friend who has mentioned something along that line," she said vaguely. "I'll write a letter."

First she scolds me for not taking responsibility, I thought, and then she takes matters into her own hands. Just like Mama!

Mama and Louise were more alike than different, I realized, but Mama lived with Papa all the time, alone on the ranch. Louise was the master of her own fate—had I read that in a poem somewhere?—and saw Papa only when it pleased him, and maybe only when it pleased her. That complicated realization put a whole new light on things for me, and I held on to it.

When Papa delivered me to the veranda of our house, where Mama stood waiting with a soft smile on her face, I hugged her fiercely. "I missed you," I said, and then in the next breath, "She's a nice lady. I—I liked her." I wasn't sure, afterward, why I felt compelled to tell Mama that.

"I'm sure she is," she said, her arms still holding me tight.

The two women had been in Papa's life for a long time. Now they were both in mine.

CHAPTER 4

In spite of all my dreams, it wasn't the Buffalo Bill show that got me off the Luckett Ranch. A letter arrived one April day, addressed to Tommy Jo Burns and bearing a return address of The Miller 101 Ranch, Bliss, Oklahoma. Papa brought it home from Guthrie one day, and I know it cost him not to open it, but the letter was sealed when he handed it to me.

"Been there awhile," he said. "Postmark is 'bout two weeks old."

I'd not been the recipient of a whole lot of letters in my lifetime, so I didn't know to look at that. The return address caused me enough confusion.

"The Miller 101?"

"Louise knows those folks," Papa said. "Big spread, east of here a ways. Owned by three bachelor brothers—Zack, Thomas, and something else, I disremember the third one's name. Go on, open the letter." Impatience was getting the best of him.

Carefully, like a child opening a Christmas present, I slit the envelope and drew out the folded paper. The message was written in an expansive but straightforward hand: "We are planning a ranch exhibition for the National Editors Association meeting in June. Could you be part of the entertainment? We would like you to ride and rope. Please answer to me directly." It was signed Colonel Zack Miller.

"Well," Papa demanded, "what does it say?"

"They're going to have an exhibition," I said breathlessly, "and they want me to be in it." I wasn't sure how I felt. Here I'd been hoping for the Buffalo Bill show, and what I got was a neighbor—well, almost—who was having a show for a bunch of editors. I wasn't even sure who editors were, what kind of gathering it would be. But on the other hand, it sure was a change from the ranch, and I wasn't about to object—or decline.

"What kind of exhibition?" Papa asked, though his eyes danced with excitement and I knew he was pleased by the offer.

"For some editors or something."

"Well, I don't know," he said. "I'm not sure if that's the thing for you to do."

I looked straight at him. "Papa," I said, "it's the thing for me to do. It's better than not ever getting invited to rope anywhere."

He huffed and puffed and said nothing.

Mama was a little harder to convince. "Of course you won't rope and ride in public like some cowboy," she said, turning to bury her face in the clothes she was folding.

"Yes, Mama, I want to do this," I said as calmly and carefully as I could.

"This is not," she said stiffly, "what I raised you for."

I took a deep breath. "Maybe not, but it's what I want to do. And I'm seventeen years old now, Mama."

She folded laundry.

The next morning, well before daylight, I crawled out of bed and pulled on my divided skirt, a wrinkled shirtwaist—who had time to worry about wrinkles at five o'clock in the morning?—and a warm shawl. It was April, but mornings were still almost fiercely cold. Then I scrawled a note for Mama and Papa: "Gone to Guthrie. Love, Tommy Jo."

Propping the note on the kitchen table, where they couldn't miss it at breakfast, I snuck out the door, ran to the barn, and feeling my way in the darkness, saddled Sam. Casey and Wilks, still asleep in the adjacent bunkhouse, never stirred, in spite of Sam's welcoming nicker and my voice, which got louder than I meant when he offered a friendly early-morning pitch or two. It occurred to me that Papa's security wasn't too great—someone could have ridden off with all the horses, and no one would have stopped them.

Once I turned him loose at a fast pace on the road, Sam forgot his early-morning friskiness and settled into getting me to Guthrie. Overhead the sky was still midnight blue, dotted by bright stars, and I would have stared upward long and hard except I knew that would lose me control of Sam. The horizon turned a faint pink just as we left the main gate of the Luckett Ranch, and by the time we were two miles down the road, the eastern sky was a deep, rosy red.

"'Red at night, sailors delight / Red in the morning, sailors take warning,'" I recited to myself. The air was crisp and clear, and I couldn't believe a storm was coming. "Come on, Sam," I whispered in his ear, and we flew toward Guthrie.

I was at Louise's before breakfast. "Need help?" I asked, as I let myself in the back door.

She whirled from the stove. A white apron covered her chambray dress, and her hair was sort of temporarily put up—good enough to get her through breakfast but not fixed enough to go shopping or such. "Tommy Jo!" Dropping the spoon into a batch of grits, she held out her arms. "What're you doing here so early?"

Walking into her hug, I told her, "I wanted to talk to you. But let's get breakfast on the table."

We served eggs, grits, bacon, and stewed apples. Most of the boarders were the ones I'd known a few months earlier. The schoolteacher, the milliners, and the printing company owner were the same, but there were new traveling salesmen. One, with a droopy mustache and pale rheumy eyes, asked me how I'd arrived so early in the morning and seemed astounded when I said calmly, "I rode horseback."

"How far?" he asked weakly.

"Fifteen miles about," I said.

"And you're a girl," he muttered, though I thought that was pretty obvious. He said nothing more for the whole breakfast and actually avoided looking at me.

I ate Louise's food with relish, my appetite increased by the ride. "Don't they feed you at that ranch?" she asked teasingly, when I helped myself to more grits and bacon. Pretending offense, I ignored her.

At last, the boarders drifted away, the schoolteacher muttering about youngsters without proper education, and the new drummer repeating "Fifteen miles before breakfast?" Louise poured herself more coffee, smiled at my emphatic no when it was offered to me, and settled back in her chair.

"Why are you here?"

"The most wonderful thing has happened," I began, "and it's awful!"

Her sudden, surprisingly deep laughter filled the room, and after just a second I laughed with her. Then we both sobered.

"You've heard from Zack Miller," she said.

"You knew?"

"Of course. I told you I would write to a friend. The colonel—that's what they call Zack—was in here some months back, told me he was planning an exhibition. So I just wrote and told him I knew the best girl roper in the Strip."

"In the country!" I said indignantly.

"You'll have to prove that," she said gently. "All right, it's wonderful! You've a chance to ride in an exhibition that isn't the Buffalo Bill show, but it's a start. What's awful? Mama or Papa?"

"Both. Papa thinks he's going with me, and Mama came as close to forbidding me to go as she could. I—I don't know what to do."

If I'd expected Louise to hand me the answer, I'd pinned my hopes in the wrong place. She just sat silently, watching me.

"Well"—I began to talk to fill the silence—"if Papa goes with me, he'll pretty soon be bossing everyone around, probably make that colonel angry. And it'll be hard for me to meet people, because Papa will be in the way. But if I ask him not to go—"

"He'll go anyway," she supplied.

"Yes. So maybe there's nothing I can do about that." With an inward shudder, I thought back to the wolf hunt and the way everyone resented me. The exhibition could turn out the same way.

"I wouldn't give up so easily," came the quick reply. "What about your mother?"

"She's hurt, angry with me. She won't talk about it, won't even listen to me. I guess all I can do is what I did—tell her I love her. But I have to go do this. If I stay on the ranch with them . . ." I shrugged, foreseeing that endless future before me.

"I think your mama will understand once you really go. But you may need my help with your father. When do you go?"

"Three weeks."

"I think you should go home and practice harder than you've ever practiced, be more helpful to your mama than you ever have, and leave your papa to me. He'll be in here before then, I can almost guarantee. Now, let's get these dishes done, and then I want to take you shopping."

In the mercantile store, Louise bought several yards each of serviceable denim and a wonderful buttery-brown wool and some soft challis just a shade lighter. Her last purchase was crisp white cotton, with three yards of lace ruffles. "For the front of the shirt," she explained. "I'll send these home with your father when he comes."

"Louise, I can't let you do that," I said, feeling that I ought to protest but thrilled at the thought of new riding outfits.

"Your mother," she said practically, "won't give her approval by outfitting you. I'm glad to have the chance."

She ended her shopping spree by fitting me with a light straw Stetson. "For summer," she told me.

By early afternoon, I had Sam saddled and was ready to ride home. We stood by the barn behind Louise's house.

"Thank you," I said. "I'll—I'll tell you all about it."

"Never can tell," she laughed. "I might show up at the exhibition." Then she hesitated. "Would that bother you? Would it be like having your parents there?"

I thought about it for a moment. "No," I said, "I don't guess it would."

"Tommy Jo," she said, "I guess I have to confess. I'd sort of hoped that if you wanted to get away from the ranch, you might come to Guthrie." In a rush she added, "I know it wouldn't do much for your roping, but—well, you always have a place here." She looked away, as though embarrassed by her own words.

"Thank you," I said, and gave her a fierce hug. Then quickly, before she saw the tears in the corners of my eyes, I mounted Sam and rode off, only turning to wave when I was a block away. She was standing, one hand shading her eyes against the midday sun, looking after me.

I waved and spurred Sam into a gallop.

The ride home was as long as my early-morning ride had been short, though we covered the same level dirt road, passed the same open prairies dotted with plum thickets, and the same ranch gates. In the morning, I'd passed no one between Luckett's and Guthrie. Now I saw an occasional rider, who raised a friendly hand to me, and one or two buggies, whose occupants looked curiously at a young girl riding alone. I waved to all and kept Sam at an even pace.

Two miles from the ranch, I watched the sky begin to darken in the west. The rain began, soft at first and then harder, until it came in a good steady spring shower. The road turned to mud, which flew up at me as Sam raced along, and the wet wind plastered my hair into my face. Off in the distance I could see an occasional streak of lightning, followed by a faint boom of thunder, and I prayed I'd get home before the real storm hit. Lightning was in the same category with wolves: it scared me, because I knew it was a real danger.

When I rode into our barn, I was chilled to the bone and so tired, I wanted nothing more than to be in my bed. " 'Red in the morning, sailors take warning,' " I repeated to myself.

"Best get up to the house," Casey said, concern showing in his voice. "Your folks are fit to be tied. Was me, I'd whip you within an inch of your life."

Wilks just watched, his look hinting that he hoped I got a hiding.

My heart sank, but I managed to say lightly, "Whip me, Casey? I'm too old to whip."

"Goin' off alone like that," he muttered. "Got no more sense than that there horse. Ain't safe for a girl."

"For a girl?" I echoed.

Just then the first crack of nearby lightning hit, startling both Sam and me so badly that he shied, I jumped, and Casey yelled, "Whoa, now! Whoa, now!" as he grabbed the reins. His look seemed to say, "See, I told you a girl couldn't handle things!"

"For a girl," he repeated firmly. "Miss Tommy Jo, don't you stand here arguing with me. You get on up there to that house and get into some dry clothes."

Papa met me before I put a foot on the veranda. "Where've you been?" he demanded, ignoring the rain, which beat down on both of us, and my sodden clothes, as he stood there in his yellow slicker.

"Guthrie," I said as calmly as I could. "I left you a note. I went to see Louise."

That took the wind out of his sails for just a moment. "Louise? Well . . ." But then his anger rose up again. "Won't be lettin' you go to the Miller," he said. "You've just shown you don't have the sense to be turned loose. I'll write the colonel."

"I'll write the colonel," I said, brushing past him.

"You tell him you aren't able to ride in his *exhibition!*" he called after me, emphasizing the word in a mocking way.

Mama sat in the rocking chair, her eyes fixed on the knitting in her lap.

"Mama?" I knelt down beside the chair, one hand on her knee. A puddle began on the floor beneath me as water dripped from my hair, my clothes, my shoes.

One hand dropped its needles and reached out to stroke my hair, wet though it was. "Your father was frightened and angry. He doesn't mind you going to Guthrie, if he's the one who decides you should go. But if you decide . . ." There was no denying the bitterness in her voice.

"And now he's decided I can't go to the Miller?" I asked.

She nodded.

"And you?"

The knitting slid to the floor as Mama wrapped her arms around me and cried, a display so unlike her that it scared me. After four or five loud sobs, she quieted and said softly, "I don't want you to go, Tommy Jo. I don't want you to leave the ranch, and if you do, I want you to go to a city and live in a fine house and be a lady." A sob caught in her throat, and she wiped at the tears on her cheeks. "But none of that is fair, no more fair than letting your papa run your life."

Now the tears were running down my cheeks as freely as Mama's. "Come with me, Mama. We'll go to St. Louis, we'll go wherever." My voice was low, in a whisper, but it echoed with intensity.

"No," she answered softly. "That's not the answer either. I . . . you ride in that exhibition, Tommy Jo."

Papa came in a few minutes later and found us huddled together, Mama still in the rocking chair and me at her feet, both of us now soaking wet, for she had hugged me tightly enough to make her clothes as wet as mine. "Any dinner around here?" he asked, but all the anger was gone from his tone.

In the end, I ran away from home. Or maybe I ran away from Papa, because Mama knew I would go. Papa thought, for almost three weeks, that he had closed the matter with his letter to Colonel Zack Miller, though I never knew what the letter said. And I wrote my own letter, assuring the colonel that I would ride in his exhibition. It occurred to me to wonder if he would expect me, for he probably wouldn't know which letter to believe.

For those three weeks, I was a model daughter. I rode with Papa and helped with the birthing when the spring calves arrived; I helped Mama with her vegetable plot, digging in the red dirt until I thought my fingernails would never be clean again; in the evenings I helped with supper and did the dishes.

And whenever I could steal a moment, I practiced my roping. With Billy gone and Papa angry with me, I had no one to walk through my loop. So I built big empty loops and kept them spinning while counting aloud to myself, pretending that a handsome cowboy was walking in and out of the loop or that a horse was thundering toward me from some distance away. I roped poor Sam until it was a wonder he didn't turn skittish every time he saw me with a loop in my hands.

But during evenings in the house, I no longer built tiny loops. I occupied my hands with mending, while Mama was busy with her knitting and Papa read his blasted St. Louis newspapers.

He never mentioned the Miller 101, and conversation was sparse on those long evenings. I had nothing to say to him.

The exhibition was to begin on a Sunday. I left home on Friday morning, once again sneaking away before daylight. I rolled my clothes into a pack that would fit on the back of my saddle. Papa had brought me new clothes—two split skirts and a crisp white shirt with a ruffled front—from Louise and handed them over without a word; these were carefully folded into a blanket and rolled, though I knew they would wrinkle badly.

This time I left no note. Mama knew where I was going, and Papa would figure it out soon enough. The fear that he would come riding after me, determined to bring me back, made me spur Sam all the faster.

I should be feeling sad, I thought, leaving home with my father angry at me, my mother heartbroken. But my spirits fairly flew ahead of Sam, filled with excitement and anticipation. I was going to rope in an exhibition—really, I decided, I could honestly call it a Wild West show. The parade in Washington flashed before my eyes, and I heard myself again being cheered by the crowd, saw myself bowing and responding.

The bowing in my mind had to stop if I was to make it to the Miller 101 in two days, and at that they would be long days. I remembered Papa saying the ranch took in three towns—Bliss, Red Rock, and White Eagle—and that it was almost due east of Luckett's place and a little north, near Ponca City. From Luckett's gate, I turned north, away from Guthrie, and rode until I came to a fork in the road. Then I headed east, figuring to meet someone who could direct me once it was daylight.

The first traveler I met was an old man driving a wagon pulled by two stubborn-looking mules. When I signaled him, he "whoa'd" the mules to a stop, pulling hard on the reins, and said, "What's a girl like you doin' out here on the road alone?"

"Going to the Miller 101," I said, trying to ignore the rest of his question. "Near Ponca City."

"That big shindig they're havin' over there, I bet. Still, a girl like you . . . I was your pa . . ."

"My pa's behind me," I said to cut him off. After all, that probably wasn't a lie. "But I just wanted to make sure I'm on the right road."

"Sure are, missy, but you got a long way to go. You get a mite closer, I bet you'll meet up with some other folks goin' that way. Gonna be a big shindig. If not, they can tell you in Ponca City, and you're headed straight there." He clucked to the mules and moved on.

The land went from flat prairie to rolling hills as I rode east, and the trees grew taller, the underbrush thicker. The day was hot and clear, and the sun seemed to beat down on me unmercifully. Well before midday, I was grateful for the canteen of cool water I'd brought and the meal of cold biscuits and pork. I ground-tied Sam and settled beneath his shadow to eat, just as Papa and I had done many a time while working Luckett's cattle. Only this time, Papa wasn't here. I was alone, and I was on my way to a great big show.

By suppertime Sam and I were both tired and ready to stop. I made a cold camp and settled myself for an uncomfortable night, using my saddle for an awkward pillow. As many times as I'd camped with Papa, I shouldn't have been alarmed by the prairie noises at night, but the owls seemed more threatening, the coyotes closer. Thoughts of hungry wolves and even desperate rustlers drove away all my enthusiasm for the show, and I wished myself safe at home. Had I been foolish to run away? I'd ground-tied Sam as close by as I could, and once in a while I'd talk to him just to hear him nicker reassuringly, which helped a little. Still, it was a long night, and well before daybreak I was up and ready to move on.

The show had grown in my mind ever since I'd talked to that old man driving his mules. By the time I nooned on the second day, other riders had joined me on the road, passing with a wave and a friendly smile. The terrors of the night were forgotten, and I figured I was headed in the right direction. At a fork in the road, an official-looking sign pointed the way to Ponca City, but a kind of home-done sign said, "Miller 101 this way." I followed the second sign.

By late afternoon, as I approached the Salt Fork of the Arkansas, which ran through the Miller 101, the road was downright crowded with riders, alone or in groups, and horse-drawn vehicles of every description, from wagons to closed-in black buggies with isinglass windows rolled up on the sides. At least two automobiles honked past us, though this time I was alert enough to get a good grip on Sam well before the smoking, noisy things came near us. Holding tight to the reins, I spoke softly into his ear, reassuring him, and he trembled with alarm but never did bolt.

As the sun began to drop lower, I asked a man on horseback how far it was to the Miller 101.

" 'Bout three more miles," he said, nodding his head down the road. "Big gate, you can't miss it. But they're not letting people in until the show Sunday. Even got a special train track laid out there, to bring them editors or whatever. But today I guess they're gettin' ready." He sighed, as though he would have given his eyeteeth to get on to the ranch early.

"I'm going to ride in the show," I said, aware that I was boasting. "I guess they'll let me in." And I left him behind me, probably thinking what an arrogant creature I was.

Within a mile, I could see tents pitched along the river. Whole families appeared to have settled in, their horses tethered nearby, their children playing happily in the red dirt, men sometimes gathered in groups to talk and chew and spit, women mostly out of sight.

My heart was nearly bursting out of my chest with excitement by this time. All these people had come to see this exhibition! I thought it was a small show for a bunch of eastern newspaper editors—maybe a hundred people at the most—and yet it looked now like the entire population of the Cherokee Strip and the Indian Territory had turned out for the day. And I was going to ride and rope!

Fear flickered through my mind, just a thin thread that came and then was gone. But I recognized it: What if my loop fell apart? What if Sam pitched and I couldn't control him? What if . . . A thousand possibilities, all of them bad, began to dance in my mind. And then I thought about Billy, and how he was sure I'd be a great roper, and how I was going to show him!

"Come on, Sam," I cried, "let's go!"

I swear he ran faster.

Once I passed the gate to the Miller—a fancy wrought-iron arch with "101" spelled out at the top—I moved onto land completely foreign to me. On either side of the road lay enormous fields, with the dirt piled up in even rows and small green shoots showing in the center of each row, plants in one section bigger than the other, as wheat, milo, alfalfa, even lettuce and onions sprouted in the early June warmth.

I passed an orchard—though I didn't recognize an apple orchard at the time—and a pasture where black and white cattle grazed peacefully—I didn't recognize Holsteins either, but I knew they sure looked different from the beef cattle at home. Coming from Luckett's, where there were only beef cattle and no trees or vegetable garden beyond Mama's little plot, I was overwhelmed.

I must have ridden several miles before an enormous house came into view, bigger and far grander than Louise's in Guthrie. I might have compared it to the convent in St. Louis, but it was not quite that large, and it was of wood, not brick, and was lots more interesting than the square and formidable brick convent.

The house was three stories high, though the top story looked to be dormer-like rooms beneath the various angles of the roof, all covered with green wooden shingles. The house itself was made of white slats with windows all around the second floor—including one oval window that riveted my attention for a moment—and a huge veranda, with a green shingle roof, that wrapped around the first floor. With its uneven roof lines—a pitch here and an angle there—and its profusion of windows, it was somehow a house of life, full of happiness.

Clustered around this house, like pups around a mother dog, were a smattering of smaller houses, all shingle, all painted white with green roofs, and all dwarfed by the big house. And beyond that, a field or more away, was an enormous arena. I rode toward it, but when I was about fifty yards from it, I simply stopped to stare. I bet it could seat a thousand people!

"You there! Move along! No tourists allowed here, and you're in the way. Look lively now!" From behind me, a voice bellowed in an unpleasant tone.

Holding Sam's reins tightly, I turned in the saddle, only to see an enormous load of wooden planks being hauled by mules, right toward the spot where we sat. I touched Sam lightly with my knees, and he moved forward and away.

"No tourists here!" the voice repeated, and then it took shape, a man of perhaps Papa's age with a bushy mustache, who stood, hands on hips, belligerently staring up at me from beneath the brim of an enormous Stetson.

"I'm not a tourist," I said, summoning all my dignity. "My name is Tommy Jo Burns, and I've been invited here to ride." Just who this rude man was I had no idea, but I wanted my tone to convey what I saw as my superiority.

"Tommy Jo Burns!" he exploded. "Well, I'll be. I'm Zack Miller, the one who invited you here. Come right down off that horse, and let's have a look at you! Where's your pa? I never could figure if you'd be here or not, what with your letter and his saying different things. But I figured if you showed up, he would, too."

Patting Sam to reassure him in the face of all this conversation, I dismounted, dropped the reins on the ground, and walked around Sam to face Colonel Miller. "My father," I said, "could not come with me."

"And you came way out here alone? A sprite of a thing like you? Lord a'mighty!" Hands still on his hips, he stood staring at me, evaluating, until I thought I was a horse he was thinking of buying. Finally, he said, "If you can rope, you'll be the hit of the show."

"I can rope," I said with great conviction.

"Well, come right on up to the house. We're puttin' the ladies up there. Mama's got rooms all fixed." Jerking his head toward the huge white house, he strode off, leaving me little choice except to follow or stand there looking dumb.

"How much do you know about the show we're putting together?" he asked as we walked.

"It's for editors or something," I said, puzzled by this talkative man. "You want me to rope."

"Right, editors. We're gonna show 'em what the real West is like—none of this Buffalo Bill business. We're gonna have working cowboys—and real Indians. Geronimo is here." He added this triumphantly, as though having the Indian chief were a great accomplishment.

"Geronimo?" I echoed. Sure, I'd heard the name, but I couldn't have told you any more than that he was a fierce Indian who'd killed more than his share of whites in days past. And now he was here at an exhibition? I shook my head.

"Yeah, Geronimo. Apache. One of the meanest and toughest, but he's a farmer now. Real calm. You'll see."

"This isn't a Wild West show?" I asked tentatively, trying to hide my disappointment.

"No, ma'am, it's an exhibition of real working cowboys—and cowgirls, of course. I hear you're the first to have that name, least officially."

"Well, maybe," I said, suddenly bashful, thinking perhaps I was presumptuous even to think of myself as a cowgirl. But then I raised my head and said proudly, "President Roosevelt called me a cowgirl. I guess that was where it all began." I didn't think it was worth mentioning those mean girls in the convent.

His scornful attitude toward the Buffalo Bill show was still bothering me as we reached the house, but I forgot about it as soon as I met Mollie Miller, the mother of Colonel Zack and his two brothers.

"They tell me you can rope like no other girl," she said, her voice in a question as though she were appraising me.

"I can rope," I said, with a sense of repeating myself. "I don't know any other girls who rope, so I guess I can't say about the others."

"Where's your father? I presumed he would accompany you."

There was that question again! "Papa couldn't come," I lied. "I came alone."

She frowned. "A young girl like you riding all that way alone. Your father should be horsewhipped for allowing that."

Now there was a thought! I prayed a silent but fervent plea that Papa would not arrive unexpectedly, for I'd have hated to see him tangle with Mrs. Miller. I began to understand why her three sons were not married.

"Come, I'll show you your room."

Without ceremony, I was deposited in a large sunny corner room with two narrow beds, a rag rug on the floor, roller blinds that were raised to let in bright sunlight, and family photographs hung in chains on the walls.

"You'll be sharing with Prairie Rose Henson," she said, plumping the pillows in a no-nonsense way as she talked.

"Prairie Rose?" Could it possibly be the girl I'd read about, the one who backed the officials down and rode a bucking horse?

"She's a bronc rider from Wyoming. One of the best. Dinner's at eight." And with that she was gone, leaving me to unpack my few belongings and wait in anticipation to meet my heroine.

I didn't have to wonder for long, for Prairie Rose—her real name was Florence—blew into the room a bit later. She wore a Stetson with a brim so wide it made mine look like a miniature, and an explosion of red curls escaped beneath it, framing a small heart-shaped face liberally sprinkled with freckles and split by a smile that threatened to turn into a giggle. I liked her immediately.

"You're Tommy Jo," she said, a statement that became cause for laughter—not deep laughter like Louise's, but a high-pitched, girlish sound. "You rope. Mrs. Miller told me you were the best girl roper in the West." She rolled her eyes toward the ceiling.

"She told me you were the best bronc rider," I replied, too shy to tell her that I already admired her greatly. Much later in our friendship, I told Rose that I'd known about her and that she'd inspired me, and all she said was, "Silly! You've got the spirit, Tommy Jo. You can go anywhere you want without me to inspire you. You just got to remember that." And I did remember her saying that, forever.

I sat on the bed I'd chosen and watched as she carelessly pulled clothes from a canvas duffel, flinging them over a chair here and on the bed there.

Being Mama's daughter, I'd hung my few things, including the new clothes Louise had made, neatly in the wardrobe.

"Yeah, I ride broncs. But I really trick ride. It's just that Colonel Miller is so bound that this be an exhibition of working cowboy skills, that he doesn't want trick riding. This time." With that she smiled, as though she had a secret plan. Prairie Rose emptied her canvas bag in minutes, disappeared into the bathroom down the hall for just a moment, then reappeared to insist, "Let's go downstairs." All I'd learned about her in those few minutes was that she grew up on a ranch in Wyoming, that she really wanted to be a trick rider, not a bronc rider, and that her pa, as she called him, had sent one of his cowboys to escort her all the way to Oklahoma. At first I thought they'd ridden all that way, and I was mightily impressed, but the truth was they'd gone to Oklahoma City by train. Rose, on the other hand, was awed that I'd made a two-day ride alone and spent a night on the prairie, and I could see that I went up in her estimation. It gave me a good feeling.

Since it was nearly time for dinner, we put off exploring until the next day and settled ourselves on the veranda to watch what was going on—some men carried long pieces of lumber, for benches perhaps, others led horses, cowboys rode back and forth, and people milled around.

"Look," I said, "at that Indian—do you suppose that's Geronimo?" I was staring at a short, slightly stooped man with his gray hair parted in the center and drawn back from his face. He wore a stovepipe hat, a man's suit that looked too big, a wrinkled checked shirt, and a scarf knotted at the neck, and he was animatedly talking with Colonel Miller. As he talked, he waved his hands in the air and pointed at himself, then the colonel, then the big top, then the sky. "Whatever can he be saying?"

"Don't know, but I do know that's Geronimo."

"The colonel said he was here," I said, trying to appear casually knowledgeable. "But what's he going to do? Ride in the parade?"

"More than that," she laughed. "They're going to kill a buffalo—one last buffalo hunt, so they say—and Geronimo's going to get to do it. I heard a rumor that Geronimo offered a thousand dollars to any white man who would let himself be scalped during the raid on the stagecoach. But I don't guess anybody's taken him up on it."

"I want to meet him," I said, half-rising to head toward him right then.

Mrs. Miller stopped me, sticking her head out of the door to announce that dinner was ready. She banged on an iron triangle, and I saw Colonel

Miller start a little and then take leave of Geronimo to head for the house for dinner. His mother must have trained him never to be late to meals.

Dinner was hearty—beef and potatoes—and it was informative, for Colonel Miller presided over the meal and turned it into a lecture session on the exhibition. "Trains start to arrive first thing in the morning, parade is at two P.M. Everyone's expected to ride. We'll meet in the arena tomorrow at eight in the morning to go over the exhibition plans." He looked around as though challenging his guests to come up with questions or comments.

No one spoke. I peeked a shy glance around the table—there were three other women besides me, Mrs. Miller, and Prairie Rose, and they looked to be older, one nearly thirty. The colonel's two brothers sat near him at the head of the table, and about six other cowboys had joined us. The Millers made no introductions, and I was left to wonder if these were other performers in the exhibition or simply cowboys who worked on the ranch. One thing was certain: There were a whole lot of workers on this ranch who weren't at this dinner table. Luckett's looked like small potatoes by comparison.

Papa showed up just before the parade—at least I guess he did. I saw him as I rode next to Prairie Rose, just behind Geronimo, who was bowing and smiling and loving the attention he got—only now he was dressed like everyone thought he should be, in a beaded vest, fringed leather leggings, and a feather-decorated band holding his hair. I was amazed at the change in him, from the kind of dumpy man I'd seen the day before. Now he rode proud in the saddle.

The parade was equal to the one I'd ridden in for President Roosevelt, and I had to keep reminding myself I was on a ranch in the Cherokee Strip and not in a big city. A cavalry band led the way, playing "Home on the Range" every so often between marching and battle songs. Geronimo and a band of Indians dressed for battle followed, and we five women performers followed him. Then came a long procession of cowboys. A stagecoach and a pioneer wagon train brought up the rear.

We paraded from behind the house along the road to the arena, and then twice around the arena, while the spectators stood and cheered, causing the horses to shy almost into each other. The editors were seated in a large group—Colonel Miller told me later they came from every end of the country, even Vermont and Maine—and they were mostly dressed like east-erners, in dark suits with boiled shirts, proper ties, and derby hats, which some of them waved enthusiastically. The arena that I thought held at least a thousand people turned out to hold ten thousand, and there wasn't a vacant seat anywhere.

I knew how Geronimo felt as he waved to the crowd, for once again I heard the roar and felt the applause and thought I'd died and gone to heaven. Those men, the editors, had probably never seen women riding in exhibition—gosh, they'd never seen a western exhibition—and they cheered loudly as we rode by. If they'd known our names, they'd have called to each of us, I was sure.

Papa was waiting outside the arena right after the parade.

"Get back on Sam. We're goin' home," he said in his strictest tone. "You don't run away when I've told you not to go somewhere."

"I'm here, Papa, and I'm going to ride."

"You're my daughter," he thundered, "and—"

I looked behind me to see what had caused Papa to stare into space and stop yelling at me. There stood Colonel Zack Miller.

"Burns?" he said, holding out his hand. "Good to see you again. Sort of expected you to arrive with Tommy Jo. Understand you've been her coach and all." He ignored the difference in our letters, the fact that Papa had said clearly that I was not coming to the exhibition.

"Uh, that's right," Papa said, taking the offered hand. "I've taught her what she knows." He beamed at me with what I considered a fake smile, and I was glad Billy wasn't around to hear Papa take all the credit.

"You'll be proud to see her perform today, then," the colonel said.

"Yessir, looking forward to that!" Papa responded.

"Well, I'll take her back with the performers now, but there's a reserved seat waiting for you next to the announcer. I know you'll have a good view."

"Thank you," Papa said, almost mollified. He turned into the arena, and still mounted on Sam, I followed Colonel Zack Miller.

I'd never roped before a big audience before—oh, sure, I'd ridden in President Roosevelt's parade, and I'd roped for Billy, but I'd never put the two together, at least not until it was almost time for me to perform.

The show began with an Indian ball game, followed by a war dance and powwow, bronco busting, and finally, the roping. Rose, as I'd already come to call her, rode a wicked dun bronc who sunfished, threw himself straight up in the air on four stiff legs, and finally reared back on his hind legs. I held my breath, sure that the horse would topple over backward, crushing Rose beneath his falling body. But she grinned and waved at the crowd as they cheered, whistled, and stomped. Prairie Rose was a hit, and there was, I knew, no way I could follow her. The roping was next.

Four of the men who'd been at the dinner table the night before were on the roping program before me. They roped running calves, and one—a short banty-legged cowboy with amazingly strong arms—roped a running buffalo. But none let horses run through their loops, and none dared to rope another cowboy.

"Ladies and gentlemen!" roared the announcer. "We now have the privilege of seeing the finest lady roper in the West—Miss Tommy Jo Burns of the Luckett Ranch in the Cherokee Strip."

I touched my heels lightly to Sam, and he moved forward, carrying us into the arena at a dignified pace. We moved to a point just beyond the center of the arena, and I dismounted. The arena was almost eerily quiet, though my heart was pounding so loudly that I thought it would break the silence. Moving slowly, deliberately, I built a loop in front of me—a good-sized loop—and when it was strong, I stepped into it and continued to turn it around me. The cheering nearly brought me to my knees. Letting the loop drop after a few minutes, I stepped over the rope and bowed deeply.

Then, my hands almost shaking, I laid out a huge loop behind me. When it was to my satisfaction, I nodded ever so slightly to the man who waited at the far end of the arena—he was a cowboy I'd met that morning at the planning sessions—and he began to ride toward me. When he was almost up to me, I heaved the loop over my head, until it stood vertically in front of me.

The horse, his rider waving his hat in the air, rode through that loop. For just a moment, there was silence in the crowd, as though everyone had collectively drawn in a long slow breath, just as the loop settled about the horse and rider. And then the audience exploded in applause. Laughing and as excited as I'd ever been, I took bow after bow.

The cowboy—he was John Mason—stepped off his horse and started toward me, and as he did I built a loop with the small rope on my belt and threw it around him, barely pulling it tight. Laughing, he tried to hold his hands up in a shrug, though he could only get them partway up because of the rope around his shoulder. The applause grew louder, but I could not bow as long as I had that rope around Mason. Finally, I let it drop, and he came over and grabbed my hand, holding it high in the air as though I were the victor in a boxing competition.

I bowed to them, and bowed again, breaking into laughter from pure joy at the applause. The editors and all those other folks from around about were cheering wildly, and my bows didn't seem likely to stop them. Off to one side, I saw Papa, grinning broadly, all his anger forgotten in reflected glory. With a sudden inspiration, I coiled my rope and deliberately built a loop. The crowd quieted as they watched. When the loop was right, I sent it sailing over Papa, and then tightened it enough to begin to pull him toward me. The crowd went wild again as the announcer said, "The little lady's father, folks! Sandy Burns!"

The Indian raid on the stagecoach followed. The Indians weren't Apaches like Geronimo, but were the Poncas who lived around the 101 and who respected Colonel Zack like a father. As a favor to him, they dressed up and pretended to be fierce, but it was really an act. The editors, however, didn't know a Ponca from an Apache, and they oohed and aahed with horror as the Indians shot arrows into the fleeing stagecoach and finally set it on fire. One horse—specially trained, I learned later—limped off after the battle, as though wounded. If the show was repeated very often, I thought, it would get expensive replacing stagecoaches and horses.

The climax of the show, though, was Geronimo's buffalo hunt. This great warrior chief shot his last buffalo right there in front of a bunch of easterners who didn't have any idea what it meant to him. But the amazing thing about it was that he shot that buffalo with a bow and arrow like he'd done all his life, but this time from a speeding automobile rather than from a running horse. The other Indians around him rode horseback and herded the buffalo toward him, but Geronimo, armed with bow and arrow, rode in a Locomobile that probably went twenty miles an hour—and he brought down his buffalo with an arrow placed just behind the shoulder. The editors would have buffalo meat for dinner—and probably none would realize that it was stringy and tough, because the animal was an old bull. And maybe none of them thought about how ironic it was for a great Indian chief to be hunting from an automobile. I thought there was something wrong about automobiles—and terribly wrong about an Apache shooting a buffalo from one.

Papa waited for me at the gate when it was all over. "Tommy Jo! You best talk to me!"

"Papa, aren't you proud of what I did?"

" 'Course I am, honey," he said, "but you still disobeyed me, and I can't let that be. We're goin' home now."

"Papa, I'm not goin' home with you," I said in deliberate tones, though I had no idea where or what I would do instead.

Prairie Rose rode up behind me just then. "Mr. Burns? You must be awful proud of Tommy Jo!"

He looked at her for a long minute, and then said with deliberate slowness, "I don't need no girl dressed like a cowboy to tell me I'm proud of my daughter."

She wore the britches and leather chaps in which she'd ridden, and the Stetson still rode large on her head. But Rose's face was purely feminine, and so was her anger at Papa. "You don't need to insult me, Mr. Burns. I know who I am." And she whirled her horse away, but not before she got off a wink to me.

"Papa! How could you?" I was at a loss for words.

"She'll not be telling you what to do," he thundered. "I'm your father, and I'll decide what you do."

I looked at Papa and realized that if I gave in now, Papa would be telling me what to do for the next twenty years. And Colonel Zack Miller and others would let him—they'd go to him for every decision about what I did.

"Papa," I said, "go home. I'm about to be a famous roper, and I won't be letting you tell me what to do anymore."

He opened his mouth wide in protest, but I spurred Sam away before Papa could answer, and much as it cost me, I never looked back over my shoulder.

Rose found me in our room, sitting staring out over the prairie. "Your pa left," she said. "I heard him tell Colonel Miller that he guessed he could take as good care of you now, and he was turning you over to him. Did you know he was leaving?"

I barely shook my head to answer no before the tears poured down my cheeks. Head buried in one of Mrs. Miller's best down pillows, I sobbed brokenheartedly. My papa was gone, I was on my own, and I hadn't even told him good-bye.

"Good-bye, Papa," I whispered. From the window, way off in the distance, I could see a solitary figure riding west, sitting straight and tall in the saddle. Papa never crumbled before defeat.

Dinner that night was to be festive, a celebration for all the editors and performers. Mrs. Miller told us, "Put on your best clothes, girls. The exhibition's a success, and we're going to throw a party tonight."

I dressed in the soft brown split skirt and white ruffled shirt Louise had sent. With my straw Stetson and a brown scarf at my neck, my outfit was, I thought, very western and very tasteful.

Rose outdid me. She wore pink bloomerlike pants, tucked into pale cream boots, a pink shirt, of a paler shade than the pants, and a cream Stetson that matched her boots. She looked, I thought, like strawberries and cream. Those red curls escaping under the Stetson added an almost devilish note, as though she could not only ride a horse standing up but do almost anything anyone dared her to.

"Come on, Tommy Jo," she said, linking her arm in mine, "we're gonna make some men look twice at us tonight."

Not to be outdone, I smiled as brightly as I could and tried to avoid clutching at her arm as we started downstairs.

To my everlasting surprise, Louise stood at the foot of the stairs, next to Colonel Zack Miller. When she saw me, her eyes lit up and she blew a kiss upward. By the time I reached the bottom step, my arm now unlinked from Rose's, Louise came forward with her arms open for a hug.

For just a moment, I froze. Then I hugged her, with that distant way you can hug when you're not sure about the reception. "Louise?" My voice asked why she was here, what she had seen, what she knew.

"No," she said, "I haven't seen your father, but yes, I saw you rope—and you were wonderful!" She spread her arms wide again, and this time I returned her hug with enthusiasm. She turned to the colonel. "I *told* you she was good!"

"That you did, Louise," he said, smiling at her with a proprietary air, "that you did." And then in that booming voice of his, he told not just Louise but everyone around, "This little lady was the hit of the celebration. Tommy Jo Burns, folks, the best girl roper in the entire United States of America!"

Blushing, I sidled up to Louise. It was wonderful that Colonel Miller thought I was that good, but I wished he'd be a little more quiet about it. Every eye seemed turned on me. And besides my embarrassment, my mind was whirling as I tried to figure out Louise's relationship to the colonel, in light of what I thought I knew about her relationship to my father. "Papa?" I said softly, looking at her.

She pulled me aside. "I heard. I'll do what I can. But Tommy Jo, you did what's important to you. You roped in an exhibition! Now let's go meet all these folks."

Festive was hardly the word for that celebration. Buffalo steaks, beans, biscuits fresh from the Dutch oven over the campfire—I ate until I thought I'd burst, and surely never mount a horse again. Fiddle players plucked out old familiar tunes, and some folks started a dance. Then several of the Indians began a chant, and old Geronimo got out in the middle of a circle and did a shuffling dance—none of us understood his movements, but not a one of us was left unmoved by the emotion that went with his dancing and chanting.

"That's a man who killed a lot of white men." John Mason, the cowboy I roped in the arena, came up behind me. "Can't believe he's here, dancing as though we were all friends." He shook his head.

"Aren't we now?" I asked, looking at him. Not much distinguished John Mason from most cowboys—maybe his round face, which gave him a babyish look that didn't fit with the toughness of his body. He was blond, and in the firelight I couldn't see the color of his eyes but I bet on blue.

Mason scowled, furrowing faintly defined eyebrows together. "Lost some family to Indians in Texas years ago," he said. "Don't suppose I can ever think of a red man as my brother." Then his face brightened, a grin taking over. "Why are we talking about hate and enemies? I came over here to tell you how impressed I was with your roping."

"Thanks," I said, looking down at the ground. I was unused to compliments, especially from young men my age, and I wasn't sure how to handle it.

"Never thought a girl could rope better than the poorest man," he said.

I bristled and glanced sideways at him to see if he was joking. He wasn't. "Why should a girl be any different?" I asked. Prairie Rose stood nearby, and I was sure, from the smile on her face, that she had heard the conversation.

"You know," he said as though surely I understood, "they're not as strong and all that."

"Strong doesn't have anything to do with it," I replied, primed now for an argument.

He threw his hands in the air, just as he'd done when I roped him. "I give in. No contest. Let's take a walk and get away from this noise."

Vaguely I saw Prairie Rose cast a sharp glance in my direction, but by then I'd nodded in agreement, and John Mason put his arm around my shoulders. We walked away from the singing and dancing, the gathered crowd with their whispers of conversation, their murmurs of approval at the dancing. His arm seemed heavy on my shoulders, although I was unnaturally aware of it. Suddenly, we were totally alone, beyond the shadows of the firelight, the eyes of the crowd.

"Tommy Jo," he whispered, "you can sure rope. And I bet there are other things you can do." The arm around my shoulders turned me toward him, and his mouth came down on mine, not soft and gentle like Billy's kiss, but strong and tough—and unpleasant. I tried to pull back, but he held me tightly with one hand, while the other explored my breasts, then yanked at my shirt to pull it out of my waist.

"Stop!" I muttered, my mouth still smashed by his.

"You'll like it, Tommy Jo," he promised, moving his lips from mine just a shade. "Just relax. You'll like it."

"Let me go!" I demanded, louder this time.

John Mason simply laughed, but he stopped laughing when the toe of my boot connected with his shinbone. I aimed high, above his boot top, and I kicked hard. His cry mixed pain and anger, and I was sure everyone within five miles heard it, including all those editors who were chewing their buffalo steaks and dancing like fools. It would serve John Mason right if every one of them wrote a story about cowboys and impropriety.

By the time he straightened up again, one hand clutching his leg, I was gone. Behind me, a threat floated on the air: "You'll be sorry."

I ran and ran, my booted feet complaining, until I reached the big house. Grateful that the house was empty and everyone was still at the celebration, I ran to my bedroom, closed the door, and flung myself on the bed, but not to cry. If I'd expected a flood of tears, I was surprised by my dry eyes. I was equally surprised by the intensity of my anger. John Mason was lucky he wasn't in front of me right then, for a kick in the shins would have seemed mild.

I was still up and pacing when Rose came in, laughing and calling good night over her shoulder. She sobered when she saw me. I'd forgotten that I must look a mess, my hair wild, my blouse wrinkled and pulled out. "What happened?"

When I briefly described the scene, she grinned a moment. "Serves him right." Then she sobered again. "I—I should have stopped you. I knew you shouldn't have gone with him." She set her hat carefully on the bureau and then plunked down on the bed. "You have some lessons to learn."

"Lessons?"

"About men."

I supposed that was true, and right then I believed she was the most qualified to teach me. "How would I have known what he'd turn out like? He was funny when I roped him in the arena, and I thought he'd be—well, like Billy." Of course, she didn't know Billy, and I had to explain all about him.

"That's the difference," she said. "You don't have any instinct about which ones are Billys and which ones are Masons." She shook her head despairingly, and the red curls bounced as though emphasizing what she said.

"And how do I develop that instinct?" I stood before her, hands indignantly on my hips.

"I guess like you develop an instinct about horses," she said.

I didn't think that was a whole lot of help. I didn't know how I knew about horses—I just knew. And just as strongly, I knew nothing about men, except maybe Papa.

CHAPTER 5

"I looked for you last night," Louise said at breakfast, eyeing me suspiciously.

"I didn't feel well," I faltered, toying with my scrambled eggs. "I went to bed early."

"Didn't feel well?" she echoed softly. "You can think of a better excuse, Tommy Jo." She picked up her plate and rose, saying, "Let's go for a walk."

I expected anger when she heard the story, anger at me for having been so dumb, anger at John Mason for what he tried. Instead, that deep laughter came first. We were walking toward the arena, where men were bustling about getting ready for the day's exhibition. Colonel Miller stood near one gate, gesturing wildly to men who didn't appear to understand him.

"It happens to most girls at least once," Louise said, still smiling. "And there was no permanent damage."

"Rose says I need to develop an instinct about men," I ventured.

Louise laughed again. "I suspect you began to develop it real fast last night."

That comforting thought hadn't occurred to me. We stopped and stared into a pasture where several horses, Sam among them, were grazing. There was one I would have been real cautious of, just because he had that look in his eye. I tried to remember the look in John Mason's eye. "Will you tell Papa?"

"It's not my business," she said, looking straight at me. "Will you tell him?"

"Probably not." It wasn't that I was afraid Papa would take after John Mason—though he might have felt obliged to do that. No, it was more that I couldn't run to Papa with my troubles, and I couldn't let him think that he had to rescue me or look out for me. If he did that, then he could still tell me where to go, what to do.

"That's probably good," Louise said, and I knew she understood my reasoning.

The exhibition that day was much like the one the previous day, but the Indians didn't chase a buffalo. The bronc riding was fast and exciting, and I was delighted that John Mason was pitched off his horse. As he limped away, I wondered if the limp came from the fall or my boot.

Rose was dramatic and impressive in her tricks again, and then it was my turn. I was much calmer this time, more sure of myself, and the loops I threw showed it. Oh, the editors and townsfolk watching didn't know, but I did.

I was taking my final bow when the crowd began to cheer anew, and I sensed their attention was on something behind me. Turning, I saw Geronimo walking slowly into the arena. Behind him came a line of solemn Indians. Still several yards from me, he stopped, pointed at me, and then made circling motions around his body. He wanted me to rope him!

The other Indians stopped and stood impassively, watching while I built my loop. Nerves had come to attack me again—what if I hit him with the rope? With great deliberation, I built the speed of my rope and then threw it. The loop sailed over Geronimo, who stood there grinning. The crowd was shouting and clapping.

I dropped the loop, and he stepped out of it, bowing to the crowd. While he bowed, I laid out a new, bigger loop behind me. Then I motioned Geronimo toward me and whispered to him. He backed off, started walking toward me, and at the right moment I threw that new loop. With great dignity and a huge smile, he walked through it. The crowd went wild again.

Later that day, Geronimo came up to the veranda where I sat with Louise, gently swaying on the swing. He was carrying a beautifully beaded vest, which he handed to me. "For you," he said. "Thank you."

My mouth was open to say I couldn't accept this gift, when Louise gave me a nudge. "Thank you," I said. "I'll treasure this." The vest was richly patterned in pale blue, red, yellow, and white beads in a design I didn't understand at all, but it fit perfectly, and I whirled once to model it. Geronimo clapped his hands in pleasure and then vanished.

"You will treasure that," Louise said. "Not many girls can claim a gift from Geronimo." She paused and stared off into the distance, but her eyes were not seeing the people who were packing to leave, the men who were working around the arena. "When are you going home?"

Home! I hadn't thought beyond my nose, certainly not about where or what I was going to do next. But of course, after two days the exhibition was over—hadn't the editors already boarded trains?—and I couldn't stay at the 101 forever. "I don't know," I mumbled.

"Maybe this is the time for you to come back to Guthrie with me. I'm leaving the day after tomorrow. Zack invited me to stay an extra day, and I'm sure you'll be welcome. We'll help them kind of wind down after all the excitement."

"Thanks" was all I could say. And then, "I'll write Mama."

That night twelve of us gathered at Mrs. Miller's dinner table. Colonel Zack was in high spirits, as he dished out beef and beans, cabbage salad with creamy dressing, fresh biscuits, and a blueberry cobbler for dessert. "A success," he said, "a roaring success. Liked it so well, I think I'll do it all over again next year." With his hat off, you could see that the colonel was balding and combed some stray hairs over the top of his head to camouflage the condition. Now as he talked, light from the gas fixture overhead gleamed on his head.

Someone clapped, and someone else suggested, "You ought to take the show on the road."

A piece of bread, buttered and covered with beans, in his hand, Colonel Zack stopped dead and raised his eyes heavenward, as though thanking the Lord. "On the road! Of course! Instead of a Wild West show like Buffalo Bill, we'll do a ranch exhibition. True ranching skills—with some showmanship thrown in, of course." He put down the bread, rubbed his hands, and began to talk rapidly of what he'd have in his show, how many horses, what kinds of acts.

I was spellbound, not only by the plan but by his enthusiasm. If I couldn't be with Buffalo Bill, Colonel Zack's show would be a sure second best. I sat waiting, I think, for an instant invitation to join.

As suddenly as he'd taken up the idea, the colonel sobered and said, "I'll think on that. It's one hell of a good idea."

My spirits fell dramatically. It was Guthrie for me.

That night as Rose and I lay in bed, talking about the possibilities of the Miller 101 road show, I said suddenly, "I want to learn how you do it."

"Do what?" she asked lazily. "Tell about men?"

"No, goose. Tricks on horseback. Can you teach me?"

"Not in one day," she said, more awake now. "But I guess I can show you some things to practice. You'll have to train your horse, too, not just you."

I hadn't thought of that. Poor Sam! If I tried to stand up, he'd wonder what on earth I was doing. I had a vision of him shying in confusion and me flying through the air. "Show me tomorrow," I demanded.

"I promise, if you'll let me go to sleep now."

Next morning I dragged poor Rose out to the arena straight from the breakfast table. She pulled on pants—"I always wear them to practice"—and I was downright jealous, even though I was wearing a practical denim split skirt. First bloomers, and now outright pants, like the cowboys wore! Sometimes I wished I could be Rose.

We caught our horses in the pasture beyond the house—Sam came willingly, and so did Rose's pinto, which she called Poor Babe. "Poor I guess because he has to put up with my shenanigans," she shrugged, "and Babe because he's my baby." As we rode up and down the road to warm the horses up, Rose warned me, "This isn't easy. I've been practicin' since I was ten."

"Who taught you?"

"Lady named Bertha Kendrick. She rode in the first Frontier Days in Cheyenne in 1897. She lived not far from us when I was a kid, and she said she saw right away I had an instinct for horses. My pa wasn't too sure he wanted me to learn this fancy stuff, but he's gone along with it."

"Must have," I muttered, "to have sent you down here. Who's the cowboy that came with you?"

"Oh," she said airily, "just one of Papa's hands. He's been busy helping Colonel Miller with the stock." Then, spurring Poor Babe to a gallop, she tossed over her shoulder as an afterthought, "I'm probably going to marry him."

Urging Sam to catch up with them, I shook my head. I couldn't figure Prairie Rose out at all, but I surely did like her.

"Demonstration first," she said when we got to the arena. "You got to teach the horse to accept different distributions of your weight. So you start by leaning out of the saddle." She rode slowly in a wide circle in front of me, leaning her upper body to the left until it was almost parallel to the ground. Poor Babe never missed a step, even when she swung quickly from one side to the other. "Start slowly," she said. "You don't have to lean that far the first time. And don't switch sides like that—I was showing off." She giggled.

I touched my heels to Sam, and when he was at a good pace, I began to lean, ever so slightly. No reaction from Sam, so I leaned a little farther, which threw him off his stride some, but he didn't buck or anything.

The morning flew—Rose told me about crouching in the saddle, the first step toward the Roman stand, but I couldn't imagine myself standing in the saddle.

"You use a strap at first," she said, "and then one day, you just let go of it. But once you do, you can't reach down and pick it up again." She laughed gaily.

She demonstrated and talked about the pickup, where you pick something off the ground while riding by at a good clip—"Good trick for you to start with once you get Sam used to your leaning"—and she showed me how to make Sam rear on his hind legs by pulling hard on the bit—"some horses will rear," she said, "and others won't, they'll just back up." Sam reared, and I was supposed to sit prettily in the saddle. The first time, I clutched Sam's mane with both hands and held on for dear life, terrified as I'd never been on a horse. But Sam never did get his front feet very far off the ground.

Rose showed me the new trick she was working on—going under Poor Babe's belly from one side and coming up on the other, while he raced around the arena. Her head came so close to his flying hooves that I held my breath, but she scrambled up on the other side and was soon seated in the saddle again.

"Still too awkward," she said. "I got to make it look like there's nothing to it, not like I'm struggling."

She could have fooled me. At the end of the morning I was exhausted and exhilarated, my clothes wrinkled and sweaty, my hair flying in wisps in my face. I sure was not a trick rider by any stretch of the imagination, and I could see dimly that trick riding was never going to take the place of roping for me. But I was determined to master a few tricks, on the theory it would make me more useful in a Wild West show.

The only sour moment in the whole morning came when I was riding, leaning out from the saddle, and looked up to see John Mason watching me from the gate to the arena. He wore a black Stetson pulled low over his eyes, but I could somehow feel his look burning at me from under that hatbrim. I remembered what Papa said once about if looks could kill.

Rose saw, too. "Ignore him," she advised.

Rose and I parted with many hugs and promises to meet again soon. Young, we saw nothing as impossible, and we only barely understood how far Wyoming was from Oklahoma. In both our minds, unspoken, was the dream of Colonel Zack Miller and a 101 Wild West Show.

It was a year before I heard from Colonel Zack, a year of hard work and practice, a year I lived in Guthrie with Louise, and above all, the year I met Bo Johnson.

Colonel Zack Miller had, it seemed, sent a carriage and driver all the way to Guthrie for Louise, and he intended to return her in the same fashion. So we tied Sam to the back of the carriage, and I rode inside with her. I'd have hated it if the carriage were closed, but it was one with a top that could be pulled back. Louise put on a huge hat and fussed about the sun, until I deliberately took off my hat to expose my face to the light.

"You'll freckle," she warned direly.

"Next year," Colonel Zack said, "I'll send the Locomobile for you."

"Zack," Louise laughed, "I'm not sure I'm ready to trust my life to one of those newfangled things. You drive it up to see me first."

"I'll do that," he said. His loud voice softened, and he smiled once again only for her. As we pulled away, he seemed to remember me and boomed, "Keep that rope spinning, Tommy Jo!"

I waved over my shoulder, and we were off.

The roads, so crowded when I arrived, were now almost empty of people, though here and there on the riverbank we could see a tent or two still up and, other places, signs where people had camped. We rode in silence, the sun beating down on us and promising a hot June day. Every once in a while I glanced at Louise, but she seemed to have drawn into herself beneath the veil that tied her hat to her head.

After an hour or so, she suddenly looked at me. "Well, was it everything you wanted?"

"Yes and no," I said slowly. "I loved riding, and the crowd. And I think Prairie Rose is the most wonderful person I've ever met."

"I think I shall have to be jealous of that girl," Louise said, and then laughed. "She is lovely. I agree. And what else?"

I took the proverbial bull by the horns. "I was asked because of you, wasn't I? I mean, Colonel Zack Miller had never heard of Tommy Jo Burns, wouldn't have known I can rope, if you hadn't written him."

"That's probably true, though not for certain. He knows your father." Mama would have looked over the far edge of the carriage at this point, but Louise turned a steady eye on me. "I introduced them."

I swallowed. "Is Colonel Zack . . ." What on earth was I going to ask her? I had no idea what to say, how to say what I thought I was thinking.

"He is a good friend to me, and an old friend."

"Like Papa?"

Without flinching, she said, "Yes, just like your papa." She saw the puzzlement on my face. "Tommy Jo, I'm not married to either of them, or to anyone else, and I'm not beholden to either of them. I can have as many friends as I want, and I'm the one who determines what my relationship with them is. Zack Miller does for me just what your father does—gives me masculine companionship without any strings attached."

"He comes to see you in Guthrie?" I asked, and when she nodded yes, I pursued, "But not when Papa comes. Or Papa doesn't come when Colonel Zack is there."

She nodded yes again. I had a lot to think about—Mama and the way she let Papa run things; Louise, who let nobody run things; me, who didn't know what I wanted but sure wasn't going to let the John Masons of the world run things. Billy flitted through my mind briefly, but I couldn't see him behaving like any of them—Papa, Colonel Zack, or John Mason.

I wrote to Mama as soon as I was in Guthrie:

Dear Mama,

The exhibition was a success. Colonel Zack Miller said I was the hit of the show, and Geronimo gave me a beaded vest. I really liked riding and roping before a crowd, and I hope I can be in another show.

I've come to Guthrie with Louise. Papa is angry with me, and I guess I'm angry with him, too, though not as bad as he is with me. But still, I

*can't come to Luckett's right now. I'll stay in Guthrie. Please come to
visit me. Give my love to Papa.*

Love, Tommy Jo

Even as I wrote the words, I knew Mama would never come to Guthrie to see me. Mama wanted her world to go on just like it was, undisturbed by women like Louise, by a daughter who wanted to ride in Wild West shows, by change in any form. But would Papa come to see me—or to see Louise? I couldn't guess.

Mama wrote me a stiff note saying she was glad I was in good hands and she would miss me. But she never mentioned coming to Guthrie, and she never suggested I come home to Luckett's.

For Louise and me, it was back to serving meals to the boarders. "Louise," I said as we did dishes that first morning, "Sam can't stay in your barn. There's no place for him to exercise. And I—I've got to find a place to ride and practice."

Her hands deep in soapy water, while I toweled and dried the dishes, she looked at me. "Practice?"

I got very busy with the plate I was drying, so that she couldn't see the blush creep up on my face. "Tricks. Rose showed me some tricks, how to practice them, and I want to try."

"Tricks," she echoed. "Like standing in the saddle?"

I nodded.

Shaking the soap off her hands, Louise reached for a towel, dried her hands, and then hugged me. "Of course you can do that! And you must! I know just the place for you to practice."

And that's how Bo Johnson came into my life. He owned a stable on the edge of Guthrie, and he'd built a small arena next to it, mostly for cowboys to practice roping. "It's a lot easier if the steer gets away and they don't have to chase him halfway to hell and back," he explained grinning.

Bo was maybe thirty years old, lots older than me, and a widower. His wife, Elizabeth, had died in childbirth two years before, and you could tell it pained him even now to talk about it. But when he talked about almost anything else, his eyes lit up with fire and laughter and joy. He was like Billy—and not like Walt Denison—in that he was kind of overgrown and gangly looking, his arms too long for his body, his hair always flying in several directions. No, Bo Johnson was not a man to stop a girl's heart—at least not until you got to know him.

"Got my name as an orphan boy, I think," he said. "Always thought I probably didn't have a name and somebody began calling me Boy. Then it got shortened to Bo, and I've been Bo ever since. Not a very dignified name, but it suits me."

If Papa first taught me to ride, and Billy taught me to rope, Bo taught me to ride, really ride, though he didn't know a blasted thing about Wild West shows or trick riding or any of that.

I went to see him the very day that Louise suggested it.

"You want to what?" he asked incredulously, standing with his hands on his hips in a pose that made him seem belligerent.

Still mounted on Sam, I said loftily, "I want to practice trick riding. Louise Turner said you'd let me use your arena."

He grinned and looked at the ground, as though trying not to let me see him laugh at me. "If Louise says so, it's so," he declared. "But trick riding? What's that mean?"

Now I was on shaky ground. I still wasn't all that sure. "I want to learn to stand in the saddle."

"Stand in the saddle! That's the most foolish notion I ever heard! Girl, you could get yourself killed that way." His alarm was genuine.

"I won't get killed. Lots of cowgirls do it. I—I just need somewhere to practice. I won't get in your way."

He waved a hand vaguely toward a barn that obviously needed repairing. Between it and where we stood was the small arena, but its fenceposts weren't quite straight, and some of the boards were sagging. Papa would have had Casey and Wilks out fixing it before daylight. "Not much anybody can do to bother me," he said. "I ain't got enough time to get it all done anyway, so I just don't worry about it."

I thought about Papa and marveled that men could be so different.

"You just suit yourself, come on anytime. If there's some ropers here 'fore you, well, you'll all just have to take turns. Now, I got to fork down some hay. See ya." He waved jauntily and turned away, leaving me sitting there.

Pure devilment went through me like a flash, and I built a quick loop with the rope that was always tied to my saddle. Carefully I sailed it over his head, aiming beyond where he was to compensate for his forward motion, and then let it catch him.

"Hey!" There was real anger in that first response, but when he saw that I wasn't going to pull the rope tight, he tried to raise his hands in the air just like John Mason had done—maybe, I thought, I should stop roping men and stick to horses!—and then he laughed aloud. "Gosh a'mighty, girl, you're good, you're damn good!"

I let the rope drop to the ground, and he stepped over it, asking, "What other tricks can you do?"

Without a word, I slipped off Sam and built a larger loop behind me on the ground, then flung it over my head and whirled it in front of me. Bo stood watching about fifteen feet away. "Come on," I said. "Walk through it."

He looked startled and wanted, I think, to look behind him on the off chance that someone else was there. With one finger he kind of pointed at himself and looked questioningly at me. When I nodded yes, he shrugged, as though this fate was inescapable, and trudged through the loop. Once through, he looked over his shoulder with a kind of surprised expression, and then walked back through again. I let the loop drop, figuring if he did that too long, my arm would really get tired.

"Never seen a girl rope like that," he exclaimed. "Or a man either. Tommy Jo, you're somethin' else. You tell me when you want to practice, and I'll be here to help you."

"Six o'clock every weekday morning," I said crisply. "Soon be too hot by ten to do anything."

He gulped and said, "Six o'clock. I'll be here."

"Louise might feed you breakfast afterward," I said, climbing back onto Sam. With a wave of the hand, I spurred Sam to a gallop—show-off stuff, I knew—and whirled away from him. But I couldn't resist the temptation to look over my shoulder once, quickly—there he stood, one hand shading his eyes against the sun, his faded shirt and jeans blending into the weathered barn behind him.

So began a year of long and hard work, a year in which Bo Johnson, with his ever-present grin and his complete awe of anything I did on a horse, became my teacher and my best friend.

"You're not moving with the horse," he'd say. "Relax and feel how he goes." Or, "You didn't prepare Sam for that one. Near scared him to death—and me, too." Once he said, "Tommy Jo, you need to relax and be with the horse, not against him. You do it when you ride, but now you're stiff as a board." I was mortified.

He particularly hated when I tried to make Sam rear, and I was reluctantly about to decide that Sam was one of those horses that wouldn't do it. He never did get his front feet much farther off the ground than he had that very first time at the Miller, and when I used a Spanish bit, with a hump that no doubt really hurt a horse's mouth, Sam neighed his displeasure—but he didn't rear back any higher.

Bo was more vocal about his displeasure. "Can't believe you'd do that to your horse," he said disgustedly. "Just to get him to jump some way the good Lord never intended him to anyway. Tommy Jo, this show business has warped whatever good sense you had."

When he wasn't displeased with me, Bo counted time, stood still for my rope tricks, applauded my successes, and laughed at my failures. The day I pushed Sam too far and he dumped me in the dirt, Bo was there to pick me up.

"You hurt?" His arms were under mine as he gently pulled me to my feet.

"No, I don't think so." I shook my head, as though to banish the fuzziness from my brain. "My own fault. I shouldn't have gone so fast." I'd tried to raise up from the crouching position on the saddle.

"Yeah, you shouldn't have," he said.

Bo's hands were on my shoulders, holding me up and steadying me, and his face was inches from mine, his eyes looking directly at me. I felt that funny fluttering in the stomach again, but just as I wondered what would happen, Bo released his hold so suddenly that I almost fell. That, I guess, was the difference between Bo and a man like Walt Denison or even Billy Rogers. But that lesson was years away for me.

"Guess you best call it a day," he said. "I'll skip breakfast this mornin'."

Most mornings he came to Louise's, and she saved us huge plates of eggs and sausage and cornbread, sometimes grits—which I despised—and sometimes wonderful brown potatoes. The three of us sat, the other boarders long gone much to our gratitude, and talked of show circuits and Wild West shows and the folly of women wanting to be performers. At least, that's what Bo always talked about.

"Can't see why you want to do that stuff, Tommy Jo. You ought to be out in town looking the young men over. Find you one to marry and have some babies and—"

"Bo Johnson, don't you even say it! You know I want to ride in a show."

He shook his head and reached for his coffee cup. "Yeah, I know it. But I sure don't understand it."

He was more intrigued by my stay at the 101. "Heard about that show," he said, "clear down here in Guthrie. You can't tell me that that old Geronimo offered a thousand dollars to any man who'd let himself be scalped."

I laughed aloud, remembering the quiet, almost hesitant Indian chief who'd presented me with the beaded vest that now lay folded carefully away in my chest upstairs. "I heard that story, too, but it was just rumor. Geron-imo would never scalp a man—not anymore leastways."

Bo grinned a little, self-consciously. "I heard he wanted to scalp a man, and he wanted a buffalo hunt. Word was they killed thirty-five buffalo. Don't know where they'd find that many these days."

"One buffalo," I said. "One old bull, so old the meat was stringy. And no scalping."

"No fooling? I really did wonder how they could kill so many." He grinned again, aware that he'd been gullible but not too upset about it.

I didn't understand the feelings I was beginning to have about Bo. Every instinct told me he was a cowboy who'd be content to be small potatoes the rest of his life, he was too old for me, he had no understanding of what I wanted out of life, he was a good friend and nothing more. But when he came close to me, I felt shivery, and sometimes I thought my loop would fall flat just because he was watching, just because I wanted more than anything else to impress him.

Louise eyed me suspiciously one evening after dinner, when we sat in the parlor. She was mending, and I was building tiny loops with a small rope. "I didn't mean for this to happen," she said.

"For what to happen?" I went on whirling my loop, honestly in the dark about what she meant.

"You to fall in love with Bo Johnson." Her eyes were on her stitches, and she never raised them to me, never gave me a smile that might have hinted at teasing.

"I am *not* in love with him," I said indignantly. "Bo Johnson is . . ." I sputtered, "Bo Johnson is old enough to be my father!"

"Not quite," she replied calmly, "and he's sure in love with you."

"All he talks about is how dumb it is for me to want to go off and ride in a show," I said. "He thinks I should settle down and marry some cowboy and have ten babies."

"Not some cowboy," Louise said. "Him."

"Pshaw. You're wrong this time, Louise. You're really wrong." Frus-trated, I threw the rope aside and strode out of the sitting room without so much as a "good-bye" or "excuse me." But that night I lay in bed and thought about Bo and the time he'd held me up, and how I could always feel him watching me, even when he pretended to be busy around the stables, and how glad I was to see him at six o'clock every morning—and how angry I was on the mornings he overslept.

"Bo?" I called one wintry morning when the corral was empty and the barn looked deserted. "Bo?" I was almost tempted to go to the small house down the street that he called home and pound on the door until the lazy thing got up. "Darn!" I said, and was tempted to say something stronger.

"Don't get yourself in an uproar" came a lazy drawl around the corner of the barn. "I got other things on my mind this morning."

"Like what?" I asked peevishly.

"Like fifteen wild horses your pa brought in here yesterday."

"My pa?" I echoed faintly.

"Yeah, your pa. They're horses for one of them shows you set so much stock by, but I got to feed 'em for a week 'fore they're shipped off."

"Where are they?" I demanded, my confidence recovered. "I want to see them!"

"Whoa, Tommy Jo! Hold on now. They're in that pasture I keep out from town aways."

"Let's go," I said, wondering why on earth he was just standing there looking at me instead of getting his horse. 'Course, Bo had no way of knowing that visions were dancing in my head, visions of Devildust, the one wonderful wild horse I'd once tried to ride.

"No practice this morning?" he asked, grinning as though he'd caught me being outright lazy.

"Maybe," I said, "practice of another kind. Are you coming with me, or am I going to ride out there alone?"

"I'm coming with you," he grumbled, " 'cause I'm worried about what you'd do if I left you alone."

Turning Sam toward the road, I spurred him into a gallop and left Bo behind, shouting wildly for me to wait for him. Instead, Sam and I ran the entire two miles out to Bo's pasture—behind us, faintly, I could hear Bo shouting. He was still far behind when I tied Sam to the pasture fence and stood, staring at the horses, who frisked around the small pasture, made lively by the cold air.

Still sputtering, Bo jumped off his horse and was beside me—for a slow-moving man, he was amazingly graceful when it came to getting on and off a horse—and began to complain. "Lord, Tommy Jo, you ain't got no more sense than a peafowl, come riding out here like the Devil was on your tail."

"No Devil," I laughed, "just the memory of one wonderful wild horse. Magnificent, aren't they?"

"Wild and untamed and pure trouble, that's what they are," he replied, but I could see the admiration in his eye.

"The red one," I said. "That's the one." I pointed to a medium-sized horse. "He's been gelded, hasn't he?"

"Yeah," Bo said, "but he looks proud-cut. Ain't tamed him down one bit." He eyed me suspiciously. "The one for what?"

"To ride," I said without hesitation.

Bo turned away, as though he wished he hadn't heard what I said.

"Bo, if you tie him to a post and help me, I can ride that horse." I tried to be my most persuasive, but I hadn't learned about looking deep into his eyes, and there was sure no way I could look helpless.

"You got to be kidding! I am not going to let you get on any wild horse!"

But of course, that's just what he did. Tied that horse to a post and held him while I got on. This time I remembered a much earlier lesson, and I went slow, talking softly to the horse, giving him time to get some sense and scent of me. Then, when I gave the signal, Bo turned him loose.

That horse bucked every way but loose, as the cowboys always say. He went straight up in the air and landed, all four legs stiff, in a spine-jolting collision with the ground. Then he fishtailed, twisting and turning, while I held on for dear life and hollered as loud as I could. This wasn't an arena, and there wasn't a pickup man to come behind me. I was on my own, with only Bo for an audience and no sure way to get off that horse.

After what seemed an eternity, the horse suddenly stopped and stood perfectly still in the arena, his head down in defeat. Touching my heels to his flanks, I moved him around in a circle. Finally, I brought him back to the post where Bo stood. Tossing him the reins, I climbed off. The horse stood perfectly still.

"Well," Bo said softly, "you ruined one good bucking horse, that's for sure."

"What do you mean?" I asked indignantly, still panting from my ride. I was sure that sweat—Mama would have said perspiration—was pouring off my face and head and that I looked a mess, but I expected congratulations on my ride.

"He's been ridden," Bo said. "Doubt he'll ever buck again quite the same. Look at him."

Grinning, I looked at the horse. He stood still, sides heaving, head down, the perfect picture of defeat.

"But I rode him!" I cried. "You wouldn't have done it! I rode that damn horse!"

"Don't swear, Tommy Jo. It don't become you." He shook his head.

"But you're right—I wouldn't have ridden him, and you did. You rode a wild horse, but I don't know what that makes you. It sure don't make you a lady." Without another word to me, Bo Johnson mounted his own big bay horse, gentle as they come, and turned back toward town, leaving me to follow as I would.

Papa was at Louise's when I returned, exhilarated because of my ride but vaguely out of sorts because of Bo, not that I was smart enough to recognize that mix of emotions in myself. But Papa didn't make me any happier.

"Tommy Jo," he said, his expression inscrutable. He sat at the kitchen table, sipping coffee, looking perfectly at home. Louise washed dishes in the background, and I couldn't interpret her expression either.

"Papa," I acknowledged.

Suddenly he stood, and taking me completely by surprise, he gave me a strong bear hug. "I've missed you," he said.

And then I was in his arms, crying gently. "I've missed you, too, Papa," I said. Well, it was almost the truth. In some ways, not having to worry about Papa was a big relief, but I knew a girl couldn't shed her father as easily as that. And I really didn't want to.

We talked then, long and hard, about what I'd been doing, about Mama, about the Miller 101, even about Bo Johnson. Somewhere in that conversation, Louise slipped away, and when I looked to her for help, she was gone.

"You got to come see your mama," he said, reaching across the table to touch my arm. "She—she thinks I drove you away."

"You did," I said, but I said it as gentle as I could, and he just shrugged.

At Christmas I went home to see Mama. At first I thought she was just the same, as though I'd never gone away, except that she was a little more withdrawn, a little less aware of what went on around her. But she greeted me with a tight hug and tears in her eyes. "Thomasina! Oh my darling, I've missed you so!" And her arms went around me again.

"I've missed you, too, Mama," I said, returning the hug. "There are so many things I've wanted to tell you."

"We have forever to talk about them, dear," she said, and then, vaguely, "I must look to the dinner."

Papa had stood silently, his look almost accusing. "She hasn't been the same since you left. I—I didn't want to tell you in Guthrie, in front of Louise, but . . . you broke her heart, Tommy Jo, just broke it in two." Papa, who never cried, looked like he might sob.

There was no way I could tell him, no way I could ever make him understand that *he'd* broken her heart long ago, and that I'd had to leave before he broke my spirit, just as he'd broken her heart. I couldn't say that it wasn't fair that she looked to me to make right what he'd made wrong, and that I loved my mother desperately but could not spend my life living out her sorrows.

"Mama? Let me help you." I burst through the swinging door—something new Papa had installed—into the kitchen.

Mama stood in the middle of the room, her apron tied at the neck, a spoon in her hand. "Help me? Oh yes, the dinner." Jerking herself back to the present, she turned to the stove and began vigorously to stir the contents of a pot. I looked over her shoulder, into a pot of water.

Fear clutched at me. "Mama? What are we having for dinner?"

Eyes clear and bright, she said indignantly, "It's Christmas, isn't it? We're having turkey and dressing and mashed potatoes and mincemeat pie."

The menu of my childhood, except that as I looked around the kitchen, I could see none of it. There was no turkey in the oven, no pie cooling in the pie safe, no potatoes simmering on the stove.

"Oh, Mama," I wailed, wrapping my arms around her and holding on for dear life. We stood that way for a long time, tears running down both our cheeks, until gently I said, "Mama, you go in and visit with Papa. I'll fix the dinner."

There was a turkey in the icebox, a small one that wouldn't take too long to bake, and the potatoes were in the bin, the mincemeat made and in the icebox. It took me five hours to make dinner, but we ate a fine meal. I had lots of time to think while I was out there working in the kitchen—Mama's early lessons and Louise's more recent training stood me in good stead—and I determined, first of all, that dinner would not be strained nor awkward. It was a holiday!

"Papa," I said, as I lit the candles, "will you ask the Lord's blessing?"

He prayed that the Lord would make us thankful for the meal that we were about to receive and that the Lord would help us to love one another, in spite of our weaknesses. I know he had Mama in mind, but I thought his prayer was particularly appropriate to him.

Mama really thought she'd cooked the meal. I guess in her mind she'd done the work, and that was all that mattered. When Papa commented on the moistness of the turkey, Mama said, "Thank you, James. I always cook a bird long and slow. Makes them juicy." Actually, I'd cooked it as hot and fast as I dared, but it was still tender and good.

Papa and I did the dishes. "You've worked hard today, Jess," he said, his tone unusually gentle for him. "You rest. Tommy Jo and I'll do the dishes."

She smiled sweetly, thanked him, and settled into the rocker with her knitting.

"Papa? Who cooks for you?"

"Some days I do it. Wilks's wife comes in and cleans the house once a week. And some days your mother's fine, and she does the cooking herself. There's just no telling. It's like she's home one day, away the next."

I bit my lip. "How long?"

"Since your letter saying you were going to Guthrie. She kept saying you'd be home tomorrow . . . and then tomorrow . . . and then the next day. And the longer it went without you coming home, the more she kind of went into her own little world."

It is not fair, I wanted to shout, for one person to make her happiness or health dependent on another! Instead, I said, "I should have come and talked to her."

"What would you have said?" he asked, the dish towel dangling from his hands.

"That I had to live my own life," I said firmly, looking Papa straight in the eye.

"You're doing that," he said slowly. "I guess maybe it bothers your mother that you're living your own life with Louise."

"I guess," I said slowly, "that's your problem and not mine."

Our gift exchange was almost gay. Mama was like a little child, thrilled with the brooch that Papa had gotten for her, excited over the shawl that I'd handworked with sequins and beads. "My, James," she said, "we'll have to go someplace special so that I can wear this. Perhaps the opera."

"Perhaps," he said softly.

Mama had made me a beautifully worked nightgown and dressing gown to go over it. "For your hope chest," she said. "I—I hope you'll use it soon."

"Thank you, Mama. They're beautiful. The work is so . . . the stitches so small. You never could get me to do that, could you?" No need to tell her that my hope chest might be just hopes for years, that I had no intention of settling down to be wife and mother as she had. Strangely, Bo Johnson's face flashed before me as I folded the gowns to put them away, but I forced his image back.

Papa was pleased with the scarf I'd knitted for him, and the afghan Mama had made him—"for his evening naps," she said. The afghan represented weeks of work, and I knew then what Mama did when she wasn't cooking or keeping house. Handwork had become her world, and she surely was good at it.

I stayed three days at Luckett's ranch. Papa was off working as soon as Christmas was over, and so I had two days alone with Mama. And I saw what Papa meant about her being different on different days. Once she startled me by saying, "I don't like it that you're living with Louise in Guthrie instead of here with us."

"Mama, it's not Louise. It's Guthrie. I can't live my life out here on this ranch. It's too isolated, too lonely. You know that."

"Yes," she said, with a catch in her throat, "I know that. But what do you do in Guthrie?" Her knitting lay untouched in her lap, and her eyes looked straight at me, intense and clear.

"I help Louise with the cooking for my room and board," I said, "and I practice my roping and trick riding, and I read a lot."

"Roping and trick riding!" Her voice was scornful, and she picked up her needles and began to knit almost furiously. "Won't do you any good, Thomasina. You need to be looking for a husband."

I thought briefly of describing Bo Johnson, just to quiet her, but I decided such deception was unfair. And no more than I could be totally honest with Papa, I couldn't say to her that I didn't want a husband at the cost she'd paid. "Yes, ma'am," I said meekly, "I'll keep looking."

When I left, Mama acted as though I were going out for a ride and persisted in talking about what we'd have for supper when I got home. Helplessly, I looked at Papa. With his nod giving me courage, I said, "Yes, Mama, I'll look forward to supper."

"You see that you come right home," she said sternly, as though talking to a ten-year-old.

"Yes, Mama," I said, hugging her tight and hiding my tears over her shoulder.

"Jess, it's cold. You best go inside," Papa said.

Obediently, Mama turned and went inside, giving me a sad little smile over her shoulder as she closed the door.

"Can you come see her more often?" Papa asked.

"Yes, I can, and I will." It still hadn't occurred to Papa what role he'd played in all this, and now he was all gentle and kind and caring for Mama, without the least bit of recognition of his own part in this tragedy.

I kissed Papa good-bye and headed for Guthrie, relieved to be away from the ranch. But I could hardly see the road in front of me, for the tears came so fast and hard. I was driving Louise's carriage, with Sam tied behind—she'd insisted, since the weather could turn bad—and I was glad the horse seemed to know its way home, for I was hardly in control of the carriage or of myself.

I was relieved to be back in Guthrie, where life seemed to go on at a more even pace.

In February, a letter came from Rose. I'd written to her two or three times since we'd left the 101 and been puzzled by her silence. Now, in her breezy tone, she explained that so much had been going on, she'd had no time to write. "I could not stay at home," she wrote. "My father insisted on treating me as a child and was unmoved by my arguments that I'd now ridden in an important exhibition and that trick riding ought to be considered my work. He thinks marriage and motherhood should be my work."

Different people with different opinions, I thought, but the problems were the same. Her father, my mother. Rose went on to say that she was living with a family near Cheyenne and riding broncs in local ranch riding shows but saw little future in trick riding.

No future for girl ropers either, I thought gloomily, though I tried to make my answer to her letter brighter in tone, telling her all about life with Louise and sharing a joke, so I thought, about Bo Johnson. I must have written more about him than I intended.

"I don't know who Bo Johnson is," she replied, "but you best grab him."

I knew who Bo Johnson was—a continuing and growing problem to me. Some days I could barely rope, being around him made me so nervous.

"What's the matter, Tommy Jo?" he'd ask, hands on his hips, a grin on his face as he stared at me. "Lose your sense of balance?"

"No, I did not," I'd reply hotly, whirling Sam around for another try.

" 'Bout fell off that horse," he said, and now there was outright laughter in his voice. "Maybe you should call it a day."

And then one day when I did quit early, Bo came up to me as I tied Sam to the rail of the corral. "It ain't workin'," he said. "I don't like you doing this, and I can't help you no more."

"What do you mean, you can't help me?"

"Just that," he said, tight-lipped, turning his face away from me. "You got to find someone else to help you try to be a trick rider." He looked at the ground, his usually cheerful face as solemn as I'd ever seen it.

"Bo?" I didn't know what I was feeling, but that fluttering sensation was playing havoc with my stomach.

Bo turned slowly to face me, and then, as though he moved in slow motion, his arms were around me, and he bent, ever so gently, to kiss me. Like they say in the novels, I must have been waiting for this moment, because there was no hesitation in my response. I kissed Bo Johnson—hard.

"I can't make you choose, Tommy Jo," he said haltingly. "I can't tell you it's either me or the Wild West shows, but I don't see any way it can be otherwise."

"Can't you come with me?" I asked unbelievingly. Here I'd found a man who loved me, a man I loved, and my dream of roping in a show was standing between us.

"No," he said shortly, "I can't do that."

There's something wonderful about that feeling of new love—it wipes out all the bitter truth that you know lurks just outside the circle, waiting to turn happiness into ashes. That bright new feeling ran all over me that morning, for I heard Bo's words and yet didn't. And when he said he couldn't come with me to the shows, I simply walked back into his arms in that foggy dreamlike state.

His response was so passionate as to scare me a bit, and yet I met him in intensity, for I'd never felt this way about a man before. One arm around me, his lips on mine most of the way, he led me into the barn, and we sank down into the hay, a welcoming soft bower. Vaguely I heard Sam nicker, but time had stopped for me. Bo's lips were on mine as he unbuttoned my shirt and reached a gentle hand inside. I never protested and wouldn't have, but suddenly he was the one who stopped.

"Tommy Jo! We got to go!" All at once he was no longer lying next to me but was standing before me, one hand brushing his hair as though to smooth it, the other making nervous circles in the air. "Louise'll be lookin' for us for breakfast."

If I hadn't felt so suddenly abandoned and thrust aside, I'd have laughed. "Louise? She doesn't pay any attention to when I come and go." That part was true.

He was more nervous than I'd ever seen a man, especially one as slow-moving as Bo. "Come on, let's go."

"Bo, what's the matter?"

"We can't act like that," he said softly, looking away from me. "We aren't married, and you don't want to marry me, and we . . . well, we just can't put temptation in our way. I mean it, I won't be helpin' you ride anymore."

"Bo . . ." But I didn't know what I wanted to say. Part of me was tempted to tell him I'd probably never get a chance to ride in a show and it was a moot point anyway. But I was smart enough, even then, to know that I couldn't settle down and marry Bo Johnson just because I wasn't sure I'd ever get a better offer. That wouldn't have been fair to him. And in the back of my mind, I think I believed that Bo would follow me wherever I wanted to go, in spite of what he said.

"Come on," he said too heartily, "let's race."

We arrived at Louise's panting and breathless and pretending to be in good spirits from our race.

"There's a letter for you from Colonel Miller," she said.

Excitement making me blind and thoughtless, I grabbed the letter from the stand in the hall and ripped it open. " 'Dear Tommy Jo,' " I read, " 'I have finally made plans to take the Miller 101 Wild West Exhibition on the road. I would very much like you to be part of the show. We will meet at the 101 on Sunday, April 25, to discuss the tour. Please let me know if you will join us.' It's signed Colonel Zack Miller. April 25—that's two weeks from now!" Hardly able to contain my excitement, I turned to wave the letter at Bo.

He was gone.

"He just turned around and left," Louise said, her voice level and without any sign of how she felt about what had transpired.

"Left?" My stomach tied itself into a knot so tight that I winced.

"Left. Shrugged his shoulders and left."

A great wail escaped from my mouth, almost as though it came from another being, and I ran to my room, sobs beating me to the door and echoing after me as I slammed it.

Later, Louise and I talked, though she mostly listened, and asked only one question: "What are you going to do?"

Astounded, I looked at her. "Go to the Miller 101," I said. I may have been heartbroken about Bo, but there was never any choice in my mind.

I left for the 101 ten days later. This time, though, I'd been to the ranch to see Mama and Papa, and I'd been to the corral to talk to Bo. Neither visit was pleasant.

At first, Mama seemed herself. "Thomasina! I'm so glad to see you. I've just baked a pound cake—your favorite—I must have known you were coming." Her face was lit by a wide smile, and I walked into a welcoming hug.

"Tommy Jo," Papa said, standing behind her, "what brings you here?"

I could have read anger or hostility into his words, but I didn't. And I didn't bristle. I simply said, "I came to say good-bye for a while. The 101's going to take a show on the road, and they've asked me to go with them."

Mama frowned. "A show on the road? You mean you won't be in Guthrie? You'll be traveling, unsupervised . . . like a hoyden. . . ."

I wasn't sure what *hoyden* meant, but I could tell from Mama's expression that it wasn't good. Behind her, Papa rolled his eyes heavenward.

"Mama, Colonel Zack will look after me, strict as Papa would." Well, it was probably the truth. "You won't have to worry 'bout me doing anything you wouldn't approve of. You raised me right."

She looked at me with a blank expression, as though she were suddenly trying to figure out who I was.

"Tommy Jo," Papa said with real regret in his voice, "there's no way I can go with you." He nodded toward Mama and put a protective arm around her.

Did my relief show? "Papa, thank you, but I don't need you. You need to tend to your work at Luckett's and take care of Mama. I'm eighteen now, and I can take care of myself." I paused a minute and grinned at him. "Or at least, I darn sure better learn pretty quick."

Papa held out his arms, and I didn't back away, as I would have a few months earlier. Instead, I went to him and hugged him hard.

But then he said, "I'll write Zack Miller tonight, tell him my concerns."

"Papa!" I wailed, but he just turned away.

I stayed for supper, which was roast that Mama had put in the oven, and potatoes and greens that Papa and I fixed while Mama sat in the rocking chair, smiling a little, knitting furiously, and speaking only when spoken to.

"What? Oh yes, that's lovely, James," she said when asked if the roast was done, and "You shouldn't stay up past your bedtime," to me when the subject of my traveling came up.

I left the ranch in the late afternoon, tears welling in my eyes for the life that Mama could have had and didn't. When I reached Louise's, I barged through the kitchen and up to my room without a word to anyone—especially Louise, who was doing dishes and gave me a long hard look—and hid myself. I was going to be a great roper, but my mother and father weren't going to enjoy it, for various reasons. It was enough to make anyone cry, and I did.

Louise came to my room later. "You all right?" she asked softly, opening the door just a crack.

I still sat in the chair next to the bed, wearing the rumpled clothes I'd worn all day. Without looking, I knew that my eyes were red and my hair wild. "I guess so," I said. "It's just not fair—and don't tell me that life is never fair. Papa used to tell me that."

"It's fair," she said, shrugging. "We get what we want. That's why we have to watch out, or we'll end up where we're headed. Your mama didn't want to deal with reality anymore, so she's gotten what she wants. It's hard on you, but—"

"It's hard on Papa," I said, though my voice held a question.

"He's probably gotten what he wants, too," she said. "He can protect your mama, without worrying about making her happy because now that's impossible. And he'll probably feel less guilty about coming to see me, or going to St. Louis, or—"

"You'll still let him come?"

She bit her lip. "I probably will. I don't owe your mama anything. But in truth, I doubt he'll come anymore. I think his energy is all taken up with your mama. She's gotten one of the things she wanted when it's too late to enjoy it."

"You'll miss him?"

"Some," she said, shrugging, "but not too much. There are other fish in the sea, as you'll soon find out, Tommy Jo."

Louise left, and I sat in front of the mirror at my dressing table for a long time, brushing my hair and staring at myself. What did the future hold? What was going to happen to me? Would I be all right without my mother and father?

My meeting with Bo did little to reassure me and created new complications in my world. He was sitting at the shabby desk in the corner of the barn he called an office, dusty papers piled around him, straw sticking out between them. Bo's attention was concentrated on a ledger open before him, and he grasped a pencil tightly in his hand, as though it would fly away if he relaxed for a moment.

"Bo?"

He threw the pencil down as he would a burning-hot branding iron. "Damn accounts. Never can figure who owes me what, but it doesn't look like enough to buy feed for the next week," he said, his voice unusually loud and angry.

Impulsively, I said, "Come with me to the 101. They probably need help." I guess I was thinking I could have my cake and eat it, too, go with the show and not give up Bo. But the minute I said anything, I knew it was wrong. Still, Bo's answer surprised me.

He stood up and brushed a hand through his hair. "I am going with you," he said. "Louise and I talked about it. Can't let you ride up there alone again." Was that a slight grin?

If it was, he turned solemn immediately. "But I ain't stayin', Tommy Jo. I ain't running along behind you."

"I never meant—"

He shook his head. "Naw, you didn't mean, but that's what it'd be. I'd be the man that followed Tommy Jo Burns, and if you get to be as famous as you think you will—and I don't doubt it'll happen—things'd get worse and worse." He paced behind that small desk, and then turned to slap the wall behind him in frustration.

"I could have made a life for you here—a life with horses, and babies, of course"—that slight grin came again and faded at once—"but that's all I can offer. I love you, Tommy Jo Burns, but I won't ruin my life for you."

I stood stock still, my mouth open in speechless amazement. No man had ever told me he loved me, and it gave me great pause. I walked through the barn, rubbing the nose of this horse and then that as they stuck their heads out the half doors in curiosity. Bo simply stayed behind his desk, framed against a wall that held harnesses and bridles and all manner of tack hung on random nails.

When I walked back to him, I was crying, not the loud sobs of recent days but tears that wet my cheeks, no matter how insistently I wiped them away. "It's—it's what I've wanted all my life," I said. "I can't . . . if I backed away now, I'd never know."

He wrapped his arms around me, comforting, warm, and secure. "I know that, Tommy Jo. I know you can't ever take the life I'm offering you. It's just the way things happen sometimes. I'm not angry, just sad."

I held on for dear life and wondered once again if I was being the world's dumbest fame-seeker. In my mind for just a second I saw a headline that read "World's Greatest Lady Roper" and below it an article that began, "The lonely figure of Tommy Jo Burns, never married, estranged from her parents . . ." I shivered.

"What's the matter?" Bo asked, releasing his hold on me. "Ghost walk over your grave?"

"Not funny, Bo," I said.

At least my parting with Louise was less emotional. "I'll come see you when you're famous," she said, and then let loose with that deep laughter. "Meantime, you're always welcome here." She stood at the back door, a clean white apron over her cotton dress, her hair neatly swept up on her head. She looked to be maybe ten years older than me, no more, a friend but certainly not another mother to me. Or was she?

"I'll write," I promised. And then, jumping out of the buckboard for one last hug, I said, "Thank you. I—I don't know that I could be doing this if I still lived with Papa."

"We'll never know that," she answered, "but I'm truly glad for you, Tommy Jo. Go show 'em what a Cherokee Strip girl can do!"

Bo drove the buckboard from the stable, a roomy and sturdy vehicle but not one built for comfort. "Best bring a pillow," he'd warned me, and we hadn't gone very far before I was grateful for the pillow that cushioned my seat. Still, Louise's little carriage wouldn't have held my belongings—"You're not just going for one show this time," she warned me, as we sewed and put together a hasty wardrobe for me. Sam was tied on behind the buckboard, and I could have sworn the look in his eye was "Oh, oh, here we go again!"

Excitement won out over doubt, and my spirits were high that morning as we started out. Bo, bless him, matched me in mood, and we chattered about the weather, how high the bluestem grass was for April, how the horses looked this spring, whether or not we'd had enough rain—anything but the Miller 101 Wild West Show and my future. It was a pleasant ride, and I loved Bo for not making me confront my decision head-on. He'd said his piece, and he said no more.

As we approached the ranch, Bo saw the same fields I had—wheat, milo, alfalfa, onions—and the apple orchards. "Apples!" he'd said to me. "They grow those up north, Michigan and all those cold places. Who owns all this?"

"The Millers," I said, a bit impatiently. "You know, the three brothers and their mother."

He looked sideways at me with a grin. "Any of those brothers single? You could do worse than to marry into this ranch. You'd get your show and everything else beside."

"Not funny, Bo."

Colonel Zack greeted us at the ranch. When I introduced Bo, he said as casually as he could, "Sure some spread you got here, Colonel."

Colonel Zack beamed. "Glad you like it. My father, he built this place. But he never thought about a Wild West show." Pride was evident in his grin. Then he added ruefully, "My brothers aren't too sure, either."

Bo ducked his head a little and muttered, "I bet not." But then he said heartily, "Must make a man proud to look out over this place." Bo was easily impressed, obvious in his amazement.

The colonel took a liking to him. "Tommy Jo, you go on up to the house and say hello to Mama. She'll be glad to see you. I'll take Bo here and show him around. We'll bring your stuff up later."

"Sure," I said, somewhat put out that the two of them were going to go off and leave me behind. Bo knew—I could tell by his look and the slight shrug of his shoulders—but he followed the colonel without hesitation.

Mrs. Miller greeted me like I was the daughter she'd never had, what with all those boys, and showed me to the same room I'd shared with Prairie Rose before. "Prairie Rose ought to be here tonight," she said. "Zack's had a letter saying she'll come, if he'll let her trick ride. And I 'bout beat him into agreeing, though he insists this is a ranch exhibition and nobody really trick rides on a ranch."

I grinned happily. "Prairie Rose's coming? I haven't heard from her in months." I might almost forget about letting Bo go, if I had Prairie Rose for company—but as soon as that thought crossed my mind, I dismissed it as unworthy.

Prairie Rose arrived in a flurry, like she always did, and we barely had time to whisper "Hello, how are you?" and "What's new?" before we were called to dinner. Bo waited in the parlor with Colonel Zack, and when he was introduced to Prairie Rose, he made so much over her that I wanted to kick him.

"Prairie Rose! Tommy Jo's sure talked a lot about you," Bo said, holding her hand and looking straight into her eyes. "She admires you, and if Tommy Jo says that, then I do, too."

I wanted to lurch across the room and break that handhold. More than that, I wanted to change my name to something terribly feminine, like Prairie Rose, and learn to charm men, the way Rose did. Bo was positively ignoring me. At dinner, he asked Rose about her riding—"Tommy Jo's told me all about your tricks, and she had me helping her practice all this winter."

Bo Johnson, I thought, why must you blabber so?

Colonel Zack gave me a sharp look. "Rose will be doing a little trick riding," he said sternly, "but you'll be roping, Tommy Jo. This ain't a circus. It's a ranch exhibition."

"Yes, sir," I murmured, "I know that."

He settled back to his pork chops and potatoes, contentedly, as though he'd made his point. I picked at my food, angry at Bo, the colonel, even

Rose. Somehow this wasn't going the way I wanted. I'd practiced almost a year so that I could be a trick rider in someone's show, and here I was at last in a show—ordered to rope and do no more.

After dinner, the men retired to the parlor for cigars, and though Rose and I offered to help with the dishes, Mama Miller sent us packing. We didn't repeat our offer, and soon we were in our room.

"Wow!" Rose said, pulling off the high-top shoes she'd donned just for dinner and rubbing her feet as if they ached badly. "He's great! Where'd you find him, Tommy Jo?"

"Bo?" I asked stupidly. "He has a stable in Guthrie. Louise arranged for him to help me practice."

"And what did you practice?" she asked with a mischievous grin.

"You know. The tricks you told me—I can pretty much stand in the saddle and pick something off the ground, and—"

"I'd have sure practiced something else," Rose said, "with a man like that."

She made me feel inadequate and stupid, and I resented it. "He wants me to stay in Guthrie," I said shortly, "and I can't do that."

Rose, by now parading in front of the mirror and examining her figure—she was wearing a corduroy skirt with a high tight waist and a sharply pleated white shirt—turned to look at me. "You mean, live in Guthrie and not ever join a show, not ever rope professionally?"

I nodded my head unhappily.

She was next to me on the bed, her arms around me, in an instant. "You can't do that, Tommy Jo! You've got to do what you do best."

"I know. I tried to get Bo to see if the colonel didn't have work for him, but he won't do that. Says he won't follow me around."

"Well," she said huffily, rising again to parade before the mirror, "it's his loss."

And mine, I thought miserably.

Next morning at breakfast, Colonel Zack said in a hearty tone, "I've tried to tempt this man, Tommy Jo, offered him job after job, but he says he has a stable in Guthrie, and that's where he wants to be."

Bo stared at me, but I managed to answer lightly, "That's right, Colonel. It's a fine stable, and Bo's happy there."

Bo hitched up the team and prepared to leave right after breakfast, and after he'd said his good-byes to everyone at the White House, I walked out with him to the buckboard.

"It's a whole new world you're moving into, Tommy Jo," he said, "and I wish you well in it."

"You could be part of it," I said, almost pouting.

"We talked about that, and I can't do it. You know that. If it goes sour for you, I'll be in Guthrie waiting. But I hope that don't happen. I hope you're a triumph, and if you ride in Madison Square Garden in New York, I'll come cheer for you."

"Promise?"

"I promise," he said, and kissed me softly on the forehead. Then he added, "You keep in touch," which almost sounded as though I were a stranger, and he was into the buckboard and urging the horses down the road. When he was a good ways beyond me, he turned to lift his hat and wave. I waved back and ran into the house.

"Honey," Rose said from her wicker seat on the veranda, "there's lots more men in this world. He's wonderful, but he's not irreplaceable."

I wasn't sure, right then, that I believed her. It was scary to send Bo off, like sending off my last link with home and a past that, however unsatisfactory, was familiar. Whether I recognized it or not, my old life was behind me, and I was beginning a new adventure. I was both scared and excited.

PART TWO

CHAPTER 6

Life has its disappointments for everyone, I guess, but it was a big disappointment to me, years later, that I'd never been a trick rider. Bo left me at the 101 in full faith that next time he saw me I'd be a famous trick rider, and I, young and ignorant of life's catastrophes, thought so, too. It didn't work out that way at all, though. First it was the colonel who kept me from trick riding, and then it was Rose herself, though she didn't know it.

"There'll be no trick riding in this show," the colonel announced firmly at our first rehearsal. "It isn't part of ordinary ranch work, and this is an exhibition. Tommy Jo, you'll rope and ride broncs. Prairie Rose, you'll ride broncs, except for the grand entry. You can do that trick business then." He turned on his heel and left us.

"I thought I got out from under my father's domination," I said disgustedly. "The colonel sounds just like Papa—we'll do this, and we won't do that." In my mind's eye I could see myself mounted on a rearing white horse—never mind that Sam was brown—in Madison Square Garden, and I didn't want the colonel or anybody else getting in the way of that dream.

Rose seemed unconcerned. "We'll win him over. You watch and see."

"What 'trick business' are you going to do in the parade?" I asked curiously.

She shrugged. "Nothing fancy at first. Got to kind of work the colonel into this." Then she laughed and whirled away from me, dancing a few steps in the dirt from sheer happiness. My, how I envied the way Rose handled men—or thought she could.

We began to practice, and I almost thought I was back at Luckett's learning to rope calves. I'd been so busy with trick roping that it had been a long time since I'd roped a living, running animal. Now I had the strength to do it right. In spite of flashes of memory about that dead bull, it didn't take too long for me to get really good at it. By the end of the week, I had beat the time of most of the men—and my calves always stayed tied until I let them up.

The colonel also had me riding broncs, as he'd said. I got on the first one fairly confident—after all, hadn't I ridden that bronco in Bo's yard? The cowboys snubbed this one for me, and I got on and motioned them to let go. Next thing I knew, I was face-down in the dirt—and darn mad about it.

"Bring him back here!" I roared. "I'm goin' to ride that horse!"

Grinning, the cowboys brought the bronc back and snubbed him again. I got on again, remembering all Papa's lessons about taking my time, remaining calm and in control. This time when they turned the horse loose and he busted in half, I stayed in the saddle until the colonel finally rang that old cowbell of his. But I had a hard time doing it, 'cause I kept trying to get my feet in the stirrups for a better seat, and the stirrups were hobbled.

Women were then riding with hobbled stirrups—tied under the horse's belly—on the theory that it was safer for them. After that ride, I never would let them hobble the stirrups for me but insisted on having them loose like the men did.

Finally after a long week of practice, we were ready to board the train and start out on the circuit. Railroad tracks, laid for the editors' exhibition, still ran from the main railroad line to the ranch, and special railroad cars began pulling onto these sidings the day after Bo left—stock cars with special stalls built for the horses, sleeping cars, baggage cars, a chair car, and a diner, which was nothing more than an empty galley with a large table in the middle—the colonel bought our meals at various stops and carried them on board. We would travel in style, or so it seemed.

We were to head north toward Wichita, with our first show in Hutchinson, Kansas. Then came Salina and Manhattan, before we swung east into Missouri and Illinois, where we'd hit several small towns before ending the tour in St. Louis in July—"before it gets hotter than hell," the colonel said.

That first show in Hutchinson was pretty tame. After the entry parade, the cowboy band played "The Star Spangled Banner," "Home on the

Range," and a stirring march that spooked at least five horses. The colonel would have to rethink his musical selections, I thought as I calmed Sam.

Then several cowboys roped and wrestled steers, rode bucking horses, and finally rode some bulls. The action was fast and the cowboys were skillful, but the crowd only clapped politely. All this was nothing folks in Hutchinson hadn't seen before. The colonel was trying to exhibit ranch skills to people who did the same thing every day of their lives.

But I could feel the crowd perk up when Prairie Rose was announced. "Yes, sir, ladies and gentlemen, the prairie flower herself, riding the meanest, toughest bronc ever to buck on this earth, a horse by the name of Twister." Twister pretty much lived up to his name, turning this way and that, leaping straight into the air and twisting before he came down. Rose, riding with tied hobbles, made the act of staying aboard look effortless, and when she stood on firm ground again after the ride and bowed daintily to the crowd, she got more of a response than all the cowboys combined. Still, it wasn't overwhelming. Ladies in Hutchinson probably rode tough broncs, too, out of necessity, not for fun, which was what they thought we were doing.

"Whew," Rose said as she came by me, still out of breath from her ride. "If this is show business, I believe I'll retire. I expected—"

"Wild cheering?" I asked. "Like the editors' show? Rose, those editors hadn't ever seen anything like broncs, but these folks ride mean horses every day." It seemed obvious enough to me what the problem was.

Rose looked at me with wide eyes, then turned to look at the crowd in the bleachers around the arena. They wore jeans and shirts, Stetson hats, boots, kerchiefs at their necks. The women wore serviceable straight skirts and shirts, and many wore hats just like ours, though several bonnets could be seen. Men and women both had lined weathered faces that told they'd been out in the sun most of their lives. They sat patiently but clearly without the excitement and anticipation one wanted from an audience.

"You're right," Rose breathed. "You're absolutely right. Why doesn't the colonel see this?"

"You tell me," I said, and then something bold came to me. "We'll have to show him," I told her. "Come over here a minute, and let's make some plans." Leading Sam by his reins, I guided Rose to an out-of-the-way spot behind the arena where we could talk. Minutes later, we both came away smiling. Sam and I headed for the arena gate, ready to begin our act, and Rose remounted her horse.

"Ladies and gentlemen, you've never seen a lady rope like Miss Tommy Jo Burns from the Cherokee Strip. She can rope 'em and tie 'em before you can blink! Tommy Jo!" The announcer's voice rolled over my name like thunder as Sam and I trotted into the arena and once around, waving at the crowd. There were a few scattered cheers and one or two waves, but once again it wasn't enthusiasm.

I roped three calves and tied them, each in pretty good time if I do say so, and the crowd applauded nicely. They understood good timing and could respect it, but it didn't excite them. Then I roped a yearling steer and Sam held him firm until one of the cowboys came in to throw him. The applause was a little less this time, and I couldn't blame the audience—what was the good of roping a steer if you had to have someone else come in and throw it for you? But the colonel had insisted, in spite of my showing him two times that I could tie my own steers.

"Nope, Tommy Jo," he'd said. "Calf is one thing, but a steer's too strong. Might get the best of you."

It did no good to tell him I'd been tying steers at Luckett's since I was fourteen, and I seethed with resentment again. But this time, I'd have my own way.

After the steer was tied, I took my hat off and waved it in the air. The crowd, at first thinking I was bowing out, clapped politely, but silence struck when I recoiled my rope and began building a large loop on the ground. I looked out of the corner of my eye and saw Rose, mounted on the dun mustang she'd brought with her, waiting patiently. I nodded my head ever so slightly, and she spurred her horse to a gallop. I stood, rope in hand, my left foot braced forward, waiting. When they were almost upon me, I hefted that huge loop into the air in front of me. Without missing a step, horse and rider rode through it.

The crowd went wild, standing to cheer as Rose turned her horse and came back toward me. Rose waved, and I, feet firmly on the ground, bowed. Colonel Zack stood on the sidelines, alternately glaring at us and staring in surprise at the crowd. I was tempted to throw a loop at him but decided it was the better part of wisdom to quit while I was ahead.

On impulse, though, I took the handkerchief from my pocket and threw it on the ground, then stepped well back. Rose saw me, spurred her horse to the other end of the arena, then turned and flew by me, reaching to grab the small cloth off the ground as she went by. The crowd roared again, and Rose, made bold by the applause, began to ride slowly around the ring. I watched her move into a crouch and then into a stand. Feet planted firmly on her saddle, standing tall and straight, arms extended in a gesture of embracing the crowd, she and her horse circled the arena. Finally, speaking softly to the horse, she bent her legs slightly and then propelled herself off the horse, to land standing almost beside me. I was overwhelmed, and so was the audience. Applause rolled over and around us.

"Here comes the colonel," Rose said sideways to me, still smiling brightly and waving at the audience.

"Oh oh!" I said, but waving my hat in the air toward the crowd, I added, "Just smile pleasantly at him."

All smiles, he came to stand between us, an arm on each shoulder, and joined us in bowing. The colonel was no fool—he took full credit for our act and our success, while the announcer roared, "Aren't they wonderful, ladies and gentlemen?"

"I'll see you in my railroad car as soon as you get the horses put up," he said to us when we were at last out of the arena, and neither Rose nor I had a hint from his tone about what he would say to us.

"I don't care," I said defiantly. "We saved the show."

"We did, didn't we?" she said, her dimples showing as she grinned triumphantly. "There'll be trick riding in the Miller 101 Show from now on, I'll bet you."

It was nearly an hour later when we presented ourselves to the colonel. We'd rubbed and fed our horses and then taken a minute or two to clean ourselves up some. "Always look your best," Rose said grimly, "even if you may be shot."

The colonel's railroad car combined living and sleeping quarters with an office. It was comfortable but far from fancy, not like those I'd seen pictured with rich wood trim, tapestries on the wall, and cut velvet upholstery. This car had a large rolltop desk in one corner, a sturdy dining table surrounded by straight wood chairs that didn't match, and a comfortable but plain sofa and chairs. A screen apparently curtained off the sleeping portions of the car, quarters for the colonel and his mother. His two brothers, not enthusiastic about this exhibition adventure and its cost, had remained in Oklahoma to run the 101. "Someone's got to make some money," I heard one of them mutter before we left.

The colonel sat at the desk, staring out the window at a rosy sunset to the west. He'd acknowledged our knock with an abrupt "Come in!" but now, as we stood awkwardly before him, he ignored us for several long minutes. Rose and I stole a couple of glances at each other, but we stood patient and still, refusing to appear nervous.

Finally, he turned toward us. "Took things into your own hands this afternoon, didn't you?" His hands played with a worn leather bridle, moving almost nervously across it, but his eyes were steady, looking straight at us.

"It was my idea," I said boldly. "I talked Rose into it."

Rose almost giggled, and I wasn't sure if she was amused or nervous or both. "It didn't take much talking. Colonel, we were about to be——"

"I know," he interrupted, "we were at the opposite end of the scale from success, and you saved us. Makes me so damn mad to be so wrong about something!" His fist pounded so hard on the table, it made him wince, and I thought to myself that a little pain was probably good for him at this point.

"You were right," he said, his tone still angry even if his words weren't, "and I was wrong. Folks don't want to see ranch skills——"

"In St. Louis they will, and maybe even over in Illinois, but not out here where they do the same things every day themselves," I said, aware that I'd been rude in interrupting him but determined to make my point.

"So," he said thoughtfully, "we either have to change the show or the schedule."

"Why can't we do both?" Rose asked. "When we're playing for ranchers and cowboys, we'll do tricks. In the cities, we'll ride and rope."

"I'm going to think about it," he said. Then, pulling himself to his feet, he came toward us and put fatherly arms around our shoulders. "I owe you two, and I'm not too proud to admit it. Angry yes, but I try to be honest. I'm grateful to you."

"Thank you," we murmured, almost in chorus.

His voice grew thunderous again. "But don't you ever take things into your own hands again. Now go on, get out of here, and let a man think."

"Rose," I said when we were settled in our own car, "I believe I've learned something tonight, something about men that I should have learned from being around Papa. They aren't always right."

Rose giggled anew, and I thought there couldn't be two happier people anywhere in the world than we were that night. The road to St. Louis, I was sure, was paved with applause and good times. I had a lot to learn about the show circuit.

By the time we reached St. Louis, the Miller 101 offered a "History and Review of the Wild West," and I was tired and discouraged. There'd been no good times. We'd played twenty-eight small and middling towns in the space of just over forty-five days, and we'd practiced day and night to perfect new tricks. Oh, we got applause—no more of that halfhearted response we'd seen in Kansas—and the roar of a crowd never lost any of its fascination for me. But I was lonely and tired of days that seemed one like the next—up early, eat breakfast, practice until late morning, then lunch, followed by a rest and more practice. By the time we rolled out for an evening performance, the day had already been too long.

Our work showed though. We presented a real Wild West show, with all the trimmings—Rose and I did an act that combined trick riding and roping, almost all the stagehands had been recruited for a mock attack on a stagecoach, the cowboys herded cattle on a trail drive while one warbled "When the Work's All Done This Fall" or "Don't Bury Me on the Lone Prairie"—the colonel had discovered that one of his hands could almost sing and, flying in the face of all his earlier principles, had incorporated music into the show. I didn't remind him about the time he'd scornfully said, "There's no music in the background when you're working on a ranch!"

We still did the exhibition acts—the cowboys rode broncs, and roped and tied steers, but now I roped Rose as she rode toward me at full speed, and I always ended my act by throwing a loop around some unsuspecting person. One night, feeling foolhardy, I threw it around Colonel Zack. I think he would have frowned if the crowd hadn't roared so, but he just kind of grinned and shrugged his shoulders. I never did it again though—usually one of the cowboys was my target.

Rose and I were usually exhausted at night and fell into whatever bed was assigned us—sometimes it was a comfortable boardinghouse in a small town, once in a while it was a sleeping bag in a tent, and occasionally it was a stiff, uncomfortable seat on the train when a schedule demanded we travel at night. After a night on the train, I awoke stiff, sore, and sure that I wasn't cut out for a career in show business.

Tired or not, Rose found it possible to fall in love—twice. The first was an older farmer—he must have been thirty-five—who lived near some small town in Missouri where the colonel had announced we'd stay for several days to practice. Most of the women who came to the show in that town looked worn down by hard work before their time, and not a one looked like she'd willingly get on a galloping horse. They were, I suspected, women who walked behind the plow to help their husbands, raised their children, fed their chickens and their families, and died early of exhaustion. Sometimes it made me glad to be on the show circuit—helped banish those longings I'd been having for Bo and Guthrie. But I worried about Rose.

"Rose, you oughtn't to be encouraging this . . . what's his name?"

Buffing her nails in the dim light of our boardinghouse room, she said,

"Mitchell. His name is Mitchell. And I'm not encouraging him. He says he's never seen a girl ride like I do."

"I'll bet," I said. "But you're going to move on in a few days and forget all about him, and—"

"How do you know I'll forget?" She whirled indignantly to face me. "We plan to correspond, and he says he might come to St. Louis."

"Rose, by the time we get to St. Louis, you'll have forgotten all about him." I lectured like an older sister, I thought, disliking my tone of voice. Still, she wasn't being fair.

"Maybe, maybe not," she said, her tone clearly implying that it wasn't any of my business.

Mitchell waited for her after the show each of the three nights we performed in this town—the colonel couldn't resist turning our practice sessions into performances, and we drew a fair crowd each night. Anyway, this Mitchell was fairly tall and fairly nice looking with straight brown hair and big brown eyes that stared endlessly at Rose. But somehow he just wasn't like the men I'd been raised around. He didn't walk the same, and he didn't even look the same. Oh, he rode horseback and sat a horse well, and he wasn't fat or anything . . . it took me days to figure it out. He was a farmer, not a cowboy. I didn't say that to Rose.

"Prairie Rose!" he'd say, with a hint of wonder in his voice. "How'd you get a name like that?"

"Named after the flower," Rose said smugly. "Grows wild on the prairie. It's hardy and beautiful."

Mitchell had never thought about girls being like flowers, I don't think. The two of them would disappear in the evening, and Rose would come sneaking quietly in way late at night, her hair messed and her clothes slightly askew.

I always pretended to be asleep, though one night I lay awake a long time thinking about Bo and wondering if I was just plain jealous of Rose.

As I predicted, when we moved on Rose lost her fascination with Mitchell and was bothered by his almost-daily letters. "How will I tell him not to come to St. Louis?" she wailed, angry that I was less than sympathetic.

The second love of Rose's summer was a more serious affair. Jake, a cowboy in the show, began to watch her. In the ring, when she curried her horse, when we ate our midday meal at the long table by the arena, even once when we went shopping in Peoria, Illinois—Jake was always there, staring at Rose. It flustered her.

"He's admiring you," I said. "I wish some man was looking at me that way." Truth was, I'd expected romance to come flying at me now that I was out in the world and Bo was back in Guthrie. But nothing even remotely like that had happened, and I was disappointed—and jealous.

She flounced her hair. "If he's admiring, why doesn't he say so?"

"Maybe he's shy." I paused to stare in a window at a display of saddles and bridles. My old saddle was worn and in need of replacement, but I was torn between a new store-bought saddle and one custom-made for trick riding.

"Tommy Jo, let's look at these parasols. I see enough of saddles every day," Rose complained.

Jake watched and waited for nearly two weeks. Then one afternoon he asked Rose to go for a ride with him. They were gone an hour, and Rose came back looking subdued and puzzled.

"Well?"

"Well, nothing. We rode out in the country, stopped under a tree, he rolled a smoke, we talked a little bit, and then we came back."

"What'd you talk about?"

"The show. His boyhood—he grew up not too far from Guthrie, as a matter of fact."

"Really? I never knew him, but I guess that's not surprising."

"No," she said dryly, "he didn't go to a convent in St. Louis." She was pacing the floor nervously. "He didn't really say much. Never said why he was watching me. And he just said good-bye and thanks when he brought me back here. Rode away without . . ." Rose didn't really know what she expected of him, but she hadn't gotten it.

By St. Louis, Rose and Jake were an item, and Mitchell had been told not to come to St. Louis. I pictured Mitchell turning forlornly to some hardworking, sturdy farmer's daughter and remembering, the rest of his life, his brief fling with Prairie Rose.

Jake was another matter—much more worldly and sophisticated about women than Mitchell. Even Rose, whom I thought so knowledgeable about affairs between men and women, was no match for Jake. He had planned his campaign thoroughly, and he'd captured the prize he wanted. Rose hung on his every move, and once he was sure of her adoration, he accepted it as his due. Jake never went out of his way to see Rose, but he didn't have to. She saw that they were together almost constantly.

"Colonel Zack says I've got to stop following Jake around," she pouted one evening, flinging herself on the bed in our St. Louis hotel room. "Says romances between show participants are distracting, not good for business. Pooh! As though I'd give up Jake just because he says so."

"Did he give you a choice—Jake or the show?"

"Not exactly. Besides, he doesn't have to. Show's over after this, and Jake and I are going north."

"North? Together?"

"North. Together," she repeated shortly. "Doesn't seem so remarkable to me. We want to be together, and Jake can find work in Wyoming or Montana. My family's up that way. And there's lots of shows up there—Calgary Stampede, Cheyenne Frontier Days."

The St. Louis Coliseum was an enormous, three-story, square red-brick building, with flags—eight of them—flying on the rooftop, which was edged by a marble cornice with abstract designs in relief. The main entrance was a great arched two-story affair with marble columns on either side, and all the windows along the first floor were similarly arched, though smaller. I thought it was a grand building. Inside, the arena was large, seating thousands.

Something unexpected happened in St. Louis. The show was a huge success, and the crowd began cheering with the grand entry parade. The colonel had hired extras in St. Louis, so now the intricate figure-eight parade was a big—and dangerous—presentation. But we got through it without a mishap, in spite of a few spooked horses under the temporary riders. The broncos reared higher and twisted more than usual, or so it seemed, as though they were spurred on by the enthusiasm of the large crowd. One rider was tangled in his reins for a few seconds, and the crowd collectively held its breath until he was freed, unhurt. The steer wrestling was similarly exciting, but no one—neither man nor animal—was hurt.

Rose began her act, as usual, with the trick of picking up a handkerchief from the ground while riding full tilt across the arena. The crowd gasped as she leaned down, but I paid no attention—I'd seen Rose do this a hundred times by now. Then the gasp became louder, and I whirled to look. Rose had missed the handkerchief and lost her hold on the saddle. The horse, still racing and now unguided, was dragging her, and with each step her head swayed dangerously near his hooves. Before anyone could move to help her, Rose arched her body, throwing it out and away from the horse, and fell onto the floor. As I went forward to comfort Rose, the crowd was cheering and calling her name.

She brushed me away. "I'm all right," she muttered almost angrily. Then, without a word, she whistled her horse to her, caught him, and was in the saddle. Carefully she threw the handkerchief on the arena floor and rode back to the chutes to start the trick again. This time she picked the handkerchief up without a problem, and the crowd went wild.

But her near-miss made me so nervous that my timing was a little off, and I came dangerously close to missing a steer when my act was on. But by the time the act ended I had control of my nerves, and this time, for my surprise victim, I chose Jake and Rose, who were standing at the edge of the arena talking earnestly and absolutely oblivious of the crowd. When the rope fell around them, they looked up in surprise, and then embraced in mock terror. The embrace, however, turned into a passionate kiss, which brought down the house and made a nice ending to our St. Louis show.

"Whew!" I said that night. "Rose, you scared me."

"Scared you! I was terrified," she confessed with a grin. "And I was mad, too. Jake saw me do that!"

"Doesn't seem to have bothered him," I said, recalling that final kiss.

"He was scared, too," she said contentedly, as though his fright proved he loved her. "But we agree that I won't stop doing that trick. That was a fluke. Nothing's going to happen to me."

Why did I hear footsteps on a grave when she said that?

Next morning, Colonel Miller called us all together at the coliseum. "I have an announcement," he said. "This show has been asked to present an exhibition at Madison Square Garden in September at the annual horse show, sort of an extra attraction. Anyone who wishes to accompany us, please see me before the train leaves."

Madison Square Garden!

"Rose?" I was breathless with excitement.

"Not me," she said. "Jake and I know where we're going."

Jake just nodded in agreement, and I stared at them in disbelief. How could they turn down such an opportunity?

Without another word, I rushed to find the colonel.

I never saw Prairie Rose Henson again.

I spent the rest of July and all of August at the Miller 101, though Papa tried to tempt me back to the ranch. I think he wanted help with Mama, or maybe the freedom to get away himself a bit, and that last almost made me guilty. I felt bad about Papa having to stay there, but then I guessed he'd gone his own way long enough, and having to take care of Mama now was some sort of justice. For me, once having made the break, I felt like I didn't dare go home again. And so I stayed at the Miller, practicing my roping and riding. Mrs. Miller fussed over me, and it was nice to have someone act motherly toward me, but I would have traded her for Louise, who treated me as an equal.

One morning while I was practicing picking up a handkerchief from the ground, the colonel strode into the arena, waving a telegram. "Telegram for you," he called, as I rode up to him. "I thought it might be important."

I took it from his outstretched hand somewhat nervously. No one had ever sent me a telegram before, and all sorts of black possibilities went through my mind, prime among them that something had happened to Mama. I was totally unprepared for what the telegram did say.

"Rose killed in arena accident. STOP. Jake." Nothing more—just that cold message in black on that yellow paper.

Wordlessly I handed it to the colonel. He handed it back after a moment, his eyes fixed on me, watching cautiously, wondering, I'm sure, if he would have to catch me as I fell off the horse.

I managed to dismount all right, but once I touched the ground my knees were so weak, I could hardly stand. Unconsciously, I took the colonel's arm and allowed him to lead me all the way to the house. Neither of us said a word, but it occurred to me that this man, who I both loved and resented, was really genuinely sad and really truly worried about me.

"Mother!" he called as we came through the front door. "Tommy Jo needs you right now."

And that motherly woman came on the run. One look at us, and she wrapped her arms around me. Only after she'd soothed and hugged did she ask what had happened, and I guess the colonel whispered it to her, but I don't remember that much of anything.

She made tea and put a splash of bourbon in it—I do remember that. I drank it slowly, staring into space, and they both let me be alone, though I was aware that they hovered nervously not too far away. Later, I realized that both of them were almost as grief-stricken as I was, but with a wisdom I hadn't yet learned, they focused their concern on me. There was nothing they could do for Rose—and nothing, the colonel told me much later, that he *ever* could have done for her, though he had wanted to.

In my mind's eye I was seeing Rose in a thousand different poses—on the back of a rearing horse, primping in front of the mirror, smiling coquettishly at Mitchell in Missouri or Jake in St. Louis, pouting when she was criticized, nearly getting her head bashed when she lost her hold on her horse, standing up indignantly to the colonel when he did something that displeased her, laughing heartily over some small thing and making everything funny by her laughter.

Slowly, at last, tears formed in the corners of my eyes, and soon I was sobbing. Only then did Mrs. Miller come and put her arms around me and hold me tight until my great wails finally subsided.

"She was my age!" I said in disbelief. "She couldn't die!"

Though she must have been tempted to tell me that there was no law about age, that good lady just let me ramble. And I did, talking on about Rose and how Jake wasn't good enough for her and how it was probably his fault. I began to blame Jake for taking Rose away, and my sorrow took the misdirected form of anger at him.

Only later did I learn that Rose had been practicing with a new horse, and when she made him rear on his hind legs, he went over backward, crushing her. When they pulled the horse off, they thought she was miraculously saved, for she got to her feet and bowed as though to an imaginary audience. Then, minutes later, she collapsed. She lingered in the hospital for two days before she died of internal injuries. A heartbroken Jake wrote me a five-page letter about it and asked that I share the details with the colonel.

"Cheyenne Frontier Days were only a week away, and she was very excited about that," he wrote. "But I'm thankful this didn't happen in front of an audience. Rose had too much pride for that."

My anger at Jake turned to compassion.

Rose's memory was with me constantly in the days that followed. The colonel and his mother both treated me like an invalid recently over an illness, until I wanted to yell at them to stop babying me.

One day an idea came to me that seemed to lift the weight I'd been carrying around—and it solved something else that had been bothering me.

"Colonel Zack," I said, barging into his office, "I want to change the way my name is billed for the show."

He raised his eyes from the papers he was working on. "To what? Folks are just beginning to know about Tommy Jo Burns."

"Prairie Jo," I said with finality.

"Now, hold on, Tommy Jo. You're taking the prairie part from Rose, aren't you?"

I nodded, almost unable to speak. Finally, I managed to mutter, "It's . . . well, it's my way of keeping Rose alive, or at least her memory. And besides, I've wanted to get rid of that masculine name for a long time. I just haven't known how."

He looked surprised. "I didn't know it bothered you."

"I want people to know I'm a girl," I said.

The colonel thought for a long time, and then said, "I understand, and

I respect your feelings about Rose." There was a long pause, while he sat staring at me pensively. Then he said, "But I think there's another way to do it. You ever see the wild white rose on the prairie?"

"Cherokee rose?" I asked. "The rose that climbs the fencerows and grows where nothing else will. I always thought that was where Rose took the prairie part of her name." I could see those hardy little flowers Mama had cultivated by the porch of our little house at Luckett's. They grew wild all over the ranch, but Mama went to great trouble to dig them up and plant them again around the posts of the porch of our house. "The only wild thing I like," she said to me once, when I was too young to understand.

"That's right," the colonel said, "I think she did take her name from the Cherokee rose. So now, if you took that name, it'd speak to your home in the Cherokee Strip—and it'd give you the feminine part of Rose's name." Offhandedly he turned back to his papers and said, "Think about it."

"I don't have to think about it," I said. "I like it."

"Cherokee Rose it is." The cigar stuck out of his mouth, and he chomped hard on it. " 'Course you got to understand that most folks are still gonna call you Tommy. They know you that way, and they can't change easily."

"Someday most folks will know me as Cherokee Rose," I said positively, "and Tommy will fade away. I can wait."

The colonel switched topics faster than a cutting horse changes direction after a runaway calf. "New trick roper's gonna join the show. When we get up to New York, maybe you and him can practice together and work out an act. Name's Rogers—ah, Will . . . yes, that's it. Will Rogers."

"Billy!" I shouted, alarming the colonel with my exuberance. "Billy Rogers used to work on Luckett's ranch for Papa, and he taught me to rope. I swore I'd be a star by the time he came back from Australia."

The colonel eyed me patiently. "He's been back awhile, working various shows," he said. "Least you made the star part 'fore you saw him. I'm giving you top billing this time."

And so I became Cherokee Rose, the world's greatest woman roper. Well, that part was to come next. I wrote Mama and Papa to tell them I'd be seeing Billy and to tell them about my new name. I thought Mama would be pleased because the name reminded me of her wildflowers, but Papa wrote that she was distressed. "She says Thomasina is a good name, and you should use it," he wrote. "I will watch for news of Cherokee Rose, but I do think the colonel could have chosen a name that didn't imply you were part

Indian." Papa never would change, I thought wearily, and Mama would never get any better. I was glad to be headed to New York.

All the way to New York, the wheels of the train sang Billy Rogers's name to me. What would he be like? Would he recognize me? Would he remember that sweet savory kiss in the pasture? I remembered every detail—his lopsided grin, the way he looked at the ground sometimes when he talked to me, the hank of hair that always fell in his eyes and the way he'd shake his head to throw it back. In my daydreams, I walked slowly up to him, and he threw his arms wide, exclaiming "Tommy Jo! I should have guessed who Cherokee Rose was!"

When I made myself admit the truth, I knew that Billy would never throw his arms around me or anyone else. That deep-grained shyness would hold him back. Still, I liked my fantasies better.

"Tommy Jo? You best come with me." The colonel shook me back to reality.

"Where?"

"Horse car. Sam's down," he said tersely, and then I read the look of concern on his face and wondered if it were for me or Sam.

"Sam? He's all right," I said loudly, convincing myself.

"I hope so," he said, "I surely hope so."

"What is it?" I demanded, as I followed him down the aisles of the swaying train, sometimes losing my balance and bumping into seats, tripping over extended feet, always remembering to murmur, "Pardon me, please."

"Sam's . . . well, he got excited."

"Excited? Why would he get excited?"

Colonel Zack looked like he wished I hadn't asked that question. Over his shoulder, he threw, "You know, the train and all."

"He's ridden on trains before and never gotten excited," I said, and then demanded, "How bad is it?"

"His left hind leg," he said. "Doc's looking at it now."

For this trip to New York, the colonel had brought along his own veterinarian, a Dr. Smith-Jones, who was, I thought, probably deliriously happy to be rescued from Ponca City.

When at last we stumbled into the stable car, I blindly shoved past the colonel to Sam's stall. I'd visited him not four hours earlier and found him fine. Now he stood, head down, left hind leg raised, blood almost dried but still dripping a little from a deep gash. Dr. Smith-Jones stood bent over the raised leg. He was a small man, with a bushy mustache, wire-rimmed spectacles, and a funny hat balanced on his head. But his hands, tracing the length of Sam's leg, were sure and strong, and I saw calluses on them.

I went closer to look, though the colonel held out an arm as though to stop me. I'd seen hurt animals on the ranch, even helped with calving, and a gashed leg wasn't going to bother me. Or so I thought until I looked and realized that it was Sam. Then I had to put a hand to my mouth, but I stayed next to Sam, patting his nose and talking softly to reassure him.

"Not good," Dr. Smith-Jones said, shaking his head. "Torn the tendon. Don't know if it's past repairin' itself or not. But he's got to keep off it for some time."

From behind me, the colonel argued, "Some time? What's that mean? She's got to ride this horse in New York in less than a week."

"Can't do it, 'less you want to cripple the horse for good," the doctor said.

"She's got to," the colonel insisted.

"No, she doesn't," I said just as firmly. "I won't ride Sam and cripple him."

"But Tommy Jo, you're the star. I've given you top billing! What're we gonna do?" The colonel looked almost desperate, and I would have felt sorry for him if I weren't so busy worrying about Sam and feeling sorry for myself. I didn't want to miss my Madison Square Garden chance any more than the colonel wanted me to miss it.

"Wrap the leg or do whatever you think is necessary," I said to the doctor. Then, turning to the colonel, I asked, "Where's the stable boy? How did this happen?"

"It's obvious," the colonel said in exasperation. "He kicked his foot through the side of the stall. See, there, you can look at the hole."

I saw jagged wood, with splinters sticking out wickedly and blood dried where it had dripped toward the floor.

"But what made him do it?" I persisted. Sam simply wasn't the kind of horse to go crazy and start kicking his stall. The other horses in the car stood placidly enough, and none showed any sign of wanting to kick out of a stall.

I put my face to Sam's, as though I expected him to tell me the truth about what happened, but of course I got no answers. Finally, the leg wrapped and the doctor declaring he'd done the best he could, I retreated to my seat, going much more slowly than that hasty rush toward disaster. I never did find out what had frightened Sam, though I never again trusted a stable boy completely.

The colonel had a different worry on his mind. "What are we going to do for a horse?" he asked not once but at least ten times.

Now the wheels sang a song to me about missing your chance, and I forced myself to remember something that Louise had told me often: "You take opportunity when it knocks, and when it seems like it's not knocking, you sit and wait. Sometimes opportunity surprises you." I couldn't get off the train and go back to Guthrie, and I wouldn't have if I could. So I didn't have much choice except to head for New York and wait for opportunity.

"Tommy Jo? I—we heard about your horse, and I just wanted you to know, well, I'd do whatever I could for you. My horse just don't rope." Belle Saunders stopped by my chair, her hand on my shoulder and her voice in my ear rousing me.

"Thanks, Belle," I said, and meant it. She would never replace Prairie Rose, but Belle Saunders was a friend and would become a better friend in New York.

One by one the others stopped: two or three cowboys, a Spanish dancer who rode bulls (the colonel was proud to bustin' for having "discovered" her in Texas), some of the women who were to be in the "scenes" the colonel planned, and finally Mrs. Miller.

"Tommy Jo, I just want you to know I'm sick about that horse of yours, just plain sick."

"Thank you," I said, grateful once again for her kindness. Then it struck me that here I was in a crisis, and I hadn't even thought about my own folks. I guess that's because I knew how Papa felt about horses: "Tore up a leg beyond repair? No room for a nonworking horse around here!" I'd seen two good horses shot before their time, and I couldn't bear the thought that it would happen to Sam.

My ranch childhood put me in a funny place about Sam. I knew enough about raising animals not to get attached to them, and I understood full well that Sam would have to be replaced and that I would come to trust the next horse as much if not more. But I wasn't Papa—I couldn't cold-heartedly abandon Sam. He'd served me too well, putting up with all my foolishnesses—learning roping tricks, trying to learn trick riding, forcing him up and down the road from Guthrie to Luckett's in blinding thunderstorms. No, in a real sense, I knew I owed my life to Sam, and I was sensible of the debt.

With those thoughts rattling through my brain and keeping me awake nights, the miles ticked away. Belle had come to sleep in the chair next to mine—a move of companionship, which I appreciated—and she snored gently, sleeping the sleep of the innocent. Sam's future didn't trouble her, and it shouldn't—but I knew that Prairie Rose would have been awake, worrying with me.

"What're you thinking, girl?" The colonel crept up behind me and leaned over the chair, his voice gentle.

"I . . . I don't know," I said, twisting to see him in the dimness of the darkened railroad car. "What does the doctor say?"

"You won't ride him in New York, that's for sure. Can't tell if he ought to be put down or not."

"No!"

"Now, Tommy Jo, you know better than to ask someone to keep a broken-down horse what can't earn its feed."

"Bo will keep him," I said, not letting him know that I had just this moment thought of that. But of course that was the answer—Bo knew about Sam, knew what he'd meant to me, and Bo cared about horses in a way that men like Papa and the colonel didn't.

"Might be," the colonel said thoughtfully. "He probably would, for you." And without another word, he turned and left the car, headed for his own private domain.

The colonel had arranged for the special railroad train to park on sidings not too far from Madison Square Garden, although he declared that we would stay in boardinghouses he'd located, and we would parade at least once through town to drum up business for the show. But Sam, blessedly, could stay in the stable car.

"There'll be a guard on duty all the time," he said. "Got to have someone, what with crime what it is in a big city like this. Whoever's watching the train can watch Sam and make sure he's got food and water."

"I'll come check him every day," I vowed.

"Like as not, Tommy Jo, you'll get too involved in the show and city life. I wouldn't promise to do that if I were you." The colonel had a tolerant look on his face, as though he understood me better than I did myself, and it made me mad.

"I'll visit him," I said distinctly.

Belle, Mrs. Miller, the Spanish dancer, myself, and three or four women I hadn't really met were staying at a boardinghouse run by a Mrs. O'Riley. "Good plain food," she told us as we arrived, "and clean rooms. But I don't allow no men in the rooms, no drinking, no smoking." She looked stern.

"Of course," we murmured in unison, meekly complying with the tyrant.

"Good. Now set yourselves down to some supper."

And we "set ourselves down" to a stew with a rich meaty gravy that outdid anything I'd ever tasted—not only did it beat anything Mama thought about cooking, but it was better than Mrs. Miller's stew, which I'd eaten aplenty of, and even better than Louise's, and that was hard to beat.

"This has a wonderful unusual flavor," I said, hoping to compliment our stern hostess. "What is it?"

"I reckon it's turnips," she said sternly, and I subsided, having always hated turnips.

I'd expected to share a room with Belle but found myself instead paired with the Spanish dancer. She was, I soon found, from Brooklyn.

"Brooklyn?" I exploded.

"That's right," she laughed. "Right back home. But do not tell the colonel." With the last words, she moved into the Spanish accent that had apparently fooled the colonel. Carmelita—her real name, she told me, was Hannah—was dark-complected, with dark hair that hung below her shoulders, curling around her face in ringlets. Her jet black eyes had a way of looking through you, but she was quick to laugh—and she was calculating.

"Hannah?" I asked, as fascinated by her deception as I was by her beauty.

"Jewish," she said. "My papa, he's a cantor in a synagogue, and he . . . he has disowned me because I wanted to be in show business." She shrugged her shoulders, as if to say being disowned mattered little to her.

I hadn't exactly been disowned, but I could sympathize. "But where did you learn to ride bulls?" I asked, for that was what it was broadcast that she would do. A nagging bit of worry was beginning to force itself into my brain.

She shrugged again. "I've never ridden the bull. I just told the colonel that because I was in Oklahoma, and I needed to get back to New York. I can ride it when the time comes."

Oh, oh! I thought. *We have a real problem here.* "Carmelita, you can't 'just ride' a bull," I said desperately. "It's—well, I've ridden some rough broncs in my life, but I'd never try to ride a bull."

"Rough broncs?" she echoed.

"Carmelita," I said directly, "what were you doing in Oklahoma?"

"I was with an actors' troupe that failed. We did Shakespeare and George Bernard Shaw and some others—even *Uncle Tom's Cabin*—but the show went bankrupt and left us stranded. The colonel's show was the only way I could see to get home." She looked pitifully helpless, but I felt not one whit of pity, for I knew the trouble that was brewing.

"Are there any others like you in the colonel's troupe?" I asked. When she shook her head to the negative, I said, "Hannah, you cannot—I repeat, *cannot*—ride a bull. You'll just have to confess to the colonel."

The Spanish accent came back in full force. "Oh, but *mi hija,* I cannot. It is a matter of honor—to be sure, you understand?"

It was, to me, a strange sense of honor. "No," I said, "I don't understand at all."

Worrying about Carmelita would not find me a new horse to ride, though, and I was getting more and more worried. The colonel, beset by a thousand details, had just waved his hand and said, "I'll take care of it," when I talked to him. But I'd carefully gone over the troupe's horses in my mind, and I knew there wasn't a one trained to rope the way Sam was. And I seriously doubted the colonel would find a good roping horse for sale in New York City.

So it was with a great deal of apprehension mixed with excitement that I went to the Garden that first day. Excitement won at first, for here I finally was in Madison Square Garden, the place of my dreams. Granted, Buffalo Bill wasn't there, but maybe that would be another time. Meanwhile I was going to ride and rope in the mecca. The annual horse show was a high society event, so the colonel told us, and they sure had turned every trick to fix up that big coliseum. Flags from all nations flew from the girders, and bunting was draped all over the sides of the arena. They'd put dirt on the floor—four feet at the turns—to make sure the animals didn't slip, and that dry dirt rose in our faces as we stood in the arena.

A cowboy stood leaning against the wall of the arena, a small rope twirling in his hand while he looked idly about. One look, and I knew that cowboy was familiar.

"Billy!" I meant to walk quietly up to him and whisper. Instead, I yelled so loudly that even the colonel turned to stare for a moment.

"Hey, Tommy Jo," he said, never moving from his spot against the wall.

"Billy, how are you? Where've you been? You were supposed to come back to the ranch!" I was full of questions and accusations, and behind them lay the unspoken question about whether or not he'd missed me.

"I'm fine," he drawled. "Been around some." He nodded his head again and then looked straight at me. "I didn't think coming back to Luckett's was such a good idea."

My mind scrambled for a minute to digest that, and then I babbled, "I swore I'd be a star by the time you came back. Guess I didn't make it."

That big slow grin traveled across his face. "No, guess not. Somebody named Cherokee Rose has top billing in this shindig."

I laughed aloud, an unladylike, hearty, happy laugh. "That's me," I told him. "I'm Cherokee Rose."

His jaw dropped, and he shook his head to throw that lock of hair off his forehead. "No kidding? How come you chose that name? You ain't Cherokee." He grinned a little bit. "Sometimes I'm called the Cherokee Kid."

"Really?" I asked. "I—well, you know the wild rose they call the Cherokee Rose . . . and I knew Prairie Rose Henson . . . and it's a long story. You can hear about it later. What are you doing here?"

"Colonel Miller invited me, says he'll make a roping star out of me." He nodded toward the center of the arena where Colonel Zack was in heated conversation with someone, pointing this way and that and raising his voice so that we could hear him, even if we couldn't make out the words. "Telling 'em how he wants it, no doubt," Billy said. "You ride a high school horse?" he asked suddenly.

"High school horse?" I'd wandered into a world for which I was totally unprepared. "Nope. Don't even know what one is."

"It's foreign," he said disgustedly. "Spanish I think. They teach the horse to do everything like lie down and roll over, and the rider doesn't hardly have to signal, leastaways not so the audience can see. Looks like the horse is thinking for itself. Colonel's got one billed, but he don't have anybody to ride it."

"He doesn't have a horse like that," I said with certainty. "He'd have told me. Besides, what does that have to do with the West?" Echoes of the colonel's insistence on reality sounded in my mind.

"Nothin'," Billy said, "nothin' at all."

"I don't have a horse for roping," I said. "Sam's torn a tendon. S'pose a high school horse can rope?"

"Nope. But a roper ain't much good without a horse," Billy said, eyes once again on the ground.

"That's true," I agreed. Six months ago—before I left home, before Rose died—I'd have been frantic, but now I could almost stand there and watch myself look for a horse.

"I'd hate to miss this chance because I didn't have a horse," I said.

Billy did what I'd been hoping he would, even if I hadn't admitted the hope aloud even to myself. "I got three horses," he said, "all trained ropers, good ropers. You can take your pick out of two of them, for an extended loan. Lucy's Luck is mine."

"Who's Lucy?" I demanded without even thanking him for the offer of a horse.

"Girl I met," he said noncommittally. "You want to see the horses?" I chose a bay named Governor. "Governor?" I asked.

"Yeah. I used to know a man named Governor. Liked him. Thought naming a horse for him was about the best tribute I could give him. You best get to riding that horse, get him used to you. Show opens in two days."

And for two days I rode Governor almost constantly, until the horse and I were both exhausted. I almost lost interest in my Madison Square Garden debut, simply from practicing so long and hard. I was the one who had to practice, not the horse—he was better trained than any roping horse I'd even dreamed of riding.

But I didn't lose interest in Billy. Trouble was, he'd lost interest in me. I could tell that from our first conversation. He was maybe one of the best friends I'd ever had—who else would loan you a roping horse?—but he saw me as a little sister. I practiced being flirty, like I'd seen Rose do, but my giggles and sidelong looks only made Billy uncomfortable. More than once, he just turned and walked away from me, twirling that little loop of his.

He really only lost his calm indifference twice. The first time was when I'd called him Billy for the umpteenth time, and he said, "I'm Will now. Outgrown that Billy name." He blushed a little, and I thought I heard belligerence—or defensiveness—in his voice.

The other time he listened, and then he comforted. It was all because of the colonel, of course. The colonel had thanked him profusely for the loan of the horse. "Don't know what we'd have done," he said. "I just—well, I couldn't scare up a horse in New York, and yet Sam—that leg . . ."

"Glad to," Billy said, cutting him short.

But the next day as I was practicing, the colonel came storming across the ring. "Cherokee!" he said loudly, and I was instantly wary. He'd suggested the name all right, but he'd never used it, still calling me Tommy Jo, and I knew by his use of my new "public" name that he had something hidden on his mind. I waited.

"Cherokee," he said, coming close, "we're gonna beef up your act. Put some trick riding in it, along with the roping. You can do those tricks that Rose used to do, can't you? You know, like picking up a handkerchief."

My heart turned to absolute stone. "No," I managed to say calmly, "I can't."

"But that man from Guthrie—what's his name? Bo, yes that's it, Bo. He said you'd been practicing all summer."

I looked at the dirt. "Yes," I mumbled, "I had. But that was before, and I had a horse trained for it. Governor's never done tricks."

"Now, Tommy Jo"—he was back to using my given name—"that's a good, calm horse. He'll do fine. And you can't let Rose's tragedy stand in the way of your career. You simply got to do some tricks. You got top billing, but a roper ain't enough for that, won't bring the people in."

A part of me wanted to simply turn and run away, throwing Colonel Zack and Madison Square Garden and my dream of Buffalo Bill to the wind, but I caught Billy watching me intently, and I drew a deep breath. "I'll give them a show worth their money," I said, looking directly at him, "but I won't do any trick riding."

"Tommy Jo! I've got this horse . . ." The colonel almost wailed, and I walked away.

Billy caught up with me. "You want to tell me about it now?" he asked.

"Yes," I said.

And so Billy Rogers and I sat on the bleachers in Madison Square Garden, and I poured out the story of Prairie Rose, our friendship, her death, my own uncertainties, my determination to be a star, equaled only by my determination not to be a trick rider. I'd done my crying for Prairie Rose, and I was darned if I'd let the colonel make me cry, so I told the story in a flat tone, with no tears. Billy looked straight into my face while I talked and never made a sound.

"You can do it, Tommy Jo," he said—and then with a grin, "Pardon me, I mean Cherokee. You can do anything you want, but you don't have to trick ride."

"Thanks, Billy" was all I could say. Years later, I never would know if I'd have been a bigger star if I hadn't listened to Billy, if I'd put my fears and convictions aside and learned to do the Roman ride. But right then, Billy Rogers gave me a gift beyond measuring. He gave me myself. I was young and thinking I was looking for romance, and bitterly disappointed that I didn't get it from Billy—not even his smushy kisses—but what he gave me was beyond that. And I've treasured it all my life.

HAPTER 7

In the end, though, I only partway took Billy's advice. "What horse?" I asked the colonel later that day.

"High school horse," he said, still angry with me. "But you don't want to be a star, you don't want to ride it." I think he assumed I didn't know what a high school horse was, and if it weren't for Billy, I wouldn't have known.

"What does it do?"

"Wha'dya mean, 'what does it do'?" He stood, cigar in his mouth and hands on his hips, staring down at me.

I held my own. "What kind of schooling has it had?"

He shrugged impatiently. "Bows, rolls over, and plays dead, trained-dog kind of stuff. Nothing to interest you."

"Show me the horse," I said.

"Cherokee"—he turned from angry to dead serious—"I want you to ride this horse and be the star, but you got to promise you won't change your mind, won't quit halfway through for some silly notion."

"I'll ride the horse," I told him.

The horse was a palomino gelding with a luxurious white mane and tail. The colonel had bought him, he told me, from a small show that went bankrupt in one of the towns we passed through on the way to New York. He was called Blaze, because he had a blaze on his forehead, but I elected to call him Guthrie.

"Guthrie? That's a city," the colonel said in disgust.

"Now it's a horse, too," I replied. "Why didn't you tell me about him when you got him?"

"Couldn't predict what you'd do," he said with a grin. "Just thought I'd wait till we were here and you had the dust of the Garden in your nostrils."

Rose had been unpredictable that way, and I guessed the colonel was confusing me with her—or taking my identification with her one step too far. But I vowed right then that top billing wouldn't go to my head, making me difficult. Without another word to the colonel, I began to saddle Guthrie for our first practice session.

"Who knows what commands he's used to?" I asked.

The colonel shrugged, and I nearly threw the saddle at him. I had twenty-four hours to figure out how to make Guthrie bow!

Somehow, between us, with some help from Billy, I figured how to make him rear on his hind legs and bow, and he was so well trained that when he saw me about to mount, he knelt down. Same thing if I swung a leg over to dismount. And so, if I never became a trick rider, I did become a star.

The colonel announced that the day before the show started, we would parade through the city—"just like the circus," he said—to drum up interest in the performances. We lined up at eleven in the morning, me on Governor, Carmelita on a chestnut horse from the colonel's general stock, Billy on his beloved Lucy's Luck. The band marched in front, blaring out patriotic songs, and the colonel rode just behind them, waving his white Stetson at all who stopped to look.

I wasn't the kid from the ranch anymore, or so I thought. I'd been to Oklahoma City and St. Louis, been to the convent, been off the farm as they say—and yet New York fascinated me. Streetcars and paved streets and electric lights were nothing new to me, but the people of New York—it seemed to me that in Guthrie or Oklahoma City the people all looked alike, most of the men like Papa, the women like Louise. Here, I saw men in tall hats and black suits, carrying canes, sometimes wearing white gloves, and then men in shapeless baggy coats and pants with hungry eyes and lean faces, women who wore scarves over their heads even though the weather was still fairly mild, and elegantly dressed women who clung to the arm of some man or another. One old woman ran in terror as she saw us approach—probably from Russia, where horses meant armies and trouble for many people, the colonel told me. I was horrified.

The babble of a thousand voices seemed to surround me. Men pushed carts through the streets, selling everything from apples to sausages, children shouted, sometimes in play and sometimes offering everything from newspapers to shoeshines, and policemen blew on whistles.

Children were everywhere, dirty, shabby, sometimes almost furtive looking, always alone or in groups but never with parents.

"Where are these children's families?" I asked the colonel later. "No one seems to care about them."

"Street children," he said. "Some are orphans, others are just neglected. Watch yourself around them—they'll pick a pocket before you know it."

I'd always thought myself poor in comparison to others my age, poor in emotional terms if not actually poverty-stricken. I remembered my envy of the convent girls who came from big houses in the city and had fathers who worked in offices and mothers who were cheerful and happy. But the street children of New York opened my eyes to an entirely different kind of poor.

"Can they come to the show?" I asked the colonel.

"Of course not," he said shortly. "They'd rob the patrons blind."

One little girl, about five, stood solemnly at the curb, watching us ride by. Her dress was too big and ragged, though one or two patches indicated someone had done their best. She followed the parade with round emotionless eyes that betrayed neither jealousy nor fear. When I waved, she raised a tentative hand in a half gesture, as though afraid to call attention to herself by waving, and yet I had the sense she desperately wanted to make contact.

I guided Governor up to her, half wondering if she would run, but she stood her ground. "What's your name?"

"Sonya," she said, and when I asked her last name, repeated, "Sonya. Just Sonya."

I fished a dollar bill from my pocket and leaned down to hand it to her. Wordlessly, she grabbed it, wrapped a tiny fist around it, and disappeared into the crowd.

Sonya haunted me for a long time.

Just before we circled back to the Garden, our parade met a funeral cortège coming toward us. The horse-drawn carriage bearing the casket was followed by four smaller carriages, each with the curtains drawn and a black ribbon on the door handle. The people all hidden, there was a sense of impersonality about the procession, no hint of who had died—young? old? peacefully? suddenly?—and no glimpse of the mourning family.

But the colonel called a halt and spoke quickly to the band, who struck up a solemn version of "Nearer My God to Thee," while we stood still in respect, the men's hats across their chests.

The story made the newspapers the next day, and the colonel gloated over the publicity.

Even though we were by far a lesser attraction than the annual horse show, our first performance was a smashing success, from the grand entry right through to the finale. Guthrie was the highlight, even though we were in the ring the shortest time of any act. He was such a magnificent animal, and his tricks looked so effortless—someone had put years into training that horse!—that the audience went wild. And I, of course, bowed and waved like a star.

But the whole show was our very best. Six thousand New York City folk were wowed by the things that most western folk took for granted—bronc riding, roping, and the like. Of course, they were at the horse show to see fancy Thoroughbred horses walk around the arena, and when the folks in the audience rode—if they did—they rode English style, sedately, in Central Park. None of them rode a horse to work, let alone a bucking bronc, or ever held a rope in their hands with a reluctant steer on the other end, or even got anywhere near a steer until it was cooked and served on a platter. We showed them the things they didn't see every day, and they loved it.

Governor performed perfectly. I felt guilty when the thought crossed my mind that he was an even better roping horse than Sam.

"He's yours," Billy said to me after the first show.

"Mine? Billy, I can't afford to buy him. I'll just ride him till Sam's leg is healed."

"I'm givin' him to you," Billy said softly. "Consider it thanking your pa, who gave me a job when I needed it." Then he grinned at me, laughter lighting his eyes as he slanted his head toward me. "Or consider it a gift to one of the prettiest girls and best ropers I ever knew."

"Billy . . . I—"

He shook his head. "Don't say it, Tommy Jo. It wouldn't ever work between us. We gotta be friends. You're gonna meet someone real soon. Feel it in my bones."

"Maybe I don't want to," I said belligerently.

"You do," he said quietly, "you do."

And Billy was right. I did want to meet someone, and it happened pretty soon.

Meantime, Billy and I were friends, but to my disgust he was fascinated with Carmelita. She didn't ride in the first three shows, sending word by me to the colonel that she was "indisposed."

"Indisposed!" he fumed. "She better get 'disposed' pretty quick, or she'll find herself out of a job. Stranded in New York, that's what. I don't need a sickly Spanish bull rider."

It took a lot of tongue-biting to keep from telling him that she wasn't Spanish, she wasn't a bull rider, she wouldn't be stranded in New York but just happy to be home, and finally, I suspected she was more frightened than indisposed.

"Carmelita," I said sternly that night, "you've simply got to tell the truth. Obviously you can't ride a bull." Actually, I hadn't even heard of many men riding a bull, but the colonel swore it would make a great exhibition event. I thought it was a dangerous idea to begin with.

Carmelita and I weren't ideally matched to share a room, for I was impatient with her deception and angry that she and I didn't get along one quarter as well as Rose and I had. Carmelita, on the other hand, was probably incensed at what she saw as my interference and impatient with my lecturing.

This time she turned from the mirror, where she was carefully applying rouge to her cheeks—something so far from my experience that I watched with fascination. "Cherokee, as soon as I feel well, I can ride the bull." She persisted in addressing me in her fake Spanish accent, trying to fool both of us, but I knew it was a ruse, and she knew I knew. That made her even haughtier.

I threw my hands up in the air and told the whole story to Billy the next day. If I'd expected him to be alarmed, I was disappointed. He laughed—not his usual slight grin, but an out-and-out loud laugh.

"Billy, it's serious," I said.

"You're right, Tommy Jo, it's real serious," he said, still chuckling, "but it isn't our problem. It's Carmelita's. I sure wouldn't want to be in her shoes—or on her bull." And he was off chuckling again.

I stalked off, still uncertain what to do.

Carmelita appeared for the matinee the third day we performed. During our practice session that morning, the colonel had been gone for a long time, and I thought he'd probably stormed over to the boardinghouse to give her what for. Whatever it was, a subdued Carmelita, dressed in a red ruffled shirt and matching split skirt, rode in the grand entry that day—on a calm and fairly well-behaved horse, though, not a bull. She looked dramatic, the red brilliant against her dark hair, but I thought the bull might have a different idea about dramatic.

When it came time for her act, I made it a point to be mounted on Governor at the edge of the arena, and I noticed that Billy, for all his laughter about Carmelita, was mounted and in the ring. The bull was snubbed to a post in the center of the arena and attended by several of the colonel's cowboys, who held him still until Carmelita could mount.

As she sashayed—there is no other word for it—across the dirt toward him, the bull's nostrils flared and he pawed the ground with one forefoot. A bad sign, I thought, but no one else seemed to pay any attention, except Billy, who nodded imperceptibly to me.

The crowd held its collective breath while she mounted. The bull, having little choice in the matter, was still, except for those nostrils, which still flared. Then, in a flash, the men melted away and the bull was free of the post. He ran a few steps, jumped straight into the air, twisting as he came down, and Carmelita flew from his back, landing in the dirt to lie still like a deflated red balloon. The crowd gasped as the bull stared at her, nostrils still flaring and that front foot pawing the earth impatiently. It seemed obvious he was about to charge an unconscious Carmelita.

Two of the men on foot in the arena ran toward Carmelita, waving their hands and shouting to scare the bull away, but they were plainly scared themselves and ready to run.

Bulls are unpredictable, and this huge animal—probably two thousand pounds—suddenly decided to visit the band, instead of charging Carmelita. The music came to an abrupt halt as the band members scattered. Without stopping a moment to think, I spurred Governor, building a loop as I raced across the arena. Vaguely I was aware of gasps from the crowd and, even fainter, the plaintive notes of a horn, warbling alone without any other instruments behind it. I threw my rope at the bull, remembering in an odd flash the last time I'd roped a bull and how it had been the cause of my being sent to the convent. This time, when the loop settled around the bull's neck, he stopped stock still, as though surprised. He was within a few feet of the horn player, but that solo music never wavered. Governor stopped and began to back up, pulling the rope tight, and I began to breathe again.

The horn was still playing. When the cowboys had taken control of the bull and I'd caught my breath, I looked up to see the band coming back, one by one, to take their places and join the horn player. But he stood where he'd always been, only a few feet from where I'd stopped the bull. I'd never seen him before, I was sure, but I was aware as I sat there that he was staring at me, even while playing. He came to the end of a bar, put down the horn with a flourish, and bowed, tipping his Stetson in a broad gesture—not to the audience, but to me.

There was nothing polite I could do, of course, but dismount and, leading Governor, go over to congratulate him on his bravery.

My congratulations didn't come out as smoothly as I'd have liked. "Why'd you do a fool thing like that?" I asked. The minute I said it, I could have bit my tongue in half. If he stomped away, it'd serve me right.

Instead, he grinned, not Billy's shy little half-grin but a wide smile that dimpled his cheeks and crinkled his eyes with laughter. They were brown eyes, deep, deep brown, under thick eyebrows. Above them was a high forehead—intelligence?—and curly hair so brown, it looked like chocolate and so curly it would have looked like a rag mop if it weren't cut close to his head.

"I thought it added to the show," he said. "Nice musical background for your roping. Congratulations on a good job."

There! He'd said what I should have! "Thanks," I mumbled. "It was—wasn't anything. I can rope pretty good." Why didn't I go ahead and tell him I admired his nerve?

"Yeah," he agreed, "you can. I been watching you. Where'd you learn to rope like a man?"

I stiffened. "Oklahoma," I said shortly. "My father runs a ranch, and Billy, uh Will, worked for him. Between them they taught me to rope." Then belatedly, I asked, "Where'd you learn to play the horn?"

"Here and there," he said. Then, turning, he said, "See you around. Name's Buck—Buck Dowling." And he was gone, leaving me standing there.

"Wait," I called, "you don't even know my name."

"Oh yes, I do, Cherokee," he said over his shoulder and kept walking.

Buck Dowling was the hero, and Carmelita was in disgrace. By the time I got back to my room that night, she was packed and gone.

"Never had ridden a bronc," the colonel fumed the next day. "Flat lied to me, she did. Should have had you riding that animal, Cherokee."

"No, thanks," I said, though I'd ridden enough raw horses in my day that I'd have had a lot better luck than Carmelita. I never did tell the colonel she lived in New York and simply wanted a way home, but Billy and I laughed over that again and wondered if she was happily settled in Brooklyn.

"It was a steer," Billy said to me quietly.

"A steer? Of course not. The colonel billed it as a bull, and there's an obvious difference," I retorted.

"Did you look?" he asked with a grin.

"No, of course I didn't look!"

"Neither did anyone else, and half of New York wouldn't know the difference anyway. It was a steer. The colonel wouldn't take a chance putting a bull out there with a slip of a girl."

I pondered that for a minute. "Would he have let you ride a bull?" I asked.

"Might have," Billy said, "but I'm too smart for that."

I didn't see Buck Dowling at all for days, except during performances, when he was in the band and I was riding, and I confess to a certain curiosity, disappointment even. When I was in the arena, I could hardly stare at him—roping and riding took every bit of my attention. Yet I thought I felt him watching me, in a way that was different from spectators who watched.

I'd about decided that I was imagining an interest on his part that didn't exist when I met him at the train after the performance one night. It was my habit to check on Sam while everyone else was cleaning up from the performance and getting ready for the next day.

"Walk with you?" Buck asked.

Startled, I managed to mumble, "Sure. Just going to check on my horse."

"I know. I've seen you each night. Don't you know that it's not safe for a girl to be wandering around New York alone at night?"

"I'm not wandering! I'm going to the train, and there's a watchman there, and then I'm going to walk to my boardinghouse with several people."

"No," he said, "I'll walk you there tonight."

He didn't ask, he just assumed, and that made me angry. "Sorry. The others will be waiting for me. They do every night."

Nothing seemed to faze him. "Well, I'll just walk with all of you then."

When I raised Sam's leg to look at his injury, Buck proved to be knowledgeable about horses, recognizing the torn tendon, guessing at the age of the wound, and suggesting that the present lack of swelling was a good sign. "Never can tell if he'll be good as new or not," he said.

"He's going back to Oklahoma to rest," I said. "Bo, a friend, will take care of him."

Patting Sam's neck and then running his hand along his back and onto his hindquarters, Buck walked around my horse, inspecting as if he were thinking of buying. "He's a good sound horse," he finally said.

"What would a musician know about horses?" I asked, laughing.

"I grew up on a ranch in southern California," he said quietly. "Been riding since I was three. I'd just rather play my horn now than try my luck on a bronc, but I still do a little of that, too."

"You're a cowboy?" I said in surprise. "I thought that getup was, well, you know—for show."

"This?" He looked down at his fringed suit of brown denim, with a holster at his hips. "This *is* for show! I'd never dress this way, 'cept this is how the colonel wants the band to look. I've got no choice."

"You talk like you've been to school," I said as we walked back to the Garden after giving Sam an extra ration of oats.

"Have been. Four years of college. My pa wants me to be a lawyer, but I just don't feel the calling."

Four years of college probably made him twenty-two or -three, four or five years older than me. What, I wondered, would Papa say about Buck? And then I wondered why that thought had even entered my mind.

True to his word, Buck walked me back to the boardinghouse, joining Mrs. Miller and Belle and several of the others. Though I stiffened in anticipation, no one sang out, "Tommy Jo has a boyfriend," or, "Look who's walking Tommy Jo home!" They seemed to accept Buck without question, and he chatted happily with Mrs. Miller about the show. So much so that I wanted to remind him sharply just who it was he was walking home.

"He's a good one, honey," Mrs. Miller said to me as we climbed the stairs to our rooms that night. "Hold on to that one."

I blushed, but long after everyone was asleep, I lay in bed, seeing Buck Dowling's curly hair and deep, deep brown eyes.

Buck really began to court me after that night, waiting at the stalls for me after every show, walking home with me every night—we soon managed to walk at a different time from the others, and we walked slowly, lingering, savoring each minute together. A feeling swept over me like nothing I'd ever known, certainly nothing Bo had ever shown me in spite of some passionate moments between us. Buck made me feel cherished, protected, loved—and slightly giddy all the time.

"See that fence?" he asked one night, pointing to a wrought-iron fence protecting someone's garden.

"The one with the points on top?" I asked.

"Yeah"—he grinned—"that one. You make me feel like I could leap any fence in the world." And he proceeded to take a running jump over the fence, while I screamed, "Buck, don't!" having visions of him landing on those sharp iron points.

He landed safely on the other side with a shout of glee, and when lights came on in the house that owned the garden and fence, we joined hands and ran laughing together down the street.

"See the things I do for you?" he asked.

Another time he picked a bouquet, stealing from someone's carefully tended fall garden to present the flowers to me with a bow and a flourish. "They're not half as beautiful as you deserve," he said, "nor one tenth as beautiful as you."

I blushed. I knew it wasn't true, but I thought he believed it, and that made all the difference to me.

Sometimes he spun wonderful dreams in the air for me, visions of me roping for the Queen of England, heralded all over Europe as America's favorite cowgirl, or back in this country, starring in those newfangled moving pictures from California. Always in these grand visions, I was wealthy beyond measure, and always, Buck was beside me.

"You've just been reading about Buffalo Bill in Europe," I accused one day when he had me riding for the queen.

"Well," he said, "you should be riding for that show, not this one."

"The 101's good enough," I said defensively, "and I've got star billing at the Garden. Not bad for nineteen years old."

"Star billing in a two-bit show that's tacked on to a horse show," he said. "You deserve better, Cherokee, and I'm going to see you get it someday."

I sighed in contentment. It seemed to me I'd been looking after myself for a long time now, nursing my own ambitions privately, and it was wonderful to have someone take up the battle for me. I guess that's one of life's hard lessons we don't learn young—no one else ever really rides your horse or does your battle for you.

The first time Buck kissed me, I knew it was different from Billy's smushy kisses and Bo's more intense ones. Buck was gentle but persistent, his mouth moving on mine in a way that made the pit of my stomach lurch and sent tingles the length of my spine.

"You've kissed a lot of girls," I said breathlessly one night, pulling away from him.

"And you've not kissed many men," he said. "That's the way it should be."

I took his word for it.

We were teased, of course. Even Will couldn't resist. "Ain't seein' much of you these days, Tommy Jo," he said. "Where you disappear to every night?" But his grin told me he knew.

The others would poke fun at us, and even the colonel harrumphed and said something privately to me about behaving and not getting in trouble. But it was Mrs. Miller who encouraged me by smiles and gentle advice. "Don't listen to them, dear. They're jealous. He's a lovely young man."

I wrote Mama and Papa a short note that night, telling them all was well, and I also wrote Louise a long letter, telling her all about Buck Dowling, right down to the tingling along my spine.

The show continued to be successful. Newspapers heralded it as "exciting," "daring," and "spectacular," and one reporter called us, "as good as the Buffalo Bill Wild West Show"—high praise in my books, but the comparison angered the colonel and made Buck say, "I told you so," which didn't quite make sense to me.

Halfway through our two-week run, the colonel called us all together one morning during a practice session. "We've gotten good reviews and people have liked us here. So I've decided to take the show on the road for the year," he said. "Anyone who wants to go with me, sign up in my office. We'll winter in Oklahoma and get on the road early in the spring."

Of course, I would have run straight to his office to be the first in line, but Buck put out a hand to stop me.

"Let's think a minute first," he said. "There's lots of other possibilities."

"Like what?" I demanded. The Buffalo Bill show in Europe was, so we heard, nearly bankrupt. If I couldn't ride with the Buffalo Bill—in spite of Buck's visions—the colonel's show was the next best thing.

"Well, we could look into some smaller shows. I could ride broncs instead of playing the horn."

I was thoroughly confused. "Why go with a smaller show when I've got top billing with this one? And why should you ride broncs when you really want to play your horn?"

Buck hesitated. "Well, the colonel . . . don't you ever feel like he's running our lives?"

I thought about that a minute. "Sure I do. But I suspect that'd be the same no matter whose show we were in. And at least with the colonel I know him, know what he's like." I was destined to be ever practical.

Buck looked at me speculatively, no laughter in his brown eyes now. "There's one more thing. Do you want to spend the winter in Oklahoma?"

Where else, I wondered, had I been planning to spend it? I'd thought I'd have to go back to Louise and spend the winter worrying about my future, but instead I'd be at the 101 with a show ahead of me. It sounded ideal. "You don't want to go to Oklahoma, do you?" I asked.

"Well, after all you've told me about your pa and all, and that fellow—what's his name?"

"Bo," I said distinctly, "and you probably won't even see either one of them if you're at the 101. I'll go to Guthrie alone."

He could tell I was getting angry, something I'd never done with him before. "Now, Cherokee, I just want what's best for both of us—but mostly for you, and I want you to think about this. Who knows what's out there for us? We could be missing the biggest opportunity of our lives, just by going with the 101. Tell me you'll take twenty-four hours."

I knew that twenty-four-hour period would include lots of Buck's persuasive kissing—getting more urgent and persuasive by the day—and that I'd be hard put to keep up my resolve, if he really didn't want to stay with the colonel. Reluctantly, I promised to wait twenty-four hours.

"Cherokee! You haven't been to see me," the colonel boomed as I sat mounted on Guthrie, waiting for the afternoon performance. "Surely you're gonna join us." He chomped his cigar to one side of his mouth and gave me a lopsided grin. "Can't do my show without my star."

"I know," I said nervously. "I just need time to think. Got to be sure I'm doin' the right thing."

"Buck's got a place, too," he said dryly and turned away.

After the show, as I was storing my gear in the box next to Governor's stall, Buck came toward me, arms open, and I walked into a tight hug and a passionate kiss. "Let's go for a walk," he said.

As we walked away, I saw the colonel, hatbrim down over eyes that were staring speculatively at us.

Years later I would realize—or suspect—why Buck didn't want to stay with the colonel, but young and green and in love, I was puzzled by it. I wanted to believe in Buck's visions, but I knew there wasn't anything better out there for us right then. In spite of all I felt for Buck, my resolve to be a star in a Wild West show was stronger than ever now that I'd had a taste of fame in Madison Square Garden. I needed that applause, that excitement, even more than I needed those wild, crazy, whirling feelings I had when I was with Buck. Leaving Bo behind had been hard and leaving Buck would be harder, but there really wasn't a choice. And Buck would leave the show—of that I was sure.

"Just tired of being a no-count musician," he'd said one night. "Want to make my mark somewhere."

"You will, Buck, I know you will," I had breathed with the fervor of young love.

Now, several nights later, I was making my pronouncement. "I'm staying with the colonel," I said, pulling away from the arms that held me tight. We were standing in the shadows of the bushes beside the boarding-house, and everyone else was already long asleep. It was a good thing Mrs. O'Riley hadn't established a curfew as strict as her dinner rules.

"I've got to," I went on, while Buck stood motionless, listening to me. "The colonel gives me top billing, and I can't walk away from that, for his sake or for my own." I braced myself for the persuasive argument that would follow.

"Sure, Cherokee, I understand. And I think you're right." He placed gentle hands on my shoulders, gave me a soft kiss, and said, "We'll stay."

My head spun until I thought I'd faint. "You'll stay?" I managed to whisper.

He laughed aloud. "Of course I'll stay. We're together, you and me."

And then I was the one who initiated the deep, passionate kissing. Our stand-up lovemaking was getting more and more frustrating for Buck. Even I, inexperienced in such things, could sense that. I could feel his hardness when he held me tight to him, and I could hear him sigh when we parted. One night he left me abruptly, saying, "I either go now, or we finish this upstairs in your room."

I remembered a similar scene with Bo, and I remembered Louise's stern words about women who were teases. I would have to make some hard decisions soon, and I suddenly wished to be young again and daydreaming about boys and their smushy kisses. Buck had awakened feelings I hadn't known existed, a craving deep in the pit of my body that could, I sensed, only be satisfied by letting him make love to me. Nice girls didn't. Rose had, I was sure, and Carmelita, too, and probably Belle. But I was Tommy Jo Burns, ranch-raised and convent-schooled, and I didn't—or did I?

About the time I was wrestling with this problem, I received a long answer to my letter to Louise. "Don't," she warned, "marry this man because you have a tingling in the pit of your stomach. Your father would whip me for saying this, but sleep with him first. Then decide if you still want to marry him, once the mystery has gone out of the physical relationship."

That didn't quiet the doubts I was having nor make my decision any easier.

Meantime, love went to my head in a disastrous way. Governor and I were roping steers—the first part of our act and the easiest, as we slowly worked up to the really showy tricks. The first two steers went well enough, my loop catching them safely and the pickup men hustling them out of the arena. But as the third steer was released, I stole a glance toward Buck . . . and my loop came up empty. The crowd laughed—a sound I was *not* used to nor pleased with—and I built another loop, spurring Governor after the steer who was headed hell-bent for the far end of the arena. Just as I got ready to throw my loop, the steer decided it was safer with the audience. It jumped the barricade and clattered into the stands, sending a handful of people scattering in a thousand directions, their screams only further frightening the steer. While the animal crashed about in the stands, I threw my loop again—and missed again. By now my nerves were shattered and my timing off. Blast being in love anyway, I thought.

With visions of trampled bodies in my mind, I built another loop, trying to calm myself. And then, magically, the steer was caught by a loop that came out of nowhere behind me.

"Got 'em, Cherokee," Will Rogers said.

That story made the headlines, too. "Cowboy Catches Steer Run Amok in Audience," and "Will Rogers Hero of the Day at Horse Show."

Will always said later that was how he became a star, and he used to say he owed his fame all to Cherokee Rose—and her empty loop.

Buck drove a bargain I hadn't expected. "Marry me before we go to Oklahoma," he said one night.

"Marry you?" I said with surprise. Sure, the idea had been in my head, one part of the decision I was facing, and I'd had Louise's warning, but I thought marriage was a bridge I'd have to cross much later. Marriage was something for older people, for Papa and Mama, not for me. "Here? Now?"

"Here and now," he said firmly. "Cherokee, something's got to give. We can't go on being half-lovers. I want us to be together. And I want to marry you—I don't want you to be, well, like . . ." His voice drifted off, but I knew what he meant, and I liked it that he felt that way. He'd made my decision for me.

But in my mind I was rereading Louise's letter. Did I really love Buck Dowling, or was I blinded by his kisses and his hands, or worse yet, was I maybe just curious?

"What could be better than a wedding in Madison Square Garden?" Buck asked.

"A wedding in the Garden?" I seemed to echo everything he said like a wooden puppet. "In front of all those people?"

He roared with laughter. "The audience? Of course not. Maybe after the last show, when it's just our people."

And that's what we did. We got married in Madison Square Garden at nearly midnight the evening of the last performance. Cleaning crews were moving through the stands picking up trash, and bored guards stood around the edge of the arena. The minister from a nearby Presbyterian church thought we were crazy—and maybe a little disgraceful—but he agreed to perform the strange ceremony.

When he asked, "Who gives this woman in marriage?" the colonel stepped forward and said solemnly, "I do, in place of her father." How, I wondered, would Sandy Burns feel about that?

The minister's words—"death do us part" and "to have and to hold forever"—seemed to echo in the great cavernous gardens, and my nerves were worse than they ever had been around a horse or a rope. At one point, I thought Buck was going to have to catch me as I fainted, but the feeling passed, and I managed to make the appropriate responses to the minister's questions about taking Buck as my lawfully wedded husband. It startled me when the minister, with ever so slight a tinge in his voice, asked, "Do you, Cherokee, take this man, Buck . . ." But I was married as Cherokee, and Tommy Jo became a young girl, tucked forever away in the back of my mind.

But when the minister pronounced us man and wife and Buck kissed me sweetly and tenderly, it seemed all right. In fact, it seemed wonderful.

Mrs. Miller was there, and Belle, and even Mrs. O'Riley, along with almost everyone from the 101 troupe. After the ceremony, they all applauded and began to drift away.

"Cherokee," Will said, "I knew you'd fall in love soon, but I didn't think you'd act so fast on it. Best of everything." He tipped his hat and wandered off.

That was the last time I saw Will Rogers for years, though I kept reading about him in the newspapers. He'd had an offer from Hollywood, out where they were making those new movies, and he wasn't going to stay with the 101. I couldn't blame him. "It was that empty loop of yours," he'd explained to me.

Buck and I spent our wedding night in my room at the boardinghouse, which seems unromantic but was very practical. I had a room to myself; Buck shared a dormitory-like room with five other men, and we couldn't afford a hotel.

Mrs. O'Riley allowed us to be late for breakfast the next morning, and I was grateful that most everybody was about the business of packing when we appeared. I didn't want to be the subject of a lot of stares and speculations, and I wondered—almost desperately—if my new status as a wedded and bedded woman showed on my face.

It must have, for Buck whispered to me, "Stop grinning," but he was grinning when he said it.

I knew that morning that Louise's warning was useless. I'd have married Buck even faster if he'd made love to me before the ceremony. Sometime during the night as his hands and his whole long body brought me a frantic, desperate pleasure, I remembered Mama and Papa and the fights that ended so quickly in their bedroom. And for the first time I understood my parents a little bit. And I knew what Louise was trying to tell me—a man who makes love to you makes you his forever, or so it seems at the time.

Of course, I wanted to be Buck's forever. The world couldn't have looked any rosier to me than it did on that October morning in New York City. I was married to a man I loved, and I was about to star in a traveling Wild West show.

I sent a telegram to Louise, signed Mrs. Buck Dowling, and wrote Mama and Papa a note. Best, I thought, give them all the news before I arrived in Oklahoma with a husband.

Once we were back in Oklahoma, I felt obliged to take Buck to meet Mama, Papa, and Louise. I'd told—or warned—Buck about all of them, but still I wondered how he'd react to my strange family, and that wonder, or worry, made me nervous. We rode from the 101 to Luckett's, arriving unexpectedly about noon on a Sunday. The day was surprisingly warm for mid-October, and Mama, a worn sweater around her shoulders, sat on the porch. She looked much the same as when I'd last seen her—maybe just a shade more tired, a few more strands of gray in her dark hair.

"Thomasina! Oh, my darling, I knew you'd come home. I tried to tell your papa to set a dinner place for you, but he said I was fooling myself." She suddenly became aware of Buck and asked suspiciously, "Who's this?"

"Mama, this is my husband, Buck."

The dark eyes glittered with suspicion. "You've got no husband, Thomasina. You're too young." Then her voice raised to call, "James? James, where are you?"

Papa came barging through the door with a loud "Here I am" that stopped in midsentence when he saw us. "Tommy Jo!" His grin was genuine but tentative, as though he didn't know how it would be received.

"Papa," I said, "this is my husband, Buck Dowling."

Papa handled the situation with good grace. Stepping down off the porch, he offered his hand, saying, "Sandy Burns, Buck. Glad to know you." Then he reached an arm around my shoulder and asked gently, "How's the world's best cowgirl?"

Maybe it was because I was married, making me independent of him forever, or maybe because Buck had taught me something about men and women, or maybe it was just time, but with a cry of "Oh, Papa!" I hugged him tight, and after a startled second, he hugged back. We just stood that way for a long minute, while Buck looked self-consciously away, and Mama hummed to herself.

"James," she finally said shrilly, "she says this is her husband."

"That's right, Jess, he is. Our little girl's all grown up and married."

Mama looked more puzzled than distressed. "But I don't remember the wedding, and I didn't make her a gown."

I went to her side. "No, Mama," I said softly, "we were married in New York, in Madison Square Garden. But I missed you something fierce."

Mama wailed as if her heart would break. "Thomasina's wedding," she cried, "and we weren't there!"

Eventually she quieted down, and I helped Papa fix a noonday meal by adding more potatoes around the roast he'd started, opening some canned peaches, and slicing some fresh bread. After we ate, Papa took Buck on a ride around Luckett's, and the two hours they were gone gave me a good chance to visit with Mama, though it wasn't much of a visit.

I guessed, as we sat there on the porch, that I never would understand Mama. Oh, I knew about how much she loved Papa and even why she never left him, in spite of all his trips to Guthrie, but I couldn't understand why she'd given up, retreated into that half-world of hers. How could she sit on the porch and rock all day, while Papa did his work and hers? For the first time, I felt more sympathy for Papa than Mama.

"Showed me where you killed a bull," Buck said grinning, "so I told him about the steer you missed in the Garden."

"Is that tit for tat?" I asked, embarrassed that Papa had heard about my empty loop. "Why not tell him about the ones I caught?"

"He did," Papa said, "he did. Bragged on you right good, and made me a proud old man. But it sure makes me jump some every time he calls you Cherokee."

I laughed, and Buck said, "I've never known her as anyone but Cherokee. Don't think I could call her Tommy Jo."

"I'm gettin' used to my new name, Papa. You will, too."

"Cherokee?" Mama said vaguely. "What Cherokees?"

There was a moment of uncomfortable silence, while Papa patted her shoulder reassuringly.

"Papa? Will you come to the show sometime, maybe when it's in Oklahoma City?"

"Honey, I'd go to Kansas City, even St. Louis to see you ride—and I'll bring your mama."

We spent the rest of the afternoon talking a blue streak about the show, with Papa listening intently to everything we described, asking questions about the people we mentioned, probing the plans for the next year. Mama's hands were busy with her knitting, and occasionally she said, "Really?" but I don't think she cared what we were talking about. Every once in a while she'd look up from her handwork to just stare at Papa, with a look so full of love and devotion and dependency that it near made me cry.

Papa said we could have my old room, but we both knew the bed there was too narrow for two, and Buck and I left in midafternoon to ride to Guthrie. When we were near to the ranch gate, I turned to wave at Papa, who stood on the porch, his big arms signaling a hearty farewell. Then I rode on without saying a word for miles, tears streaming down my face.

Finally, Buck said, "It isn't ever like you want it to be when you go home again, Cherokee."

"I know. I just . . . well, I want them to be happy, and they seem so pitiful."

"I don't think they're pitiful," he said. "At least your pa's not. He's a fine man, proud of you, good to his wife, and fairly happy. I don't know what more you want."

Buck made me see Papa in a new light. Finally, I said, "He liked you."

"I liked him," Buck said, and I thought my world sure was in good shape.

Louise and Buck took to each other instantly, as I'd known they would. Far be it from Louise to fuss over a man—instead, she sized him up with a long look and said, "You think you're man enough to keep up with, uh, Cherokee?"

Buck grinned. "I sure aim to try, ma'am."

"You'll probably do it," she said, and led us to the kitchen where she put me to work on a pie while she floured steak and fried it with potatoes and onions. We ate with the boarders—just like old times—and sat in the parlor talking until near midnight.

Louise filled me in on the news of Guthrie—which wasn't much, considering I didn't know too many people there—and we retold the story of our adventures in New York, how we met when Carmelita's bull ran amok into the musicians, how we married in the Garden late at night.

"Sandy upset?" she asked. "I haven't seen him since before you left."

I wasn't surprised that Papa didn't come into Guthrie anymore. "No. He and Buck got along fine. Mama cried 'cause she wasn't at the wedding."

Louise just nodded. Her sympathy never had been with Mama. "You going out to see Bo?"

"Should I?"

"You owe him that, child."

Bo had been part of Tommy Jo's life, and now I was Cherokee, and married, but I guessed Louise was right. I went to see him alone the next morning, leaving Louise and Buck chatting over coffee.

"Tommy Jo!" Bo ambled out of the barn when he heard me ride up. "Didn't know you were coming back." He shaded his eyes against the sun with one hand and reached the other out for my hand. "Gonna get down for a minute?"

"If that's all right," I said, feeling awkward about the news I had to impart.

We walked toward the barn together, Bo asking small questions like "How was New York?" and getting small answers like "Fine."

"Tommy Jo, there's somethin' I got to tell you," he said all in a rush. "I met this girl—now she ain't like you, but she's a fine little girl, and—"

I laughed so loudly that Bo stopped in his tracks and stared at me, hands indignantly on his hips.

"It ain't funny," he protested.

"Oh, Bo, yes it is," I said. "I came out here to tell you I'm married."

He didn't exactly laugh like I had, but he grinned. "Married? Well, I'll be . . . you beat me to it, Tommy Jo. I was worrying how to tell you, and all the time . . . well, don't that beat all!"

"Why didn't Louise tell me?" I asked.

"I reckoned it was mine to do. We talked about it before. But Tommy Jo, I want you to know something." Bo looked at the ground, avoiding my eyes. "I'm here for you always, anytime you need me. I . . . it ain't that I don't love you, and I guess you know that."

I threw my arms around him. "And I love you, Bo. But we're better off this way. And thank you."

When I was mounted again and ready to ride back to town, I said, "Bo, my name's Cherokee now. Cherokee Rose."

"After Prairie Rose," he said instantly, and it struck me that Bo was still one of the few people who really understood me.

"Yeah, after Prairie Rose. See ya, Bo."

"See ya, Cherokee."

Buck and I spent two days with Louise—almost a honeymoon, since she left us strictly alone unless we came looking for her. We stayed in bed half the day sometimes, wandered the streets of Guthrie looking in stores and splurging on silly things for both of us—an oak-backed dressing table set for me, silver-backed hairbrushes for Buck, things we never needed.

"We'll have to be more practical," he said. "Colonel doesn't pay us all that much."

I giggled. "This is a one-time honeymoon shopping spree!"

"As long as it's just us, we can spend what we make," he said. "But when we have a family, we'll have to watch our pennies and nickels."

A family! Buck and I had never talked about children, and somehow the idea had never occurred to me. I couldn't see myself raising babies, and just as I didn't want love to get in the way of my riding and roping, I sure didn't want motherhood to.

The look on my face must have been a clear map to the thoughts in my brain, because Buck laughed and asked, "Don't you know how babies are made, Cherokee? What do you think we've been doing since we were married?"

"Making love," I retorted, "not babies."

"Can't always separate the two," he said complacently. "I sort of hope it won't be too long now."

My heart lurched. I should have known, I told myself later, that I was too happy. The Lord just doesn't let folks have everything all at one time—seems like he always puts at least one cloud on the horizon, and he sure had put a black one on mine. From now on, I'd worry about pregnancy and watch my monthly time like a hawk. Would I think of that every time Buck touched me?

"Buck, look at that hat in the window," I said, almost frantic to change the direction of my thoughts. "The one with the pheasant feather headband—I want it to wear in the show." It was a brown Stetson with a high crown, a large brim, and a hatband woven of feathers, with two feathers sticking jauntily into the air.

"And you shall have it," Buck said, dragging me into the store.

I talked to Louise about my new fear late that night, having sent Buck to bed on the true excuse that some girl talk was needed. "I just figure if I keep roping and riding, it won't happen," I said.

"You mean it won't take?" she said with a smile. "You going to get rid of a baby by riding so hard it won't stay around? I don't think you can count on that, Tommy Jo, and I don't think it would make you happy. There are remedies, folk medicines and such, but they're chancy."

"I don't want a baby!" I surprised even myself with the ferocity of my reply.

"Are you going to let that fear ruin your marriage? Are you going to stop sleeping with Buck?"

"I've thought of that," I mumbled, "and that's not what I want either."

"It's trite and corny, child, but we don't always get all the things we want."

"Or even half of them," I interrupted petulantly.

"My best advice is to love Buck as much as you can and leave your life in the hand of fate to a certain extent. At least, don't let this fear dominate your life."

We talked a few minutes longer, and I hugged her as I went up the stairs, saying truthfully, "I don't know what I'd do if I didn't have you to talk to."

"Never thought I'd be mothering a grown girl," she laughed, "but I like it."

I woke Buck when I came to bed, and I think I surprised him with my passion that night, but I made love to him frantically, as though to keep my fears at bay.

We left for the 101 the next day, and once we were back there, we were into a whole new routine. The colonel put us all to work. Buck had worried about staying at the 101—"Colonel can't feed all of us for months till show time, without getting anything for it," he'd said, and I assured him it would be all right. It was: The colonel put Buck to work cowboying, cleaning stalls, doing general work that needed to be done.

My job was to sew costumes with Mrs. Miller, a chore I didn't mind too much. If we'd been making fancy clothes with ruffles and tucks and the like, I'd have rebelled. But we made western-style clothes. As the colonel added a new member to our group—he was out recruiting all the time—we measured him or her and began a new wardrobe. 'Course some of the new ladies had to sew with us, and that gave me a chance to get to know them.

New York had been a disappointment to me in one way. I'd never found another Rose, never felt close to anyone in the show except Buck—and that was so different that I didn't think it counted as friendship. Somehow I thought there should be a camaraderie among us, particularly the girls, but in New York there had been only Carmelita and me and Belle, who was nice enough, but somehow we never developed a real close friendship. I longed for Rose or Louise or some new friends, so I eyed each newcomer hopefully.

"We're gonna add to this show," the colonel said heartily at one of the meetings he called. The troupe had grown so, with his new recruits, that breakfast meetings could no longer accommodate everybody. Because I was an old-timer, as it were, Buck and I lived in the big house and ate with the colonel and his mother and brothers. But most of the new troupe lived in hastily built dormitory buildings and ate in a mess hall. When a norther blew through in February and Buck and I were warm and comfortable in a very private bedroom, I felt sorry for the others.

The colonel wanted to add relay races to the program, for one thing. "I been checking out other shows," he said, "and they have ladies riding relay races. Good event. Gets lots of interest. That's why I've hired so many of you girls." He nodded at the new riders, of whom there were seven. "Teams of four, counting Cherokee."

My new companions were another Belle—Belle from New York had elected to return to her family's ranch in southern Oklahoma rather than join the 101 traveling show. This Belle was from Montana and had short dark hair, enormous wide eyes, and a kind of solemn look on her face all the time, but she could ride. I'd seen her top off a feisty horse early one morning, and I was impressed.

Then there were Jane and Jo, seventeen-year-old blond twins from Colorado, raised on a ranch and perfectly at home on any horse you put before them, full of giggles and high spirits. Dixie Bell—surely that wasn't her real name!—came from southern Oklahoma, but I suspected she was a little like Carmelita, a town girl who pretended to be ranch-raised. Still, she could ride and rope, and she'd be an addition, if she didn't prove as untrustworthy as Carmelita. Fay Harrison, from Kansas, was the tallest girl I'd ever seen, near as tall as Buck, with blond hair that hung in natural ringlets down to her shoulders and bright blue eyes that looked at the world with laughter, even when she fell off her horse, which she did during her first tryout.

I didn't know the last two girls at all yet—Bonnie Adams and Grace Carroll. The colonel had come back from St. Louis with them in tow only a few days before this meeting.

Two things about all seven of these girls—they took the term cowgirl for granted as their proper title, never knowing that it had been coined for me, and I didn't tell them. And they all called me Cherokee, thought it was my name. In a way it was like Tommy Jo was dead and gone—and that gave me a qualm or two.

"We're gonna add some other things," he went on. "Acts, kind of like little dramas. With music in the background. Buck," he said suddenly, "that's gonna be your responsibility. You and me, we'll dream up these acts, and then you can fit some music to go behind them."

Buck grinned, and I knew he liked the idea of being part of the planning. "What kind of acts, Colonel?"

"You know—Indian massacres and attacks on homesteads, and stuff that shows people what the Old West was like."

I put my hand to my mouth to stifle laughter and wondered if Rose was looking down from heaven on this scene. If so, she'd be laughing and saying, "I told you so!" The colonel had come a long way from that show that he declared would be nothing but authentic work done on a real, working ranch. Little dramas indeed!

Those were happy days for us. Buck spent long hours reading history books and poring over sheaves of paper on which he plotted his little dramas. Usually I was allowed to comment and contribute, as long as I kept the needle and thread in my hand busy.

"Custer's Last Stand has been done too much," he'd say. Then, reading from a book: "How about this? In 1873 the Grand Duke Alexis was visiting here and wanted to go buffalo hunting. So the army sent Custer to lead the party. How about that for a skit?" And so eventually the show had a skit showing Custer leading this prince, who had an atrocious fake accent, over plains made of green carpet, in search of buffalo.

And, of course, there was the massacre scene, but Buck decided that too many homesteads had been attacked onstage and instead we'd do a wagon-train scene. He read somewhere about some freighters who were killed by Comanches in Texas—the Comanches almost got General Phil Sheridan—and he invented an act he called "The Salt Flats Massacre."

By April, the show was ready to go on the road. The cast totaled nearly fifty cowboys and cowgirls who doubled as soldiers, beleaguered wagon-train drivers, Russian princes, whatever the script called for. Only the Indians were real—seventeen men of the Poncas, who lived on and around the 101, rode with us.

One night as we lay in bed, Buck leaned a lazy arm around me and said, "Cherokee, you were so right. Coming with the colonel was the best thing for us to do. I'm going to listen to you from now on."

I shivered before I could stop myself. Buck, thinking I was cold, began to warm me, and my doubts melted away. Lesson number two: When a man makes love to you, you forget your worries, even about him. For one clear second there, I had seen the future, and it frightened me.

CHAPTER 8

By the fall of 1908, Buffalo Bill was back from Europe, his show in disarray and debt, his longtime partner, James Bailey, dead. In Madison Square Garden, he gave a farewell speech, bowing out of the Wild West show business forever. But then he immediately teamed up with another smaller show, Pawnee Bill's Far East, and they toured the country together. Their show, familiarly called the Two Bills, grossed a million in one year, and Buffalo Bill was out of debt again. But the tour was, so Cody insisted, "a farewell exhibition."

It struck me as ironic that I was touring with the show that was in a large sense competing with Buffalo Bill, when all my life I'd meant to ride with him. The colonel was careful to take the 101 far from wherever the Two Bills Show was playing, but it was a big country, and there were plenty of audiences for both of us. Colonel Miller and the 101 did all right in show business despite the competition.

Buck and I went all over the states with that show for six long years. I was the star, and Buck kept on plotting his little dramas—sometimes he'd ride in them, like the time he took over the part of Custer when the regular cowboy sprained his ankle. For one show Custer had short dark curls instead of the long blond ones that everyone knew him by. Buck also became sort of the colonel's assistant manager, taking more and more responsibility for the smooth running of the show. That meant the show revolved around the two of us in a lot of ways—sounds immodest to say, but it was true—and we were sort of the golden couple of the Wild West. It was a heady time. We traveled forty thousand miles, did more than eight hundred shows in forty-two states, and by the time the show left for Europe in 1914, we were different people, with a lot of different experiences behind us. But that gets me ahead of my story.

Our first big show on the road was back in St. Louis, and it fooled me into thinking all our shows would be in big grand coliseums, that we would always stay in comfortable boardinghouses, and that the road would always be smooth. It wouldn't turn out that way at all, but in St. Louis I added Buck to my act—by accident at first, and then, with the colonel's blessing and Buck's reluctant agreement, on purpose as part of the show. The audience loved it.

I'd given up my trick of roping someone by surprise at the end of my act—too cute, I'd decided—but that night I took a notion to rope Buck, and I caught him, horn and all, by surprise. But Buck was game—he laughed, and arms pinned to his side, he still tried to play his horn.

"The little lady's husband, folks—Buck Dowling!" the announcer roared, and then nothing would do but that I pull Buck in, like I would have a steer. I tied the rope to Governor's horn, dismounted, and slowly walked toward Buck. Of course, he did what no steer ever did and walked toward me. When we met, I kissed him soundly—thinking Sandy Burns would never approve this public display—before I loosened my rope. When he was free, Buck held the horn in one hand and me in the other and returned the kiss soundly. Then hand in hand, we bowed to the cheering audience.

The colonel was waiting for me after the show, his face stern. "Took a big chance, didn't you, Cherokee?"

"It worked," I said defiantly, and only then did he break into a grin.

"It sure did," he said enthusiastically. "You can do that every show from now on."

"Anybody ask me?" Buck said plaintively, and we all laughed.

Later that night, in the privacy of our room, I asked, "Buck, did you mind my roping you?"

He took the hairbrush I'd been using out of my hand and began brushing my hair. "No," he said slowly, "not really, but it did make me feel like your trained dog."

I whirled toward him. "I'll never do it again!"

"No, Cherokee, it worked. The audience loved it. That's what counts, so we'll do it every time from now on. Turn your head."

I turned my head, and he continued to brush. After a minute, I said, "You're more important than the show, and what's between us matters more than whether or not an audience claps. I won't do it again."

Standing behind me, Buck looked into the mirror and into my eyes as they were reflected there. Finally he said, "No, Cherokee, we'll do it, for lots of reasons. It won't change what's between us."

I shuddered, but it would be years before I understood that Buck saw something I didn't, maybe knew me better than I knew myself at the time.

From St. Louis we went to every little town in Missouri, or so it seemed to me. That was a particularly rainy spring, and the long gray wet days faded into each other, punctuated by miserably cold nights and performances in the mud at outdoor arenas to sparse crowds made unenthusiastic by the chill. Even the food we ate was depressing: cheap cafés where the idea of steak was to cook it until it was like leather, boardinghouses that made up for a scarcity of meat with lots of potatoes and turnips, and long nights when we were just plain hungry because there was no place to eat. Sometimes on the train at night, when we'd boarded right after a show and hurried off to the next town, my stomach would grumble so loudly that Buck would laugh—and that would make me mad, adding anger to hunger for an unpleasant combination. Even so, it was the rain that was the worst.

"Weather doesn't break, Colonel will cancel the show," Buck predicted one night as we slogged through the mud to our tent.

We were in Hannibal, Missouri—Mark Twain country—for three days, and the colonel had put up tents for all of us. "Tents, or sleep on the train," he said with forced cheerfulness. "No money for boardinghouses."

And now Buck was telling me the tour might be canceled. "Did he say so?"

"No. I just think it's logical. Crowds have been off, gate's down. Makes no sense to keep on losing money."

"You don't know the colonel," I said. "His brothers back at the ranch, well, they think they make all the money so he can lose it on the road. And maybe they're right. Damn!" I was looking so intently at Buck as I talked that I walked right through an enormous mud puddle, splashing dirty gray water on my boots and the chaps I still wore.

"Here"—he laughed—"stand still." And Buck, that most patient of men, took out his bandanna and wiped off my clothes.

"I've been wanting angora chaps, but I sure wouldn't wear 'em in this weather." I'd had my eye on the curly white angora chaps that Fay Harrison wore, and I really did covet them.

"Better stick to rough-outs until the weather clears," Buck suggested with practicality.

"I wouldn't care if the show did close," I said defiantly. "I'm tired of being wet and cold and dirty. You ever try to rope and tie a calf in the mud?"

"Yeah, that's why I play the horn."

I swung an impatient fist at him. Buck flinched, then took off on a run, and I gave chase.

"You'll get mud on your clothes again," he warned over his shoulder, "and this time I won't wipe it off."

We landed in our tent in a wet dirty heap, shedding our clothes in a pile on the wood flooring and heading for bed without delay. It was the only warm dry place I'd been for days—but that wasn't why either one of us hurried. I'd put aside my fears of pregnancy, vowing not to let anything ruin the physical intimacy between Buck and me. And nothing did—not the thought of children, the possibility of the show closing, or the mud outside. Buck and I forgot the world the minute we were alone together.

Tying a calf in the mud was bad enough—the little beasts threw mud all over you as they struggled to get away—but relay races were worse. The horses tended to slip in the soft soggy ground, and their hooves churned up mud and dirty water. We had an act the colonel called "Pony Express" where four girls raced each other, on four separate mounts each. It was complicated—and hard to do in a small arena—but each of us stood at our post around the edge of the arena. If you think of a clock, we were posted at 12:00, 3:00, 6:00, and 9:00. Each of us had a cowboy to hold the other horses. When we had circled the arena and were heading toward our starting point, the cowboy would slap the second horse into motion. The point was to dismount from the first horse, bounce on the ground and take a flying leap to land on the second horse, which was already in motion. It took exact timing and a lot of nerve—the cowboys always said that was why they just held the horses and refused to ride in such foolishness.

I wasn't riding the night Bonnie Adams's horse lost its footing in the mud. His forelegs buckled, just as though someone had put a trip wire in front of him as he ran, and then, almost in slow motion, he pitched slightly forward, and Bonnie was flung forward, luckily not enough to fly over the horse's head. While we all held our breath in fear, the horse fell to one side, pinning Bonnie's leg beneath him. Too close behind them came Belle, her horse going too fast to stop. At the last minute, Belle's horse shied to one side, almost crashing into the board wall that edged the arena, and then did an awkward jump over the fallen horse and rider, his hooves clearing them by inches. Behind that, Fay Harrison and little blond Jo desperately fought to turn their horses into the center of the arena.

There was absolute silence in the arena, except for the whinnying of frightened horses and the soft tones of riders trying to calm them. Bonnie's horse mercifully lay still for a moment, too stunned to try to right himself. If he had struggled to get up, he'd have hurt her worse.

Buck was one of the first to get to Bonnie, and he said later she was singing "Home on the Range" softly under her breath when he got there.

"Singing?" I was incredulous.

"So she wouldn't cry out," he said, "and maybe to quiet her horse."

Bonnie, whose leg was badly crushed but not broken, stayed perfectly still while several cowboys pulled her out from under the horse and then stood back while the animal righted himself. He stood, head down in bewilderment, but all four legs planted firmly on the ground—no legs broken. Beside him, Bonnie, supported on each side by a cowboy and covered with mud, waved to the audience, and at last the silence was broken by applause. The crowd was thin that night, as it had been for days, but the noise they made sounded louder than the biggest crowd I'd ever seen in Madison Square Garden.

"Ladies and gentlemen, Miss Bonnie Adams," the announcer roared, "and her horse, Samson. What a strong man he proved to be tonight!" That loud dramatic voice went on to praise the cowgirls who avoided even greater disaster with their tight control of their mounts, and the cowboys who ignored their own safety in the rush to save Bonnie. "Ladies and gentlemen," he concluded, "what you have seen tonight is the best of what the Wild West has to offer—a comradeship and concern for fellow performers and for animals that is absolutely unselfish. There're no finer folks on this earth, ladies and gentlemen, and I urge you to tell them once again how much you admire their courage." The applause swelled again, and I wished the announcer would be quiet.

Bonnie couldn't ride for a week, but she came to every show and sat in the stands.

"You scared to ride again?" I asked. It was the question on everyone's mind—that she'd been so spooked by what had happened that she'd lose her nerve.

"Yeah," she said, "I am. But soon as this leg mends, I want the colonel to put me in the 'Pony Express' again. Can't scare myself out of doin' something that I love."

I hugged her tight, hoping that I'd be brave enough to feel the exact same way if I got hurt.

I almost did get hurt one night, and it caused a row between me and Buck. A steer I was roping decided to act more like a bull—instead of running, it turned and started to charge Governor and me. I had a moment of panic—I couldn't very well turn and abandon the steer, but I sure didn't want him plowing those horns, short as they were, into Governor's side or my leg. Buck tried the trick that had worked before—playing his horn loudly—but the steer was oblivious. He had begun by walking deliberately in our direction; then he stopped and pawed the ground, just like a bull getting ready to charge. Just as he began to move forward—at a good pace—another rope sailed out and caught him. One of the cowboys had roped him from the opposite direction, and with both ropes on him—pulling in different directions—the steer was pretty much stuck right where he was. The cowboys finally got him out of the arena, and the colonel later admitted he sold him to a butcher right away.

Buck was angry about the incident and turned his anger toward me. "You can't do that, you know, just disregard people who care for you."

"I didn't do anything I don't usually do," I said hotly. "It was the steer, not me!"

"I don't care! How do you think I feel down there with the band, watching while you nearly get yourself killed?"

"I didn't nearly get killed, and if you don't like it, don't watch."

We lay rigid in the bed that night, careful not to touch each other, going to sleep with only a murmured goodnight. In the middle of the night, though, Buck reached for me, and as I turned into his embrace, he whispered, "I just don't want anything to happen to you." And then the world disappeared for us again, as his hands brought my body awake and alive with wanting.

Life went on—we were in Wisconsin, Illinois, Michigan, and Ohio in the next three or four months—and I thought little about Belle. The colonel gave me star billing all along the way. Headlines in local papers screamed, "The Miller 101 Featuring Cherokee Rose and Her Amazing Rope Tricks!" or, "Cherokee Rose, World's Greatest Cowgirl, to Perform Here!"

Before and after shows, little children would clamor for my autograph, and the colonel generally had me stand in front of the arena for a while and sign programs or tickets or whatever they had.

I loved it! I loved having those little children look up at me and breathe, "Golly, you sure can ride, miss!" or "I wish I could learn to rope." When they asked, I'd tell them quick stories about growing up on a ranch and learning to ride before I could walk—well, it was only a slight exaggeration. The faces of the city kids would turn pure green with envy, and I wished for each of them a childhood on a ranch.

I was a heroine to the grown-ups, too, though in a different way. Sometimes a man would sidle up and ask if he couldn't show me the town or a good time, but Buck seemed to have some kind of special intuition, for at just the right instant he would appear next to me, asking "Cherokee, you need anything?" and I'd smile graciously and introduce my husband. The man generally was gone before I could get out Buck's name. The rest of the time, while I signed, Buck sat on a stool behind me. "Watching you," he told me. "I'd never get tired of that." It gave me a good secure feeling to know he was there.

But it was the women who surprised me. Generally they wanted to talk more than they wanted my signature, and the request for an autograph was just an excuse for a brief conversation. Invariably the first question was "Are you married?" and I'd say yes and nod at Buck, and then they'd give him a long stare.

"He doesn't mind?" The question from a pale woman in a faded dress was typical. Two children clung to her skirts, the little girl crying for ice cream and her brother trying to smack her into silence, while the mother, oblivious of them, talked to me.

"Buck's proud of me," I said quietly. "He's in the show, too."

"But he's not the star like you are," the woman said, shaking her head.

No, I thought, that's true, he's not—but I was too busy to ponder that right now.

"You have children?" she asked, glancing for a minute at the two clinging to her but neglecting to recognize their quarrel.

"No, ma'am," I said, and bit my tongue before I added, "not yet."

"I wish . . . I wish I could do what you do," she said. "You're free, and I envy you."

I hadn't rightly ever thought about being anything but free—I had been free as a child on the prairie, and I was still free, even with Buck. It was one of the blessings of my life I took for granted, until all those sad-faced women started asking about my life—and reminded me of Mama, who never had been free. I wanted to hug this particular woman and tell her . . . no, I didn't know what I'd tell her.

Late that night, I said, "Buck Dowling, I'm glad I married you."

Startled, because I almost never spoke about love or what was between us, Buck replied, "I'm glad, too. Any special reason you brought it up right now?"

"Just been thinking," I muttered, "about what most women's lives are like."

He laughed aloud. "Not like yours, Cherokee, not at all like yours. 'Course, soon's as we have a baby, you'll get a little better idea of how the other half lives."

Buck talked a lot about having a baby, and I usually just listened and tried to agree without having to sound enthusiastic. Nothing ever would make Buck Dowling leave me, I knew that, unless I said, "Buck, I don't want children." Deep down inside, I knew that Buck wanted children even more than he wanted me.

It wasn't that I didn't want children exactly. Part of it was that I'd simply never been able to imagine myself as a mother. Seeing myself in the future had never been a problem for me—hadn't I always seen Tommy Jo Burns right where I was now, starring in a Wild West show? Only part I'd missed was the identity change from Tommy Jo to Cherokee. But motherhood, that was something different.

The other part, of course, was that pregnancy would interrupt my riding. While I was sidelined for three months or more, Dixie Bell or Fay Harrison or some girl I'd never heard of might take my place, and I might never get it back. Maybe, I thought once in a while, if I could find a baby in a basket, like Moses in the bulrushes, I could raise it and make Buck happy and keep on riding. Miracles, however, don't grow on trees—or in bulrushes—and I knew that.

But every time Buck made love to me, I thought about it, and every time he asked about my monthly time being so regular, I shuddered a little. If I was lucky—in my own terms—and failed to conceive, then I'd be unlucky in love and disappoint Buck. It was a dilemma I still hadn't come to grips with.

In Ohio, we ran into trouble with the Society for the Prevention of Cruelty to Animals.

"Threatening to close us down, that's what they are," the colonel said one morning in Cleveland. "Damnedest bunch of nonsense I ever heard of. Cruelty to animals . . ."

"Cruelty? What kind?" I asked, tagging along behind him as he paced the hallway outside the arena. "We treat our animals very well."

" 'Course we do, Cherokee, 'course we do. This is just some bunch of do-gooders, saying the horses and cattle don't have a choice in the matter. They're forced to do these things. When did you ever know a steer to make a choice?"

"I remember one that chose to run at me," I said flippantly, and then regretted it, because the colonel gave me a really black look. "Sorry."

"They claim it's cruel to rope and tie a calf, and unnatural—that was their word—unnatural to race a horse. Good Goda'mighty, what those people don't know about the West would fill a book. Here I am trying to show 'em what it was like, and they're claiming it was cruel. Next thing you know they'll outlaw cattle raising and ranching and—"

"Colonel, your blood pressure," I said. "Calm down. They can't close us, can they?"

"They've gone to get a court order," he said. "If that works, they can."

"Well, we'll just go on to the next town," I said prosaically.

"And what if the do-gooders in the next town get word of this? It could follow us all across the country. Every town we go to, they could stop us."

I couldn't believe that, but maybe I underestimated the people he called do-gooders.

In the end, the judge they applied to sent an inspector to watch a show and see how the animals were treated, fed, housed, and so on. A prim-looking matron from the SPCA, wearing a fur-trimmed black cloth coat and a large black hat with feathers on it, sat through the show with the inspector, her lips pursed in disapproval, her jaw set. When a steer was roped, she would poke him and say, "See? You see that?" Finally, I saw the poor man rubbing his arm, as though it were sore from the constant poking.

Buck caught me staring at her and asked mischievously, "Where'dya think she got the fur and the feathers? Did those creatures have a choice?"

I laughed aloud and went to tell the colonel, but he was too distracted to be amused.

She tagged along through the inspector's tour of the animal quarters, too, lifting her long skirt to keep the hem out of the muck and wrinkling her nose as though the good barn smells offended her. I followed at a respectful distance, and once when she turned to look at me, I smiled and said "Good evening," but she just turned away without a word. I thought she was probably the world's unhappiest woman ever.

The inspector reported to the judge that the animals were well treated and he saw no cruelty, so the judge refused to sign a restraining order and the show went on. But the publicity had hurt us, and the crowds were a little lighter than we would have liked. We left Cleveland a day early.

It was after the Cleveland show that Bonnie Adams came to me about Belle. Belle with the dark hair and wide eyes decided she had a crush on Buck, and she was none too subtle about it. "Buck, will you carry my saddle?" "Buck, are these chaps too long?" "Buck, be sure to play your best for me when I'm racing tonight." Sometimes when she said these things, she'd lay a light hand on his arm, or she'd look at him a minute and then cut her eyes away flirtatiously. Once I saw her leg brush his as she walked by him, and then she said with exaggerated politeness, "Oh! Pardon me, Buck."

Buck was only human. He was flattered by her attention and angry when I teased him about it. "Buck," I said in a syrupy-sweet voice, "be sure to play your best—"

"Cherokee, she's just being friendly."

"Friendly?" I hooted. "Buck Dowling, you are not that naive. She's got a crush on you, and she's doing everything she can to make something happen between you two."

"That's not true, Cherokee. She's a friend of yours, and none of these girls would do anything like that."

In truth, Belle was not a friend of mine. I hardly knew her, and liked her less than any of the other girls. Dixie Bell was the only other girl who was married, and the two of us were a little apart from the girls who roomed together and shared secrets late at night. Still, I felt close to them, and sometimes we all went in a bunch to eat dinner—on those nights, Buck would go out with the cowboys, and both of us liked those evenings apart.

"Makes coming back to you even better, Cherokee," he said one night. "I like missing you."

"And besides," I giggled, "we can trade gossip."

"Not funny," he said. "Were you polite to Belle?"

I'd taken supper at the boardinghouse where most of the girls were staying in St. Paul, Minnesota, while we were there for a week. "I didn't have to be. She wasn't there."

"Where was she?"

I sat straight up. "Buck Dowling, maybe she was with you. Maybe you didn't really eat with Mike and Joe—maybe—"

"Cherokee," he said patiently, "if I wanted to go to supper with another woman, you'd be the first to know about it. I promise you that."

I laughed aloud. "I know," I said. "I just wanted to see if you'd get upset."

Then he was angry that I'd tricked him, and he turned his back on me. Belle, I thought, could become a real problem if I weren't careful of the way I acted about it. What Belle did had precious little to do with anything.

By the time we closed in St. Paul, Belle had been reporting in sick for almost a week now, forcing some of us to ride doubles in the relays, and we were all getting fed up with her.

"She can't be that sick," I said to Bonnie. "What's the matter with her?"

"She's pregnant," Bonnie said matter-of-factly. "Pregnant, and scared, and miserable."

"She can still ride," I said. "She sure doesn't show." Then it dawned on me I was on the wrong track. "Who's the father?" I asked suspiciously, my mind going back to her play for Buck.

"Not Buck." Bonnie laughed, and I indignantly said, "I know that!"

"But," Bonnie went on, "that may have been why she made a play for him—get herself a good steady man she could claim as the father. I don't know who he is. She won't tell."

"The colonel know?"

"No, not yet. I told her she's got to tell him quick, so's he can find someone else, but she doesn't have anywhere to go. Her family's real religious, and they'd throw her out. 'Least, that's what she thinks."

I had no sympathy for Belle, probably because I'd never walked in her moccasins. Tell me about a young girl whose father was domineering, her mother weak, and her home unbearable, and I was full of sympathy—I knew that kind of trouble. But in my smug self-righteousness, I thought Belle's troubles were her own fault—she shouldn't have been sleeping with a man she wasn't married to. Besides, my pa, for all his faults, would not have thrown me out if I'd appeared on his doorstep pregnant. Disobedient, yes, but pregnant, no. "Well," I said, "she's made her bed."

"It's a bed a lot of us could have made, save for good luck and some honorable men," Bonnie said dryly, and I had the grace to blush.

"Don't know what I can do about it, though," I said.

The gossip got to Buck before the colonel, and he was more upset than

I'd ever seen him. He paced our little tent one night in his long johns, while I sat huddled in the bed wishing he'd join me.

"She's just a kid, Cherokee, and now she's got no place to go. I—well, we've got to help her."

"Colonel would probably let her go to the 101, now that Mrs. Miller's back there." The words came out of my mouth without my even thinking of them first, surprising me as much as they did Buck.

"Cherokee, my love, you're a wonder. Of course that's the answer! She can help Mrs. Miller down there until the baby comes, and then—"

"And then she and the baby will have to go someplace and build a new life. I suppose she could come back to the show," I said reluctantly, "but I don't know how the baby'd do."

"How can she raise that baby alone?" Buck demanded, as though it were all my fault. " 'Course if she were in the show, we could all take care of it."

"Buck Dowling, if I didn't know better, I'd begin to believe that rumor that you're the baby's father."

What I'd intended as a joke fell flat. Buck looked at me long and hard and said, "I'm not the father, and you and I both know that. But I care about that baby."

When he came to bed, Buck never touched me, and we both tossed and turned all night.

I could have predicted what happened next. Buck took matters into his own hands—without even consulting Belle, which I thought was pretty high-handed—and went to the colonel. The colonel was not pleased—he'd always made a big point that no breath of scandal would touch his show. "Good clean entertainment by wholesome honest folks—a show for the whole family," he always said. Belle's little problem tarnished that image, though I was sure all those families in the audience would never know that Belle was expecting, let alone unmarried, unless the colonel made too big a fuss over it and some small-town news reporter, desperate for a story, found out.

A tearful Belle was called in to the colonel's office, in Buck's presence, and offered sanctuary at the 101 in Oklahoma. Buck described the interview to me later.

"Buck's idea," the colonel said gruffly, his scowl canceling any idea of sympathy.

"Buck, I'm in your debt." Buck didn't tell me this part, but I interpreted Belle's reaction for myself and could picture her falling into his arms.

"She did not," he told me indignantly. "She was grateful and re‑lieved."

"What's she going to do after the baby comes?" I asked innocently.

"Don't know," Buck said. "We're still mulling that one over."

"We?" I yelled, louder than I intended. "Who is we? You and Belle? Or you, Belle, and the colonel?"

"Cherokee, I'm just trying to help."

There was a big silence and a deep distance between Buck and me for days after Belle left, and I damned her for creating it and myself for making it worse, but it didn't ever occur to me to blame Buck. Oh, we mended our fences and went on being lovers and friends both, but that memory was always there. Our whole relationship had shifted, be it ever so slightly, and would never again be quite the same.

CHAPTER 9

I thought we could forget about Belle and go on with our lives, but I guess for both of us anger and resentment lingered just under the surface. It came to the top one night when I sailed my loop toward Buck, just as I'd been doing for a long time now at the end of the show. It settled gently over his shoulders—but when he should have walked toward me, Buck pulled back, pulling the rope tighter about his shoulders. His reaction took me so by surprise that instinctively I tightened the rope from my end. The crowd began to snicker and then to laugh outright.

"The lady's caught him," the announcer said, his bravado voice covering the uncertainty he felt at this strange turn of events, "but the gentleman doesn't appear to want to be caught."

The look on Buck's face was enigmatic—maybe he was teasing and playing with me, or maybe he was serious. Either one, I thought, was out of place in front of a sellout crowd in Des Plaines, Illinois. But how was I going to get us out of it?

I could drop the rope, but that would look silly. Buck could suddenly start walking toward me—I prayed he would—and that would make it all right. Or we could stay there, in a Mexican standoff, until the crowd wearied and went home.

Buck finally grinned and began walking toward me . . . slowly.

"The little lady's husband, folks," the announcer said, relief plain in his tone. "He's been funnin' with her, but here he comes. Buck Dowling!"

Buck slid the rope down over his body and waved his arms to the crowd, which was now cheering. Then he came and planted a distant kiss on my cheek, grabbed my hand, and together we bowed to the audience.

At last the performance was over.

"Buck Dowling, what were you doing?" The minute we were in our own room in the current boardinghouse, I demanded an answer.

He shrugged and avoided looking at me. "Just thought it was time to change the routine."

"Don't you think," I asked coldly, "that you could tell me before you change the routine?"

"I—I didn't think you'd agree."

A premonition swept through me, one that I didn't like and pushed to the back of my mind as quickly as I could. "We've always talked about the show and how it should go."

"I know. Somehow it's different lately." He looked as unhappy as I felt.

"All right," I said, "let's talk about how we should change it. What's wrong with my roping you?"

Now he downright squirmed. "Aw, Cherokee, it makes me look—well, it makes me look like a henpecked husband."

He might as well have thrown a pail of ice water straight in my face. I had to take a deep breath and think a minute. Finally I asked, "Is this about the show, or about what's between you and me?"

"How can you separate the two?"

He was right. I had no idea whether I'd even look twice at him if I were a schoolteacher and he a banker and we met on some city street. Oh, I'd think he was cute, but beyond that . . . Our whole lives were bound up in the show, and maybe, just maybe, it was the thing that held us together—well, besides the physical part.

Sandy Burns had not raised a coward. "Buck Dowling," I said, my voice gathering strength from my determination, "what are you trying to tell me?"

"I don't know," he said miserably, "but I gotta change something. I can't keep blowing a horn while you . . . well, you know, Cherokee. I thought it would be different. Maybe I don't know what I thought, but I thought things would change."

"And you'd be the star?"

He was quickly indignant. "No, that's not it. I don't necessarily want to be the star. But maybe I want to wear the pants in this family."

"I thought you did," I said. I knew honestly, in my soul, that I had made every effort to see that Buck Dowling was the head of our two-person family. When the colonel came to me with problems or suggestions, I always deferred to Buck. And the colonel kept increasing his responsibility, so that Buck played an active part in the management of the show. As far as we were concerned, he chose where we stayed, how we lived, even how we spent our money, even though that money was in large part my earnings. And Lord knows, in our personal life Buck was the leader. I wasn't sure I knew where Buck's problem lay.

Suddenly he came to me and took me in his arms. "I don't know, Cherokee. I don't know what's the matter with me. Just an itch in my soul I can't seem to scratch. You can rope me anytime you want."

But it was a long time before I ended a show by roping Buck Dowling.

Outside the arena, life went on. Buck and I were still lovers and friends. If the passion between us seemed a little less, I attributed it to having passed the first flush of new love—and it seemed to me we'd enjoyed that honeymoon period longer than most people have a right to expect. There were still many nights that we rushed back to our quarters, oblivious of the rest of the troupe, longing to be in our own cocoon.

But more often Buck would say, "I'm going for a beer with the fellows. You all right going home with the girls?"

"Sure," I'd reply, and I'd be sound asleep when he came home, only to be awakened by his probing kisses and persistent hands.

Sometimes in those months toward the end of the season, I thought Buck Dowling was making love to me in order to prove a point to himself. But I said nothing. I was scared.

"We'll winter at the 101," the colonel announced in late September 1912. "Get ourselves together for the next season—new acts, new costumes. Got to spiff up the show every year." His voice was hearty with enthusiasm. The Miller brothers back in Oklahoma may have complained about the financial drain of the Wild West show, but it had lost none of its charm or importance for the traveling brother. In spite of señoritas who couldn't ride bulls, horses who got down with colic, and cowgirls who were unexpectedly pregnant, the colonel was having the time of his life.

"Cherokee," he said, as we turned to leave the general meeting that morning in the arena in Des Moines, Iowa, "I got an idea for you and Buck."

"Good," I said. "Better tell it to Buck." I hadn't roped Buck since that awful night, but I sure had made it a point not to make one decision without him.

"Cherokee," the colonel said, "you're the star here. You're the one the show depends on. You and I have got to talk."

"Buck," I said, controlling my voice, "is my husband. He's the one we've both got to talk to."

So Buck and I were both called into the colonel's railroad car the next night, while the train sped through the Iowa night. It was one of those nights we were condemned to sleeping upright in the coach car, so both of us were delighted to be summoned, even briefly, to more comfortable quarters.

"Cherokee. Buck." The colonel nodded at chairs in front of his desk and lifted a decanter of brandy. Buck accepted, and I declined, having never acquired a taste for hard liquor. But I noticed that Buck sipped his brandy cautiously and kept an eye always on the colonel.

"I've had a thought for a winter show," the colonel said. "Vaudeville."

Buck laughed aloud, as though it were a good joke. "We don't sing and dance, Colonel. And we sure don't do blackface."

The colonel grinned back, the two of them enjoying a joke, though I remained puzzled. "Not what I had in mind, Buck. I think we could do kind of a miniature Wild West show on the small stage."

"You want me to rope a calf on a stage?" I asked incredulously, forgetting my resolve to remain quiet and let Buck handle the meeting.

"No, no," the colonel said. "But you could do trick roping. Thing is, you could do it on a stage inside, where folks could come in bad weather. You could work all winter long. Buck could play with a small band to back you up."

Lord, I thought, he could have chosen any one of a thousand other ways to say that! Just as I thought Buck would storm out of the car in anger, he said, "Not a bad idea, Colonel. Tell me more."

And they fell to discussing what could and couldn't be done on a small stage.

As we left the colonel's car, late in the night, Buck turned and said, "We will get to go to the ranch for a little time off, won't we?"

The colonel hesitated, saw the look on Buck's face, and then agreed quickly. "We'll all go to the ranch in November, and you can stay until after the holidays. I won't make any bookings until January. Folks are looking for new entertainment then."

"I didn't know you were so all-fired fond of being at that ranch," I said later. To me, time at the ranch meant that I'd have to go see my folks, I'd get a visit with Louise, and I'd get some warm wonderful time being catered to in Mother Miller's house. But Buck had never seemed as at home there as I felt.

"Want to check on Belle," he said without apology. "That baby's due in October."

A great silence fell between us, and I said no more.

We arrived at the ranch early in November, and Mother Miller greeted us with a newborn infant in her arms.

"Isn't she darling?" she asked of nobody in particular. "This is Sallie May, just two and a half weeks old."

Buck reached out and took that baby as though he'd been holding tiny babies all his life. "Isn't she beautiful!" he breathed, and then, turning to me, said, "Here, Cherokee, take her."

I felt as awkward as a barren cow trying to suckle a motherless calf. "She *is* beautiful," I said, never reaching an arm to take her because I was sure I didn't know how to hold a new baby. Wasn't there something about supporting their heads?

Buck gave me a funny look, and finally I reached a tentative finger out to stroke her forehead. It was the softest thing I'd ever touched, maybe like old sheets that have been washed and washed until they're buttery soft. And she had this fine fuzz of gold hair all across her head. When she gurgled, I drew my hand back in alarm.

Buck laughed. "She's fine, Cherokee. She liked that." Then, turning to Mrs. Miller, "Where's Belle?"

"Upstairs resting. She hasn't been doing so well since the baby came. Can't seem to get her strength back."

Without another word, Buck bounded up the stairs, loudly calling, "Belle? You get out of that bed now!"

Mrs. Miller gave me a strange look and then said, "You two have the usual room, Tommy Jo. You might as well go on and get settled."

Without another word, I hoisted my duffel and headed upstairs. As I passed a closed door, I could hear the murmur of voices—Buck and Belle. Their talk was followed by the tinkling laughter of a woman.

Without meaning to, I slammed the bedroom door behind me.

"How's Belle?" I asked, striving for casualness, when Buck finally came to our room, dragging his own duffel.

"She'll be all right," he said. "She just needs to stop feeling sorry for herself and get on with things."

"Sorry for herself?" I asked.

"You know, new baby and no way to support herself. What's she going to do?"

"I don't know," I said. "What *is* she going to do?"

"She'll be all right here for a while," he said, and then Buck Dowling, who knew me better than anyone, came over and put his arms around me. "You jealous of her baby, Cherokee?"

"No," I answered truthfully, "but I'm uncomfortable around it. I—I don't know how to handle babies."

He laughed aloud. "You'll learn. Just wait till we have our own. You'll learn real fast."

"Yeah," I echoed in an empty voice, "real fast." Without another word, I began to dress for dinner.

It soothed my soul some to be among those gathered at the huge 101 dining table again, though I thought of Prairie Rose and how it didn't seem right to be at the ranch without her. Still, the food was hot and hearty as always, and so was the company.

"Got great plans for this winter, don't we, Buck?" Colonel Miller asked heartily, and Buck jumped to attention, equaling him in heartiness as he replied, "We sure do, we sure do!"

"Tommy Jo, dear, are you as enthusiastic about this vaudeville business as these men?" Mrs. Miller put her question gently, and I had no way of knowing if she knew how close she came to the mark.

"Oh, of course," I said too quickly. "It'll be great to work all year—though, of course, I'll miss being here."

"Of course," she said. "How's your family?"

"Mama's not doing so well, or so Papa writes. I thought I'd go see them and then go down to Guthrie in a day or two. That is, if you don't need me," I added hastily, looking at the colonel.

"No, no, you go on and get your visiting done. We can do without the two of you for a few days."

Both Buck and I looked startled. I opened my mouth but couldn't think of what to say. Buck was quicker.

"I'll probably just let Cherokee go by herself," he said. "I think her family likes to have her to themselves."

I shot him a quick look but could read no ulterior motive on his face.

We spent the next few days unpacking from the tour, sorting costumes that needed mending from those that needed replacing, untangling tack, making a list of props that needed repair. The colonel pretty much stayed in his office and let Buck handle the allocation of work, and Buck was everywhere, issuing orders, making demands, acting like it was his show.

"Cherokee, that rope is fraying—best get a new one. Bonnie, see if a new feather won't fix that hat. Jake, can't we paint over that fake front so the settlers' cabin looks a little more real?"

Not a month earlier I would have been filled with happiness that Buck was doing more than blowing his horn. He was taking on responsibility and showing a talent for organization. And best of all, he was feeling better about himself. I remembered his words: "I gotta do more than blow my horn!" But now a corner of my mind resented him. It wasn't that I thought he was taking over or replacing me on the colonel's list of most valuable people in the troupe. As a matter of fact, I didn't know why I felt the way I did. But there was that little lingering black cloud in my mind, and it was growing. It was time to get away for a few days.

"Buck, you really don't mind if I go alone to see my folks and Louise?" I sat at my dressing table, brushing my hair, while Buck concentrated on some paperwork before him.

"What?" He looked up as though I'd brought him back from a far place. "Oh, no, Cherokee, I really think it would be best. I got a lot to do here."

"Yeah," I said dryly, "I noticed you've been right busy."

He got up and came toward me, taking the brush out of my hand as he often did. "You miss me?" he asked softly.

Maybe I was wrong. Maybe everything between us was right, and I ought to stop manufacturing trouble. "Yes," I whispered, "I guess I have been missing you."

"Let's not let that happen again," he said, bending to kiss my neck and work his way up toward my ear, while I sat shivering in anticipation.

The morning I was to leave for Luckett's, Belle appeared at breakfast. Her entrance was dramatic, to say the least: she wore a wrapper of richly printed cotton—no chintz for our Belle!—and her hair was swept back and up, with a few loose curls falling around her face, to give just a hint that she was still an invalid. Still, I detected a little rouge and gloss on the lips.

"I just got tired of being confined in that room," she said, almost pouting, "and Sallie's asleep, so I thought . . . may I join you at break-fast?"

Well, of course every man in the room jumped to help her to a seat. Buck won, the first to reach her, hold out his arm, and help her into a chair. She favored him with a wide smile and a look that went deep into his eyes.

"Thank you, Buck." Then turning to me, "Cherokee, Buck tells me you're leaving today for a little bit."

"Just a little bit," I mumbled, unconsciously mimicking her word choice. Buck frowned at me, so I became more conversational. "I'm going to see my family for a few days."

"Aren't you lucky to have family to visit," she said.

Nastily, I thought to myself that she was playing on the fact that everyone knew she had been disowned and couldn't go visit her family.

Before I could say anything else, the faint sound of a baby crying floated down the stairs. As Belle said, "Oh, my," and started to rise, Buck said, "I'll get her. You stay still." And he bounded up the stairs, returning a minute later with the baby nestled contentedly in his arms.

Now I knew Buck had spent a lot of time with Belle and the baby ever since we arrived at the 101. He regularly and without apology went in to see them before dinner and supper both, and he regaled me at night with accounts of how darling the baby was, how she smiled at him—I didn't tell him the one truth I knew about babies' gas pains being mistaken for smiles—how she followed him with her eyes when he was near her. I had told myself it was clearly a love affair between my husband and a three-week-old infant, and that the mother was no part of it. And I really believed that, maybe even thought Sallie would fulfill his need for a baby and I'd be off the hook.

But now, seeing him standing there holding that baby, I drew in my breath sharply. There was a sort of radiance about Buck, a happiness I'd never seen, even in the wildest days of new passion between us. I saw clearly that Buck would never be a whole person until he had children of his own—and the thought whirled in my brain like a dervish.

"Here, Cherokee, you hold her and let Belle eat." He handed Sallie to me, ever so gently, holding her head and moving my hands until they were placed under the baby to his satisfaction.

She fit comfortably into my arms and snuggled down as though perfectly content, and I liked the feel of that little warm body next to mine. *What, I thought, is happening to me?*

"You gonna sing to her, Cherokee?" asked one of the cowboys, a grin on his face.

"Don't want to scare her," I retorted quickly. But my quick voice was enough to start the baby crying, which unnerved me completely. With a red face, I handed her quickly back to Buck, who simply talked softly to her, walked in a circle for a bit, and soon had her back to quiet contentment.

"Oh, Cherokee," Belle laughed, "you'll have to learn about babies. Buck tells me you two are hoping to start a family."

While I roused in indignation that Buck had been talking to her about our intimate life, the colonel nearly choked on his coffee.

"Cherokee?" he said in a strangled voice, and I knew he had a vision of his show closing while the star had a baby. "Do you . . . is there something I should know?"

Maybe it was the tension around the table that got me, but I began to laugh, and the more I tried to stop, the harder I laughed, until tears were streaming down my face. I was the only one that knew how close my laughter was to sobbing.

Meantime, Buck jumped in. "No, sir, it's just—well, you know, every young couple would like to start a family. And we will, someday."

I threw my napkin on the table and ran up the stairs, followed by a great silence. I knew, behind me, they all sat with their eyes glued on me.

I went straight to Guthrie. I wasn't ready to face Mama, and I needed Louise. I went alone, riding off while Buck was busy so that he wouldn't insist on accompanying me or sending someone with me. I'd ridden from Luckett's to the 101 alone all those years ago—it seemed like a lifetime but it was really only six years—and I would ride back now by myself. I needed to be alone.

But the prairie was of little comfort. The day was warm and sunny for November, and I shed layers as I rode, stuffing my jacket and then my sweater into the duffel I'd packed behind me. Instead of reveling in the beauty of the day, I began to feel sweaty and uncomfortable.

The grasslands seemed to have already withdrawn in preparation for winter. There had been a pretty hard frost a week or so earlier, and the grass looked brown, the bushes bare, the landscape uninspiring. I guess that just as I wanted my honeymoon to last forever, I wanted it always to be spring on the prairie, with the bright green of new grass and the crazy-quilt colors of the wildflowers. Today, it was all brown and gray, unfortunately suited to my mood.

Louise greeted me with open arms and a wary look. "What's wrong?"

"What makes you think something's wrong?" I countered lightly.

She shrugged and turned to light the flame under the coffeepot. "Maybe it's your red eyes—or maybe it's that you aren't due here for several days."

I sat down at the table in the kitchen and began toying with a spoon, but I couldn't say anything.

"Are you pregnant?" she finally asked.

It was, of course, the question that burst the dam. Between sobs, I managed to convey the opinion that it might be better if I were.

"Better than what?" she asked. Louise never hovered. She never reached an arm to comfort or console, or spoke in soft tones to quiet me. She was practical and matter-of-fact—and I knew that she cared desperately about me and whatever was wrong. It was like having the proverbial rock to lean on.

"Better than having Buck Dowling fall in love with someone else just because she has a fatherless baby."

The coffee having warmed, she poured herself a cup—I still couldn't stand the bitter stuff—and sat down. "You better begin at the beginning," she said.

Between sobs, I told her about Belle and the baby and the time Buck had rebelled when I roped him and how happy he was with the baby. I must have blathered like a baby myself.

"Tommy Jo, you knew this man wanted children right from the start," she said, wasting no sympathy on me. "You thought you could ignore it and it'd go away, and now the whole big problem has come up to hit you in the face."

"It's Belle's fault," I wailed, having completely given up my good sense in favor of self-pity. "If she hadn't gotten pregnant—"

Louise hooted. "I imagine she feels that way a lot of the time too. But if Belle hadn't brought the problem to a head, something or someone else would have. You can't hide your head in the sand anymore."

"What," I quavered, "if I never do get pregnant. It's been four years."

"What if?" she said. "You win, Buck loses."

"I lose too, because Buck . . . well, he . . ."

"He won't stay with you, if you don't give him a baby? Good possibility. So?"

"I love Buck Dowling," I said automatically.

"That's not what I asked. Do you want to spend the rest of your life with him?"

"Yes," I said, far too quickly.

"Tommy Jo," she said, rising from the table, "you're going to have to do some hard figuring: about how much you want to be a star in a Wild West show, how much you want Buck Dowling, what you're willing to do to keep either one. May be that one will have to be sacrificed to the other, and you're going to have to choose. I can't do that for you." She turned lightly away. "Besides, I have a noonday meal to fix. Here, start on those potatoes."

And so I sat at Louise's kitchen table and peeled potatoes and thought long and hard about life's choices.

Dinner at Louise's table was like dinner at the 101 table—familiar and comforting. The drummers were different but still the same—men with empty lives who traveled from place to place, never at home anywhere but always ready to grab on to anything of interest. When one of them leered at me and asked if I'd care to walk out after supper in the evening, Louise let me defend myself. I did, so quickly that he never looked at me again during the whole meal.

"Me?" I said innocently. "My husband wouldn't approve."

"But," said the drummer, "he let you come here alone."

"He knows I can take care of any fools I might meet on the road," I said.

The two lady milliners still lived in Louise's house, and they approved of me not one whit more than they had before. "You're doing what?" said one, while the other murmured, "Your mother must be worried unto death."

I wouldn't treat them the way I did the drummer, and I reminded them that I was married.

"But those wild horses," said the second one. "You could be hurt."

"Yes, ma'am, but it's not likely. I know what I'm doing."

She clucked and went back to her meat and potatoes. She must have thought how safe it was to be making fancy hats for town ladies. I thought it so dull, I couldn't even bear to think about it.

After Louise and I had cleaned the kitchen in companionable silence, I asked about Bo. I'd shipped Sam to Bo's stables, and much as I wanted to know about Bo himself, I also wanted to know about my horse.

"He's fine," she said noncommittally.

"Fine?" I demanded. "What does that mean?"

She turned toward me, the soapy rag in her hands dripping onto the kitchen floor. "Means he's married, seems to be happy, goin' along like he always has." She paused a long moment. "That man loves you, Tommy Jo, and that's a responsibility you'll have the rest of your life."

"He has a corner of my heart, Louise, always has. I'm glad he's happy, but I'm not jealous. Should I go see him?"

She thought a minute. "No. That might just stir up trouble. That girl he married—well, she hasn't a lot of self-confidence, and I reckon it would bother her more than a little if you were to come calling."

I shrugged. I would have liked to go to the stable to check on Sam, but I understood what Louise meant, and I surely didn't want to cause any trouble.

But the next morning as we lingered at the kitchen table after breakfast, the dishes still undone and the kitchen a mess, there was a knock at the door. When Louise called out, Bo stuck his head in the door.

"Mind if I come in?"

Louise jumped up. "Of course not, Bo. I'll get you a cup of coffee."

"Bo!" I said, rising and holding out both my hands in real honest delight to see him. "How's Sam?" was the first question out of my mouth.

"He's fine, just fine," he said, apparently glad for a way to begin the conversation. "Leg's healing nicely. You can probably ride him again if you want."

"Sam deserves a better life than that," I laughed. "I want him to be fat and happy at your place."

Bo just nodded.

"How'd you know I was here?" I asked.

He grinned self-consciously. "You know Guthrie. Word travels. Fact is, the wife went to pick up her new bonnet, and the ladies at the millinery store mentioned a visitor at the boardinghouse, and she—well, she put two and two together, and she told me about it."

With relief I thought that must mean that "the wife" wasn't jealous of me. "Well, how nice," I said. "I hope to meet her."

Bo shook his head. "I don't think that's what we ought to do, Tommy Jo. She knows about you, and she knows I'd have married you if it'd worked out. We've made our peace with it, but, well . . ." Then he brightened. "We got us a little one, a fine boy, named him Thomas."

I winced inwardly but didn't ask about the name. Instead I probed for the usual things a father will brag about—how old the child was, how he took to horses, and so on. Bo talked on awhile with great pride, and then asked me about the show and about Buck, and it was my turn to talk. I did so cautiously. There was no reason to let Bo Johnson know about the distance that was growing between Buck and me. And with Bo so proud of his new son, I wasn't about to tell him that I couldn't—or wouldn't—get pregnant.

Bo stayed a long time, probably close to two hours, and then, with a kind of reluctance in his voice, he said, "I best be getting back to the stables. Can't take a whole day's vacation. Sure good to see you, Tommy—uh, Cherokee."

I took his hand in mine again and echoed, "It's good to see you, Bo. Take care of my horse for me, and tell him I'll come see him soon." But I wondered when I could visit Sam, if a jealous wife stood between me and Bo.

He ducked his head as though bowing slightly, put his hat on, and was out the door before either of us could say another thing.

Louise had busied herself with the dishes and dinner preparation all this time, but I knew she'd heard the talk. Still, she waited for me to say something, and I was a long time doing it. Instead I sat at the table brooding, thinking that Bo and I, who had once been the closest of friends, now had a distance, an uneasiness between us. It struck me as sad, but I didn't know what to do about it. Why, I wondered, did men have to be your lovers or nothing? Why couldn't Bo and I have kept the friendship between us, even though each of us had other lovers? At twenty-two I was far too young to know the answer to that question, but I was also blind to my own ignorance, in the way of the young.

I stayed with Louise five days and then, reluctantly, rode out for Luckett's. When I left, Louise simply said, "I'm here when you need me."

With great bravado, I smiled as I said, "And I probably will, sooner or later."

I rode slowly, as though I didn't want to go to see my parents. Papa had written from time to time, and his letters were full of a sort of forced cheerfulness. Mama was not, I gathered, getting any better. Louise had told me, though, that Papa never came to see her anymore. She would hear, from time to time, that he'd been in town on business, but she never saw him.

When I rode through the gate at Luckett's I was overcome with a sort of nostalgia. This was the place I'd grown up, the place that held all the memories that mattered to me—except maybe the 101 and Buck—but the place that had shaped me. And now, I could scarcely bear to come back there.

My mood, already darkened by Buck and, more recently, by my encounter with Bo, did not lift, and I thought perhaps there was something about life that doomed us to unhappiness. Vaguely I remembered the sheer joy each day had brought when Buck and I were new to each other. Now that joy seemed a faraway dream.

No one came to greet me when I rode up to the house, but when I shouted "Hello the house!" Papa came slowly out the door. When he saw me, a great smile spread over his face.

"Tommy Jo! Get down off that horse and come here right this minute." He held his arms open wide, and I went willingly into them.

"Papa! I've missed you!" It was a treat to be able to say it truthfully.

"I've missed you, too, Tommy Jo. But we surely have been proud following the show and hearing all about you. Where's Buck?"

"He stayed at the 101. Things to do. We're getting ready to take the show to the vaudeville stage, and he's got a lot of planning to do. Besides, I thought I'd get a better visit if I came alone."

Papa hugged me, and I swear he turned his head to hide a tear. "Come inside," he said. "Your mama's in bed, but she'll be glad to see you."

"In bed?" I asked.

"She spends most of her time there now," he said gently. "Seems like she just doesn't have the energy to get up and move around."

"Papa!"

"Shhh, Tommy Jo. It's all right. She's not unhappy." That seemed to be all that mattered to him.

Seeing Mama was a shock to me. She had lost weight until her face looked drawn—gone was the beauty that I remembered from my childhood. Her skin had an unhealthy paleness, and her eyes were dull, their brightness forever dimmed. And her hair, that lovely dark hair, had turned not only gray but limp and lank. It hung about her face, though I could tell that someone—Papa?—had tried to comb it. It was neat and clean, but that was all you could say for it.

"Mama, it's me, Thomasina." In my effort to awaken something in her, I reverted to the name she'd given me at birth and had always insisted on calling me.

"Thomasina?" She reached a hand toward me, and I bent down until she was stroking my forehead. "Have you been out riding on the prairie?"

"Yes, Mama," I said. Well, it was the truth. I had ridden on the prairie to get there.

"I'm glad you're home safe, darling. Remember the day you killed that bull?"

I thought Papa would choke behind me, but I managed to say softly, "Yes, Mama, I remember."

"You mustn't do that again, Thomasina. You've been to the convent now."

"Yes, Mama, I've been to the convent." Tears were welling up in my eyes.

Papa murmured something about dinner and left the room, and I sat there by Mama's bedside, holding her bony hand, for an eternity. Once in a while I had to brush a tear away, but mostly I managed to smile and talk brightly to her, though I generally had to pretend that I was eight years old again.

When Papa stuck his head in to say that dinner was ready, I asked, "Mama? Will you come to the table?"

"Oh, no, dear. Your papa will bring me something. I . . . well, I'll just stay here."

"She gets up sometimes and acts like she's all right," Papa told me over a meal of beef stew and bread—he had turned into a credible cook with Mama's illness. "But she more and more just stays in bed. I—I don't know what to do other than let her do what she will."

"I don't guess there is much you can do," I said, wanting in a funny way to lift his guilt just a bit. "How do you do your work around the ranch?"

He laughed ruefully and nodded toward the desk, which had always been at the center of the house and was still cluttered with papers. "More and more, that's the kind of work I do. I've got hands to do the riding and roping—what you used to do for me." His voice grew a little wistful, but then he was quickly back to the present. "Luckett doesn't seem to mind, and the ranch's still turning a handsome profit."

I had worried some about Papa losing his job because he couldn't pay enough attention to it, and I was glad that didn't seem to be a danger.

As if he'd read my mind, Papa said, "Luckett says I got a place here as long as I need it, long as I live." Pride was evident in his voice, as well it should be, for Luckett's generosity was a reward for work well done. "You'll always have a home to come back to, Tommy Jo."

I laid an appreciative hand on his arm and didn't tell him Louise's house was now the home I retreated to when I needed solace and comfort. We never did mention Louise the whole day I was at home, although Papa must have known that I had been there.

"Buck let you ride down here alone?" Papa demanded as I prepared to leave the next morning.

"He didn't have a choice," I said, stiffening a little. "I left without telling him. Besides, Buck doesn't tell me what to do."

"Someone," Papa muttered, "ought to see that you have some common sense. I'm gonna call Wilks to ride with you, least partway. Roads ain't safe for a woman alone."

"Papa," I said firmly, "I'll leave while you're calling him. I want to go alone. I need to think." I looked at his worried face and laughed, as though to banish his fears. "I'll be fine, really I will."

I hugged him and was gone. When I was almost to the gate, I turned to look, and he was standing by the house, still waving one big arm.

That ride back to the 101 may have been the bluest time of my life. I sank into self-pity as I thought about all that was wrong with my life and those around me—Buck and our growing distance over the complicated issue of children, Mama growing weaker by the day and Papa being so brave I sometimes thought he was blind, Louise letting me know that I had to sort it all out for myself, and even Bo, letting me know in his own gentle way that he still loved me. I had, I thought, made a royal mess out of a lot of things.

My mood seemed to darken with every mile I rode, and I recognized that I'd be in a foul mood by the time I reached the 101. Somehow I got to thinking about what Louise would have said about that, and I had the proverbial moment of inspiration—Louise would have raked me over the coals with her tongue. I'd have gotten no sympathy from her. Life, she'd have told me, is what we make of it, and if mine was in a blue period it was up to me to pull it out, by the bootstraps if I had to. Well, I was mixing metaphors in my mind, but I suddenly knew clear well what the message was and where the truth lay. I had flat been feeling sorry for myself, and it was time to change directions.

I rode long and hard and reached the 101 at midnight, having stopped only long enough to water and rest my horse. When I rode up to the house, Buck was sitting on the porch railing staring down the road. Was he watching for me?

He was casual. "Hey, Cherokee. How's everything in Guthrie and at the ranch?"

"Fine," I said cautiously. "Louise and Papa said to tell you hello. Mama's just the same, maybe a little worse."

"I'm sorry." He stood up and came slowly down the stairs. "I missed you, and I caught holy hell from the colonel for letting you go alone." He stood close to me but didn't reach out a hand in my direction. There were none of those intimate gestures by which he had so often possessed me. It was like Buck knew he was dealing with something new between us.

I grinned just a little. "Did you tell him it wasn't your fault? I'll be sure he knows."

"I told him," Buck said slowly, "that you could take care of yourself and that I damn sure was not going to go with you when I wasn't wanted."

I raised my eyes to meet his. "Thanks, Buck. It wasn't that I didn't want you. I just—"

"I know, Cherokee, I know." And now he did reach out toward me, not with a tentative hand or a gentle gesture but to pull me toward him with two strong arms. I buried my head in his shoulder as he hugged me and said softly over and over, "Cherokee, I missed you."

"I missed you, too," I said, and realized that it was true.

"You two gonna stand out there all night," the colonel demanded loudly. "Buck, put up that girl's horse. I got to talk to her."

"Yes, sir," Buck said, laughing. "Anything else, sir?"

"I'll let you know," the colonel grumbled. "Cherokee, you come in here."

He didn't, of course, have anything much to say. He just wanted to make sure that I was back in one piece and ready to go to work. I convinced him.

Late that night Buck and I lay in bed talking. We had had our private reunion, and I had only fleetingly wondered if the chances of pregnancy were in any way mathematically related to the amount of passion involved. But now, spent, he seemed to want to talk. We'd talked some about the coming vaudeville season and a little about Mama and then it occurred to me that I hadn't asked about one thing that had really stood between us—Belle and the baby.

"How're Belle and the baby?" I asked.

"Baby's fine," he said. "She's really . . . well, you'll just have to see, Cherokee, but she's the smartest little thing, for one so tiny."

Just as I was about to accept that I still had Belle and Sallie as rivals for his affection, he added, "But Belle is really getting on my nerves. She's after me every minute: Would I do this, would I hold the baby because she's so happy when I hold her, could I talk to her about what she should do with her future. Lord, Cherokee, I didn't take that girl to raise!"

I smothered a grin. But then I asked more seriously, "Would you take Sallie to raise?" The wild thought had gone through my brain that we could adopt the baby, solve Belle's problem for her, and give Buck the child he wanted, all without interrupting my career. 'Course I hadn't thought about what raising a child could do to a career.

Buck began to stroke my hair with one hand. "Cherokee," he said, "I know what it cost you to say that, and, yes, I have thought about taking that baby to raise. But I don't think it would work right. Belle . . . well, she's unpredictable. Maybe flighty is the word. But she'd always know who had her baby, and she'd never let us alone. Sallie would never really be ours, and I don't think that'd be right for us or for the baby."

"You're sure?"

"Yeah, I'm *real* sure."

I went to sleep that night in Buck's arms, happy to be with him again. I was about to banish that little black cloud that floated over my head.

CHAPTER 10

We began serious work for the vaudeville show.

"You know," I said one day, "we can really take advantage of Guthrie as a high school horse. He's trained to do tricks that would be terrific on the stage and don't need the space of an arena."

Buck grinned. "You're right. We can work a whole segment of the show around that. But Cherokee, you still gotta rope. The audiences will expect it."

"What," I asked, "do I have to rope?"

"Me," he said with a grin.

The little black cloud was gone, Buck and I were happy, and Belle had left for Chicago where she said a friend would take her in until she could get on her feet. Buck missed Sallie desperately, but he was clearly relieved to be rid of Belle, and he did not go back to talking about when we would have our own child.

The colonel was sending three railroad cars on the vaudeville circuit—one for the troupe, one for the stock, and one for stage props. He himself was staying behind. "Got to see where we stand," he explained, "plan ahead for the next season. I want . . ." He looked almost sheepish as he continued. "I want to see if we can't take the show to Europe in a year or two."

"Europe!" I echoed. "Am I really gonna get to rope for the king? And use my convent French?"

The colonel grinned. "You might, Cherokee, you just might. But I have to work on my brothers, convince them I won't lose the ranch for the sake of the show. Buck will be in charge when you all are on the road."

Buck was trying to look humble and doing a poor job of it. One look at him told me he already knew that the colonel was going to make that announcement. It didn't bother me, for I certainly wanted someone else to be in charge.

"But Buck," the colonel went on, "you remember that Cherokee is the star of the show. She's got a say in things, too."

Buck grinned at him—maybe too quickly—and said, "That won't be a problem, Colonel. Cherokee and I pretty much see things the same way."

I nodded my head in agreement. Right then, it seemed like the truth to me. Funny how love, or stars, or the moon, or something can blind us.

I practiced every day—twirling a loop, building a larger one that Buck and I could walk in and out of, putting Guthrie through his paces of kneeling, playing dead, raising on his hind legs—all the kinds of things I thought would work in vaudeville. A part of me missed the rough stock and the relay races and the excitement of the Wild West events, but I told myself this was only a brief vacation. Come spring, I'd be back on the bucking horses, throwing big loops and roping calves.

One day I caught Buck behind the barn—literally—with his guitar. I'd been currying Guthrie and thought I heard singing from somewhere—I think it was "Home on the Range." Puzzled, I let myself out of the stall and followed the sound. There was Buck, sitting on a stump, strumming his guitar and singing all by himself.

I listened for a minute without letting him know I was there. He wasn't Enrico Caruso, but he had a nice voice, soft and gentle, sort of like what you thought a real cowboy might sound like if he sang. 'Course I'd never known a real cowboy to sing, but the audience wouldn't know that. When Buck came to the end of the song, I clapped.

"Cherokee! I didn't know you were there." He was clearly embarrassed.

"Did you mind?" I asked, walking toward him.

He jumped up from the stump. "No . . . yes—no, I'm just still pretty self-conscious about singing."

I laughed. "You shouldn't be. It was good. Every woman in the audience will want to take you home with her—but I won't let them." I linked my arms through his, and he put a companionable hand on mine.

"Thanks, Cherokee. The colonel insisted a singing cowboy was essential to the act, and he elected me. No objections allowed."

"You can sing to me, and then I'll rope you," I laughed.

That's just how we did it. Buck opened the show by riding across the stage, playing his guitar and singing "Home on the Range," "The Yellow Rose of Texas," and a couple of other favorites. He wore an outfit no respectable working cowboy would have been caught dead in—tan pants and a tan shirt with dark brown cording and embroidered flowers on the yoke, a brown Stetson and shiny brown boots that had clearly never been used for anything more strenuous than sitting astride a horse and singing. He was, as Bo would have said, a "dandy." I thought that once as I watched him go through his act and then wondered why Bo came suddenly, unbidden, into my mind.

As Buck neared the end of his last song, I rode Guthrie onstage from the wings, waited until the audience was applauding, and then sailed my rope over his shoulders—he was always careful to hand the guitar to someone just before I threw my loop.

Inevitably, the audience gasped, and Buck pretended to look confused for a moment. This time there was no bell-toned announcer to interpret for the audience, to roar "The little lady's husband, folks!" Vaudeville was much subtler, and the audience was left to make their own interpretations when I slowly drew Buck toward me—both of us still ahorseback—and we met to lean across the horses and exchange a chaste kiss.

Buck rode off, and I did some fairly standard rope tricks, stepping in and out of my own loop and such. Then Buck came back, and I built a loop around the two of us. That of course called for another kiss, and I began to feel that I was in a romantic comedy rather than a Wild West vaudeville show.

We opened in St. Louis at the old Orpheum Theatre. The first thing we did on arriving in the city was go to the theater to look at the stage. Outside the theater displayed posters billing "Cherokee Rose and the Miller

101 Wild West Show—first time on stage! Thrills, excitement, real western adventure!" The poster had a picture of a girl who looked vaguely like me—only she looked like she was twelve years old.

"That's not me!" I exclaimed indignantly.

Buck was amused. "Have I married myself a child bride?"

"I want my picture to look like me *now*," I said, "not like I did when I went on that wolf hunt with Roosevelt. Do I look at all like that?"

Buck studied the poster a long minute, then turned to look at me. I wanted to remind him that he should know what I looked like without having to stare at me!

"Sort of," he said. "You don't quite look twelve. Maybe sixteen." He ducked my upraised hand and went on, "It's the blond hair, Cherokee, and—well, gosh, you're gonna make me feel silly. But you look sort of sweet. Maybe innocent is the word I want." Then he took a big step away from me before he said, " 'Course I know you're not innocent, and you're sure not always sweet!"

I knew, no matter what he said, that I had grown and changed a lot in recent years, and I did *not* look like a twelve- or sixteen-year-old cherub. I was tall, like my parents, and still very fair, like Papa. At twenty-two I was still as skinny as I had been as a kid, and I fully expected to stay that way—after all, Mama was still pretty thin and they say a girl gets those traits from her mother. But I also knew that all the things that had happened to me—Bo, and the loss of Rose, and life on the road, and yes, Buck—had changed me, and that that change showed in my eyes, maybe even in the expression on my face when I wasn't onstage. No, I wasn't twelve years old in spirit any more than I was in body.

That night when I thought Buck was sound asleep, I stood in front of the long mirror in our hotel room without a stitch of clothes on and took a good look at myself. I hadn't reached any conclusions when I heard Buck murmur, "Looks pretty damn good to me!"

Next day we did a dry run of the act. "I don't like it," I said after I rode Guthrie on to the stage. "We'll be too close to the audience for their safety or ours."

Buck told me not to worry. "I've designed a portable fence," he said. "It'll hang from the usual theater rigging—up where the curtain is—and go between the stage and the orchestra pit. So if a horse gets unruly, it can't go toward the audience. Safe as can be, sweetheart."

I wished I believed him. Somehow I had trouble envisioning an audience watching me through a fence. But of course, that's what happened. By opening night, there was dirt spread several inches deep on the stage floor, and that fence hung between us and the audience. I held my breath in anxiety.

We really were in vaudeville.

The first night went better than I could ever have hoped. There were hitches, of course—the band started to play just as Buck began singing, completely drowning him out, and I, from nerves I guess, came close to missing him with my first loop. But the audience was enthusiastic and responsive.

Our act was preceded by some more traditional vaudeville acts—singing and dancing, which, in theater language, "warmed up" the audience. I laughed when I heard that and told Buck we'd learn a whole new way of talking.

"Nope," he drawled, "we'll probably teach those singers and dancers a vocabulary they never heard before."

After Buck and I did the opener together, I came back on the stage and did some fairly basic rope tricks, mostly while mounted on Guthrie. Then I put Guthrie through his paces—rolling over, kneeling for me to mount, and all that, and ending with him rearing back on his hind legs, which was always showy and splendid because he was such a magnificent horse.

The exciting part of the show came when the cowboys brought in the rough stock. They actually roped a calf on that tiny stage—and caught it before it made it off the other side. But I held my breath when they rode the rough stock—to see a bronc bucking and kicking on that small stage scared the living daylights out of me. Nothing happened, beyond some folks in the front row getting dirt kicked in their faces.

At the end of our act, we were called back for extra bows, and the audience called out for Cherokee and Buck. So I took my rope and built a loop around the two of us again. It became the standard close for the show as well as the opener.

"Whew! I'm tired," I said when we were finally back at our hotel.

"It's gonna work," Buck said. "It's really gonna be a good show, Cherokee!"

"Yeah, but it sure is hard on my nerves."

"You'll get used to it."

I did get used to it, but it seemed I was always anticipating trouble, always waiting for a bronc to get out of control, a calf to break loose from the rope. It's good I didn't know the old theater wisdom that wished actors to "break a leg"—I'd have taken it literally.

"Cherokee, you worry too much. Look how perfect everything's going. We got good crowds, and they like us. The act is getting better every time we do it. Nothin's gonna happen."

We played Springfield, Peoria, and Rockford, in Illinois, working our way north into Wisconsin and finally coming to Milwaukee, from where we'd head down into Chicago.

It was in Milwaukee that Buck had his wonderful idea. "Cherokee, the show needs a new punch. Why don't you ride one of the broncs?"

"On that small stage? Absolutely not." There was no use talking further about it, as far as I was concerned.

Buck was smart. He shrugged and let it go. But the subject kept coming up again and again. Sometimes it was, "If we had a girl to ride a bronc . . ."

"Call Belle," I said nastily one day.

"Now, Cherokee, you know I don't want anybody but you in the show. You're the star!"

"I'm the star that won't ride a bronc on a small stage," I said.

The colonel met us in Chicago. It was the first time he'd seen the show actually performed, and he was impressed and full of praise. "I knew you could do it," he said heartily. "Cherokee, you pleased with the routine?"

"It's fine," I said. "Seems to please the audiences, and we're getting some good publicity in almost every town we go to."

Buck nodded. "Sometimes," he said, "I think we need to add a little more drama to it. You know, something the audience doesn't expect."

"Can't do an Indian massacre or a stagecoach holdup on the stage," I said sarcastically. I knew what he was headed toward.

"I've tried to get Cherokee to ride a bronc," he told the colonel, "but she refuses. Says the stage is too small."

It angered me that Buck would try to work around me, use the colonel to force me into doing what he wanted. "I don't think," I said, my voice shorter than I intended, "that you should agree to do something you're not capable of." I wanted badly to remind the colonel of Carmelita, who claimed she could ride a bull. Hadn't he learned anything from that lesson?

"But you can ride rough stock," the colonel said, obviously intrigued by the idea. "You ride better than most of my cowboys, and if they can ride on the stage, so can you."

I saw through him at once, of course. He was trying to play up to my pride in my riding. It wouldn't work, I told myself.

The subject was dropped for a day or so. And then it came up again, with the colonel pressing me to give it a try, while Buck sat back and watched with the satisfaction of a man who has put the wheels into motion and has only to watch the action play itself out.

I refused again, and the colonel shrugged.

The third time he brought it up, he was more clever. He spoke to Buck, knowing that I would hear every word—we were, after all, sharing breakfast in a hotel dining room. "I been talking to a little gal from Texas. Says she'll ride anything anywhere. You know those Texas girls. I'll bet she can do it."

"You think she'd ride a bronc on the stage?" Buck asked, wide eyes innocent.

"Bet she would," the colonel replied.

"All right," I said, standing up suddenly, "I'll ride the damn bronc. But you two be warned—if anything happens, it's on your heads."

They both began to protest, until I wanted to paraphrase Shakespeare for them—"Methinks you doth protest too much!"

"Now, Cherokee, we didn't mean . . ."

"Cherokee, I don't want you to do anything you don't want to. . . ."

"I'll ride the horse," I said and walked away, leaving the two of them to gloat.

After that, I rode a bronc at the end of the rough stock portion of the show. It meant, among other things, that I was onstage for almost all of the Wild West act, a fact that probably escaped Buck. But I sure knew it when I left the theater at night, more tired than I'd ever been after any performance.

"I won't ride with the stirrups hobbled," I said.

"Now, Cherokee, that's the way women ride."

"Women," I said, "don't ride rough stock on a stage. If I'm going to do this, I'll do it the way men do."

"Just trying to make it safe for you," Buck said.

Relations between Buck and me had been frosty for days. I felt I'd been tricked into a ride I didn't want to make and, worst of all, by my own husband. It came to me slowly that he was putting the show before me—or before what was between us. And then of course, that was a puzzle—did I admire his professional dedication, or did I want him to be a husband first and Wild West show producer second, or the other way around?

I didn't have to deal with such philosophical nuances to know that I was angry at Buck Dowling. And he didn't have to wonder if I was or not. At night, I lay tightly curled on my side of the bed and mumbled a distant "Goodnight" to him. And he, too proud to do anything else, replied, " 'Night," and turned his back to me. We were in a Mexican standoff.

I rode a bronc onstage the first time in Chicago, but I rode it without hobbles—and I stayed on for eight seconds. Nothing bad happened. The horse bucked and pitched enough to give the audience a thrill but not enough to shake me loose from its back. Contrary to my certain expectations, we did not fly through Buck's fence to land in the audience, though I did look with worry a time or two at the band in the unprotected pit below. We could easily have pitched off the stage to land on those poor musicians. Lucky for us we didn't.

The audience was on its feet when I finished the ride, and flushed with a double success—staying on the bronc and overwhelming the audience—I took a long deep bow with an enormous grin on my face.

"See?" Buck was quick to say. "I told you it would be a real pick-me-up for the show."

I wouldn't—couldn't—give him the satisfaction of agreeing, but we did reconcile that night. It occurred to me, even in the midst of passion, that we might better talk out our differences than wash them away with physical love. But I said nothing and, subconsciously, moved a slight emotional distance further away from Buck Dowling.

It wasn't me that got into the trouble I anticipated from riding rough stock in a confined space. It was the musicians who got the worst of it, but I ended up in the middle of the fracas. Fortunately, the colonel had gone back to Oklahoma by the time this happened.

One of the cowboys—an Oklahoma ranch boy named Hank—was on a bronc named Spitfire who lived up to his name by sunfishing or twisting like a fish on a line. He twisted too far and went off the stage and into the pit with a great crash, scattering the musicians while the audience screamed in panic. The noise only frightened the poor horse more, and he began to thrash about, trying to get to his feet. He could not, of course. There wasn't room for him to right himself, even if one hind leg hadn't been stuck right through the cello.

Watching from the wings, I saw in my mind for one brief second Buck Dowling bravely playing his horn while an enraged bull contemplated charging him. But I was instantly back to the present and into action, knowing what I had to do without thinking about it. Two cowboys beat me to the pit and began to try to quiet the horse while Hank, fortunately only dazed, freed himself from the thrashing animal. But the more the cowboys tried to quiet him, the more terrified Spitfire became. They could not, without risking life and limb, get close enough to get the cello fragments off his hoof.

I went straight for the downed animal's head and, using all the body strength I had, sat on it, bending my face down next to his ear. Simultaneously I began to croon softly to him, while biting gently on his ear. It was an old trick Billy Rogers had taught me—the horse will be so concerned about saving his ear that he will stay very quiet. Old-timers used to "ear down" bucking horses to allow riders to get safely mounted.

Spitfire quieted immediately, though I could feel his flesh trembling in fear. Working quietly, the cowboys freed his leg, loosened the saddle, and cleared all the chairs, music stands, and instruments away from me. All the while I talked to the horse, and the cowboys talked to me. "Just one more minute, Cherokee. . . . Can you hold on, Cherokee? . . . When I give the signal, Cherokee, you jump clear." Though we were quietly working to calm the horse, the audience was in a turmoil, and waves of noise seemed to rush over me.

Beyond the cowboys' quiet talk and the frantic buzzing of the audience, I heard one loud, anguished cry of "Cherokee!" Buck had been in the dressing room when the accident happened. Now, if I trusted my ears, he stood directly above me at the edge of the stage. I prayed that he would not repeat that wail, and he didn't. All I could think was that the loud cry was instinctive and then his practical side took over. What I heard next was his voice—calm but loud—pleading for quiet from the audience.

"Folks, we've got this under control, but we need your help. We've got to ask you to be absolutely quiet until this horse is freed." I could picture him holding up his hands, begging for cooperation. The audience never did become absolutely still, but the noise level dropped a good bit.

It seemed an eternity that I had that horse's ear in my teeth and felt him trembling beneath me, wondering all the while if fear was going to make him forget about his ear and explode into frantic action. But then, softly, came the call, "Jump clear *now*, Cherokee," and jump I did.

For a moment, Spitfire was stunned and lay still. Then, kicking and neighing, he struggled to his feet. Miraculously, he seemed to stand on all four legs, none broken. He was spent, and once righted he stood quietly, head down. I went quickly to him and began stroking his nose, assuring him in soft tones that I wouldn't bite his ear anymore.

Buck took over, telling the audience that the horse was fine, the rider was all right. Would they please, he asked, take an intermission and clear the theater briefly, so that we could get the horse out of the musicians' pit. A little grumbling followed, but soon the theater was almost empty. The cowboys used several wide planks to build a ramp up which they could lead Spitfire. He was retired from action for the day and given an extra ration of oats.

I got a tongue-lashing. Oh, not right away. Not until we were back in our hotel room.

"Damnfool thing to do," Buck stormed. "Scaring the life out of me, risking your own life."

"We saved the horse, didn't we?" I asked edgily. "What else did you want me to do? Stand there and watch that horse thrash about until it broke a leg or two and had to be destroyed, probably right there in front of the audience?"

"*I* could have gone down into that pit," he said. "There was no call for you to do it. You're a girl, Cherokee! Sometimes I think you forget that!"

There was no sense telling him how illogical he was. He wanted to take advantage of my being a girl, having me risk danger when I rode a bronc onstage, but he was furious when I took a risk that, to me, was much more justifiable. Maybe, I thought, he was angry—jealous?—that I had been the one to do the so-called courageous act. It was supposed to be a man who saved the day in a tight situation, not his wife.

"Would you have eared him down?"

"What?"

"Would you," I asked patiently, "have bitten his ear?"

"Hell, no, I wouldn't have bitten some horse's ear."

"Good thing I was there," I said, and turned away.

The newspaper headline the next day blared "Cowgirl Saves Horse!" and "Cherokee, the Heroine of the Day!" We made the front pages of the Chicago papers in stories that would surely increase attendance at the show and maybe even call for a longer Chicago run. Buck took one look at the papers, threw them across the room, and stormed out. I didn't see him again until show time that night, and by then I had decided he would have to come to me. I was through apologizing. And this time we would talk.

It wasn't until we arrived in Detroit that we talked, and by then it was almost time to go to Oklahoma. We had been to Michigan City and Grand Rapids between Chicago and Detroit, and Buck and I had been outwardly polite, especially in front of the rest of the troupe, but inwardly frosty. At night, we slept carefully so as not to touch each other, and I wondered about the feasibility of separate hotel rooms.

Finally, after the first show in Detroit, Buck spoke. Maybe he was prompted by the fact that the show was only a medium success. The audience had been polite, but not enthusiastic the way that crowds in earlier cities had. Our timing was off—the timing of the whole crew—and I knew it was because the trouble between Buck and me was spreading throughout the entire show. If Buck hadn't spoken, I would have—and the results might have been very different.

"Cherokee, we got to talk," he began tentatively. "We can either let this thing sit between us like a permanent wall, or we can talk about it."

"I'll listen," I said, willing to be cooperative.

"So I've got to talk?" For a moment I thought he was going to be angry, and I bristled defensively. But then he said, "Maybe I was wrong to get mad at you. You didn't jump into that pit to scare me or make me angry."

"You weren't even in my thoughts for a second," I said, and then I chuckled. "Yes, you were, too."

He was startled, uncertain. If I was taking this lightly, the temper he was holding in tight control would flare out.

"Just before I jumped, I remembered the first time I ever saw you—playing your horn while that bull pawed the ground and eyed you, the bull that Carmelita couldn't ride."

He grinned sheepishly. "So we're both too brave for our own good. It's just that—Cherokee, I don't want you doing things that a lady shouldn't."

I took a deep breath. "I'm not just a lady, Buck, and I'm not just your wife. I'm a cowgirl and a performer. I grew up ahorseback, and I'll probably always act instinctively around horses. You're right, someday it may get me killed, but I can't do anything else." I wanted to add, "And I sure can't think about what you'll say before I throw a rope or spur a bronc. There isn't time." But I didn't say that. Nor did I ask if he was embarrassed by me.

Buck sat in our hotel room's lone chair, his elbows on his knees, his hands locked in front of him, and his eyes fixed on those locked hands. At long last, he raised his head. "Am I wrong to want a wife and a family, like every other man?"

I drew a deep breath. The question of babies was about to come up and get me again. "You're not wrong," I said slowly, "but that's not who you married. And to tell you the truth, Buck Dowling, I don't think that's who you are. If a rose-covered cottage was what you wanted, you wouldn't have been so pleased when the colonel put you in charge of this show. You like the traveling and the show as much as I do. It's just that you want me to be two people."

"Two people?"

"Right. The cowgirl you married, who can ride and rope, and who even lets you force her into riding rough stock on a stage, and at the same time, a wife and mother who raises the children, cooks the meals, and waits for you to come home at night. You can't have both, Buck, and you better decide which one you want."

I picked up my coat—a luxuriant fox that Buck had bought me in a moment of feeling rich and on top of the world—and left the room, headed I didn't know where, but anywhere away from Buck. It wasn't that I was angry at him or in a hurry to get away from him, but I thought he needed to think, *really think,* about what I'd just told him. As a matter of fact, my own insight had surprised even me.

Buck was asleep, or so I thought, when I returned. I had actually spent the evening in the hotel restaurant, talking to the cowboys and giving a casual answer to their questions about where Buck was. They were not used to seeing us apart, another thought that gave me pause.

I undressed quietly and crawled carefully into my side of the bed, prepared to lie still even though my thoughts were tossing and turning. But a hand reached gently for me, turning me toward him, and Buck soon began to stroke my back, wordlessly. His hands became more insistent, moving to my stomach and my thighs, and I could not have kept myself from responding if I had wanted to. Trouble was, I wasn't sure I wanted anything else but Buck Dowling's hands on me.

When we were spent, sweaty and panting in each other's arms, he said, "All I want is you, Cherokee. If we never have babies, so be it." Then with a chuckle in his voice, he added, "And if you never cook me a meal, I'll probably live to be an old man."

Indignant, I squashed a pillow over his face. "I'm a *good* cook," I said. "I can make mayonnaise."

"Who wants to eat mayonnaise every day?" he asked, now laughing aloud.

And we made love again, our passion this time full of fun and lightness. For all that Buck and I had been through, that was one of our better nights together.

We were on the vaudeville circuit for fourteen months, from early 1912 to the spring of 1913, with a return to the Wild West show and outdoor performances during the summer months. But we played on stages in almost every town of any size in the Midwest, moving as far east as Ohio and as far west as Kansas, even once dipping down into Texas, which I fully expected to be a different land. It wasn't, but the people were louder and they bragged more. Still, they took us into their hearts, and I vowed to return to the Lone Star State someday.

Buck and I were riding a seesaw during those vaudeville days. Sometimes we were lovers and friends, just as we'd started our marriage, but other times there was a tension between us—not the electricity of attraction but a tension that threatened at any moment to break into open warfare. We were professionals, and we knew we had to work together, so most of the time we kept it under control.

Oh, there were momentary flashes, and then we'd see the troupe watching us warily, trying not to stare and yet curious to see if we could perform the opening rope trick without killing each other. Usually one or the other of us took the proverbial bull by the horns and made the first advance, and we patched it up, whether we'd quarreled about something that happened in the show or Buck's tendency to spend a *lot* of money or the sorry kind of a hotel I'd booked us into. We never quarreled about children, but the subject was always there, lurking beneath the surface.

That second winter, we went to Oklahoma for the holidays. "No audience over Christmas," the colonel had wired, though he was quick to tell us when we arrived at the 101 that he had booked a New Year's Eve show in Oklahoma City. I figured to spend Christmas day with my parents, then go on to Guthrie and pick up the show in Oklahoma City.

"You want to go?" I asked Buck.

"Don't you think," he asked coldly, "you could have worked out your plans with me? I am half of this marriage, though sometimes it doesn't seem like it."

I was stunned—and rightly taken to task. "You're right," I said, "and I apologize. Would you like to go with me?"

"I'd like to spend Christmas here at the 101," he said, but his voice had a petulance about it that made me think he was deliberately being contrary. If I'd said I wanted to stay at the 101, he'd have been for Luckett's or even Guthrie.

"Buck," I said gently, "my parents are getting on, and my mother is not well. It's important for me to spend the holiday with them."

"She won't know you've been there."

"No," I said patiently, "but I'll know."

"And do we have to go to Guthrie?"

Once, in one of our arguments, he had accused Louise of turning me against him, filling me with unworthy thoughts about being an independent woman. I had reminded him that Louise had always treated him with nothing but courtesy, but he carried a lingering feeling that she was the enemy.

"You don't have to go to Guthrie," I told him. "I do." I wanted to add that he sounded suspiciously like he was whining.

We went together, though at first I wished he'd stayed at the 101. I was afraid he'd be unpleasant around Papa, though I should have known better. They shared a kind of bond that I never could understand, let alone anticipate.

Our visit went as well as could be expected. Papa, knowing in advance that we were coming, had cooked a big turkey dinner—wild turkey, of course—and had even decorated a small tree. Under the tree was a miniature rearing horse that he had carved for me out of maple he got who knows where—it was exquisite in every detail and much resembled Guthrie.

"It's Guthrie," I breathed.

"Close as I could come," he said with satisfaction. Since Papa had to stay home so much with Mama, he'd taken up whittling and gotten right good at it. For Buck, there was a handsome plaid flannel shirt and a new band for his Stetson. He was obviously pleased.

We'd brought Papa a smoking jacket, which he declared far too grand to ever be worn, but I assured him back east men wore them around the house. It was velvet and elegant, and I thought Papa deserved a touch of elegance in that tiny ranch house that now bounded his life. For Mama, I brought a warm afghan—she had plenty of blankets, but I wanted her to have one that would remind her of me when she wrapped it about her.

Mama had failed a great deal since my last visit—isn't that how people say it? "She's failing fast." I didn't want to hear it, and I didn't want to think about it, but the clear picture was before me. In three days, she recognized me just twice, both times with great joy and exclamations that clearly indicated she thought I was about twelve years old. The whole visit she assumed Buck was Papa's hired hand and gave him peremptory orders to which he always replied with appropriate subservience, so that she thought he really would go muck out the barn when she told him it needed doing and Mr. Burns should not have to do it.

"Sometimes," Papa said, "she has trouble breathing at night. I—I don't know what I'll do if something happens in the middle of the night."

I squeezed his hand and said, "You'll do whatever you can, Papa. The Lord's will be done." The words were trite unless they revealed a deeper religious conviction than I had, but I meant them nonetheless. I figured Mama was in the Lord's hands, and it was only a matter of time. No doubt she would be happier when he called her home, and she was already beyond thinking of the effect on those of us left behind.

When we left, I knew I would not see Mama again, and that the next time I saw Papa, we would bury Mama. I held her tight and stroked her hair and left with tears in my eyes. Papa said nothing but gave me a strong hug.

If anybody had asked me when I was growing up, I'd've said that I would be close to my mother all my life and never reach any kind of closeness to my father. "A daughter is a daughter, all of her life." Funny how things turn out.

Our visit in Guthrie was more strained—Buck and Louise danced around each other like sparring partners in the boxing ring, and Louise and I never did get a private visit. We shopped some, with Buck ostentatiously buying me a new hat with a feather in the hatband and a wonderful buttery-soft silk shirt. But his largesse did little to impress Louise. She could sense the rift between us, and she had no sympathy for Buck.

The last morning we were there, we sat late at the breakfast table, though I knew Louise itched to be up and about, doing the dishes, starting the noonday meal. Still, she was the one who lingered, when I would have risen to help out.

"You seen Bo?" she asked with sudden directness.

"No, you know I haven't."

She ignored that. "His wife is not well. Doing poorly, as they say. I suspect she won't live long. She had a pregnancy, but the baby died. I don't know what went wrong, but something."

I was thunderstruck. I'd carried this vision of Bo living happily ever after with this person he'd married, whoever she was. "I—I don't know what to do."

"I don't think you should do anything. I sure don't think you should go out there. That would upset Ruth. She knows pretty much about you."

Ruth, I thought. *Was she as plain as her name?* "Tell him," I said, "that I asked about him."

She nodded, and only then, having said what she wanted, did she get up to do the dishes. I helped her, while Buck sat in the parlor and practiced new songs on his guitar. He'd never said a word about Bo, though he knew full well who Bo was and what he'd meant to me.

"Gosh," he said as we rode south from Guthrie, "am I glad to be away from all your family! Sorry, Cherokee, but that's an honest statement. I feel like I have to watch my every step with all of them. Makes me tighter than a drum. I'm feelin' better already."

What could I possibly have said in reply to that? I simply spurred my horse and raced him down the road.

As we neared Oklahoma City, we realized that we were out of date. There were few horses on the road and many, far too many automobiles. One driver honked indignantly at us, spooking Buck's horse until it took off through a pasture. Buck hung on for dear life, sawed on the reins, and yelled angrily. When he finally had the horse under control and rode back to where I waited, he was visibly angry.

"Damnfool! Doesn't he know horses had the roads first? It just ain't right for automobiles to be taking over everything!"

I laughed aloud at him. "No, it's not, but I guess we're going to have to accept progress in whatever form." I remembered the car that had spooked my horse when I rode with Mrs. Roosevelt in Washington all those years ago, and I decided that Buck and I had been insulated against the changes taking place in the country. We'd gone from city to city by train and rarely ridden in automobiles, though by that year—1912—more and more of the darned things were appearing on the roads.

That was nearly the last trip Buck and I ever took by horseback—and almost the last trip we ever took together.

The show went well in Oklahoma City—after all, weren't we on home territory? Weren't we the local stars? For a week we played to capacity audiences who stood and cheered for us after each performance. Papa even came down from Luckett's for one performance, having asked a neighboring ranch lady to stay with Mama, and he beamed with pride when he was introduced to the audience as my father. A photographer took a picture of Papa, Buck, and me, our arms around each other's shoulders, showing the world what a close happy family we were. So much for photography!

From Oklahoma City, we went to Bartlesville, then on into Missouri, where we played Joplin, Springfield, Jefferson City, and finally Kansas City. Then we worked our way up into Iowa, playing Des Moines, Cedar Rapids, Ames, and Sioux City. The plan was to work our way east then, across the top of Illinois, and close the show with a grand performance in Chicago.

It was in Chicago that my marriage to Buck fell finally and utterly apart—though we stuck it out almost two years after that. The last night of the show, when we had closed in triumph, on a high note, the cowboys begged and cajoled until Buck agreed to celebrate with them.

"You mind, Cherokee? I really think I ought to go." He was apologetic and charming.

In truth, I did mind. There were no girls in the troupe for me to celebrate with, and since this was clearly a boys' night out, I would simply have to go back to the hotel room alone and pack our clothes so we could leave for Oklahoma the next day. But Buck didn't do that very often, and I decided I'd best be a good sport about it.

"No, no," I said, "you go on. Just behave yourself." I added that almost as a joke, an afterthought, a way of teasing, but he shot me an alarmed look.

"You don't have to tell me that," he said tightly.

"Of course I don't, Buck, I was just teasing." I reached to kiss him lightly, but his utter lack of response told me I'd made a serious error. It was one of those times I wanted desperately to have a chance to replay the last three minutes of my life and to write a new script.

Packed and organized, I finally went to sleep. Buck came in well after midnight, pounding on the door and shouting my name because he'd not taken a key.

"Hush!" I said as I opened the door. "You'll wake everyone in the hotel."

"Don't care if I do," he said belligerently, and I knew immediately he was drunk. It was a new experience for me—I had never ever in our years of marriage known Buck Dowling to drink too much. But there he was, weaving before me and talking far too loud.

With a lurch, he reached for me. "C'mere, Cher'kee. You know what we're gonna do?"

"I," I said coldly, "am going to sleep. You may do what you wish."

"No, no, you aren't gonna sleep. You and me, we're gonna make some babies."

My blood froze. No drunk, not even my husband, was going to make love to me. And the mention of babies—the topic that hadn't come up in months—alarmed me. Had the boys been teasing him about our childless state?

"Buck," I said bluntly, "you're drunk."

"Never been more in control," he said. "That's it, Cher'kee . . . control . . . I'm takin' control of our lives. It's 'bout time I acted like a man."

Someone had sure planted a bad seed in his mind! "Buck, don't touch me!"

"Now, Cher'kee, you can't tell me that. I'm your husban'."

Buck Dowling had never laid a hand on me, never even been a rough lover, and I could not believe he would hurt me. Yet there was about him now something I didn't recognize, a look that frightened me. I glanced around the room quickly, looking for something with which to defend myself if it came to that, but I saw nothing, other than a lamp that was far too heavy for me to lift.

He came toward me, weaving a little but obviously strong in his determination, pulling off his shirt as he came. "C'mon, Cher'kee, get out o' that nightgown."

"Buck," I warned, backing away, "don't come any closer to me."

He stopped, surprised at the strength in my voice. But then he seemed to recall his mission and moved forward.

Panic rose in my throat for just a minute, but I was used to putting panic beside me and dealing with horses and cattle. Surely I could do it with my own husband. I'd seen enough fights in my day—cowboys behind the stands at the shows, mostly—that I knew what to do. I waited until he was close enough, and then I raised my knee hard. I didn't quite have the heart to hit him in the crotch—instead, I plowed my knee, with the full force of my body behind it, into his stomach, and when he doubled over, the air going out of him with a great "Ooomph!", I swung my fist upward. I meant to hit his chin, but my aim wasn't very good and I clipped his cheekbone, just beneath his eye, with more force than I intended. With one plaintive cry of "Cher'kee!" he wilted.

I let him lie on the floor and went to bed, though I tossed and turned all night, listening for him to waken, wondering what he'd do. Maybe I should have fled, but I had nowhere to go. Surely, I thought, he'll be sober when he awakens and realize what he did.

Although he moaned and groaned during the night, it was nearly daylight before he came to consciousness. I sensed more than heard him when he sat up, groaned, and tried to stand. In the dark, I saw that he was unsteady and holding his head.

"You all right?" I asked. "Want the light?"

"No! No light. I guess I'll live, but I must've been a damnfool last night." He wandered around the room for some time, then came to sit gingerly on the far side of the bed. "Cherokee, I—I'm not sure I remember everything . . . but did you hit me last night?"

"You were going to force me," I said levelly. "Yes, I hit you—hard!"

"I remember that," he said, shaking his head, "but I don't remember forcing myself on you."

"You didn't get the chance," I said.

It developed that Buck had no permanent damage, but he did have a tremendous headache and a dilly of a black eye. The shiner, I told him, was my fault; the headache, his.

As we sorted out our emotions, it was clear to me, though Buck didn't realize it, that liquor had released in him some angers he'd been hiding—about my being the star, about babies. They were differences we probably couldn't ever reconcile, and I knew right then and there the marriage was over.

But lots of times we put aside what we know, afraid to face it. And Buck was so contrite, so apologetic, so overwhelmed that he had been drunk and brutal—well, nearly so—that it hardly seemed right to say, "That's it, the marriage is over."

Instead, I said, "Buck, we're going back to Oklahoma. We'll . . . let's just see what happens."

He touched me very tentatively. "Cherokee, I love you."

No, Buck, I thought, you don't. But I didn't tell him that.

When we met the crew at the train, there was lots of catcalling and joking about his eye. "Walked into a door," he told them jauntily.

And so we headed back to the 101.

CHAPTER 11

Back in Oklahoma, things seemed normal, almost. If there was a strained distance between Buck and me, we kept it in the privacy of our bedroom. With the Millers and all the others, we were just as we'd always been, working together, planning the next season's show.

At night, lying stiff next to each other in bed, Buck and I were strangers, distantly polite, until at last one night he turned to me with almost a wail. "Ah, Cherokee, how long's this gonna go on?"

"I don't know," I answered softly.

Buck's hands were tentative, almost scared, as he reached for me. When I didn't pull away, he became surer of himself, and soon he had drawn me into his passion. But it was not the lovemaking of our early marriage, and I knew that things between us would never be the same again.

"Had a letter from Belle," Colonel Zack announced at dinner one night. "She's in California—Hollywood—making them new moving pictures."

"That so?" Buck was instantly alert. "How'd she get to doing that?"

"Don't know, but she says a lot of Wild West people are out there. Says it's pretty good money."

Buck turned to look at me, the question obvious in his eyes.

"Nope, Buck," I said, "I'm an Oklahoma girl. I'll travel where I have to, but I'm not going to California."

He laughed, as though to put the subject aside with lightness. "That's my Cherokee, always ready for a new adventure."

I could easily have gotten angry about it or indignant—after all, I considered myself adventuresome. Buck just didn't know how lucky he was—or what dull women he could have been married to. But I didn't think it was worth trying to tell him at that point.

"Well," the colonel drawled, "I sure hope you're both adventuresome. I got an adventure for you."

"Madison Square Garden again?" I asked with a smile.

"No, Cherokee, something better. England." He said it with a straight face, and I knew instantly that he wasn't joking. Silence hung heavy over the dinner table, until finally his mother echoed faintly, "England?"

"That's what I said. Maybe even France."

"You're serious," Buck said, stating the obvious.

"Never been more serious," the colonel told him. "We leave in March. Gives us from now till then to get a show ready that's fit for a king."

England! Ever since the Buffalo Bill show went abroad, I'd dreamed of riding in England. And France! I remembered thinking I'd never get to use the French I'd struggled so hard to learn. Me, Tommy Jo Burns, from Luckett's ranch out in the middle of nowhere in Oklahoma, going to ride for the King of England. My heart did a flip-flop, and I suddenly discovered that I was shaking as though I were cold. Pure excitement.

"How long?" Buck asked, and the tone of his voice told me he was not as enthusiastic about the prospect as I was.

"Maybe a year," the colonel said. "See how it goes. We get the crowds I expect we will, we'll stay awhile. Costs a lot of money to get over there, so we better make it worth the getting."

Buck said nothing but looked at his plate. Later that night, we didn't talk at all about the overseas tour, and I knew that we were both consciously avoiding it. Neither of us had to tell the other that we were on opposite sides.

Papa called the 101 about a week later. I was in the arena, working out Guthrie, so Mrs. Miller took the message and then sent someone to look for me.

"It's your mother," the new young cowboy said. "You pa says you best come home right away. She's real poorly."

At that moment I understood the urge to shoot the messenger, but I thanked him as politely as I could and headed for the barn. Buck was there, checking out some tack, and his instant response was to ask if I wanted him to go with me.

"No," I said slowly, "I think I have to do this alone."

"I'll ride most of the way with you," he said. "I never did like having you ride back and forth alone."

"I'll be grateful for your company," I told him.

But I was poor company myself. We rode in silence, not because of distances between us but because I was lost in thought, remembering Mama at various times in my life, wondering how serious "poorly" was, hoping Papa was being an alarmist.

He wasn't.

Buck rode with me until I was almost within sight of Luckett's, though for the last ten miles I'd been urging him to turn back, knowing he'd have to sleep on the road.

"No," he said, "I'm gonna see that you're there."

I almost gave in and suggested he come on to the house with me, but something held me back. If Mama was really bad, it was a time to be just the three of us. Maybe if it had been a few years earlier and I'd still been madly in love with Buck Dowling, I'd have felt differently. But this was now, and that was how I felt.

With both of us ahorseback, Buck leaned over and gave me a peck on the cheek. "You can call if you need me, Cherokee," and he was gone, riding that horse too fast and too hard, considering all the miles it had already come.

I walked Governor into the ranch, going at a snail's pace to delay the inevitable.

Papa had seen me coming and was waiting on the porch, hands shoved into his pockets, the expression on his face unreadable. I dismounted and looped the reins over the hitching rail.

"Papa."

"Glad you're here, Tommy Jo. She's sleepin'. Been sleepin' for three days now."

I went up the steps and into his arms. "What's the doctor say?"

"He doesn't. Says she could leave us anytime. Or she could come out of it and outlive you and me both. Just no tellin'."

I went into the bedroom where Mama lay sleeping so peacefully that I hesitated even to take her hand. But I held that limp hand loosely in my own rough one and spoke as softly as I could, telling her I was there and that I loved her.

I sat an hour or more, with Papa creeping in and out of the room. I'd nod, and he'd leave as quietly as he came.

But then Mama opened her eyes—kind of fluttered them open—and looked directly at me. "Thomasina?" she said in a clear voice.

"Yes, Mama, I'm here."

Papa must have been hovering outside the door, listening for our voices, because he was back in the room right away. He went to the other side of the bed and knelt down, taking her other hand in his and saying in the gentlest voice I'd ever heard from him, "Jess, I love you."

"And I love you, James Burns," she said softly. Then she turned her head ever so slightly in my direction. "I'm proud of you, Thomasina. And I love you." As though the words had cost her a great effort, she closed her eyes.

"Papa?" I asked, alarm creeping into my throat like bile.

"She's all right," he said, and only then I saw that his fingers were lightly laid on the pulse in her wrist. "She's just sleeping."

We stayed that way, both of us at her bedside, for hours. I heard Mama's prized clock strike midnight, then one and two. Still Papa and I barely moved.

"She's gone," he said. Although his announcement was sudden, almost unexpected, it came softly, almost like a prayer.

"Gone?" I asked, disbelieving.

"Pulse kept getting weaker," he said, "and I knew there was nothing you nor I could do about it. I chose not to tell you, Tommy Jo, but I knew it was coming."

I laid my head down on my mother's chest and cried bitterly, Papa standing over me and stroking my hair. When I looked up, I realized that he still held her hand tightly clutched in his.

Buck and Colonel Zack came for the funeral two days later. Louise was there—I didn't know how Mama would have felt about that—and so was Bo. Even Mr. Luckett came over. But beyond that, there were few people to stand at the graveside and mourn Mama—only the cowboys who worked for Papa and the Methodist minister from Guthrie who performed the ceremony because Louise had bullied him into coming, even though we were not his parishioners. We were nobody's parishioners.

When he said, "Ashes to ashes, dust to dust," I looked around and saw not a tear, save on Papa's face. No one had known Mama, and she'd kept it that way. In spite of our differences, I clutched Buck's hand tightly. *He* knew me, and he'd have cried if it was my funeral. I found that a comforting thought.

Louise had sent food ahead with someone from town, and I'd spread it out in the house, so we had the traditional open house after the ceremony. Everyone tried to say something nice about Mama, but since they hadn't known her, they were hard put, and mostly the men ended up patting Papa on the shoulder and saying nothing. Louise simply said, "You know where I am if you need me," and I thought it was probably the most helpful comment of the day.

Your mother's death doesn't leave you in a day or two. It was a burden I would carry around with me for months, even years. But Mama used to say, as she shelled those infernal peas or worked on a piece of quilting, that being busy was balm for the soul. She was right—getting ready for the "world tour," as the colonel called it, put my grief to one side, even if it didn't make it go away.

We would leave in March—"First ship to cross as soon as the weather's clear," the colonel said, and I knew he'd have gone in January if he could have persuaded a ship's captain to brave the winter Atlantic. It would turn out that crossing in March was bad enough.

Dinner-table conversation ranged from what acts we would perform to the size of the troupe we would take with us.

"Can't just stick to Wild West subjects anymore," the colonel said. "Buffalo Bill's got all that eastern stuff in his show."

"Eastern?" I echoed.

"Not New York east," Buck said impatiently. "He's got Cossacks—you know, Cherokee, Russian soldiers—and a few years back he even reenacted that rebellion in China. Boxer Rebellion, they called it, I think, though I never did understand why."

I didn't want a history lesson from Buck Dowling. "I think we should stick to what we know," I said deliberately. "I don't want to ride in veils like I was in a harem. I want to do western things."

Buck's temper flared—you could tell from the way his eyes flashed—and he opened his mouth, but the colonel interrupted him. "Now just wait, you two. How about meetin' in the middle? We can—and should—do American subjects, but we can put in something like Paul Revere's ride."

"What's that got to do with the Wild West?" I asked.

"If he hadn't ridden, there wouldn't be a Wild West," Buck said, but the colonel went right on, "It's got everything to do with America. And those folks over there—they're not gonna be sure what's West and what isn't."

"I bet they remember Paul Revere," I said dryly, "and not with good memories."

In the end, we added Paul Revere's midnight ride in a skit that somehow also included Betsy Ross and the first American flag—I really did think that was waving our revolution in England's face a century and a half later and not good politics. But we also put in Daniel Boone, Davy Crockett, and the Alamo, and we agreed to do a massive reenactment of the Battle of Little Big Horn, involving about sixty soldiers and Indians.

"We got to call it 'Custer's Last Stand,' " the colonel insisted. "Nobody will recognize Little Big Horn."

I listened to all these discussions half in wonder and half in anger. What had happened to the colonel as a western purist? Where was that man who wouldn't even let Prairie Rose do any trick riding and who insisted on riding and roping as they were done on working ranches?

The colonel wanted a *big* show fit for royalty, and he showed a certain intensity as he went about recruiting new performers. He didn't hesitate to court performers from the Two Bills Show—that combination of Buffalo Bill and Pawnee Bill and their respective troupes. When those shows were slowly sinking, the colonel seemed to be able to promise the glamour of a show that was thinking big, on its way up, bound for the glory of England. But there were few stars left in those shows, and even fewer who would desert for the colonel. In the end, most of his riders came from ranches in Oklahoma and Texas. That pleased me, for they were men and women who had grown up riding and grown up western—no more fake señoritas from Brooklyn, or even Annie Oakleys who'd been raised in Ohio. We could boast a certain authenticity.

Then there were the Indians. They came from all tribes—Sioux, Comanche, Cherokee, and more—but the colonel would bill them all as Sioux. "They were the main ones at Custer's Last Stand," he growled. "Can't be confusing the audience with all those different tribes." I wondered if the Comanches knew he was passing them off as Sioux.

We also had a few *vaqueros* who rode silver-studded saddles and wore elaborately sequined and beaded outfits. They also had the most wicked-looking spurs I'd ever seen, which made me leery of the men. Fortunately, the colonel still remembered the lesson of the señorita; these *vaqueros* had no female counterparts.

The troupe was to number no less than seventy-five men, forty women, and fifty horses—not as big as Buffalo Bill at the height of his glory but much larger than the 101 had ever been, certainly large enough to give a spectacular show.

The new girls who began to arrive at the ranch interested me. They called themselves cowgirls, which sent my mind reeling back across the years. But these cowgirls were young, most had never ridden in a show, and many had literally never been off the ranch. At twenty-four, I felt more like a mother hen than anything. They came to me for advice and information.

"Don't you get scared when there's an audience?"

Yes, I told her, but that makes you ride and rope better. If you didn't get a little bit scared, you wouldn't be any good.

"What if your loop falls apart?"

You build it again, I told her with a smile.

"Has that ever happened to you?"

Laughing, I assured her it had. She was eighteen, a pretty but nonde-script girl named Pearl, come from Sweetwater, Texas, because her pa heard about the show. Her ma, she said, absolutely forbade her to go, but her pa had helped her run away in the night.

"I feel bad about Ma," she said, her lips beginning to tremble, "but I couldn't pass up a chance to ride for the King of England. I wrote Ma the nicest letter I could, but I ain't heard from her yet."

I bit my tongue to keep from correcting the grammar and wondered what stories all these other girls brought with them.

I was less interested in the cowboys. They were mostly eighteen or nineteen and looked amazingly innocent to me. They, in turn, apparently considered me too old, married, and the star of the show—they cut me a wide swath. I caught one, a slightly older fellow with blond hair that hung almost to his collartop, looking at me from time to time with laughter in his eyes, and once when I caught him, he raised an imaginary toast. I waved back and turned away, slightly embarrassed.

The cowboys lived in tents that winter, and the girls in two makeshift buildings the colonel had thrown up. Buck and I, the only old-timers and the only married couple, stayed in the main house, a fact that increased my distance from the girls even more. I never did, that long winter of practice, become close to any of those girls.

At Christmas, Buck and I went by carriage to see Papa and then took him down to Guthrie with us, where we all had Christmas dinner at Louise's generous dining table and afterward, with the few boarders gone back to their rooms, exchanged gifts in her parlor. It was strange to me that for the first time in several years I was part of a family at Christmas, and that was only because Mama was gone. I guess her shadow hovered over each of us in a different way, but we were quietly happy. Buck and Louise seemed to have signed some sort of truce, I guess out of deference to Mama's memory and Papa's grief—and mine. But it was only a truce. I knew that when I caught Buck watching Louise with real anger in his eyes, and by the way she ignored him except when she strained to say, "More turkey, Buck?" or "Another piece of pie?"

Buck and I left Papa at Louise's when we headed back to the 101. It was a cold blustery day, with the wind sweeping across the prairie as though it came direct from the North Pole. I was wrapped in an old buffalo robe that Mrs. Miller treasured and had insisted we take in the carriage, so I was snug and warm and even a bit sleepy, though the bouncing of the carriage over the rough road kept me awake. It would be a long day.

"Strangest family I ever saw," Buck said. He drove a team of horses with such a careless attitude that I sometimes wondered if he was in control as much as he should have been. Now he held the reins loosely and hunched down so that his elbows rested on his knees. He wore a warm greatcoat and had a blanket over his knees, but I knew he wasn't as warm as I was. Maybe the cold was making him philosophical.

"Your father's mistress is more like a mother to you than your own mother was. Doesn't that make you feel disloyal?"

I wanted to hit him. "No," I managed. "Mama understood about Louise."

"You mean she understood about your father going to see her," he probed.

"No," I said softly. I knew Mama had never understood that, and Papa had only chosen between them once Mama stopped trying to force him to choose, once she was too ill to care what he did. Then he had been a devoted husband, and this Christmas was the first time he'd been back to Louise's. "No, she only understood about what Louise did for me."

"Would you understand if I were interested in another woman?"

Would the man never stop? "Are you?" I asked wearily, wishing this interminable ride would end.

"No, no," he said quickly. "I just wondered—well, you know, if tolerance ran in your family."

I didn't know what to say. A year earlier I would have given him a stern warning not to test either fate or me, but now I wasn't sure if I cared if he looked at another woman or not. It might be a relief, and it might settle once and for all what was between us.

We rode most of the rest of the way in silence. And it was indeed a long day.

It was also a long winter, from January to March. If I thought I'd worked hard before getting ready for past shows, I didn't even know the meaning of the word. The colonel was merciless, and I doubt I slept eight hours any night those three long months.

We were up at dawn and in the arena by eight in the morning, no matter the weather. We rode and roped and paraded and raced in wind, sleet, and snow.

"Weather's always bad in England," the colonel would say cheerfully. "Got to get used to it." He wore an enormous fur coat and a Cossack-style hat pulled down over his ears on cold days and seemed impervious to discomfort.

I, on the other hand, was often miserable and prayed for that occasional bright day when the temperature rose almost to the sixties and you thought it wouldn't turn ugly again.

We had two long practice sessions daily, morning and afternoon, and evenings were spent working on costumes—at least the girls worked on costumes, while the men built props, repaired wagons and tack, and painted backdrops.

"I'd rather work on the tack than sew," I complained to Buck one night. "And I'd be a lot better at it." I had found him in one of the large sheds the colonel used for storing props. Buck had a hammer in his hand and three nails in his mouth, which he had to take out to talk to me.

"Cherokee, all the other women are sewing. Can't you just for once act like everybody else?"

Stung, I turned away from him and went back to my sewing in the house. I mended old costumes and put together new ones until my eyes were so blurry, I couldn't see the stitches, but I knew that my work was never neat enough to have satisfied Mama.

By the first of March, the costumes were ready, the sets designed, and the props prepared, with most all of it loaded onto the special train cars the colonel kept on the 101. He called a general meeting.

"We leave the 101 by train for New York City on March tenth," he announced. "We depart New York by ship on March twenty-first, arrive in England approximately ten days later. We will be there until late October, come home just before the Atlantic storms start in again. That's eight long months, folks, and I want each of you to think about that. Be sure you're prepared to be gone that long."

I thrilled with excitement at the thought—eight months in England and Europe! Impulsively I grabbed Buck's arm. "It's more than I ever dreamed of, Buck. Just think, we're going abroad! When I was in the convent in St. Louis, all those little rich kids used to talk about going abroad, and I always thought it was something I'd never get to do. I'd never get to use that French I worked so hard to learn!"

"Yeah," he said with a noticeable lack of enthusiasm.

"Buck, you aren't as excited about this as I am." I'd known that ever since talk of England first came up, but I'd managed to ignore it. Sometimes I'm a real slow learner.

"No, I'm really not, Cherokee." He bit his lip and looked away. In front of us, the colonel was still addressing the whole troupe, talking about arrangements and places I'd never heard of, like Shepherd's Bush in London. But the colonel had lost my attention now; I was puzzled by Buck.

When the meeting broke up, the colonel pulled me aside and asked me to meet him in his study. "You hear every word I said, Cherokee?" he asked, sitting down at his desk and pulling out a cigar.

"No," I said slowly, "I really didn't. I got distracted." I perched nervously on the edge of one of the chairs facing him. A small fire burned in the grate, giving the room a hot closed atmosphere, and I began to feel uncomfortable, as though I wanted a deep breath of clear fresh air, preferably cold.

"I know you didn't," he said, but both his tone of voice and his expression were kindly. "I saw you talking to Buck. What'd he say?"

I wondered just what the colonel knew that I didn't. "He just wasn't too enthusiastic about the tour," I said slowly. "He never has been."

"He doesn't want to go," the colonel said flatly, blowing a great cloud of blue smoke toward the ceiling. "Says, as a matter of fact, that he isn't going."

My instinctive reaction was one of panic. How could Buck not go? But it took me only a minute to put reason before instinct. The latter came from having been married to Buck for several years now and assuming that we had to be together all the time. Reason told me that we weren't very happy together, and I might have a better time on the tour if he *didn't* go along. But there was still the troubling matter that he'd told the colonel instead of me.

"Has he said that?" I finally asked.

The colonel had been patient, looking away while I sorted this thing out in my mind. Now he turned back to me and nodded to indicate a yes. "Couple days ago. I told him to take it up with you."

"He hasn't." What more could I say?

"Didn't figure he would. Cherokee, that boy's . . . well, *scared's* not the right word, but he doesn't want to cross you, and he doesn't know what he wants."

"But he doesn't want me?"

"Not necessarily. But maybe he doesn't want always to take second billing to his wife. Besides, do you really want him?"

I did a thing so unlike me that it puzzles me to this day. I burst into tears, clasping my hands over my mouth to hide the great roaring sobs that wanted to escape.

The colonel was uncomfortable and didn't know quite what to do. He heaved himself up from his desk and came around to where I sat, only to stand rather awkwardly patting my shoulder and saying, "There, there." Finally, after a long minute, he went in search of his mother.

Mrs. Miller came in and closed the door firmly behind her. "Don't need that fool son of mine right now," she said. "He's got no more idea what's troubling you than if you were a horse with a bellyache. Matter of fact, he'd be better at handling that."

With great efficiency but no lack of compassion, she handed me a fine lacy handkerchief for my eyes. I took it, but then was hesitant to use it.

"Go on, it's just lace. Not near as important as you are, dear."

So I dried my eyes and tried to sit up straight, and Mrs. Miller pulled another chair up close to mine and took hold of my hand. "I won't pretend to know what's bothering you, Tommy Jo"—the use of my old name almost sent me into wails again—"but I know you need a woman to talk to. Not me. I think you best go to Guthrie. She understands you better than anyone, and from what my sons tell me, she's a savvy woman."

It flashed through my mind that this wasn't easy for Mrs. Miller to say. As a mother, she may have resented Louise in her own way, just as Mama resented her. Maybe it was no easier to have your sons run after a woman in town than for your husband to—it was just different.

We sat in that room for a while, until I could get some control back, and then she said, "There's no one in the house right now. You go on and splash water on your face, get your appearance back."

I did as she told me.

But I couldn't let it go. Something in me made me confront Buck that night as we dressed for bed. "The colonel says you don't want to go on the tour."

"I tried to tell you that today." He sat on the edge of the bed, skinny yet strong in his underwear, and for just a moment I felt a flash of longing. But then I was angry again.

"Why didn't you tell me before you told him?"

"I didn't think you'd understand."

"What I do understand," I said distinctly, "is that our marriage is over." Even as I said that in an accusing tone, putting all the blame on him, I felt a twinge of guilt. Maybe the marriage was over because I wanted it to be, not because he did.

"I don't know that's true," he said, "but I guess some time apart might help us figure that out."

"You don't mean for me to stay back just because you're going to?"

He was almost too quick to answer, jumping up from the bed to stand in front of me. "Not at all, Cherokee. This is important to you. You've got to go."

"Will you . . . stay here . . . at the 101?"

Now he was truly uncomfortable, pacing the room like a caged animal. I watched him, remembering how not very long ago I had thought him perfect, thought I couldn't live without him. I simply waited.

"No," he said slowly. "I been thinking. Well, Cherokee, you know I want to—want to give Hollywood a try."

So that was it! He wanted to go to the moving pictures! Or, and this thought struck me belatedly, did he want to find Belle and little Sallie? I could think of no clever thing to say, so I simply looked at him—and he damned himself.

"Now, Cherokee, it's not what you think. I've heard from Belle a time or two, but she's simply been telling me what opportunities there are out there for someone like me, a cowboy who can sing."

It didn't seem worth my while to ask why Belle should be looking out for opportunities for him when he was apparently well settled with the 101. I simply said, "I hope you find what you want, Buck. I'm going to England."

"Well," he said, belligerence rising in his tone, "I'm not. I don't have to go just 'cause you do."

It dawned on me that I had done it all wrong. I hadn't given him the cause to get angry, the reason to storm away from me. He *wanted* me to accuse him of infidelity with Belle—emotional, if not physical—because then he could get angry and separate himself from me in high dudgeon. I had let him down.

"No, Buck," I said, "you don't have to go. I think it would be better if you went to Hollywood. But"—and I measured my words carefully in my head before I said them—"I doubt there'll be any marriage for either of us to come back to."

"Cherokee," he said, "don't you threaten me."

There, I had given him what he needed. He took his clothes for morning and left to seek one of the empty bedrooms. Buck Dowling and I never shared a bedroom again after that night, though I couldn't have known that at the time. It wouldn't have made me sad.

In spite of Mrs. Miller's advice, I didn't go see Louise immediately. I guess I thought I had figured it all out in my mind myself. But I went to Luckett's and Guthrie for a last visit before we left. This time Buck let me go alone and never said anything about worrying about me. In fact, he didn't even say good-bye.

My visit to Luckett's was a waste of time—Papa was down in Guthrie. I spent the night in an empty house, strangely enjoying the loneliness and the memories, and then rode to Guthrie the next morning.

When I let myself in the kitchen door, there they sat at the kitchen table, like an old married couple who've been sharing breakfast for years.

"Tommy Jo!" Papa was up out of his chair and hugging me in a flash.

"I came for a visit before we go abroad," I said, still wrapped in his arms. "But I didn't know I'd find both of you at one place. I'm glad I did."

They laughed, and I thought it wonderful that none of us let guilt or old ghosts trample on us. Louise fixed me a breakfast bigger than I needed. We talked of the tour and the acts that were planned—I was rather vehement about my objections to Paul Revere and Betsy Ross—and then we talked about traveling by boat to England and all the other things that could possibly come up.

At long last, Papa said, "Where's Buck?"

"Back at the 101," I answered noncommittally. Neither one spoke, but I could see the question on both their faces. "He's not going to England. He wants to go to Hollywood."

Nobody jumped up and threw their arms about me, nobody said how sorry they were, nobody said anything for a long minute, until Papa finally uttered, "Damn fool!"

Rising to refill her coffee, Louise said philosophically, "It's about time." When Papa glared at her, she shrugged and added, "Tommy Jo knows it. Buck wasn't going to last a lifetime. You're not brokenhearted, are you, Tommy Jo?"

I almost laughed aloud. "Not now," I said, "but I was pretty surprised when it happened." Then I thought about it a minute and said, "But I guess now *relieved* is the word I'd use."

Papa stared like we were both out of our minds, and the more he looked at us, the harder the two of us laughed.

Colonel Zack had told me that he had a job in the troupe for Papa if he wanted, managing the stock and generally seeing that things went well. I'd meant to make that offer to Papa, but seeing him sit at Louise's table, I knew I wouldn't do that. He was where he belonged. The past was behind both of us, and I was headed off to a new adventure. No need to take my papa along.

"Don't forget," he cautioned as I rode away, "you're still a married woman. I expect you to behave as such."

"Yessir," I said, and kissed his cheek. He didn't need to say that. Getting involved with another man was the last thing I wanted for a long time. What I really wanted was to be myself.

We sailed from New York on March 21, just as the colonel had said, on a ship called the *Lusitania*. Little did we know that the ship would make headlines on its next trip, and that we should well be grateful not to have been on that crossing. The *Lusitania* was a luxury ship, built for wealthy people like all those girls in the convent. We, of course, stayed in the belly of the ship in the smallest berths they had—third class or whatever they called it. Whatever, it was so humble that I swore I heard the horses kicking right next to us. Even so, I wondered that the colonel could afford all this.

"Got bookings in England already," he said, "clear through the summer. Don't you worry about money, Cherokee."

So I stopped worrying. But I didn't enjoy the crossing one bit, nor did I get to partake of all that luxury. I was seasick before we even steamed out of the bay in New York, and I stayed gruesomely sick the whole voyage, lying in my bunk and wishing I were dead as the ship pitched from side to side. It did little to comfort me when the colonel came to check on me periodically and each time repeated, "It's an unusually rough crossing, Cherokee."

"Then why," I wanted to demand, "are you upright and healthy looking?"

The one thing I wanted to hear from him was that Guthrie and Governor were safe and well cared for, and the colonel assured me of that. Back in Oklahoma, he'd been doubtful that I should bring my own horses, but I convinced him that I performed best on them—roping from Governor and doing tricks with Guthrie—and that we wanted the best possible show for the King of England. He'd given in reluctantly, saying, "I hate the responsibility, Cherokee. If anything happens to either of those horses—"

"What could happen to them?" I'd asked, as though the question were foolish.

Now, lying in a bunk bed and barely able to care for myself, I began to worry inordinately about the horses and curse myself for having brought them. It became a daily ritual for the colonel to tell me that he'd just been to check on my horses and that they were doing much better than I was.

The other girls in the show were kind to me, bringing broth—about all I could stomach—and checking on me. Sometimes they tried to tell me about the marvelous buffet they'd enjoyed or the dance on the deck, but I simply groaned and turned away.

Pearl, the Texas girl who'd run away from her mother, usually brought me the broth or tea. Sometimes she'd wring out a cold cloth and put it on my poor throbbing head; other times, she'd sit quietly by my bed, never saying a word but giving me the sense that someone was there, someone cared.

When I began to get a little better toward the end of the voyage, we talked some. I asked if she'd heard from her mother before we left, and she said,

"Yeah, she wrote. But she wasn't in a forgiving mood. Maybe she'll feel different in a year."

"Are you going to keep writing her from England?" I asked.

"Why should I? She ain't gonna write back."

"Maybe she isn't going to write back," I said, enunciating every syllable as carefully as I could, "but she is still your mother. Mine's dead. I can't write to her."

Pearl really had a good heart, and now she was conscience-stricken. "Oh, Cherokee, I'm so sorry! I—yes, I'll write to my ma." She was silent for a minute, and then boldly she said, "I don't talk right, and I know it."

"I can help you."

"I wisht you would, Cherokee, I really wisht you would."

"It's *wish*," I said, "not *wisht*."

And there began the friendship that meant much to me in England.

It occurred to me one day in the depths of my misery that it was fortunate that Buck wasn't with me. He'd have been disgusted with a sick wife. And then it came to me that I was disgusted with myself. I'd never been sick before, and it struck me as a kind of weakness. With that thought in mind, I struggled out of my bed, dressed, and powdered my nose—a look in the mirror was almost frightening—and made my way along the passage, headed for the upper deck.

Fresh air would clear my head, I told myself. But I barely had one foot on the stair when a wave of nausea sent me back to my room.

"Some people just get more seasick than others," the colonel assured me. "I asked the captain."

But he did get so worried that he sent the ship's doctor to see me. That kind man said, "Miserable, isn't it? Drink as much broth as you can, and don't worry about it. Another four days we'll be in England, and you'll be all right."

When we finally docked and the ship was absolutely still, I crawled out of bed and Pearl helped me put on the first clothes I laid my hands on. They seemed to hang as though on a scarecrow, and I needed no doctor to tell me I had lost weight during these ten days.

The colonel had booked us into a small London hotel run by a motherly woman who, once she heard my story, took it upon herself to nurse me back to health. She tucked me into bed—literally—and brought me oatmeal and toast and tea, after I told her I could not face another cup of broth.

"Lordy, lordy, child, no more broth," Mrs. Duncan said. "I'll get ye some good Scottish oatmeal. Goes down on even the rockiest of stomachs." Her Scottish burr seemed to thicken as she talked.

That night I slept in a wonderfully soft bed that stayed still the whole night long, and I awoke feeling like a new person. But by the time I was dressed and presented myself in the common room—that's what they called the dining room—I was weak as a kitten.

"No energy, lovey," Mrs. Duncan said. "You need to build yourself back up. You'll nay be ridin' them horses today."

"Mrs. Duncan's right, Cherokee. You're not going to ride for several days. You just build your strength back up." The colonel was becoming downright considerate, just when I'd have thought anxiety about the forthcoming show would make him unbearable.

I spent a luxurious four or five days. Mrs. Duncan was a natural mother—she'd raised five strapping boys, she told me—and she fluttered over me every minute. Whereas Mama would have wrung her hands and worried, Mrs. Duncan was calm and forthright about my need for food and rest. And while Louise would have prodded me into thought and action, Mrs. Duncan let me be.

In the end, I prodded myself into some introspection and decided that seasickness had been my mourning period for Buck. But it was over, and I was ready to get on with my adventure in England.

"Cherokee! Cherokee!" Pearl burst into my room late one afternoon when I was taking one of my several daily naps. "We've been invited to high tea!" She paused, a funny look on her face. "Whatever d'ya suppose high tea is?"

I laughed aloud. "I don't know, Pearl, but we'll find out, won't we? I wonder what one wears?" In my mind I was thinking of full ball gowns and coiffed hairdos and all those things I didn't have and knew nothing about—I knew just enough to know that high tea was fairly formal.

"We've been told to wear our western duds," Pearl said. "The whole point, says the colonel, is to see us as we really are."

"Well then, Pearl, let's get out our best duds!"

We plowed through our clothes, slinging garments this way and that as we sought our best silk shirts, our dressiest split skirts. "No pants," I said firmly.

"Jodhpurs?" she asked.

"Nope. Split skirts. But our best hats." Mine was a wonderful cream-colored felt Stetson; Pearl's was a lesser known model in brown beaver, a truly gorgeous hat that she said her pa had bought for her. We wore them high at the crown, not creased like cowgirls do today.

The day of the tea we knotted silk kerchiefs around our necks and pulled on the fanciest boots we owned. Finally dressed to our satisfaction, we looked in a long mirror in Mrs. Duncan's private quarters. She was as anxious as we were that we make a good showing, and inviting us to use her mirror was her way of helping.

"Not bad, Pearl," I said as I stared at our images. "Not bad at all."

"Oh, Cherokee, what will I say to an Englishman?"

"I don't think they talk much," I said. "You'll have to do all the talking. Tell them about Texas—they'll love it!"

And so we went to high tea. My English adventure was about to begin.

CHAPTER 12

I don't know what I expected, but high tea was different from anything I had ever dreamed of. Pearl and I went with a group from the show, including the colonel, who had forsaken his usual business suit for a long-jacketed black suit, a starched white shirt with a boiled collar, and a string tie—I accused him of looking like something out of the Wild West fifty years ago, and he admitted sheepishly that he had dressed for show. The members of the band wore their tan uniforms piped with brown velvet, and for just a moment I expected to find Buck in their midst, so familiar was the outfit. But I shook my head to clear it and reminded myself—with regret or relief, I wasn't sure—that Buck was on his way to Hollywood. The other cowboys wore clean denims and starched shirts, and every head sported a carefully creased Stetson.

When we arrived at the estate outside London to which we'd been invited, we were shown into a huge ballroom. You could have fit Papa's house into it five times, with room left over. The walls were paneled in a dark wood—mahogany, the colonel whispered when he saw me touch one tentatively—and the big tall windows with curved tops were hung with rich red velvet drapes. The floor was of patterned wood—parquet, the colonel said—with rich rugs on the floor—Oriental, the colonel whispered.

"I know," I whispered back, wishing he would stop treating me as though I'd just come in from the ranch for the first time. Maybe I didn't know mahogany from teak, but I did know about Oriental rugs—Louise had them in her house.

Pearl was not blessed with even my slight familiarity with the richness we were seeing. "Gollee!" she said too loudly. "Would you look at the size of this room!"

I smiled frostily at her, desperately wanting her to lower her voice and yet not wanting to hurt her feelings by saying so directly.

She must have gotten the hint, for her next words were sort of breathed into my ear. "Them curtains are velvet!" she said. "Wow-ee, I never did see so much richness."

"*The* curtains," I whispered back, "are velvet."

"That's what I meant," she answered, grinning and undaunted by my correction. "*The* curtains are velvet—and they got no moth holes in them."

I gave up and began to look at the people assembled in the room. Because they spoke English in England, I had supposed that the people would look pretty much like us, only they wouldn't be dressed western. I was wrong—they were dressed funny. The men wore suitcoats as long or longer than that strange one the colonel wore, but where he had a string tie, they wore puffed silk scarves. I saw at least two men with monocles, countless with mustaches and goatees, and several with canes, though as far as I could tell, they all walked perfectly fine without any help. I'd have thought they'd get tired of carrying those canes around.

The women, though, they were dressed as though they were going to a fancy dress ball in New York City—and here it was only late afternoon. Their hair was sleek and shiny and obviously well cared for, making me feel that my casual curls were a little country—and they wore so many strands of pearls that I wondered there was an oyster left in the ocean. Their dresses were of silk and satin, elaborate with beads and lace and trim. But it was the expressions on their faces that most intrigued me—they were clearly amazed by us and uncertain how to react, so they ended up looking snooty.

Fortunately I found out through conversation that they weren't really that way, or at least not all of them.

"How do you do," I said to one woman who looked to be just a little older than me. She was blond and pretty in a kind of fragile way, and she was clutching a stemmed glass of something kind of yellow. "I'm Cherokee Rose," I said in my most pleasant manner.

"Cherokee?" she echoed. "The star of the show?"

"Yes, ma'am, I guess I am."

She held out a welcoming hand. "I'm so glad to meet you. We're all so looking forward to your show. I can't imagine doing all the things you do from the back of a horse."

"Do you ride?" I asked.

"Oh, yes, every day, in the park."

Well, nothing would do but to make arrangements to ride together the next day. Just as we confirmed our plan, Pearl found me.

"Cherokee, you got to see this food. I—I never seen anything like it."

I smiled fleetingly at my new friend—her name was Lady Charlotte MacLeod.

"Try the sherry," she said softly as I made my excuses and turned away.

The food that had so amazed Pearl was far different from cowboy fare, and there were great tables piled high with it—sandwiches that, upon tasting, proved to have cucumber and watercress in them. I knew about watercress because Mama had grown it at home by an old dripping faucet, but hers was never as pungent as this. And there were platters of a pinkish-looking whole fish, which the butler or someone carved into the most delicate thin slices I'd ever seen and sprinkled with small black things.

"Smoked salmon with caviar," the colonel said, sidling up behind me.

I wondered if I dared try it and decided I'd be missing an opportunity if I didn't. I never could figure out which taste came from what, but the whole thing—served on a tiny piece of toast—was salty and tangy and delicious. Pearl took one bite and began to look for some acceptable way to rid herself of it—she finally had to make a beeline for the ladies' room.

A harpist played gentle music in one corner of the room, though she was almost drowned out by the buzz of so many people talking gently among themselves. It wasn't that any one person was loud—far from it—but the cumulative effect was a loud hum.

I drifted through the crowd, avoiding Pearl when I could and then feeling so guilty that I sought her out. But in between times I talked with an aging earl who told me that as a young man he'd spent a year or two in "the American West—fantastic experience, absolutely fantastic. Made a man of me, it did!"

I looked obliquely at him and could not see that he looked like he'd ever benefited from the West as I knew it, but I said nothing and listened attentively as he told me about his experiences on a Texas ranch. Oklahoma, I told him carefully, was just above Texas. I let him interpret *above* any way he wanted.

I wandered through the room, talking to this person and that—a middle-aged woman whose knowledge of America was so slim that she thought the Sioux still were scalping people right and left, a young man who rather leered as he asked what I did for amusement when I wasn't riding, a young girl of fourteen or fifteen, probably on one of her first social outings, who declared it her everlasting ambition to be as free as I was.

And when she said that, it occurred to me that I was indeed free—not in the sense she understood it, but I was free from Buck. I didn't have to worry who he was talking to, what he thought about my talking to someone else, what he might say when we got back to our rooms. I was deliciously free to be myself, to talk to whomever I wanted whenever I wanted. I had a wonderful time at that high tea.

"If that's food," grumbled one of the cowboys on the way back to London, "I'm a rabbit. Wasn't nothin' there a man could properly introduce to his stomach."

Pearl agreed. "I feel like I haven't eaten. Colonel, are we gonna get supper tonight?"

The colonel agreed that there would be supper at the inn, but when he turned to me, I said, "I filled up on salmon and those little bitty roast beef sandwiches and that nut bread—it was richer than anything my mama ever thought about baking."

By then, Pearl and I were sharing a room, since I'd recovered my health and every way we could cut corners and save pennies was important to the colonel. As we readied ourselves for bed, she said, "Cherokee, you just simply amaze me. I mean, eatin' all that stuff like you enjoyed it."

"I did enjoy it," I said. "Pearl, you're going to have to open yourself up to new experiences—new people, new tastes, new everything—or you're going to be in England without ever really being here."

She nodded wisely. "Yes, ma'am, Cherokee. You're right. You're soooo right!"

I had no idea how much she understood.

The next day I rode on the royal bridle path with Lady Charlotte MacLeod. It was an experience, right from the bridle path itself down to my amazing visit with her graciousness, as I kept trying to call her. Finally she said she thought Charlotte would do, if she could call me Cherokee. Feeling like an awkward country bumpkin, I allowed as how that would be fine.

Because I'd already revealed my lack of sophistication, I was hesitant to ask Lady Charlotte—that's what I finally settled on, and later I learned it was correct—who all these people were on the royal bridle path. Were they all royal? I couldn't believe that, for the place was so crowded that I was afraid even Governor, the best-behaved horse I knew, would begin to shy.

And these people rode funny. I knew about English saddles, of course, and how they didn't have the horns, and I knew that the ladies would be riding sidesaddle, the men wearing jodhpurs and high boots. After all, hadn't I once ridden with Mrs. Roosevelt in Washington, D.C.? But I was unprepared for the seriousness with which they rode. When I was riding just to be riding, I kind of loafed along in the saddle, letting Governor go at a good walk and have his head, while I enjoyed the weather or built one fantasy or another in my mind.

Not Lady Charlotte. She rode at a trot the whole time, standing high in her stirrups with almost every step the horse took—posting, they call it in English riding. I greatly admired the amount of exercise she was getting, but going very far at a trot frankly wore me out, and I was hard put to talk while we were riding.

Lady Charlotte had me beat there, too. She kept up a steady conversation, mostly telling me about her life. She had two children who were being raised by a nanny—she visited with them every day for tea. I bit my tongue to keep from asking if that was the only time she saw them, but I gathered it was. Her husband was a barrister—lawyer, I guess—and she usually only saw him on weekends. They went their own separate ways. Since Lady Charlotte had a thick British accent—she probably thought my Oklahoma twang was unlettered—and spoke rather rapidly, I wasn't sure I was getting all that she said, but somehow I got the impression that her husband had a "friend" with whom he spent much time. That made me think of Buck and how he thought perhaps he could have his pie and eat it too—apparently Lord MacLeod did just that, but it didn't seem to bother Lady Charlotte. "We have our own lives," she said.

I nodded as wisely as I could.

After that ride, Lady Charlotte was my friend, and I was always glad to see her at the parties we went to.

With the show set to premiere before the king and queen in less than three weeks, we were practicing the better part of each day, getting the animals accustomed to a new arena and learning its limitations ourselves. One morning as I arrived for workout, the colonel stood talking to a group of somber-looking Englishmen.

"Don't saddle up yet, Cherokee," he said gruffly.

Puzzled, I went to the stands and sat and watched from a distance. The colonel was obviously angry with these men, gesturing widely as he talked. I couldn't hear what he said, but I could hear his raised voice.

The men, on the other hand, stood calmly, almost without moving, and seemed from a distance to be talking without moving their lips much.

How, I wondered, could two groups react so differently in a disagreement, the group of men so calm and the colonel so impassioned? And what could they be arguing about? Of course that answer should have been obvious to me, and it was the minute the colonel stomped over toward me and said in a loud voice, "The damn humane society!"

It seemed they wanted us to stage a special performance for their inspection or approval, the very idea of which sent the colonel into rigors.

"I think we best do it, Colonel," I said. "They'll see that we do treat the animals well, and it'll be all right. If we refuse, who knows what kind of trouble they might cause?"

In the end that's what we did—put on an entire performance of the Wild West show for a group of five sour-looking Englishmen who never moved a muscle during the entire show except to make notes on the pads they carried. We were left with no idea whether they were damning us with faint praise or outright condemning the entire show—the colonel had made it plain to me that, should they wish, they had the power to ban the show in England. In which case, we would be headed home in disgrace, and the colonel—and the entire 101—would be bankrupt.

They neither damned nor praised. They quibbled about the calf roping, but they applauded, generally, our treatment of our horses and in fact were downright curious about Guthrie's training. Deliberately showing off, I gave them a demonstration of all he could do, hoping that they would be so impressed, they would forget to worry about calves being caught in a loop. For heaven's sake, I wanted to thunder, how else do you catch a calf? In a calmer mood, I sincerely urged them to visit a working ranch in the American West. Meantime, at my most humble, I hoped they would enjoy—and approve—our show.

They did. Just days before the scheduled premiere, we received word that the humane society had approved the show. Now all we had to do was draw the applause of a king.

There is nothing like a royal performance to bring on a case of nerves—especially in the show's producer. The colonel, who had been so kindly lately that it almost made me nervous, went quickly from father-figure to tyrant.

"Cherokee, if you don't make that entrance more spectacular, the king's gonna die of boredom! Make that horse step!"

I glared at him and retreated to try the entrance again.

When he picked on Pearl, I'd almost had too much. She was in several of the reenactment scenes, always in minor parts, since she was not a trick rider or roper and, in truth, was only a middling rider of any kind. Her only virtue was that she wasn't afraid of horses.

"Make that horse run for its life!" the colonel shouted. "There're Comanches after you! If you can't ride to save your life, you better ride to save your job in this show!"

Pearl quirted her horse, urging it on to greater speed, but the only effect—for some reason I never did figure out—was to make the horse pull up abruptly and begin to buck. Pearl held on like a trooper, but the colonel was furious.

"Get that horse under control!" he yelled, and I wanted badly to tell him we all knew she'd do that as soon as she could. In truth, Pearl quieted the horse fairly quickly, but when it stood, panting, the colonel yelled so loud, the horse almost offered to buck all over again.

"Get off that horse," he yelled, "and come here!"

From where I stood at the edge of the arena, I wasn't close enough to see that Pearl was shaking with fear and nerves, but instinct told me that was exactly her condition. When she got off the horse, I knew. She managed to dismount all right and ground-rein the horse, but when she started toward the colonel, her legs almost buckled. She caught herself, and I could see her use every ounce of her nerve to straighten. Then, step by slow step, she walked toward him. Those of us standing and hunkering around the edge of the arena held our breath collectively.

I couldn't stand it. As Pearl walked slowly across that long distance to the end of the arena where the colonel had fixed himself a chair, I suddenly ran toward him, beating her there by a second or two.

"Colonel," I said, "go easy on her. She didn't do anything wrong. The horse bucked."

"Can't have a horse buck when it's not supposed to in front of the king," he growled. "Cherokee, you leave *me* to run this show!"

My temper flared. "You can run it without me if you're going to treat people that way. That's a scared young girl who's doing the best she can—and her best is pretty good. You need to take a deep breath and tell yourself kings and queens are just people like you and me." With that, I turned on my heel and walked away from him.

Pearl, who had heard every word, stood openmouthed behind me. The colonel sat motionless for a moment, too stunned by my anger to say anything, though as I walked away I half expected a dagger in my back. But finally, he looked at Pearl and said wearily, "Go put your horse up. We'll do it again tomorrow." It was as close as he could come to saying he was sorry.

By the time we played for King George V, Queen Mary, and their royal party—Empress Alexandra of Russia, the Princess Royal, and her daughter Princess Maud—we had a better show than we'd ever had before. I couldn't help wondering what Russian royalty thought of the Cossack scene, but they were generous in their applause, so maybe it was all right. The Paul Revere/Betsy Ross scene was still shaky, but the attack on the settlers' cabin would take your breath away. When the Indians attacked, the mother took two young children and escaped through the brush—all right, brushy scenery—while the father and two young sons called for their rifles and fought a desperate battle on the front stoop of the cabin. The mother and youngsters were supposedly in the background but were clearly visible, watching with horror as their menfolk fought off the Indians. In real life, of course, those menfolk were goners, but in our scene they triumphed, and the Indians fled. Whoever said art had to mimic life hadn't seen many Wild West shows!

I had wanted Pearl to ride for me in the act where I roped a rider coming toward me, but she was so unnerved by the colonel's anger that she couldn't do it. One of the new young cowboys rode through my loop, but I didn't rope him afterward and I sure didn't pull him into a loop with me. The romanticism that Buck and I, as a pair, had given the act was gone, but the king wouldn't know what he was missing, and the act was still spectacular in a land where they used ropes only to tie animals to this post or that. I had another of my brief flashes of missing Buck, but it didn't last long.

The only stipulation for the command performance for royalty was that there could be no guns in the show. That hampered us in a few acts—the fighting in the reenactment of Custer's Last Stand had to be all hand-to-hand, but that was no problem, and neither was the attack on the settlers' cabin. I was glad to be rid of the popping of the guns and the acrid smell of smoke from the blanks they fired.

On the night of the royal performance, the grand parade began the show as usual, only this time each of us dismounted, led our animal by the reins, and bowed low in front of the royal couple, who sat, naturally, in an ornate box constructed especially for them. They graciously bowed—well really, they sort of just inclined their heads—as each performer came before them, but the whole process made the show almost an hour longer than usual.

When I wasn't riding, I watched the king and queen to see how they reacted. They couldn't have been more delighted—when the settlers' cabin was attacked, the queen clasped her hand over her mouth in horror, and when a cowboy roped and threw a steer, the king clapped vigorously, and I could have sworn he said, "Bully, bully!" which reminded me of Theodore Roosevelt. But the really telling sign was that the queen kept taking snapshots. Toward the end of the show I happened to look up and see one of their wait-persons—or whatever they are called—reloading her camera.

After the performance, we took an unaccustomed curtain call, with the audience applauding loudly and standing in ovation. But when the king looked at Queen Mary, then held out his hand, and the two of them stood in recognition of what we'd shown them, I thought I'd burst with pride.

The next day the headlines in the London newspapers read, "King Stands for the Cowboys!" And we girls came in for a good mention. The article read, "Red Horn Gulch has come to London and settled at the Stadium, Shepherd's Bush, where, among the many inhabitants of the wild and woolly west are a bunch of the most wonderful cowgirls ever seen east of St. Louis."

Royal approval got the show off to a tremendous start. We played for the king and queen in mid-April, and after that we played three times a week to large crowds well into the summer. When we weren't performing, it seemed we were at a party every day. The British, I decided, really knew how to enjoy life, though their idea of fun was fairly formal and restrained. But one dance stands out in my mind.

It was at the home of an earl—a great big estate with a huge ballroom. We had, as always, been asked to wear our western clothes, so we dressed in satin shirts and split skirts, with Stetsons on our heads.

"I get tired," Pearl complained, "of bein' a freak. Seems like they want us to dress this way so they can poke each other in the ribs and wink about our clothes."

I knew exactly what she was feeling. We were on parade, and though the interest was kindly, it was tinged with an attitude that plainly said, "We would never dress like that." We were curiosities.

"Well," I said slowly, "just think how dull it would be if we weren't there!"

"They're used to dull," Pearl said.

As usual, the Englishmen were wearing white ties and tails, and the women were formally coiffed and dressed. We all stood around, rather awkward, while we nibbled those bits of food they put out and listened to the band playing sedate music.

"I say," said a gentleman who wandered up next to me, "do they dance much in the American West?"

Startled, I looked at him. "Dance? Of course we dance."

"The waltz?" he asked.

I must have looked at him as though he'd just fallen off a horse and hit his head. "No," I said slowly, "we don't waltz much. Do you know 'Turkey in the Straw'?"

He looked faintly amused. "No, I don't think that I do."

Devilment overcame me. "You just wait here a minute," I said. With his murmured "Of course" echoing in my ear, I made a beeline for some of the cowboys from our band, whispering my message into first this ear and that. One by one, they nodded, and then, like a parade, they headed for the orchestra, which was playing that slow dull music that nobody could have danced to.

I watched with my hand over my mouth as one cowboy reached for the violin and another took the cello and so on. In minutes, the cowboys had displaced those staid English musicians. Then they struck up "Turkey in the Straw."

Hurrying back to my Englishman, I heard Tex Johnson, our band leader, call out, "Ladies and gentlemen, let's form a square."

The Englishman stood where I'd left him, a look on his face that wavered between amusement and uncertainty. Without hesitation, I grabbed his hand and pulled him into the square that was being formed by three other cowgirls who had simply grabbed the nearest man—always making sure, of course, that he was an Englishman. Pearl had by the hand a pale young man with spectacles who seemed inclined to stumble over his feet, but she simply pulled him along.

"Ladies and gentlemen, bow to your partners and allemand left," Tex called, and we girls showed our partners how to do it. There was a dry run or two before they got the hang of it, but it wasn't too long before we had those dignified Englishmen dancing in a square—and all the other guests stood around and applauded. That was the best dance I went to the whole time we were in England—and I never did learn to waltz.

The colonel, who had missed the party, was visibly nervous the next day. "Cherokee, I don't think you should have done that. These Englishmen—they've got real strict ideas about what's proper, and they might be offended."

"They had a wonderful time," I said flatly. "I think we ought to try it more often, maybe stage some square dances."

He backed away in a hurry. "Now, Cherokee, don't be gettin' any ideas. We're visitors in this country."

"And aren't we showin' them a good time?" I asked heartily.

Shaking his head, the colonel walked away.

The cowboy with the blond hair who was always staring at me also sought me out after that party, and there was laughter in his voice as he said, "That was some trick last night, making those Brits dance a square. I admire your style, Miss Cherokee."

"Why thank you," I said. "I—"

"You don't know my name. I'm Jim. Jim Bones. Born down in Texas, been with the show just since the colonel started planning this trip."

"I know that," I said sharply. "And I've noticed you before."

"Good," he laughed. "I've noticed you a whole lot. Next time you want to square dance, why don't you call me 'stead of one of those stiff Englishmen. I'll show you a good time."

He winked at me with the confidence of a young man and swaggered away, and I watched him amused. He probably could show me all kinds of good times, but I just wasn't interested. In spite of myself, I held him up on one side of an imaginary picture in my mind and Buck on the other side—and Buck came out the better, simply because he was older, enough so as not to be so cocky, enough to know that life wasn't all laughter and flirting.

After that day, when we were at a party, I would sometimes find Jim at my elbow. "Ready to dance?" he'd ask, or "How about walking out on the balcony with me, Cherokee?" Sometimes I would walk out and listen to him talk about his home in Texas, and how he wanted to earn enough money to go back and buy a ranch and raise a family. But until then, he said, he wanted to have a good time.

"And are you having a good time?" I asked.

"Right now I really am, ma'am," he said, leaning toward me as though he'd try for a kiss.

I backed away just enough so that he had to step quick to catch his balance and avoid embarrassing himself. But even that made him grin, and I admired that youthful happiness in him.

Still, when Jim began to pay attention to one of the younger girls and she returned his favors, I wasn't disappointed. He still grinned at me when I caught him watching, and I toasted him with that imaginary glass.

In spite of the parties and the good attendance we had, England was not a happy place to be that summer. The winds of war were blowing across

Europe, though I certainly was not nearly enough aware of international politics to recognize the threat. Still, I knew that the colonel read the newspaper each morning and shook his head with worry.

"Gonna be trouble here," he said one morning. "I don't know but what we should go home now, while we can."

"What kind of trouble?" I asked.

He shook his head. "Don't rightly know. These Europeans, they're all crosswise with each other, all the old governments shifting and forming new governments and new allegiances. Everybody's angry at everybody else. It's too much for any one man to understand."

Alarmed, I asked, "France is still France, isn't it?"

He looked disgusted. "Of course it is, Cherokee."

"And will it still be safe for us to go there in September?" I badly wanted to go to France, though the only reason I could think of was that I wanted to try my convent-school French.

"Far as I know now," he said. "I just got this feeling, like there's trouble hanging over our heads."

The colonel's premonitions got a lot worse in late June. "They've shot this archduke—Ferdinand of Austria—in Serbia," he said. "There's gonna be trouble come from that."

"Why?" I asked.

He shrugged. "You know these Europeans. You don't kill their royalty and get away with it."

It seemed too simple to ask if they couldn't just arrest the Serbians who'd done the killing and that would be the end of that. I put the whole thing out of my mind for a few days.

But then I rode with Lady Charlotte early one morning in July.

"Austria is blaming Serbia for the death of Archduke Ferdinand," she said tensely.

"So the colonel told me," I said, "but that doesn't affect you, does it?"

"Everything affects us," she said almost bitterly. "Europe is too small, the countries too close together for any of us to remain isolated from trouble."

"But you're not in Europe," I said, puzzled. "There's that water between you and them."

"The channel," she said decisively, "is not that wide."

At the end of July, Austria and Germany declared war on Serbia, who was soon joined by her allies, Russia and France. I was still naïve, thinking Britain was a different country—maybe in the back of my mind I thought so because they spoke English—and wouldn't become involved. Then, on August 3, Germany invaded France. There went our French tour, though I'd known for a week or more that it was out of the question. On the fourth, England entered the war.

"What now?" I asked the colonel at our usual breakfast together.

"We cancel the show and head for home as soon as we can get passage on a ship," he said.

Unfortunately, he didn't get that passage soon enough. When I went to breakfast three days later, the colonel was the most dejected man I had ever seen. He sat at the table, shoulders slumped, head down, and never raised his head even when I approached and said "Good morning."

"Colonel? You all right?"

"No," he whispered hoarsely, and then he reached into his coat pocket to hand me a letter.

I unfolded it slowly and saw that it was from a sergeant, and it had a heading that read "Impressment Order under Section 115 of the Army Act." With panic rising in my throat, I read,

> His Majesty having declared that a national emergency has arisen, the horses and vehicles of the 101 Ranch Show are to be impressed for the public service, if found fit . . . and will be paid for on the spot at market value to be settled by the purchasing officer. Should you not accept the price paid as fair value, you have the right to appeal to the County Court . . . but you must not hinder the delivery of the horses and vehicles, etc. The purchasing officer may claim to purchase such harness and stable gear as he may require with the horse or vehicle.

"They can't do that!" I exploded, my growing panic having burst into the greatest fear I could remember since the bull ran over the embankment when I was a youngster. "They can't have Governor and Guthrie!"

The colonel raised tired eyes to me. "I guess they can," he said.

"No! A trained high school horse and the best roping horse I ever had are not going to war, just to be shot on the battlefield." I flung the letter down at him and ran from the room. Actually, though my departure may have seemed impetuous, I knew exactly where I was going—to see Lady Charlotte.

"Oh, my dear!" Lady Charlotte clasped a well-ringed hand over her mouth. "I—I'm so sorry!"

"Thank you," I said briefly, "but I need your help. I've *got* to get Governor and Guthrie back. They're, they're trained and valuable, and I can't do my act without them." In spite of myself, I felt that I was about to break down completely in front of this sophisticated woman who always showed such control. I clenched my hands into fists so tight that my fingernails dug into my palms.

"I don't think that will be possible," she said slowly. "The king's order cannot be changed."

"Couldn't the king make an exception for two really special horses?"

She almost smiled. "And one really special cowgirl?" Then she became serious again. "The king, of course, can do anything he wants. He is, after all, the king. But I suspect that he will not be allowing exceptions. If he starts that, every lord and earl in the country will want his favorite jumper spared."

I could understand that, but I could not—would not—give up. "How would I put this before the king?"

"Oh, dear, I have no idea. The whole world's gone topsy-turvy this week, and nothing is as it should be. The king, I hear, is very preoccupied."

"I should suppose so," I murmured. "But he enjoyed our show—he even stood for us. Surely . . ."

She walked over to the tall windows of the library and stood looking at the formal gardens, which were now, in August, a maze of bright colors and deep green in intricate patterns. I tried to wait quietly, memorizing the pattern in the rich rug on the floor, but I itched with impatience. At length, she turned to me and said slowly, "Perhaps the queen."

"The queen?" I echoed dumbly. "She surely can't contradict her husband's orders."

"No," she said, smiling again ever so slightly, "but she does, I believe, have his ear. I have a cousin who is a lady-in-waiting to the queen. Let me see what she thinks."

"Thank you," I said with true gratitude, even as I wondered how to say that this was not something to be studied deliberately in the British fashion—considered from every angle and finally acted on a month from next Christmas. "They are coming for the horses tomorrow," I said tentatively.

Lady Charlotte understood me clearly. "You may, Cherokee, have to give them up temporarily. My advice would be to let the authorities take the horses with the others. It will be no trick to find out where they are stabled." She saw the stricken look on my face and came to put a comforting arm around my shoulders. "They won't ship them overseas in a week or less," she said. "We do have some time."

"Thank you," I said again, with an impulse to throw my arms around her. I settled for grasping her hand in both of my rough ones.

They came for the horses the next afternoon. The colonel tried to get me to stay at the hotel, but I refused. Instead, I insisted on leading each of my horses to the horse van myself—and as I led them, I whispered in their ears, telling them this was temporary and that they'd soon be going back to Oklahoma with me. Guthrie whinnied and shied with nervousness at the strange handlers and unfamiliar van, but Governor was calm, and I told myself they had both understood my whisperings.

Still, I thought my heart would beat right out of my chest as I watched the van drive away.

"Cherokee?" the colonel asked.

"I'm all right," I said, turning to him. "Are you?"

He shook his head. "I don't know. It's the damnedest luck a man could have. I've booked passage for us in two weeks. Best I could do. Everyone's in a hurry to get out of this country."

Two weeks! I was afraid he was about to say two days. Surely two weeks would give me time to free my horses.

I began to hound Lady Charlotte. Had she heard anything? What did her cousin say? How much longer did she think it would be? I made a nuisance of myself.

"Cherokee, Cherokee! You need to learn patience," she said. "Some things cannot be rushed. My cousin said she would talk to the queen if the opportunity arose. She can do no more."

When, I wondered, would the opportunity arise? What did ladies-in-waiting do, and how often were they close to the queen? Did they comb her hair, help her at her toilette, serve her tea? Did they really have opportunities to whisper in her ear, make special pleas? And if so, maybe this cousin had pleas of her own and didn't want to use up her credit asking for my horses.

I lived in a fog and cried myself to sleep more than one night during the next week. Strangely, I found myself wishing for Buck, wishing he were in the bed next to me so that he would put his arms around me and whisper into my hair that everything would be all right. But Buck wasn't there—he was in Hollywood—and if everything was going to be all right, I had to make it work out myself.

Meantime, the days were creeping by too fast. Each individual day was endless. Before, I'd spent my days rehearsing and my leisure time riding on the royal bridle path, but now I had none of those things to do. I tried reading but couldn't keep my mind on the words in front of me. Pearl and I went shopping a time or two, but nothing interested me, and wartime shortages were already beginning to show in the stores as people began to stock up against a long siege. Everywhere the mood was grim, and that made the days longer.

And yet each night I realized that another day had gone by without any word, any progress, and our sailing date was drawing ever nearer.

Once I almost went to the offices of the *London Daily News*. A fantasy had been festering in my brain for two days in which the newspapers made a big splash story about the poor American girl who was about to lose her trained horses to the war—maybe they'd even run a photograph of me on Guthrie as he performed. There would be a loud outcry of public sympathy, and the king would have no choice but to return my horses. A small voice of reason told me that the king would indeed have other choices, and that he might become so angered by such a tactic that he'd ship the horses to the glue factory.

As a matter of fact, a newspaperman did interview the colonel. He, with more tact than I had and less emotion, simply said that we were behind the war effort and proud to be able to help the British people.

"Is the show bankrupt?" I asked bluntly one morning. "Now that we have no horses."

"They paid us fairly well for the horses," he said. "We'll lose the income of an extended run, but then we won't have the expense either. No, the show's not bankrupt yet. But this war is going to be felt in our country, too, Cherokee. Nothing is ever going to be the same again—and that probably applies to Wild West shows as much as anything else."

When the horses had been gone eight days—and our sailing date was exactly a week away—I began to despair. In fact, I spent one whole day in bed.

"Cherokee?" Pearl asked in the softest voice she could manage. "You all right?"

"Yes," I muttered, and pulled the covers over my head. "Just leave me alone."

"I could bring you something to eat—maybe some tea."

"I hate tea!" I said rudely. "Just leave me alone."

"It's them horses, isn't it?" she said, mostly to herself.

Within minutes of her departure, the colonel was knocking on the door. "Cherokee? Can I come in?"

"If you must," I said, pushing up to a sitting position and covering myself with the blankets.

"What's the matter with you?" he demanded.

"I just don't feel like getting out of bed," I said belligerently. "And I guess that's my right. There's nothing I have to do if I do get up, so—"

"Cherokee, this isn't you. All I can think is that Pearl's right, and you're grieving over those horses. That's a blow—a bad one, and I admit it. But we can get you more horses. We can even train another high school horse. What I can't replace is you."

It was as close as he could come to saying that I was important not only to the show but to him, and I was touched. But I was also still too sunk in self-pity. "I don't want other horses. I want Guthrie and Governor," I said stubbornly.

"Cherokee, if I have to drug you and carry you onto that boat next week, I'll do it!" he thundered.

I just stared at him, and pretty soon he retreated. My mind was incapable of thinking about next week, about what I'd do if the sailing date came and I didn't have my horses back.

That night I apologized to Pearl. I'd been rude and ugly when all she wanted was to help me, and I was properly ashamed of myself.

"Land's sake, Cherokee," she said, "it ain't nothin'. We all get down now and then."

But she, I thought, never got down. She was always Pearl.

I made it to breakfast the next morning and tried to apologize to the colonel. When he asked if I was feeling better, I promised him that I'd try to be polite and added, "I appreciate your . . . well, you know." Apologizing was as hard for me as caring had been for him.

That morning I was in my room writing to Louise—a self-pitying letter, I'm sure, though I later crumpled it and put it in the trash—when a great roar erupted downstairs. I could hear the colonel bellowing, "Cherokee! Cherokee! You come down here right this minute!" The urgency in his voice was unusual, even for that most mercurial of men.

Maybe it was instinct, and maybe it was the pent-up tension, but I was suddenly so breathless that for one brief second I thought I might faint for the first time in my life. Then I was on my feet, out the door, and running toward the stairs. "What is it?" I called, my voice preceding me.

"Your horses!" he shouted. "The king has made an exception. He's returning your horses to you!"

I nearly fell down the stairs, ending up in a trembling mess before the colonel, who finally had to reach out a hand to hold me. "Your horses," he repeated. "They're yours. You can take them back to Oklahoma."

And then, his arm around me to steady me, I collapsed into a great mass of sobs.

The colonel and I went to the designated stables for the horses that day, and he rode Governor while I was on Guthrie. We took them to a livery stable near the hotel, and I ordered—really ordered!—the colonel to make arrangements for their passage on our ship. "If they can't go, I won't go," I said stubbornly.

He shook his head. "Cherokee, quit fighting. You've won. The horses will go." Then, looking sideways at me, he said, "And I'm proud of you. Sandy Burns will be, too."

I hadn't thought about Papa during this whole long thing, but now I realized that yes, he would be proud of me for standing up for myself, for making things go the way I wanted them to.

"I have to go see Lady Charlotte," I said.

There was little I could do to repay her kindnesses, but I urged her to come to Oklahoma.

"Oklahoma?" she said. "It sounds too strange, too foreign. But"—with a shrug—"you never know. Maybe I will one day. Meantime, my dear Cherokee, it's been a new experience for me to know you. And I've enjoyed it."

"Me too," I said.

We sailed on August 21, with Governor and Guthrie safely in the hold. As the ship steamed out of the harbor, I looked back at England with some pain and some pleasure. "I'll never come back here," I told Pearl, "but I'm glad we've been here."

"Me too," she said, "but ain't the food awful!"

CHAPTER 13

Buffalo Bill's show was failing. Profits went down a little each year during his string of "farewell exhibitions," and the Two Bills Show had dissolved. Those years we were in Europe Buffalo Bill toured with something called the Sells-Foto Circus. When I heard about it from the colonel, I nearly cried for the demise it represented for my hero.

"He's not a spring chicken, Cherokee," the colonel said gruffly. Then reluctantly he added, "But he's still got the name."

Buffalo Bill would turn out to be the answer to the colonel's dilemma about reorganizing the Miller 101 Wild West Show after we lost all our animals in England. But we didn't know that as we headed home across the ocean, and we were a dismal bunch.

Our crossing was smooth and I was not troubled by seasickness at all, though I'd approached the ship with dread. Crossing to England, when I'd been full of excitement, I'd have enjoyed being on deck, sharing our anticipation with the colonel and the others. But now, when I was physically able to be on deck, there was little to share but a sense of failure.

None of us talked much. We stared at the ocean, and sometimes we cast furtive glances at each other. But there was little to be said. The colonel sat in a deck chair, hands folded over his stomach, eyes closed. If spoken to, he responded, sometimes politely and sometimes gruffly. If left alone, he remained silent.

"Colonel," I asked one day, "did you get paid enough for your horses?"

"Nothing's enough," he grumbled.

"Colonel," I said, my voice as threatening as I could make it, "can you run the show next year?"

He sighed. "I can. Question is, do I want to?"

"Don't you?"

"I don't know." He shook his head, as though bewildered. "Do you want to be in it?"

Until that very moment, I'd known of course, without a doubt, that I wanted to be in the show, no matter where it was, what shape it was in. The Miller 101 Wild West was my life—what else would I do? But when the colonel asked that, a great shudder went through me. After a long pause, I said, "I don't know. I—I thought I did. But maybe . . ."

"Maybe we're all tired," the colonel said. "Maybe we should not even think about it for a month."

"Won't that be too late to get bookings?"

"It's already too late," he said, "or it would be most seasons. But I predict that this war will change a lot of things, maybe even people's appetite for entertainment."

I thought about that a lot during the next days. If I didn't ride in the show, what would I do? The answer was always the same: Go home to Guthrie. And yet I wasn't ready to spend the rest of my life in Guthrie, Oklahoma, not after I'd ridden for the King of England.

"Did you ever hear from Buck while we were in England?" Pearl asked one day as we leaned over the rail and watched a school of fish swimming alongside the ship. Behind us people were playing shuffleboard as though they had not a care in the world. I wanted to shout and ask them if they didn't know there was a war on, and what they were going to do when they got home.

"Buck?" I asked, surprised that she would be that curious. Pearl had always been real good about not prying into anybody else's affairs, and while her question was logical, it still startled me. "No," I said quickly, "not for a while. Why?"

"Well," she said with great practicality, "I was wondering what you're going to do when we get back to Oklahoma."

"Go back to the 101 and see what the colonel plans, I guess," I said. "You?"

She almost broke down. "If the colonel cancels the show, I'll have to go back to Sweetwater. And I might never get the chance to be in a show, to ride—to get away from home." Something had released a stopper in her, and the words came tumbling out. "I'll probably have to marry Donnie Slaughter and have lots of babies and wash clothes and cook—and I'll never learn to rope and ride like you do!" Her last words nearly came out in a wail of anguish.

"You don't have to marry anyone," I said with more anger than I meant.

"But what else could I do?" She was in tears now, but my sympathy for her was mixed with frustration. "You married Buck, didn't you? Why'd you do that?" Accusation crept into her tone.

"Because I loved him," I said firmly, "and surely not because I didn't have anything else to do. I always had something else to do. It—it just didn't work out like we thought it would," I finished lamely.

"I *know* how it would work out with Donnie Slaughter," she said darkly and stormed off, angrier at herself than at me but not knowing it.

She set me to thinking about Buck, of course. I had heard from him only occasionally while we were in England—three letters from Hollywood and then, to my surprise, a more recent one from the 101. "I'll be here when you get home," he wrote cheerily, and as I read, I'd wanted to demand what had happened to Belle and the beautiful baby Sallie. Now I wondered if he'd really be there, and if he were, what I would do about it.

Somehow we docked in New York, transferred our few belongings—and Guthrie and Governor—to trains, and headed home to Oklahoma. It was a long depressing trip, and I don't think I'd ever been as tired as I was when the cars at long last pulled into ranch headquarters.

Buck was there, waiting at the siding, and he came looking for me as we began to leave the train. "Cherokee?" He held his arms out for a welcoming hug, and not knowing what else to do, I walked into them.

"Buck? Why aren't you in California?"

"Didn't you get my letter? I came back here to wait for you."

Something made me look long and hard at him. "I got the letter. Why did you really come back here?"

He turned away. "Ah, Cherokee, I wasn't . . . well, it just didn't go like I thought in Hollywood. Belle—well, she exaggerated about the work out there."

I didn't have to ask if Belle had exaggerated about anything else, or if maybe Buck had made something up in his mind that wasn't really there.

"Let's go up to the house," I said, and turned away without waiting for him, but he fell in beside me without hesitation.

"Mrs. Miller put us in our usual room," he said softly.

"Good. I'm exhausted."

Mrs. Miller had dinner waiting for us—pot roast with rich brown gravy, mashed potatoes, green beans from her garden, light bread, and for dessert a peach cobbler. I picked at it and ate maybe two bites of everything.

"Cherokee?" she asked. "Are you all right?"

"Just tired," I said. "Would you excuse me?" As I rose from the table, Buck stood as though to follow me. "No, Buck, you stay and enjoy your dinner. I'm just too tired." And I nearly ran up the stairs to throw myself, fully dressed, into the bed. I was asleep within seconds.

It must have been late when Buck came in. I had no sense of time except that I had been sleeping soundly for a while.

"Cherokee?" His voice was tentative, and the hand that reached for me was even more so.

"I'm sleeping," I said thickly. "Just let me be."

"Cherokee, I'm your husband, and you've been gone the better part of a year. I'd think—"

"Then," I muttered, "you'd think wrong. Go sleep somewhere else, Buck."

That was probably the final straw that broke our marriage, though I really didn't do it deliberately. I was telling Buck the truth when I said I was tired—I just left out the part about not wanting him to touch me. I guess he got the message anyway. But I was truly too tired to care, and I slept until nearly noon the next day.

"Buck left you this," Mrs. Miller said when I finally made my way downstairs.

"Left?" I asked stupidly.

"He rode out this morning. Took everything he has with him on a pack horse. Says Zack can pick the horses up in Guthrie after he catches the train west."

I fingered the rough sheet of paper in my hand, looked down at the familiar scrawling handwriting, and then, reluctantly, unfolded the paper to read the message silently to myself.

Cherokee,

*What I suspected is true. It's over between us. I'll keep in touch and let
you know where to send the divorce papers. Please know that I really
loved you, and I'm sorry.*

Buck

*P.S. It's not Belle, believe me. She was a mistake, and I feel sorry for
Sallie.*

The last lines almost made me laugh aloud, but my laughter would
have been tinged with great sadness—for Buck, not for me. I knew that my
spin in the spotlight was bound to be brief, but I was even more aware that
Buck had never had his moment, and never would. Unless he left the show
circuit, he would always be a second-rate player, and that made me sad for
him. I thought about Buffalo Bill, failing and in ill health, and knew that at
least he had had the grand success of his show, for years and years, to carry
into old age as a comfort. Buck would never have that.

I left for Guthrie that day.

Louise put me to work in the boardinghouse—making chicken-fried steak,
washing linens, setting the table, all the thousand chores that went with
running her home for others. It was mindless work, and it kept me from
thinking. She, bless her, asked no questions and made no false conversation.
Some mornings we went from the noise of breakfast—with the milliners
chatting away about this hat for that lady and so on and the drummers
planning their day aloud—to the subdued quiet of dinner without exchang-
ing a word between us. It was comforting to me that we could work that
way.

If Louise never asked about Buck, she did tell me about Bo. "His wife
died some seven or eight months ago," she said one morning when we were
doing dishes.

"I've got to go see him," I said immediately.

"I'm not sure that's the right thing," she said slowly. "He's pretty torn
up, from what I hear."

"And I couldn't make him feel better?" I asked, somewhat put out
with her.

"I'm not sure that's the kind of feeling better he needs," she said, never acknowledging my bad temper.

In the end I didn't see Bo that time I was in Guthrie.

On the fourth day I was in Guthrie, Papa came blowing in the kitchen door just before the noonday meal. "Tommy Jo? Where are you?"

"Here, Papa," I said quietly. "How'd you know I was here?" I turned suddenly to look at Louise with accusation clear in my eyes, but she simply shrugged as though to say she had no idea how he knew.

Papa told me himself. "Colonel Miller," he said loudly. "He had a rider going to Guthrie to pick up some horses and had him stop by the ranch to tell me where you were." He gave me a big hug, as expansive as he was, and then held me at arm's length. "Where'd that no-good husband of yours go anyway? Never did think he amounted to a hill of beans. Colonel's man told me he's the one left the horses in town."

If I hadn't wanted to cry so bad, I'd have laughed. As it was, my voice was shaky with emotion when I said, "I don't know where he is, Papa. He's just gone."

"You grievin'?"

"Not," I said, "like you grieve for Mama. I don't miss him. I don't even know what I feel, except sad."

"Thing to do for sad," he said, "is keep busy."

Now I really could smile. "Louise wouldn't think of letting me do anything else," I said. "I've been busy."

"She's pretty good help," Louise said with a smile, "but she doesn't make much conversation with my boarders. The ladies still think she's stuck on herself."

"The hell with 'em," Papa growled.

Papa stayed the day, and in the late afternoon, with supper simmering on the stove and the chores all done, we sat at the scarred old kitchen table and had a serious visit.

"What's next, Tommy Jo? You gonna give up this Cherokee business?"

"I don't think I can, Papa. It's who I am."

"Colonel don't get his show together, there won't be no place for Cherokee." Papa looked almost hopeful as he spoke. "I could use a good hand at Luckett's."

I took his big hand in one of mine. "Papa, I can't go back to Luckett's. I just can't. Right now, the show is all I know, and I'm hoping the colonel will get it back together in a month or so."

He stared at me a long time without saying anything, then shrugged and turned to Louise to ask some banal question that had nothing to do with anything. The subject of my future was closed, as far as he was concerned.

Papa didn't stay the night. It dawned on me, with some glimmer of amusement, that he wouldn't stay with Louise when I was under her roof—some fine line of morality that Papa drew in his own mind and would not cross. I might have thought it silly, but I didn't—I appreciated it. He hugged Louise just as he hugged me and then rode out toward Luckett's.

"I feel almost guilty," I told Louise. "He'd have stayed if I weren't here."

"Don't waste your emotion on guilt," she said. "He's all right."

The colonel sent me a message two days later: "Miller 101 will team up with Buffalo Bill Wild West. Come immediately."

Louise looked at me with a question when I read it to her, but there was no question in my mind. I was going back on the show circuit. And I was glad about it.

Louise never said a word, so I didn't know if she was glad or sad about my going back to the show. She did say, as I saddled Governor, "I wish you'd get over this notion that you can ride all over the countryside by yourself and be safe."

"If I didn't do that," I told her, "I'd be dependent on other peo-ple—and I can't do that."

"Bo would have a fit to find you riding back to the 101 alone," she said.

"He's grieving, and he doesn't need to know," I said. "But tell him I'm real sorry about his wife, will you?"

She nodded.

It was not a wonderful day to be riding across the prairie—early September in Oklahoma can be blast-furnace hot, the heat rising in great gusts to blow in your face. The sky was blue and cloudless, so that the sun beat down on me relentlessly, and I was soon wiping sweat from my face with my kerchief and taking frequent sips from the two canteens I'd brought with me. The prairie was burned brown by the summer's heat and had none of the beauty that I found in it on glorious spring days. I had to hold myself back from pushing Governor faster than I should, just to get the long ride over with. By pacing him—and myself—I rode to the 101 without camping, but it was a sixteen-hour day, and I was exhausted when I rode into the ranch just after one o'clock in the morning. I'd nibbled on the cornbread and roast beef Louise had packed for me, but I was hungry and tired.

I tried to sneak into the house—into the kitchen, specifically—but

Mrs. Miller must have slept with one ear cocked. She was in the kitchen before I got the door firmly shut.

"Cherokee? Honey, you all right? Hungry?"

"Hungry," I admitted, and soon found myself sharing a midnight snack with her. Pretty soon the colonel wandered in, his pants apparently pulled on quickly under his nightshirt.

"Cherokee," he said. Far be it from the colonel to be exuberant in his welcome! "Glad you're back. We got to get to planning our show."

"Don't we have to plan it with Buffalo Bill?"

He looked startled for a minute. "Naw, not really. He's got half the show, and we got half." There was a long pause. "Our half will be better."

"His half," I said slowly, "won't be real western stuff, you know. He does all those acrobatic acts—Japanese and all—and that business about the Russian Cossacks. General public won't know which half is whose, Colonel. How're you going to feel about a show that isn't pure western?"

He sighed and rolled his eyes heavenward. "Cherokee, you have to make some compromises in this life." Then he grinned, almost mischievously. "And I'm willing to compromise a lot to tie into Buffalo Bill's name. It's going to be the Buffalo Bill and Miller 101 Wild West."

I grinned at him. "Yes, sir!" All the years I'd wanted to ride with Buffalo Bill, and now I was planning to outdo him. What strange turns our lives can take!

Next day I noticed that the colonel's brothers—Thomas and George—were mighty scarce. Oh, sure, they came to the dinner table—who could miss Mrs. Miller's cooking?—but they said little and they left as quick as they could. Specifically, they avoided looking at Zack or talking to him. And Mrs. Miller acted real nervous every time her boys were together.

"Colonel," I demanded as we walked out to the barn after supper, "what's going on with your brothers?"

"Never miss a thing, do you, Cherokee?" He stopped and stared across the fields. "They think it's time to get out of show business. Think the trouble in England was an omen. We've lost enough, George told me."

"Have you?" I asked.

"Yes," he said, "but that doesn't mean I want to quit. I—I don't know how to explain this, but I can't quit. I don't know what I'd do if I had to come back here and do my share of running the ranch and never go on the road again. I just don't know." He shook his head. "George and Tom, they don't understand that."

I took his arm, a rare gesture of affection between us. "I understand perfectly," I said. And I did.

The tour did not start out well. The night before we were to leave Oklahoma, a driving rain set in, and by morning the ground was mud and muck.

"We'll load the horses next," the colonel said from the depths of the slicker he wore against the wetness. "Cherokee, you go get Guthrie." In the same breath he ordered several others to go after specific horses, and we all turned to do his bidding.

I wasn't paying enough attention as I led Guthrie out behind one of the new cowboys, who led a skittish young horse. When I should have been watching that horse in front of me, my mind was wholly occupied with wishing I were drier and warmer. Suddenly, without warning, the horse in front spooked. I never did know why—maybe just rain hitting him in the face—but he whinnied and shied away from the cowboy who held him. I wasn't quick enough to pull Guthrie away, and my horse was thrown off while trying to avoid the tangle in front of him. With a frightened sound of his own, Guthrie slipped sideward. It was all straightened out in seconds, the cowboy got his horse under control, I calmed Guthrie, and we started again through the mud to the railroad cars. But Guthrie limped—badly.

"Colonel!" I called, and he came sloshing over, splashing mud every which way as he walked. "Guthrie's lame."

"Lame? How could he be lame from stepping out of the way of a spooked horse?" Anger made him indignant.

"Mud," I said. "He must have pulled a muscle."

The colonel sighed. "Get him on into the car and then rub it down. It'll mend by the time we get to New York."

I wasn't so sure about that, but I coaxed and urged Guthrie slowly to the car and up the boarding ramp—that part wasn't easy at all, and I wouldn't have gotten it done if that horse hadn't trusted me as much as he did. Finally, he was in a stall in the stable car, and I went to fetch the liniment.

The whole trip east, I kept that bottle of liniment in Guthrie's stall and rubbed his leg down several times a day. We stopped the train to exercise the horses once a day, and I couldn't see that the strain was improving any. But I didn't mention it to the colonel. No sense in leaping my bridges until I came to them. Still, I was worried.

The heavy rain from Oklahoma moved east with us, as though a dark cloud hung over the train the whole way. For two and a half days I stared out at a dull gray landscape, towns where the people had retreated inside, a sky that looked perpetually threatening.

"Wish it'd quit raining," Pearl said. "Makes me feel bad, like maybe the show's not gonna be a success."

"Bite your tongue," I said more sharply than I meant to. "The show will be fine. Weather's got nothing to do with it." But inside I didn't believe that. I knew, for one thing, that people are less inclined to go anywhere but home in rainy weather. And that even animals—let alone people—are affected by falling barometers and high humidity. Everything goes better on sunny and pretty days—including Wild West shows.

When we finally got to New York, the colonel had hired hands to unload the horses. "You all go on and get settled in the hotel," he said magnanimously.

"I'll take Guthrie out," I said evenly, "and see that he's settled."

The train had stopped at Grand Central Station, as close to Madison Square Garden as it could, but we would still have to lead the horses several blocks through the city, and I was worried about Guthrie making that distance.

"Cherokee!" The colonel sounded out of patience. "Guthrie'll be fine. The men will be careful."

I walked up close to him, so that his new hired hands couldn't hear me, and said, "Colonel, you don't know these men. You just hired them. I am *not* turning a lame horse over to them. In fact, I have my doubts about letting them lead Governor, even though he's perfectly sound."

In the end, the colonel led Governor and I took Guthrie, who still limped badly. It was a long slow walk to the barns at the Garden.

"He can't be ridden in time for rehearsals," I said.

"What do you mean, he can't be ridden? He's got to be ridden, Cherokee! The show depends on him." The colonel's face was turning red.

"It had better not," I said calmly, " 'cause Guthrie's not being ridden until his leg is completely well. If he limps much longer, I'm going to insist we call a vet."

"A vet!" I could see the dollar signs spinning around in the colonel's mind. "Now surely, Cherokee, that isn't necessary. . . ." His voice trailed off, and then he said the oddest thing. "I sure wish Buck was here."

I knew what he meant. He wished Buck were here to talk some sense into me. I didn't even dignify that with an answer. Buck would have made no difference in my reaction to Guthrie's lameness, and Buck would have understood me much better than the colonel. For a fleeting instant, I, too, wished Buck were there.

We met Buffalo Bill—Colonel Cody—the next morning. It was a terrible letdown for me. All my life I'd carried this picture in my mind of the dashing Buffalo Bill, dressed in his white suit, his hair and beard flowing, his eyes sparkling with life and adventure. He was the hero of my childhood dreams, and I thought him invincible. I saw instead an old and tired man, worn down by financial worries and fear of failure. He still had the beard and long white hair, and he still wore white suits, but there was no sparkle in his eyes.

"Zack," he said, greeting the colonel, "it's good to have you with us. I know this show'll be a great success."

"I hope so," was the fervent answer. I thought maybe Colonel Zack was praying aloud as he spoke.

The Buffalo Bill show was definitely on the skids. We could see it in the shape of the equipment—tack hadn't been repaired, sets had been quickly and clumsily repainted—and we could also see it in their people. They were amateurs—I don't think there was a westerner among them. These were show people, come to make a living, without knowing or caring for what they were portraying.

"They'd as soon be playing Shakespeare as a Wild West show," I whispered to the colonel, but he pretended to ignore me.

We rehearsed—and we rehearsed. Colonel Cody was not happy with anything—not his performers, not the music, and, most of all, not me. "Where's that high school horse of yours?" he demanded.

"Lame," I answered. "Not at all ready to ride."

"You'll have to ride him lame," he said, his tone clearly telling me that he would brook no argument.

He got an argument nonetheless. "Colonel," I said, speaking slowly and distinctly, "I will not ride any lame horse, let alone my own trained horse. But I will give you a good show. I have another horse, you know, the best trained roping horse I've ever seen—and I can ride rough stock if I have to." The minute that was out of my mouth, I wondered why in the world I'd said it.

It didn't take Buffalo Bill a second to respond. "You'll have to," he said. "I've billed you big in this show—you're the star—and you'll have to live up to that top billing."

So that was the high point of the show. The announcer roared, "Here she is, ladies and gentlemen, Miss Cherokee Rose! She'll be riding the previously unridden wild horse, Devil Dancer! Riding him bareback! Watch the young lady for the thrill of a lifetime!" The crowd—what there was of it—shouted their approval.

Trouble was, Madison Square Garden was only about half full. I knew Buffalo Bill and Colonel Zack had publicized this show every which way, with newspaper ads, flyers, and a parade through the city that they'd forced each of us to take part in. Yet the crowd was nowhere near what it should have been. I was puzzled, but getting ready to ride Devil Dancer I had no time to ponder it.

At least the Garden had chutes, so there was no need to snub Devil Dancer to a post in the arena. In the chute, I let myself down on the horse and felt his muscles tighten. When I was settled, my feet tucked into the stirrups, and my hand in the grip, I nodded and the gate swung open. Devil Dancer hesitated just a minute, as though sizing up the situation, and then exploded out of the chute into the middle of the arena, where he put on a good show of sunfishing and pitching, with his back humped like a camel. Each time he landed on all four of his stiffened legs, the shock of the landing went through me like a sledgehammer. It was a long ride, though it was only six seconds—the prescribed time for women, as opposed to the eight seconds men rode.

When I had slid onto the hazer's horse and then down onto solid ground, with Devil Dancer running mad circles around the perimeter of the arena and the hazers chasing him, the crowd roared. And in spite of the sparseness of the audience, the noise seemed deafening to me.

I hadn't been truthful with Colonel Cody about how long it had been since I'd ridden rough stock.

Pearl was concerned about me—and Colonel Zack was furious!

"Dumb fool thing to do," he ranted. "Could've put yourself out of commission for the whole season. Then where would I have been?"

I looked sideways at him. "Where would *I* have been?" But then I got more serious. "It was either that or ride Guthrie while he's lame, and you know it."

He hemmed and hawed and finally said, "The lameness any better?"

"I think so. I expect I can ride him in a week or so. Meantime I'll ride Devil Dancer—or another one of Cody's bucking stock."

"You better," he said dryly, "stick to Devil Dancer. At least you know what his tricks are."

"I sure do," I said, rubbing the sore muscles in my upper arm, muscles I'd strained holding tight to that hand grip.

After a minute I asked the colonel the question on my mind. "Why was the audience so slim tonight? Doesn't Buffalo Bill's name draw people anymore?"

He shook his head. "I don't know. Worried me a lot, too. Maybe it's this war climate we live in. People are too preoccupied to be entertained."

"And maybe," I said hesitantly, "Wild West shows are . . . well, old-fashioned, out of date. How can you get caught up in Indians and cowboys when the kaiser is threatening all of Europe?"

He looked startled. "Cherokee, you're a deep thinker. You may be right. But that's why I renamed the old artillery show. Now it's the 'Military Preparedness Pageant.' Figured that would appeal to people's sense of patriotism, of getting ready for the war that is inevitably going to involve us."

"Is it really, Colonel?" I asked seriously. I hadn't figured out that the war that had driven us out of England might follow us back to the States.

"I'm afraid it is, Cherokee. I can feel the tension in people and see the poor attendance at our shows."

The crowds were never what we anticipated, and the show lost money right from the first performance. But we plugged on, closing in New York City and opening in Boston for a one-week run. Then it was on to Atlantic City, Atlanta, and Chicago. Everywhere we played to small audiences, and the two colonels grew more worried with each run of the show.

Colonel Cody hovered like a shadow around the show—an old and tired and desperate man. He rarely spoke to any of us but rather seemed to be watching, hoping for a miracle—that big success again—that we couldn't give him, though not through any fault of our own.

Sometimes he'd talk to the colonel. I'd see them standing close together at the side of the arena before a show or even early in the morning when we were taking care of the animals and making ready for the day's performance. Later, the colonel would tell me about the conversations.

"The acrobats," he said disgustedly. "He thinks the acrobats will draw a crowd."

Grudgingly I admitted that they were indeed unusual, bending themselves into shapes that were absolutely impossible for the human body, and flying through the air in ways that God surely never intended. "But," I added, "it's not western."

"I know, I know," the colonel said. "You told me that before."

I didn't want to say I told you, so I was simply quiet.

Every once in a while Colonel Cody would try to be my friend, and I never knew what to make of that. "Cherokee," he'd say almost too heartily, "you're the backbone of this show. If anybody can draw the crowds in, you can. We've got to do it, girlie."

I didn't like being called girlie, and I resented the implication that I could be drawing more crowds in somehow. I was doing my darnedest—and the poor crowds had nothing to do with my performances. But I don't think Buffalo Bill ever understood that.

The whole time we were with his show, Buffalo Bill made me feel sad—sadder even than either Sandy Burns or Buck Dowling did, and that was saying a lot.

Guthrie's leg was sound again, and I thought he was putting on a terrific show, but then Governor gave me the scare of my life. He refused to eat one day in late November, turning indifferently from the oats I put in his bucket, and when I studied him I thought he looked like a rag doll—limp, without the spark that gives a horse pride and carriage. Well, at least a horse like Governor.

"Colonel, I'm worried about Governor. I'll sleep in the stall with him tonight." We were in Atlanta, and the barns were adjacent to the coliseum. Our hotel, small and modest, was more than a mile away.

"Cherokee! You can't do that. It's not safe for a young woman alone."

"There's no choice," I said. "Come look at him yourself."

It was late in the evening when I dragged the colonel back to the barn. By then Governor was standing with all four legs spraddled, looking totally dejected. He'd stare at us a minute, and then turn his head as though to look at his stomach.

"Colic!" we both said in chorus.

"We'll both be here all night," the colonel said, "and even then who knows if we can save him. You sit and rest, Cherokee. I'll start." And he began to walk Governor in a large circle in the open part of the barn. Periodically Governor would balk, pulling back on the lead rope.

"Wants to lie down and roll," the colonel said, "but it won't do him any good. We just got to keep him walking and see if we can't untwist that gut."

I nodded. I knew only too well about horses and colic, and the twisted gut that could literally explode inside an animal and kill it. Bo had once told me, "If only a horse could burp, it could relieve some of that pressure. But it can't. It's like its insides are frozen—can't burp, can't eliminate, can't make anything happen. And they're in terrible pain."

It was Governor's pain that bothered me the most. That most gentle-manly of horses should not suffer! Watching the colonel walk that poor miserable horse around and around, I periodically thrust my fist into my mouth to stifle the urge to scream. At last, huddled on a bale of hay, I slept a little. When I woke, the colonel was still walking in circles.

"My turn," I said, rising groggily. "He any better?"

The colonel shook his head. "No, but he's not any worse, either. I'd like to be chivalrous and tell you I'll keep on, but I can't. I'm dead on my feet."

I took the reins and began that monotonous circling. If it's monotonous for me, I thought, what can Governor think of it? By now he was following me docilely, though he still turned his head in the direction of his stomach every once in a while. I thought maybe he was just a bit better.

It was a long night. The colonel and I took turns every hour or two, napping a little when the other walked the horse. All I could tell myself was that if it was long for each of us, think how it must be for poor Governor.

About six o'clock in the morning, Governor stopped dead in his tracks. My heart leaped into my mouth, and I could barely frame that frantic call, "Colonel!" Then, before I could say anything, the horse moved its bowels. I'm not sure I had ever been as glad to see anything in my life. The crisis was over.

"Colonel," I said as we walked to the hotel for breakfast, "don't ever ask what can happen next."

He patted my arm comfortingly. "I won't, Cherokee. I figure we've had all the troubles we can by now."

In Chicago, we had to cancel the "Military Preparedness Pageant." Mayor Big Bill Thompson saw it on the program before we arrived and immediately objected in loud tones. Chicago, he informed the two colonels, had the sixth largest German population of all cities in the world, and he wasn't about to flaunt military preparedness in their faces. His city was hoping that peace would win—a vain hope, I thought, but I was not allowed to voice my opinion to the mayor.

In Chicago, we were the Chicago Shan-Kive and Round-Up instead of the Buffalo Bill and Miller 101 Wild West Show.

"What's Shan-Kive?" I asked suspiciously.

Colonel Cody shrugged. "Loosely translated, it means 'good times.' "

"In what language?"

"One of the Indian dialects. I don't have any idea which one." The colonel walked away, effectively closing the conversation.

We went three weeks without any pay.

"Gate's just not good enough, Cherokee," Colonel Zack said to me dismally. "I hate it, but there's no money. You know I'll never let you want—and I know you won't bolt. But there's some I'm not so sure about."

"I'll stick, Colonel," I assured him. Then, trying to lighten the moment, I added, "Long as I get fed regular, anyway."

The colonel almost smiled, but he didn't have the heart.

"When you think we're gonna get paid?" Pearl whispered to me late that night. "I can't be workin' for nothin'."

"You thinking of quitting?" I asked. It went through my mind that Pearl had nothing better to quit for—either way, she'd be without money, and this way she had shelter and food. I suspected she'd heard that veiled threat from someone else in the show and now was trying it on for size herself.

"Well," she said, drawing the word out into two long syllables, "maybe not quite yet. How long you think this can go on, Cherokee?"

"Till the gate's better," I said, thinking the answer was obvious. "Instead of worrying about our pay or lack of it, we really ought to be worrying about what we can do to get bigger crowds to the shows."

Pearl sighed. Such complicated thinking was beyond her.

Five people did quit the show—three cowboys, one of the girls who rode in relay races and acted in the skits, and one stable hand. "That many fewer mouths to feed and worry about," the colonel said, but his tone was bitter, and I knew he felt betrayed.

"Colonel, it'll be all right," I ventured, wishing I could believe it even as I said the words. "The crowds'll come back.

The colonel was as wrong as he could have been when he said he thought we'd had all our troubles. The final catastrophic blow came in December as our train hurtled through the night between Chicago and St. Louis.

"Sure seems this train is in a hurry," Pearl said nervously.

I peered out the window into the dark night. I had always loved seeing the houses and towns go by. Sometimes I made up all kinds of stories about people who lived in those houses, their lights lit against the night. They are home and safe, I would think, and I'm far from home, suspended between one place and the next. Sometimes I envied their security, but then I remembered that I was Cherokee Rose, riding with a Wild West show. And now not just any Wild West show, but the Buffalo Bill and Miller 101 Wild West Show.

"Train does appear to be going kind of fast," I said, "but I suppose the engineer knows what he's doing."

The words were no more out of my mouth than our car came to such an abrupt halt, with the terribly loud crashing and grinding of gears and metal wheels, that I was thrown into the aisle. Behind me, Pearl gave a piercing scream as she was flung into the seat in front of where we'd been sitting.

For a moment, we were surrounded by noise—grinding metal, screaming voices, and even—from the horse cars—frantic whinnying. Then, eerily, the world became silent, except for the horses.

"Pearl?"

"I'm all right, Cherokee. How about you?"

I moved tentatively, and pain shot through my right shoulder and down the arm. "I think I did something to my shoulder. But I'm all right, too. We . . . we've got to see about the others."

In the car with us, people were stirring about, moaning and questioning, but no one seemed badly hurt. I pulled myself up and found that the pain in my shoulder was so sharp, it made me draw my breath in quick. Finally, I discovered that if I held my right arm close to my body with my left hand, it was bearable.

"The horses," I said to Pearl. "We've got to see to the horses."

Outside, that momentary stillness had been replaced by a chorus of frantic voices. Over it, the horses could still be heard whinnying desperately. Railroad cars were tilted at crazy angles on either side of the track, and men were walking back and forth swinging huge flashlights and calling aloud to each other, though somehow the sense of what they said didn't make it through to my mind.

Pearl clung to me as though to salvation. Once I had to tell her sharply not to grab my right arm, and then I was contrite for my tone of voice. "It hurts, Pearl" was all I could say.

It was morning light—and too cold—before we sorted it all out. The colonel told me that Guthrie and Governor were all right, but four horses had been lamed and two others had legs so badly broken, they had to be destroyed.

"The people?" I asked.

"Everybody's accounted for. Some are pretty seriously injured. They've been taken by wagon to the nearest hospital."

"What happened?" I asked, feeling dumb for asking. Obviously, the train had stopped suddenly—that was what happened.

"Best I hear," he said, "the conductor had been drinking. Got to going too fast, and then had to stop too suddenly."

I shuddered to think that we had all put our lives in the hands of a man who had drunk too much. When I realized the train was going too fast, I should have done something—but what would I have done? Who would have listened to me?

The colonel rescued me from my feelings of frustration and helplessness. "Cherokee, why are you holding your arm that way?"

"I think I did something to my shoulder," I admitted reluctantly, "when I fell out of the seat. Maybe sprained it."

"Maybe fractured it," the colonel said darkly. "You're going for medical attention right now."

And so, with the colonel and Pearl escorting me, I left that scene of destruction, its picture indelibly imprinted on my mind.

The shoulder was dislocated, not broken, but putting it back in its proper position hurt like six demons, and I think for once in my life I screamed—loudly—at physical pain. Afterward I was embarrassed, but Pearl kept telling me to hush. And then I slept so long that it was a day later when I awoke in a small-town hotel somewhere in Illinois.

That was the end of the Buffalo Bill and Miller 101 Wild West. I never saw Buffalo Bill again, but Colonel Zack told me he was a broken man. The train was the last in the series of disasters that had hit his show, and he was quitting.

"And you?" I asked as we rode back to Oklahoma by train—thankfully a train that was going slower.

"Tom and George haven't left me any choice." He smoothed a crumpled telegram that lay on his lap. "I'm goin' back to farming and ranching. I'm sorry, Cherokee, but there's no show."

"It's all right, Colonel. I'm ready to quit," I said, and meant it. "I'm going to Guthrie and hide from the world."

Pearl sat behind us, staring blankly out the window, and I remembered about her and Donnie Slaughter. Turning I said, "Pearl, you come to Guthrie with me. Louise always has another vacant room."

Colonel William F. Cody died in January 1917. I cried when I heard the news, but I think I was crying as much for myself as for him.

CHAPTER 14

The colonel sent us to Guthrie in a covered buggy, with a driver. "Louise threatened me if I ever let you ride across the prairie alone again," he said, and I wanted to ask what she had threatened him with but thought better of it. As we left and I turned to look back at him, I saw him brush a hand across his eyes—cinders got in them, no doubt.

I was grateful for the buggy. The weather had turned cold, and a fine rain was falling as we left the ranch. Even under cover, it would be a miserable ride. I tucked the buffalo robe tighter around myself and Pearl, then turned again for one last look.

To me, leaving the 101 was a lot more painful than leaving Luckett's had been. Sure I'd grown up at Luckett's. But I'd really grown up—some might say the word was *matured*—at the 101. Here I'd found my dreams of the Wild West show, here I'd found, and left, my husband, and here I'd been at home for almost ten years. Tired as I was after our last bad tour, and ready as I was to give up show business, I still felt a great lump in my throat. When I brushed my hand across my eyes, I knew it wasn't cinders. It was plain honest tears.

Pearl felt no such attachment to the 101, but she was plainly anxious. "Now what kind of a place is this we're going to? And who is this lady?"

I looked at her out of the corner of my eye, wondering just what she was thinking. Somehow I didn't want to tell her that "this lady" was my father's mistress—or once was—but then I thought that might be the least of Pearl's fears about Louise and her boardinghouse. I almost giggled to think that Pearl might totally have misunderstood the concept of the boarding-house—but then I was indignant. Surely she couldn't believe that I would spend weeks and months of my life at a house of ill repute—especially not with my father's blessing.

"Louise runs a boardinghouse," I said carefully. "She has some perma-nent boarders, like two ladies who run a millinery shop in Guthrie, a man who teaches school, and a printer and a lawyer. And then she takes in drummers as they go through Guthrie, so sometimes there are six people at the dinner table and sometimes there are ten or twelve."

"And she's not a relative of yours?" Pearl's round face puckered into a frown, as though she were struggling hard to understand. Her hair was blown by the wind, her nose was red from the cold, and she looked like a young—and vulnerable—child.

"No," I said. Vulnerable or not, she was beginning to wear out my patience. "She's a family friend." Well, maybe that was stretching the truth a little, but not too much.

"I don't know, Cherokee. I been thinking maybe I just ought to go on home and marry Donnie Slaughter."

"How do you know he'll be waiting?" I asked, hiding a grin.

"Oh, he will," she said. "He wrote me not long ago that he was still waiting."

"Do you want to marry him?"

She stared out the isinglass window at the rain-blurred prairie. "I don't know that I don't. I've 'bout given up on a career in Wild West shows."

I wanted to tell her that was smart, 'cause Wild West shows were pretty much a thing of the past, at least if the troubles of the Miller 101 were any indication. Instead, I said, "Well, there's always rodeo."

She flashed me a quick grin. "I can't afford to ride without a paycheck and hope I get some of the winnings. And," she added ruefully, "I'm probably not good enough ever to touch the winning money anyway." She sighed. "I've got to earn my keep. And if I can't, then I've got to be married to Donnie."

I didn't think life should be made up of such narrow choices, but I didn't say anything, and pretty soon she went on. "That means a baby every year, and lots of hard work on his family's ranch. But we'd have somethin' between us—and I do like him." Her eyes got a faraway look.

I resisted the urge to tell her she was talking herself into marriage. She made me think of my time with Bo. I'd made the exact opposite choice, and I knew my life would have been different—and somehow lacking in something—if I'd settled down with Bo before I tried my chances. Pearl had tried, but on a minor scale, and she hadn't found it wonderful. Maybe she would be better off with Donnie Slaughter.

Louise's welcome was warm but matter of fact, as was her style. With her usual efficiency, she soon had Pearl installed in the bedroom next to the one I usually occupied. "If business picks up," she said practically, "you girls will have to share a room."

We had arrived late, after supper was served and cleared away, but once we were settled in our rooms, Louise dragged us to the kitchen for a supper of leftovers—slices of roast hen, mounds of whipped potatoes, and vegetables that she had canned the previous summer. Pearl and I, too long on travelers' fare, ate like we'd not been fed in a month, and Louise watched us with amusement.

"I'll have to talk to Zack about the way he fed you," she said.

Pearl was too quick to answer. "Oh, he fed us fine, he really did. It just wasn't never as good as this." She helped herself to another serving of potatoes.

Next morning, Pearl met the boarders. There were some changes since I'd first sat at that table—the printer had married and moved into his own home, and the lawyer had given up on Guthrie and moved to Oklahoma City. But the teacher was still there, and so were the milliners, who had not changed their thinking about me one iota. They thought I was shocking, and they still whispered to each other while throwing obvious glances in my direction. I tried to kill them with kindness.

"Ladies, may I bring you a second helping of chocolate cake? More cream in your coffee?" They had both gone to fat in recent years, and I knew it was from eating Louise's desserts and putting too much cream in their coffee. Now they both shook their heads, as though they had practiced together, and protested that they never indulged in sweets. I knew better.

"They're rude," Pearl exploded that night when she came into my room. "They don't like you, and they don't hide it!"

"They're jealous, in a way," I said slowly, brushing my hair and staring in the mirror, wondering how anyone could be jealous of me. "They haven't had the nerve to do anything but make hats and live in a boardinghouse in a small town. They resent you and me because we've been out in the world."

Pearl laughed the hardest she had since the train wreck. "If only they knew," she said, wiping tears from her eyes. "I can't believe anyone finds us glamorous."

"Maybe not glamorous," I said, "but free and independent."

She thought long about that, and I watched her—by looking in the mirror—as she chewed her lip and stared at her hands. Finally, she spoke: "We have been that, haven't we, Cherokee?"

"Yes, Pearl," I said, "we have been free—except, of course, for the colonel."

"He doesn't count," she said quickly.

I wanted to tell her that if she married Donnie Slaughter, she'd never again be that free, but I didn't think it was my place.

Bo came just as we were finishing breakfast dishes the third morning we were in Guthrie.

"Tommy Jo." He stood in the doorway, his hat held in front of him by both hands, his voice solemn—and a little nervous.

"Bo!" I cried, impulsively rushing toward him with my arms spread for a hug. "I am so glad to see you!" Then I remembered what Mama would have called my manners and stepped back, saying, "I was very sorry to hear about your wife."

He still stood there, awkward as sin. "Thank you . . . thank you very much. How are you, Tommy Jo?"

"I'm fine," I said, "just fine. And I want you to meet my friend Pearl. She was in the show with me."

Bo inclined his head. "Pleased to meet you, ma'am."

"Me too," Pearl said, casting obvious sidelong glances at me. "I—I guess I'll just go on upstairs now."

I began to laugh. "Pearl," I said, "you don't need to leave us alone. Bo and I, we're *friends*." I emphasized that last word, and Bo nodded quickly. "Bo, sit and I'll get you some coffee."

Pretty soon Louise joined us, and the four of us sat at that old kitchen table talking—except Pearl, that is, who was uncharacteristically silent and kept giving me weird glances. Bo told me about his stables—thriving since some horse-racing people had moved into the area—and I told him about the decline of Wild West shows and the tragedy of Buffalo Bill. As we talked, we relaxed and fell into our old relationship.

"Buffalo Bill," he said. "Why Tommy Jo, that man's been your hero forever. That's sad for you."

"Yeah," I agreed, "it is. And yet maybe if it hadn't happened, I wouldn't have ever been ready to give up being in shows."

"You ready to give up now?" Bo asked, his eyes deliberately avoiding mine.

"I think so," I said truthfully. "For now, anyway."

Bo began to fidget, as though he'd overstayed his welcome. "I best be going. Work to do, you know," he said. "Pleasure to meet you, Pearl. And Louise, good as always to sit at your table." He paused. "Tommy Jo, I'm glad to have you home. You come out to the stable anytime."

I realized I'd forgotten to talk to him about the most important business of all. Rising quickly from the table, I said, "Bo, Colonel's going to have Guthrie and Governor brought down here, first fair day he has a loose cowboy. Can they board at your place?" Quickly I added, "Usual rates, of course."

"No rates," he said flatly. "I'd be proud to have them." And then he was gone, out the door and onto his horse before any of us could say more.

"He's in love with you," Pearl said dramatically.

I was almost angry as I turned from the window where I'd been watching him ride away. "He is not!" I said. "Bo and I are just—well, we're old friends."

"Sure," Pearl sniffed. "I think you ought to marry him."

"And I think you ought to marry Donnie Slaughter," I shot back.

"Maybe I will," she said, turning to the dishes in the sink, "maybe I just will."

And that's exactly what Pearl decided to do—leave Guthrie to go back to Sweetwater and marry Donnie Slaughter. She announced her decision some four or five days after Bo's visit.

"How can you?" I screeched. "How can you give up everything you ever wanted to settle down and raise babies and work on a ranch?"

"I'll have Donnie lovin' me," she said stoutly. "You might think about doin' the same with that Bo fellow."

"I'm not ready to give up show business!" I shouted, and then stopped dead in my tracks as I heard myself. It hadn't been a week since I'd told Bo I was ready to give up, and I'd believed it then.

Pearl was looking at me with a grin. "I didn't think you were," she said.

"I thought I was," I answered slowly, "but I guess I'm not. Why are you?"

"It's not show business," she said, "that changed my mind. It's this boardinghouse, and those two ladies who make hats. I can see myself growing old like that, living in a house that's not my own, with other ladies—what's the difference if they're trick riders or milliners? And no children, no family, nothing to show for what I've been or where."

"Maybe," I said, "that's why I'm not ready to give up show business."

Pearl turned serious now. "That's all right for you, Cherokee. You're better at it than I am, and you could probably make a living at rodeo. But I can't. I'm going home to marry Donnie Slaughter, and I think you probably ought to stay here and marry that Bo fellow."

We fell into each other's arms. "No, I won't do that," I said as I hugged her. "But I thank you, Pearl. You've helped me see myself better."

There we stood, our arms around each other, tears streaming down our cheeks, and big grins on our faces.

"What in tarnation is going on in here?" Louise demanded as she entered the kitchen.

"You better sit down," I told her, as I went to pour her a cup of coffee.

The colonel had had my horses delivered to Bo's stable, and I went out to see that they were settled.

Bo praised both horses in his own understated way. "Don't look too bad, Tommy Jo. That one"—he motioned toward Guthrie—"looks a little high strung. But this one, he's a fine ropin' horse, looks like."

"He is," I said. "I'll show you." And we spent two hours in the calf lot, me showing off what Governor could do, and Bo trying his darnedest to confuse that horse by mixing calves around and causing distractions. Governor never lost track of what he was supposed to do, and my rope flew cleaner and better than it ever had. I knew that going back to shows was the right thing.

When I finally dismounted and led Governor back to the corral, Bo said, "Wasn't you that had the talent all this time, after all. It was that horse."

I threw a handful of hay at him, and he walked away, laughing. I was glad Bo was in my life again, even though I was planning to move on again and leave him behind. He just didn't know that, and I didn't see any need to tell him until I knew what I was going to do.

Pearl was gone before Christmas, and we—Papa, Louise, and me—enjoyed a quiet holiday. I was, as they say, gathering my forces, but quietly.

"Sure nice to see you so contented, Tommy Jo," Papa said, leaning back in the most comfortable chair in Louise's parlor.

"Louise makes it easy to be content," I said, looking sideways at her in a quiet plea for conspiracy. Louise knew me better than anyone, and she knew I was simply waiting for the right opportunity.

The milliners had gone to visit relatives for the holiday, and we pretty much had the house—and Christmas dinner—to ourselves. Louise barely knew how to cook for only three people.

"Goin' down to Fort Worth pretty soon," Papa said to neither of us in particular. "That young whippersnapper Walt Denison is putting together a rodeo."

"Walt Denison?" I echoed. "Name's familiar."

Quietly Louise said, "Son of one of the biggest ranchers in North Texas, though he's no whippersnapper anymore. Must be your age, Cherokee, maybe more." She hesitated a minute. "I used to know his daddy."

Was there anybody's daddy she hadn't known at one time or another? Papa, who might have taken offense, simply grinned at her. It pleasured him some, I figured, to have for himself a woman who had so many opportunities—and who had, to whatever measure, settled down with him.

"You remember, Tommy Jo. He was on that wolf hunt with Roosevelt, all those years ago."

Suddenly it came back to me, and I saw those laughing dark eyes as clearly as I had when I was fifteen. "He was older than me, and when he tried to kiss me, I pushed him away."

Papa laughed. "Might be he'd remember that all these years."

I shrugged. "Doesn't have anything to do with how I ride and rope."

"No, but he might want a lady with spunk for his rodeo."

"Rodeo!" I scoffed. "It's not going to make it. Colonel Miller tried showing real ranch work, and nobody was interested. People want entertainment, the kind of thing we gave them in the Wild West show."

Papa was patient. "Miller's problem was he tried to make ranch events into entertainment. These days rodeo is competition."

"Competition?" I repeated.

"Yeah. Cowboys compete against each other for the best roping times, the best ride on a bronc. It's like it was when rodeo first started back in the 1890s in Pecos, when a couple of cowboys challenged each other. It's a whole different thing from all that fancy stuff the colonel and Buffalo Bill did."

"Could I compete?" I asked.

"Far as I know, there's not many ladies' events. The ladies stick to trick riding and such stuff."

"I can rope better than most men," I said with determination.

Papa grinned. "That you can," he said, and said no more. He knew me well enough to know when he'd planted the seed.

Silently I vowed I'd go to Fort Worth and see Walt Denison.

Papa rode into Guthrie early one day not too far into the new year. I was dusting and straightening in the parlor when I heard Louise sing out, "Well, hello, Sandy Burns. Come to see that daughter of yours?"

Papa's answer was muttered so that I couldn't hear, and I immediately took myself into the kitchen. We hugged and said how glad we were to see each other, even though it hadn't been more than a week since we'd last visited.

"Did you come to see me?" I asked.

"Of course," he said. "But then I'm goin' to take the train to Fort Worth, see what that Denison boy is up to with that rodeo, just like I told you. They got that great coliseum in Fort Worth. Ought to be a real show. You want to go, Tommy Jo? We can sit in the stands and watch all them poor cowboys tryin' to make a livin' out of ridin' and ropin' in a contest."

Louise threw me a sidelong look as I laughed aloud. "Yes, Papa, I do. I really do. But Papa, I don't want to sit in the stands. I want to take Governor, and I want to be one of those doing the roping."

He threw his hands in the air as though he were exasperated, and then he turned on Louise. "I thought you told me she was through with show business!"

Louise just shrugged, but she had the grace to blush a little, too. Now I knew what I'd always suspected—the two of them were in touch about me without ever telling me. It was like having parents fuss over me, only now I was too old for that. And besides, Louise was my friend—not my mother! But no matter, they both knew all along they'd get me to Fort Worth.

Papa persuaded me to leave Governor behind, seeing as how we were going by train and the rodeo wasn't until the end of the month. I didn't argue much, since trains and horses were a bad combination in my mind. Trains and people weren't all that much better.

"You think this train is going too fast?" I asked. It seemed to me that the landscape was flying by, with hardly time for me to make out the bushes and dips in the prairie. We'd soon be coming to the Arbuckles—those mountains that cut across lower Oklahoma, separating it from Texas—and I shuddered to think about the train climbing that grade.

"What?" Papa roused himself from a nap. "Seems fine to me. Makin' good time."

I fidgeted and squirmed in my seat, finally making Papa so uncomfortable, he couldn't sleep. "Whatever's the matter with you, girl? I never in my life saw you afraid of anything, and now you act like you're afraid on a train. It's not even your responsibility. Someone else is doin' the ridin'."

"That's just it," I muttered. "If I was driving this train, I'd know we were safe."

Papa harrumphed and advised me to take a nap, but I couldn't. We passed the Arbuckles safely, and I held my breath while we rattled across the trestle over the Red River. Then we went flat out, fast as lightning, across the flat prairies of North Texas, where grass seemed to stretch to the horizon in every direction, broken only here and there by clumps of pitiful trees, stunted by wind. We stopped in two towns—Gainesville and Denton—and then the train picked up speed for the last run into Fort Worth. When it finally slowed again, I breathed a sigh of relief. When I was ready to bring Governor to Fort Worth, we weren't coming by train, that was for sure!

Walt Denison greeted us when we got to the coliseum in Fort Worth. "Mr. Burns, 'course I remember you." He still had the dark curly hair and the dark eyes, though they didn't seem to have quite the same sparkle. He was taller than I remembered, and though I didn't recall the slight build of his youth, I was aware that he had fleshed out, as they say. He didn't have the slender look of a man who rode working horses every day for a living. Instead, he looked like a man who ate and drank well but was still young enough not to show any ill effects from it. "And this is your daughter—ah, don't tell me . . . Bobby."

"Tommy Jo," Papa said, his voice rather curt.

"Pretty much I go by Cherokee these days," I said.

That stopped him in his tracks. "Cherokee? Cherokee Rose who rode with the Miller 101?"

I nodded, trying hard to hide my pleasure that he knew who I was.

"Well, I'll be. Never would have guessed that the famous Cherokee was that little girl I met on a wolf hunt. You have come a long way, ma'am." He eyed me from top to bottom, and I wasn't sure whether to be flattered or offended.

We were standing in the arena of the Cowtown Coliseum, a structure now ten years old and still one of the largest show arenas in the country. Outside it was a large, impressive-looking building, fronting on a brick-paved street where traffic was still more ahorseback than motor driven and where cowboys strode along the street on their awkward heels, their spurs jingling. Inside, the building seemed huge, its roof so high that I craned my neck to look upward. The arena was ringed by hundreds—thousands?—of wooden seats, just waiting for spectators.

"You gonna stage a rodeo in here?" Papa asked incredulously.

"Yessir," Walt said, "world's first indoor rodeo. Cherokee," he said, turning to me, "you'll ride, won't you?"

I shrugged, feigning indifference because I figured it would never do to let him know that was why I had come to Fort Worth in the first place. "What's the prize money?" I asked.

"Just don't you worry about prize money," he said expansively. "We'll make you a special act—entertainment. Pay you a salary."

"I want to enter the competition," I said steadily, though from the look on Papa's face, I thought maybe he was going to kick me.

Walt looked surprised too. "Well—well, fine. But we don't have any women's events."

"I'll rope against the men," I said flatly, watching his reaction carefully.

I'll give him credit: he didn't react instantly. "Let's talk about that over dinner, folks. You be my guests, and I'll treat you to the finest steak you've ever sunk your teeth into."

Papa agreed immediately, and so I too murmured my thanks.

We had taken rooms at the Thannisch Hotel just a block from the coliseum, and we retired there to prepare for dinner. I dressed carefully—a serviceable brown denim split skirt, a crisp white shirt, a brown and gold scarf knotted at the neck, and my best light-colored felt Stetson.

"Tommy Jo, can't you look like a girl?" Papa complained when he saw me.

"I want Mr. Denison to know that I'm a roper, not a girl," I said.

"You might be both," he muttered.

We had dinner in the hotel dining room, opulent with red brocade curtains, flocked wallpaper inside walnut frames, and plush-covered chairs at the heavy wooden tables. When Papa ordered the biggest steak on the menu, Walt never blinked but simply ordered the same thing. I settled for a much smaller steak.

"Cherokee," Walt said, staring directly at me, "you ride for my new rodeo, and I'll make you more famous than Buffalo Bill ever could have."

That broad boast made me edge back into my chair a little, and Walt saw that. "I really will," he said. "This rodeo is going to be the start of something big. We're going to get away from that show business that they've always had—the Buffalo Bill kind of stuff, only on a smaller scale. We're going to have rodeo—competition between real working cowboys." He paused a minute, then added, "And cowgirls, of course. There'll be published rules, entry fees, prize money—not much, but some purses."

Papa jumped right in. "Tommy Jo, you best sign on with him."

What Papa didn't know and wouldn't have believed was that I was more knowledgeable than he about show business. "I'm not looking to be famous," I said slowly. "I got over that with Buffalo Bill. But I do want to ride and rope, and I like an audience. But if you hire me as entertainment to do trick roping, I'll be just what you said you were getting rid of."

"We've got to have some entertainment," he said emphatically. "You'll be the star."

I sighed. It wasn't exactly like being the star of Buffalo Bill's show, but it was better than working in a Guthrie boardinghouse and letting my horses forget all they knew. "I want to compete," I said. "I can rope against men, and I'll ride in relays if you have them."

His eyes danced with laughter now. "No rough stock?"

I shrugged. "I can if you want, but I don't have to."

"No rough stock," he said, reaching over to cover my hand with his larger one ever so briefly. Before I could protest or move my hand, he had moved his, the gesture so slight as to be beyond reproach.

Over a long dinner—with many shots of bourbon for the men—we agreed that I would do a trick roping act and would participate in the calf-roping competition. I'd be paid a salary for the act for the show's duration—only a week, but it was more handsome than anything the colonel had ever paid me—and I'd not have to pay entry fees for the competition, though I was as eligible as anyone else for the prize money.

"We'll be down here in . . . let's see, two weeks, little less maybe," Papa said too heartily, and my heart sank. I had freed myself from him all those years ago when I first went to the Miller 101, and now I'd have to do it all over again.

"Papa, you can't be away from Luckett's that long. I can take care of myself."

"Louise says you need chaperonin' and an escort to get down here," he said, then added almost plaintively, "Besides, I want to see the show at least once."

"You'll be my guest," Walt said firmly, "but don't worry about Cher-okee—ah, Tommy Jo. I'll see that she and her horses get here."

I realized that Louise had talked to both Papa and Colonel Miller about not letting me ride from place to place any longer, and I could hear her saying, "But Cherokee, the world's changing. It isn't safe like it was when you started out." But Papa would want to come by train, and I wasn't putting my horses on a train ever again.

"I don't want the horses on a train," I said, expecting that to exasper-ate both men. "We were in a bad train wreck, and I just don't want to chance it again."

Papa harrumphed, and I saw a cloud pass over Walt's face, but he was instantly charming and reassuring. "Of course," he said. "I'll send a couple of men to escort you down—say two weeks from today, weather permit-ting."

"Might make it a day or two earlier," Papa said, "just in case the weather don't cooperate." I knew he was simply trying to be part of the transaction, but Walt handled it gracefully.

"Yes, sir, Mr. Burns. You're exactly right. We'll do it on the six-teenth."

Papa nodded his approval, as if anyone needed it.

We worked out the details and rose to leave. Walt laid a gentle hand on my arm and turned to Papa. "With your permission, Mr. Burns, I'm going to take your daughter dancing."

I opened my mouth to protest. He had simply assumed I wanted to go dancing with him, and I knew it had never occurred to him to ask. I wasn't used to dancing, and even more, I wasn't used to having my life run by someone else, even to the slightest degree. But something stopped me—maybe it was a flash of thought that told me dancing with Walt Deni-son would be pure pleasure.

Papa was nonplussed, but he managed to sputter, "No, no objections. You young ones have a good time. This old man will just go on to bed."

I could tell by the way he held himself as he walked away that he was offended, maybe even jealous. He didn't want anything going on without him, particularly not a romance of his daughter. Papa never looked back and barely called a gruff "Goodnight" over his shoulder.

We didn't dance. We went to some private club where Walt was apparently more than well known, and we sat at a tiny table in a dimly lit room and talked. He drank more bourbon—I was amazed at the amount he could apparently contain without any ill effects—and I sipped at a cham-pagne cocktail.

"Champagne cocktail?" I asked. "I've never heard of that."

"Gentle," he said. "A lady's drink. You'll like it." And so without really asking, he ordered for me.

It was good, I had to admit. That strange bittersweet taste—he told me it was a concoction called bitters—mixed wonderfully with the bubbles of the champagne as I rolled both over my tongue. I took only one drink and made it last a long while, afraid that any more would affect me or, as Mama would have said, make me forget that I was a lady.

Walt asked about my riding, and I told him, not even realizing how pleased I was to find someone who wanted me to talk about myself. I poured out my indecision—first wanting to leave show business, then knowing I had to ride again. And when I was equally honest about my feelings about men—"I'll never marry again!"—he roared aloud with laughter, so that several others in the club turned to look at him.

"Me either!" he said loudly. "Once was enough." But when I asked him to tell me about his marriage, he just shook his head and said he didn't see any sense in talking about unpleasant things.

He sat with his arm casually on the back of my chair, while I perched, almost nervously, on the edge of the seat. Every once in a while his arm would stray over to touch my shoulder, but then it would move again to the chairback. When we talked, he locked his eyes onto mine, his expression sincere and intent. I began to wonder if I would have to fight him off at the door to my hotel room. A vision of yelling for Papa flitted through my head, making me let forth a slight giggle.

"What is it?" Walt asked, but I shook my head and refused to say.

I was wrong. At my door, he gave me a quick kiss on the forehead and said, "We'll be great together, Cherokee. I'll be in touch." And he was gone—without a word about seeing me again before Papa and I left for Guthrie.

I didn't know if I was relieved, miffed, puzzled, or disappointed. "Walt Denison," I said aloud to myself, "is a practiced ladies' man, and you best keep him clear out of your life."

Sometimes we don't listen to our own best advice.

Next morning Papa and I had breakfast in the hotel dining room. "You're lookin' sleepy, Tommy Jo. You out late last night with that Denison boy?"

It tickled me that Papa called him a boy, when he was at least thirty. "Yes, Papa, I was, and I didn't sleep too well. Strange bed and all that, you know." But it wasn't the strange bed. I'd lain awake far into the night, alternately trying to figure out Walt Denison and lecturing myself about being a fool for getting involved with any man, let alone one so obviously sophisticated and practiced in the ways of romance.

"He get outa line?" Papa demanded.

"No, Papa. He was a perfect gentleman," I said, wondering if that was why I was upset.

"If he wasn't," Papa threatened, "he'd have to fight Sandy Burns, and I can still hold my own against a boy his age. Soft, that's what he is." Papa, having yesterday thought Walt Denison was the answer to my prayers, was now making him an enemy.

"Papa," I said, "he's a fine man, and I think he's going to produce a good rodeo. He's certainly being generous to me, and I'm grateful for another chance to ride."

"Sort of a comedown for the star of the Buffalo Bill show," he muttered, "riding in a local rodeo in Fort Worth."

"No it's not," I said. "It's not a local show, like those little ones that are around here all the time. It's the rodeo with the Southwest Fat Stock Show. And besides, it's just a week—then I can be in Guthrie the rest of the time." Those words hit home like an arrow—the show *was* just one week. What was I going to do with the other fifty-one weeks in a year?

Papa went with me to Louise's when we got back to Guthrie, and before I could tell her anything, he was bragging about how I was going to be the star of the rodeo and how he'd arranged it all with that "young whipper-snapper Denison." Louise looked sideways at me a time or two but listened attentively to Papa, murmuring "You don't say" or "Well, I'll be" every once in a while, to his great satisfaction.

"All right, Cherokee," she said, once he was safely out of earshot on his way back to Luckett's, "let's hear the truth."

"I'm going to ride in the show for a week. I'll do a trick-roping act, but I'll also enter the competition." I shrugged. "That's all there is to tell."

"No, it's not," she said, pulling me up from the kitchen table where we'd sat with Papa and marching me into that parlor filled with cushions and patterns and plush chairs. "You sit there." She nearly pushed me into a chair and then chose the footstool near it for herself, so that she perched almost at my knees. "What happened in Fort Worth that changed the look in your eyes?"

I laughed. "All right. I met a man. But I think, well, I think I'm foolish to think about him, for a lot of reasons."

"But you can't stop thinking about him? And he's that Walt Denison that tried to kiss you when you were fifteen?"

I nodded, and slowly I told her about my evening with Walt Denison. "I'm not going to have anything more to do with him," I ended emphatically. "He's not right for me. He's used to ordering women around."

"May be," she said, "but he's attractive, and you're attracted to him." She sighed and stood up, rubbing at her lower back as though it pained her. "There's no telling why we're attracted to some men, Cherokee, even though every rational thought tells us that he's the wrong man. I've given up puzzling it out." Hands on her hips, she turned to look at me with a broad smile. "If I were listening to my brain and not my heart, I wouldn't have another thing to do with your papa."

We both laughed then. But as we parted for the night, she said, "You might as well ride this one out, Cherokee. You're not going to walk away from him without seeing if you get thrown."

I tossed fretfully before falling into a restless sleep, but my last conscious thought was that I was not going to let a man mess up my life, not even Walt Denison. *You are,* I lectured myself, *behaving like an adolescent, and you know better.*

Next morning Louise was not herself. When I stumbled into the kitchen at six, she was staring at the roll dough as though she didn't know what to do with it, and there was no coffee made.

"Louise?" I asked.

"Oh, Tommy Jo, I think you'll have to help me this morning. I can't seem to . . ." Her sentence trailed off as she grabbed the edge of the sink and stared straight ahead, her teeth biting into her lip.

"What is it?" I cried, almost frantic.

"My stomach," she said, and then I could see her ease some, the tension leaving her, apparently as the pain passed. "I must have eaten something," she said lightly. "It'll pass. But I would appreciate your help right now."

"You sit down," I said, as I started the coffee. She obeyed and sat at the kitchen table, where I could glance at her from time to time as I kneaded the rolls and stirred the oatmeal. She would seem fine until a pain seemed to grab her, and then, even sitting in a chair, she'd almost double up.

"Louise, you go on up to bed. I'll send for the doctor."

"No," she muttered, "no doctor. I . . . I'll be all right." But she went up the stairs, haltingly, to her room. I would have helped her, but some sense told me it was more important to her that I have breakfast ready for the boarders.

They ate, curious about where Louise was and why I wasn't sitting with them. But as soon as I had them served, I was up the stairs into her room. She lay on the bed, eyes staring at the ceiling, her skin sort of pasty and pale, wet with a cold sweat. A wave of pain would pass over her, causing her to grit her teeth and cling to the side of the bed, and then she would relax, obviously spent from the ordeal.

"The doctor's coming," I said. "I sent Mr. Coconaur for him before I'd let the poor man eat breakfast."

She turned her face toward mine. "No hospital," she said through clenched teeth. "My mother . . . she went to the hospital . . . died. I need calomel."

"Calomel?" I knew it was a laxative, and I knew that Louise's pain came from something too serious for calomel to cure.

"Calomel," she repeated, her voice firmer.

"I'll go get it," I said, and left the room, knotting a fist into my mouth in fear. Nothing could happen to Louise! I wouldn't let it!

Dr. Munson arrived before I had a chance to leave for the druggist's, and I met him at the door. "She wants calomel," I said. "I'm on my way to get it now."

He put a restraining hand on my arm. "Let me see her first."

I left the room while he examined her, and was in the kitchen cleaning up from breakfast when he appeared. "It's her appendix," he said. "It hasn't ruptured yet, but there's no time to waste. Thank God you didn't give her the calomel."

I turned toward him, my look obviously a question.

"Stimulates bowel activity," he said curtly. "Would have ruptured it instantly and spread infection throughout her belly. We most times can't save them when that happens."

"Now what?" I asked.

"We'll have to remove that appendix right away."

"She says she won't go to the hospital," I told him. "Says her mother died there."

Clutching his medical bag, the doctor gave me a long look. Finally, he spoke. "Young lady, the days when I did surgery on the kitchen table are long past. We can save her at the hospital, or at least give her a fifty-fifty chance. If she doesn't go, we'll lose her for sure."

"She'll go," I said, heading for the stairs. Once in her room, I began to put together a few of her things—a warm gown, a hairbrush and personal items, the small Bible she kept by her bed.

Between bouts of pain, she watched me warily, but the pain was now almost constant, and she was reduced to a pitiful moaning state, making small sounds like a cat in pain. Every instant I thought fear would make me bolt from the room, but then I would straighten up and continue. With her things gathered, I went to the bed and took her hand. She clasped mine with the ferocity of someone desperate for help.

"You're going to the hospital," I said. "Dr. Munson says it's the only way he can save you."

She nodded grimly and kept her grip on my hand. When they carried her out of the bedroom in a makeshift stretcher made of blankets, she was still clutching my hand, and I near fell down the stairs trying to keep that hold and yet stay out of the men's way. Dr. Munson had arranged for a flat wagon to transport her to the hospital—luckily it was a balmy day for January—and saw to all the details. Though things moved quickly, it seemed hours before that wagon pulled away from the front of the house.

Word travels fast in a small town, and before I could leave to follow them to the hospital, Bo arrived.

"Just heard about Louise," he said. "How is she, and what can I do?"

I told him, briefly, all that I knew, which wasn't very reassuring. "You can—if you would, Bo, would you ride for Papa?"

"I'm gone," he said, and he was.

I sat on a hard straight chair in the hospital hallway, alone, waiting for the doctor who had been gone, I thought, far too long. Occasionally a nurse came by and smiled briefly at me, but pretty much I was alone. I longed for Bo and Papa and maybe even Pearl, and I was terrified of losing Louise. If she was gone, I thought I'd be alone. Papa, the colonel, Pearl—none of them counted like Louise.

After what seemed like hours, Dr. Munson came down the hall. He wore his dark suit with the vest and the gold watch chain hanging across his belly, and the absurd picture arose in my mind of him fastidiously operating in those very clothes, without getting a bit of blood on himself. I silenced my urge to ask him what he wore in surgery.

"She's a very sick lady," he said solemnly, "but her appendix didn't rupture. I think she'll be fine. The next twenty-four hours should tell us."

"What can I do?"

"Sit with her, let her know you're there, give her the will to live. After a day or so, you can start feeding her broth. But for now, your presence is important."

That's where Papa and Bo found me, sitting beside Louise's bed in a darkened room, holding a limp hand and willing her to open her eyes and look at me. I was more frightened than I had ever been on any rough horse. It was more like the fright I knew on a runaway train, because I had no control over what happened.

"How is she?" Papa asked in what he thought was a whisper.

I shrugged and pointed to the sheet-covered figure, which seemed to lie with the stillness of the morgue. Only if you looked closely did you see the rise and fall of her chest from shallow breathing.

"Louise," Papa suddenly said in a loud voice, "you wake up and listen to me. I'm not gonna find another woman who cooks pot roast like you do, so you just gotta get outa that bed and go home again."

In horror I reached to silence him, but he brushed me away and nodded toward the bed. Louise's eyes had opened ever so slightly, and as I watched with held breath, the corners of her mouth lifted ever so slightly. Then she closed her eyes and fell asleep again.

"She heard me," Papa said with a great deal of satisfaction.

"And so did everyone in the hospital," I countered. "Couldn't you be quieter?"

"Be damned about other people," he said. "I wanted to be sure she knew she's important to me. How else could I tell her?"

I looked at him with surprise and some measure of respect for his judgment, and when I looked, I saw tears in his eyes. I let go of Louise's hand long enough to give Papa a big hug. "Go on," I said. "You and Bo go look after the boarders, and I'll stay here."

"No," Papa said, "there's no way I can cook for them spoiled people. You go feed them supper. I'll stay here."

It made sense to me, and I went, with Bo following me. We put together a meal of scrambled eggs, fresh vegetables, and some leftover pies. We answered the boarders' questions, reassured them that Louise would be fine, and finally—the boarders retired for the night and the kitchen clean—collapsed at the kitchen table.

"I've got to go back to the hospital," I said, feeling that I didn't have the energy to get myself upstairs to bed, let alone to the hospital.

Bo took a sip of his coffee and looked at me over the rim of the cup. "Don't you suppose if they needed you, they'd've called?" There was no sarcasm in his voice, just an honest question.

I nodded. "But she needs to know how much I care."

"She knows," he said. "You need to go on to sleep. I'll stay on the couch down here, case you need me."

Too exhausted to think, I went over to where he sat and bent my head to lean against his. "Bo, I don't know where I'd ever be without you."

He reached up to pat my hand without saying a word, and I turned and forced my way up those stairs and into bed, where I slept without waking until dawn.

Bo found me in the kitchen fixing breakfast, when he straggled up from the couch, his hair going awry in a thousand directions. I laughed before I thought, and embarrassed him as he tried desperately to slick it down with spit.

"Go upstairs to my room," I said. "There's a brush and a rag for your face."

By the time he returned, the boarders were eating flapjacks—"No eggs," I explained, "you had them for supper last night, sorry"—and I had the kitchen running smoothly.

When the last person was fed and the dishes put up, I untied my apron and announced that I was going to the hospital. Bo went with me, and we' found Papa asleep and snoring loudly in an uncomfortable chair by Louise's bedside.

When I whispered, "Louise?" her eyes flew open, and she reached for my hand.

"Cherokee . . . I'm glad you're here. I . . . I thank you for bullying me into coming to the hospital."

"You're all right!" I said, with no question in my voice.

"I will be," she said softly. "Might take some time."

By now, Papa was awake. "She'll be fine," he said, once again too loudly, "and I'm ready for some pot roast."

Louise reached a hand out to pat his and smiled gently.

"Louise, I'll stay until you can run the boardinghouse again," I said, even though a picture of Walt Denison rose in my mind as I said it.

She shook her head ever so slightly. "No . . . the Fort Worth rodeo . . . you've got to go ride. Sandy'll run the boardinghouse."

Papa harrumphed and snorted and finally said, "Well, I can hire someone to do it, and I'll see that it's done right. You go on, Tommy Jo, and ride in that show. Don't guess I'll be going, though."

I felt guilty at the sense of relief that flooded through me at that statement. "All right, Papa," I said, "if you're sure . . ."

As Bo and I left the hospital that evening, I realized I was off on another adventure—or was it a wild-goose chase? Bo didn't say anything until we got back to the boardinghouse, and then he left me with the words, "You go chase that dream, Tommy Jo, but you always know I'm here. I'll have Governor and Guthrie ready to travel whenever you say."

He was gone before I could wipe the tears out of my eyes.

CHAPTER 15

The war in Europe did not leave Fort Worth untouched that winter of 1917. The Canadian government had established three airfields for the training of pilots, and the city bustled with such tidbits as the fact that dancer Vernon Castle was training at Hicks Field while his lovely dancer-wife, Irene, stayed at a hotel in the city. When he was killed in the crash of his training plane, the whole city grieved with his widow.

There was talk that the city would allocate land west of the city for an army camp to be called Camp Bowie, and the city's stockyards already showed increased activity in the trading of horses and mules. Everyone knew that the United States would enter the war almost any day.

But you'd never have known it from the stock show and rodeo—the atmosphere spoke of a city without a care on its mind and nothing more important than the debut of its most prominent daughters. The Fort Worth rodeo was like no show I'd ever ridden in because they mixed debutantes and cowboys. It was the strangest combination I'd ever heard of.

Society's annual crop of young ladies, ready to be introduced to society, made their bows on the opening night of the rodeo, circling the arena in open wagons and waving happily to the crowd. Fort Worth's cream-of-the-crop were in the audience to applaud their daughters and to see and be seen.

This was the most important event of the social year. I was absolutely flabbergasted.

After the wagons circled the arena twice and the national anthem was properly played, the queen of the rodeo—a Miss Helen Breedlove—was escorted to her throne by one of her formally attired escorts, a handsome young man whose hands and face looked soft, as though he'd never done a lick of real work in his life. Miss Breedlove had a gilt crown and an enormous fan of peacock feathers that echoed the electric greens and blues of her satin gown. She presided over the rodeo sitting on a throne at one side of the arena, her train artfully draped to trail below her.

The other members of her court—six of them in equally elaborate outfits—clustered in a semicircle behind her. These girls—not a one of them over eighteen—wore elegant formal gowns of satin and brocade, each with long trains and many sequins and bugle beads. Behind them, in formal clothes, stood the young men of the court, so young I suspected some didn't even shave yet. Fortunately for all, the queen's throne and the attendants' chairs were high enough above the arena that the young people were spared clods of flying dirt or, worse, the danger of a runaway animal.

They made a stark contrast to the clothes, walk, and appearance of the rodeo contestants, and they made me feel awkward and uncomfortable, even slightly tomboyish, as though I lacked ladylike graces next to these ethereal creatures.

"I'd like to get one of them to walk through my rope," I muttered to Walt Denison. Truly I was thinking of the trick I used to do with Buck, and I explained as much to Walt.

His eyes were laughing as he shook his head in the negative. "No, Cherokee, not these girls. It just wouldn't work." He turned to leave and then whirled toward me, "And don't try it as a surprise." His voice was light, but this time his eyes were deadly serious.

"Me?" I pretended innocence.

"You," he said. "I already know you well enough to be pretty sure the thought crossed your mind. Don't try it. And," he added wryly, "don't rope me either." Then he was gone.

I was nervous, more nervous than I'd been before a performance in a long time. I told myself it was because I'd been out of the ring for so long, but deep down I knew it was because of those high-society girls looking imperiously down on me—or at least that was how I interpreted their rather absentminded gazes in my direction. What I didn't admit to myself was that I was nervous because Walt Denison was watching.

The announcer's voice had the same deep and dramatic tones of every show announcer I'd ever heard. "Ladies and gentlemen," he'd broadcast, the words rolling off his tongue, "Cherokee Rose, lately from a triumphant East Coast tour with none other than the late great Buffalo Bill." I bit my lip at the word *triumphant,* but when the lights turned on me, I managed to smile and wave to the audience. I was mounted on Governor at the edge of the arena, waiting to go on.

I began with simple tricks—first, still mounted, I built small loops in either hand and kept them going on both sides of Governor. Then I raised two large loops over my head that seemed to have a life of their own, finally settling around Governor before dropping limply to the ground. Dismounted, I built a loop around myself and walked in and out of it, then built a large loop and called for Governor to walk through it. Gradually I worked up to the high point of my act, where I built a huge loop on the ground behind me and swung it just in time to catch three horsemen who rode abreast the length of the arena toward me. The crowd loved it, and I breathed a great sigh of relief—I could still perform.

"Ladies and gentlemen," the announcer roared, "the little lady can ride as well as she can rope. As an encore, she'll show us some of her trick riding."

Startled, I turned to look at Walt. This wasn't part of the program, and I didn't have Guthrie saddled or ready. Walt just grinned and gave me a thumbs-up sign with one hand. The other hand held Guthrie's reins.

The audience probably thought I was milking the moment for every ounce of drama as I walked slowly toward Guthrie and stopped to pat his nose and talk to him. In truth, I was thinking of what I would do and then telling the horse about it. After I led him to the center of the arena, Guthrie knelt down before me without my ever giving a command. Instead of mounting, I ordered him to roll over and play dead, which he obediently did, just as though he'd been doing it every day for the last six months.

After a few more ground tricks, I mounted and had Guthrie prance around the ring demonstrating different gaits. Grateful that an encore could be relatively short, we ended with Guthrie rearing on his hind legs, then bowing low to the audience.

They loved it. I took a quick look at the queen and her court and found them on their feet cheering, the slightly bored looks gone from their eyes. Behind them the young men clapped vigorously. Then I looked at Walt Denison and saw he was regarding me with a serious stare, his eyes thoughtful, his hands in his pockets as all about him clapped and cheered. My heart jumped just a little as I wondered what was on his mind.

I had no time to ask, because there was a major mishap when the

rodeo came to an end that night. The queen and her attendants were escorted back down their special set of stairs and into the wagons for a departure that was to be almost as grand as their entrance. Once again, the wagons
circled the arena two or three times, so that the crowd could again applaud
the young ladies. This time I was asked—ordered?—to ride behind the first
wagons, so that I too could see and be seen.

On the second loop I found I had to touch my heels to Guthrie to
make him keep up with the two wagons of young people. It seemed to me
they were going pretty fast for where they were—and what they carried. Just
as I was considering breaking out of line to spur ahead, all hell broke loose:
The first wagon, carrying the queen and the other girls, took a corner
almost on two wheels and turned over, dumping the girls onto the dirt floor
of the arena.

The air filled with the horrified screams of the audience, cries from the
girls, neighing of horses, and the sound of wood splintering as the wagon
broke apart. Vaguely I could hear the driver of the second wagon hollering
to his horses, and I knew he was sawing on the reins. Without thinking, I
rode Guthrie away from the confusion, then ground-reined him and ran for
the thrown girls.

Helen Breedlove was on her feet—weaving as though dazed, but on
her feet—and I passed her to go to a girl who still lay face-down on the dirt,
unconscious. Hands reached from behind me to grab her, and I shouted
"No, don't move her!"

"Got to get her out of there," said a desperate voice behind me, and I
turned to look at the wide eyes of a very frightened young man. He was a
member of the court and had ridden in the second wagon. "She's my
sister!" he screamed.

I stood up and grabbed his hands. "If you move her, you could hurt
her badly—permanently. Trust me, I know these things from having ridden
in shows. Wait, there's bound to be a doctor in the audience."

As a matter of fact, there were three doctors in the audience, and they
came bounding down the stairs. None carried the reassuring little black bag
one looks for—why would they take their bags to the rodeo?—but each had
an air of competence.

One, a man in his forties and dressed as properly as the young attendants—why did these people dress formally for a rodeo?—knelt by the boy's
sister. After a long minute in which his fingers listened to her pulse and
probed her extremities, he looked up and said, "She's just unconscious. May
be nothing more than fright. I think she'll come around in a minute."

The young man slumped so that I was afraid of having to hold him up.

Sure enough, the girl began to stir within seconds and after a few minutes was sitting groggily on the ground. The doctor examined the pupils of her eyes and announced that she was in no danger but needed rest and comfort. As I watched, her brother swung her into his arms and headed out of the arena with her. At the door, where rodeo officials had blocked the crowd, they were greeted by a pair of obviously frantic parents.

None of the other girls was hurt seriously, the worst being a painful broken collarbone, which was put into a temporary sling on the spot before the girl was sent to the hospital. The others suffered cuts, bruises, and severe cases of fright.

Finally, the excitement and confusion dissipated, and my own heart rate returned to normal. I led Guthrie out of the arena and back to his stall in the barns. Grateful for the solitude, I brushed him down and talked soothingly, telling him—and by extension myself—how calm he'd been, how proud I was.

"I fired the man who was driving the wagon," a voice said behind me. "On the spot. Threatened to send him to jail."

Walt Denison leaned against the door of the stall, still dressed in the suit he'd worn at the rodeo—a compromise between cowboy clothes and formal attire?—but now he looked tired and disheveled, a look I didn't usually associate with him.

"Good," I said, uncertain what else I could say or do. "I . . . I'm sorry."

"Don't be sorry for something you had nothing to do with," he said shortly. "You did a good job. Lotta women would have panicked, but you kept your head. Let's go have supper."

Go have supper? Put the whole thing behind us that quickly and go to a restaurant as though nothing had happened? I couldn't believe my ears.

"My place," he said. "There's always a meal waiting for me, and it's usually enough for two giants." Then he relaxed just a little. "I'm tired, and I don't want to be around people." The laughing, always charming Walt Denison had been replaced by a man who was upset, tired—and human.

I must have hesitated for just a minute, because for the first time he smiled ever so slightly and said, "It'll be perfectly proper. I have a vigilant housekeeper."

He watched with fair patience while I finished with Guthrie and moved on to curry Governor. "Can't you find someone else to do that horse?" he asked, his patience finally exhausted. "I'm hungry . . . and tired."

"I take care of my own horses," I said firmly.

He threw his hands in the air in exasperation but then settled down on a bale of hay and seemed to take a catnap. I ignored him until, at last, I said, "All right, I'm ready." Of course, I hadn't changed clothes or cleaned up, but I decided that wouldn't bother me if it wouldn't bother him. It apparently didn't.

Dinner was roast chicken and boiled potatoes with a congealed salad, all kept appropriately warm or cool by the housekeeper who now, instead of vigilant, appeared to be absent, probably sleeping in her room somewhere in the vast house to which Walt had brought me.

We ate in a spotless white kitchen—the cabinets and even the pie safe were freshly painted white, the gas range was white porcelain enamel, the countertops white tile, the curtains white organdy. Only a brown and green diamond-patterned linoleum floor brought any color into the room. It was as neat as it was clean, with rows of glasses and plates, carefully aligned, visible behind glass-fronted cupboard doors. For a fleeting moment a vision of Louise's kitchen flashed across my mind, with its black iron stove and bright chintz curtains, wooden countertops, and that scarred wooden table around which I'd spent so many hours.

Even exhausted, Walt Denison was ever the gentleman, holding my chair for me, pouring champagne, waiting until I lifted my fork before he took his first bite. The housekeeper must have been forewarned about me, for the kitchen table—white with an enamel surface, of course—was carefully set with two places. We ate off fine china and sipped champagne from crystal flutes.

While we ate, Walt talked about his childhood. His mother, dead now five years, had been socially prominent in Fort Worth, and her lavish entertaining left her little time for Walt and his younger brother, Joey, who was now away studying law at the University of Texas. His father had spent most of Walt's youth at his ranch in North Texas, and he'd taken Walt with him as much as he could, determined to toughen the boy and turn him into a rancher.

"He taught me to ride when I was five," he said, "and to take care of myself alone in the outdoors by the time I was twelve. He wanted me to be just like him."

"Are you?"

"No, I like the city better. He's disappointed, but I figure producing this rodeo keeps me close to ranching, enough to take the edge off his disappointment."

"What will you do when the rodeo's over?" I asked.

He shrugged, then smiled slightly. "Take you to New York to cele-brate?" He made it a question, and I evaded the answer.

"I meant, what will you do for work?" I felt prim and prudish even as I rephrased my question.

He shrugged again. "I have an office in the livestock exchange, trade cattle for the old man and a few of his cronies. Keeps me busy, keeps my hand in."

I thought of Papa, who still worked hard from dawn to dark and would never have the luxuries and comforts that Walt took for granted, and the colonel, who could work a lot less than he did but was driven, not by money, but by a need to work. Walt was a different kind of man, one that I didn't understand, one that perhaps frightened me a little. I didn't realize how a touch of fear could heighten attraction.

We moved into the library, a room lined by shoulder-high bookshelves with leaded-glass doors. Above the bookshelves a tapestry of browns and greens covered the walls, and the same fabric had been used on a rocker and a straight armchair. The ceiling was patterned plaster, and the windows were hung with heavy brown drapes, with sheer panels under them. It was rich—but dark and depressing.

The embers of a fire glowed softly in the fireplace grate, and Walt pulled the rocker close to it for me, then settled himself lazily on the floor at my feet.

"Is that your mother?" The portrait, rather small, hung not in the place of honor over the fireplace but to one side, near the double doors, which led, apparently, into the living room. The woman was fair, with perfectly groomed hair brushed away from her face, and eyes that even by the artist's hand looked hard as ice.

"That's her," he said noncommittally. He seemed content now simply to stare at the embers, with their occasional small bursts of flame, and to be quiet. I took his lead and leaned back, closing my eyes and very nearly drifting off into a nap.

At length he roused. "You can sleep in the guest room. Mrs. Andrews made it up."

Mrs. Andrews—the absent vigilant housekeeper! He had planned this all along! I opened my mouth to protest, but he interrupted.

"She keeps it made up, changes the linen once a week whether any-one's been here or not. And no, I won't bother you. You'll be perfectly safe."

"I wasn't very worried," I said, "but I have nothing with me."

"You'll find what you need," he said. "First room to the left at the top of the stairs." And then he was gone, without so much as a goodnight or by-your-leave. Puzzled, I sat for a long time, rocking slowly, staring at the dying embers, and wondering where he'd gone. I could have sworn I heard an outside door close and an automobile engine start. Finally I reasoned I had no other choice but to go upstairs and go to bed. Walt was not going to reappear.

The bedroom in which I found myself was much brighter than the rest of the house, with canvas-covered walls of pale blue, a border in a rose motif, and floral chintz curtains and bedspread that picked up the rose pattern. A soft rosy-pink carpet covered the floor and welcomed my tired feet as I pulled off my boots. Carefully laid out on the bed were a fresh lawn gown and a warm flannel robe, both white and both obviously new. In the adjoining bathroom were all the toiletries a woman could ask for, and I wondered how often Walt brought women home, then sent them to this room. I knew I would never ask, but I also knew there was something increasingly strange about this man who'd thrust himself into my life.

It was daylight when I wakened, though apparently a dull day, so that I could not tell from the light whether it was seven or ten in the morning, or even noon, though I doubted the latter. I stretched and contemplated, with dread, the thought of pulling on last night's dirty clothes. But when I crawled out of bed and pulled the robe around me, I saw that while I slept, someone had put a perfectly new outfit—underclothes, divided skirt, starched white shirt—on the trunk at the foot of the bed. It made me wonder who'd put it there—the mysterious Mrs. Andrews?—and how soundly I'd slept.

I found Mrs. Andrews in the kitchen. She was what you'd expect for a housekeeper—middle-aged, plump, and not particularly cheerful, though she served me eggs, bacon, and toast with good grace and would have added potatoes if I'd not protested they would be too much.

"Mr. Walt ate them," she said rather righteously.

"Where is he?" I asked.

She lifted her shoulders as if to say it was none of her business. But then she admitted, "He'll be back soon. He said for you to wait."

Walt arrived before I finished my breakfast, and his usual good humor, missing the night before, had been restored. "Miss me?" he said, and I swear I thought he was going to lean down and kiss me on the forehead in a sort of paternalistic gesture.

Then, oblivious of Mrs. Andrews, he sat down at the kitchen table and handed me a small box. "I've been out shopping for this," he said. When I hesitated, he urged, "Go ahead, open it."

I untied the strings slowly, pulled the paper away, and lifted the lid of a ring box. It could be nothing but a ring, and yet I hoped it would be a silver and turquoise, or a birthstone—he wouldn't know that mine was ruby—or something without significance. It wasn't, of course. It was a single gleaming diamond, larger than I could imagine, set in a white gold band. I looked at it, fingered it, trying to get myself together. At last, I raised my eyes to find that he was staring intently at me.

"Well?" he demanded.

"Well," I said slowly, "I don't know what to say."

He laughed aloud. "I'm not surprised. But I figured we were going to get married sooner or later, and it might as well be sooner."

I noticed that Mrs. Andrews was once again absent rather than vigilant. And it struck me as strange that I was sitting across the table from a man who had courted but never kissed me, a man I barely knew. My instinctive response was to say yes, though every reasonable fiber in me shouted no.

"I—I still don't know what to say."

"Try yes or no," he said, leaning back in his chair and looking at me with almost bored impatience. "Of course, I'm betting on yes."

Stalling for time, I was. "How can you think that? We barely know each other. . . ." My voice drifted away. I wasn't going to say anything about the platonic nature of our attraction to date, partly because I wasn't sure that was true. I flat didn't know how I felt about Walt Denison.

"Because we're a good pair," he said confidently. "You know the horse and ranching and rodeo side of my life, and I'll be purely delighted to show you the society side, with you on my arm as my bride."

I had a sudden vision of all those society girls making their debut, while I watched in my split skirt and Stetson. "I wouldn't know how to behave or dress properly for such people," I said honestly.

"That," he said triumphantly, "is part of the fun. I'll teach you."

I felt like an overaged and awkward Pygmalion. "I won't give up my riding," I said in a tone that I hoped was determined but that sounded threatening even to my ears.

"Aha," he crowed, getting up from the table to strut about the kitchen, "that means you're thinking about it. Go ahead, put that ring on."

Any other man, I thought, would have put it on my finger himself. "Give me twenty-four hours," I said.

"Twenty-four hours it is." He had the air of a king granting leniency to a subject.

There was a time I would never have thought of marrying Walt Denison. I was the star in a Wild West show, my future glowing with promise. But now I saw things less brightly. Buffalo Bill was dead, the 101 show was disbanded, Wild West shows were a thing of the past, and life in Guthrie yawned before me like an endless eternity. Here was a chance to keep on riding and roping in the show ring. But there was, of course, more to it than that.

I would like to think that my decision to marry Walt was made with a certain amount of passion. Certainly, it was not a decision made with what I considered my usual practicality, nor was there anything adventuresome about it. The truth, which I avoided facing, is that marrying Walt Denison was a decision of default—I had no better choices, or so I thought at the time. Maybe Walt knew that all along and didn't care. Not that I wasn't attracted to him. There was that strange mixture of fascination, puzzlement, and a trace of fear.

In any other circumstance, I would have run to Louise for advice or at least talk. If I followed my usual pattern, I would have told Walt I needed a week, not twenty-four hours, and I would have flown like a homing pigeon to the boardinghouse in Guthrie. But Louise would have told me what I already knew intellectually: Something was wrong, and I shouldn't marry him. I didn't want to hear that—and I didn't want Louise to point out my own folly to me.

Sometimes instinct—or emotion or whatever—overrides what you know in your head, and you don't want to listen to the truth. It's easier to follow your heart than listen as your head warns you against something you want to do. Why did I marry Walt Denison? For all the wrong reasons.

It took over six months for my divorce from Buck to go through. I had done nothing about it—Walt was the one who dragged me to a lawyer and shepherded—hounded—me through the legalities. I divided my time between Guthrie and Fort Worth during that six months.

In Guthrie, Louise and I played a game of pretense—neither of us talked about the wedding. The night I finally told her that I was marrying Walt, she made the only pronouncement she would ever make on that subject: "Cherokee, I never thought you were a fool. But you're still running from Sandy Burns and Bo and Guthrie, and most of all from yourself. You aren't going to find the answer with Walt Denison."

I opened my mouth to let forth an indignant denial, but the words died in my throat. Instead, I grabbed a broom and began the most vigorous sweeping the parlor rug had seen in some time.

After that, we never mentioned it again. Louise, who should by all rights have helped choose my wedding dress and trousseau and planned whatever celebration there would be, never even asked about the plans. When the time came, she would not attend—by mutual but unspoken agreement.

Papa, on the other hand, talked incessantly about the wedding—except, of course, in Louise's presence, where even he had the wits to be silent. But to me, he was effervescent. "My little girl, marrying into the Denison family. You got yourself a fine man there, Tommy Jo, a fine man." Forgotten was what he well knew—that I wasn't his "little girl" and hadn't been for some time—and also forgotten was the time he nearly had to fight Walt Denison, Sr., because he had taken me on a hunt. In some strange way, I think it elevated Papa that his daughter was marrying the son of Walt Denison, whose lands were nearly as large as the legendary Waggoner DDD Ranch. Papa, because of the marriage, rose—in his own mind only, of course—from the status of foreman to an equal among cattle barons.

But I couldn't suggest that to Louise, either. One truth I knew: I wasn't marrying Walt Denison for Papa's sake. Was I maybe marrying him for his own sake? Was there something in me that wanted to make him an ordinary man, erase the puzzlement and fear?

When I was in Fort Worth, Walt continued to court me in a rather formal manner—and I continued to sleep, alone, in that comfortable and very feminine bedroom. It worried me that he was not a passionate lover, and I began to convince myself that once we were married, I would show him the pleasures of love. I would waken or free whatever it was that was hiding in him and holding him back. We most fool ourselves, I think, when we begin to see ourselves as saviors.

Finally, we were married in the chapel of the First Methodist Church in Fort Worth. Both our fathers were in attendance, but a church secretary was pressed into service as my attendant. I could have called Pearl, but somehow that seemed inappropriate, after my lectures every time she talked about going home to marry Donnie whatever-his-name-was.

"What God hath joined together, let no man put asunder," the minister intoned, and my stomach turned over. Then he said, "You may kiss your bride, Mr. Denison," and Walt lifted the short veil away from my face and gave me a perfunctory quick kiss. Then, hand in hand, we walked out of the chapel, followed by our fathers, who were busy congratulating themselves on a perfect union. I looked once or twice at Walt, but his attention was focused on getting the chauffeur to bring up the car—a new Ford—so that we could have a celebration dinner at his club, our fathers included, of course.

We left that same afternoon for a honeymoon in New York, traveling there by train. Walt had rented a bedroom compartment, of course, and after an extravagant supper in the dining car, Walt escorted me back to the compartment.

"You take your time changing, my dear. I'll just be in the club car."

Nervously I changed into a gown and peignoir set I'd bought—shopping for your trousseau alone, I had discovered, was no fun. I put on fresh cologne, scrubbed my face until it shone, and brushed my hair, remembering uneasily how Buck had liked to watch me and sometimes took the brush in hand himself. Still no Walt.

For a while I stared out the window, watching dark trees and occasional lights flash by, listening as the train bellowed its way through crossings. When I'd see a house, out there in the emptiness of northeastern Texas with its windows lighted, I'd imagine a family comfortably settled for the night, all together, and then I would wonder what I was doing on a train hurtling toward New York—me, who had vowed never to ride a train again. Finally I crawled into bed, never intending, of course, to sleep.

It was dawn when I woke, startled into consciousness by Walt dropping his shoes on the floor. He sat on the edge of my bunk, and when I stirred, he reached out a gentle hand to reassure me.

"It's just me, Cherokee. Sorry I was so long, but I won two thousand dollars in the parlor car." He smelled of stale liquor.

"Won?" I asked groggily.

"Five-card draw," he said, as though sure I'd understand. "You just go on back to sleep, and I'll crawl into the upper berth."

I was awake enough now to be alarmed. My bridegroom had spent his wedding night playing poker, and now he was crawling into the upper berth. Uncertainly I told myself that the berths were narrow and uncomfortable, and our marriage would be consummated in a luxurious suite in a New York hotel.

I was right, sort of. We stayed at the Waldorf Astoria in a suite with a living room and a bathroom, and we celebrated our first evening with a dinner of pheasant and roasted vegetables, some of which I was sure I'd never seen before. Champagne flowed, and Walt was an attentive bridegroom, more so than he'd ever been before.

"I am so lucky," he said, "to have convinced you to marry me. I'll make you glad, my darling, I really will." With that he stood just enough to lean over and kiss the top of my head.

"I'm glad already," I said, though I knew my voice lacked conviction.

In truth, I began on the train to question what I suddenly saw as a six-month impulse. My head, too late, had won over my heart. Still, the fat was in the fire, as Louise would have said, and I was obliged to carry on.

"I . . . I worry about being able to fit into your world." I had never, in previous trips to New York, been to the Waldorf Astoria, but I didn't think I needed to describe for him the boardinghouse where Buck and I had stayed, nor the tents I had slept in in other cities too many times.

By the time the waiter took the dinner table away, I was light-headed from the champagne and willingly agreed when Walt suggested I change into something "more comfortable." The next thing I knew, as I returned to the parlor, he swept me into his arms and carried me into the bedroom. At first, I snuggled into his embrace, thinking at last that passion had overcome him.

It had—but not in the way I anticipated. He was a rough lover, quick and determined and oblivious of my pleasure . . . or pain. His clothes came off in an instant, and mine as quickly—with a rip to my new peignoir. Then it was strong demanding kisses, harsh hands on my breasts, and a sudden thrusting for which I was unprepared. I tried valiantly to match his intensity, but somehow he had gotten off to a better start than I had. Almost too soon, panting with completion, he rolled off me and said, "Thank you, Cherokee. Thank you."

We both lay still for several minutes, I in frustration and he, I supposed, in satisfaction. Then his back to me, he slipped back into his clothes before turning to kiss me. "You just get some rest. I'll be back soon."

Once again, it was dawn before he returned, and this time I feigned sleep. I didn't want to hear how much he'd won. But I knew I was now seeing a side of Walt Denison I hadn't seen before but that, instinctively, I'd known existed—and had ignored. That flash of humanity the night the girls were dumped in the dirt was just that—an unusual flash, not characteristic of the man. Drinking and gambling ran his life, and that was why I felt that tingle of fear when I was with him. The tingle had turned to a warning alarm, and it no longer heightened the attraction—it only deepened the despair. And I knew I wasn't going to bring anything new to this man's life. Cherokee, the reformer, was a dead idea—and a poor joke.

During the day, when he was sober, not gambling, and not rutting, Walt Denison was a wonderful escort—charming, attentive, knowledgeable about a side of New York I'd never seen, and best of all, proud of me.

"This is my wife, the famous Cherokee Rose," he would tell people at cocktail parties, in restaurants, even once to strangers in the lobby of the hotel, to my everlasting embarrassment. "You'll remember, she rode with the Buffalo Bill Wild West Show. Starred in it."

Most of the people he introduced me to in New York City were friends of his, through what connection I never could discover. But they were high-society folk who neither knew nor cared about Buffalo Bill's show. Their eyes would glaze over while they smiled and said, "How nice," or, "So glad to meet you," or worse yet, "You are the lucky one, Denison."

Walt took the vague praise as his due. He had taken me to elegant dress stores and sat for hours on the chaise provided for men while I tried on one gown after another. "I like that one," he said, "but get rid of the green one. Blue, Cherokee, that's your color. A smoky, sexy blue."

I blushed to think he found anything about me sexy, for our private life had not improved one bit.

The first night he asked me to go with him when he gambled, I was flattered.

"You'll bring me luck, Cherokee," he said, and I believed it, still willing to do what I could for this strange creature who had become my man. "Wear that smoky blue dress."

It was a tight clinging chemise that hung straight, as though I were a boy with no curves, and ended in a draperylike fringe below my knees. A headband with matching feather was meant for my hair—though I thought it looked ridiculous—and my outfit was completed by white gloves and patent leather pumps that hurt my feet.

I knew little of poker or blackjack and could not follow the action of the game, but I stood loyally behind Walt until he cautioned me that the other players might think I was looking at their hands and somehow signaling him. Then, with a paternal pat on the rear from him, I retreated to a seat on the edge of the room.

Walt's concentration was intense, but periodically he would call to me to come and hold his hand. I'd bend over, my ear near his mouth, and he'd whisper, "What should I do?" When I shrugged—I obviously knew nothing about the game—he would chortle with laughter and say, "You're right, Cherokee, you're absolutely right." Afterward I would never be sure if he'd won or lost the hand, but I was increasingly sure that he was drinking a lot of bourbon, straight.

He won that night, won what must have been an enormous amount of money. It was nearly morning as we rode in a taxi back to the hotel, and Walt could not stop chortling about me as his "good luck piece." Once in our room, he took me with a swiftness that took my breath away—and left me feeling bruised and empty. The act of mating had become another of his triumphs.

Days—and then weeks—went by with much the same pattern. We slept until early afternoon, though I was often a fidgety, restless sleeper, simply because I had no activity in my life. Then we ate brunch at a fashionable restaurant or occasionally in our room, spent the afternoon shopping or visiting with Walt's friends, had dinner in our room, and then he left for whatever game was going that night. I either went with him or stayed in the room, though increasingly I preferred the latter. Walt would return in the small hours of the morning, usually drunk, often demanding. And then the next day would begin again. . . .

I began to face what I'd done. I'd married an alcoholic gambler, a spoiled boy of a man who wanted to show me off like a charm on his own personal bracelet of life. If I'd thought that marriage to him meant more opportunities to ride in the show ring—and honesty forced me to admit that that had crossed my mind—I was totally wrong. Walt Denison didn't care if I ever rode again—and worse, he didn't care if it mattered to me. And if I'd married him to bring some sort of normal relationship to his life, that didn't matter to him, either. He was perfectly content in his present state.

The society side of his life—and the gambling—were going to dominate our marriage. We would eventually go back to Fort Worth, but life would change little from what I was seeing in New York City. I would maybe ride once a year for a week, when the stock show was in town, but that was it. We were in the gambling business, not the rodeo business, and I was an ornament, an attraction, not a star. Which kind of eternity was longer—Guthrie, or Fort Worth with Walt?

Unbidden, Louise crept into my thoughts. No, I told her angrily, the conversation all in my mind, I haven't been thrown! In truth, though, I was being dragged, like a rider whose hand is caught in the bucking strap—a much more agonizing thing than a good clean throw that landed you in the dirt, gave you some bruises to get over, and let you get on with your life. This time I knew that there were no hazers to rescue me. If I was going to get away from this, I'd have to do it on my own.

In the dark hours of the night, while Walt gambled and I lay sleepless in an expensive hotel suite, I made up my mind to leave him, to admit that I had let myself fall prey to a six-month impulse, to publicly say that I'd made a mistake—a *bad* mistake. As far as I could tell, it would be a cheap price to pay for saving my self-respect. I thought I would leave when we finally went back to Texas.

"Walt? Walt, aren't you ready to wake up?" It was three o'clock in the afternoon, and I'd slept only fitfully in the ten hours we'd been back in our hotel room. Walt had slept like the dead, the leaden sleep of the drunk.

"Huh? Cher'kee? Why're you waking me?" He ran a hand groggily over his eyes.

I went to the window and opened the curtains, letting the sunlight of a winter day stream into the room.

"Oh, don't!" He truly sounded like a man in pain as he turned to hide his eyes in the pillow.

"Walt," I said, "when are we going back to Texas?"

He sat up in the disheveled bedclothes. "Texas? Why're you in a hurry to go back there? I'm winning in New York—you're helping me. You're my good luck charm." He looked sincerely puzzled that I did not understand all this.

"I want to go to Texas," I said. Left unsaid was the fact that Texas was closer to Oklahoma. Once there, I could get myself home. Walt gave me little money of my own, and I saw no way to go from New York to Guthrie, short of wiring Louise for money, which pride kept me from doing.

He was coming awake now. "Now, Cherokee, we'll go back to Texas pretty soon. I've just got to ride out this winning streak."

Our lives, I thought, were conditioned by the images of a ride—sometimes a good ride, sometimes a bad one, but always a horse in the center of things.

"I don't want to wait until you lose," I said, though in truth I cared little if he won or lost.

He honestly looked alarmed. "Don't say that," he said. "You're my good luck charm. You can't talk about losing."

I turned my back on him and lifted the phone to order room service.

By the time the dinner arrived, Walt was shaved, dressed, and back to his sophisticated self, jollying me into happiness—or so he thought.

"Come on, Cherokee, try some pâté. You'll like it, I know." He held out a toast point slathered with a gray substance.

When we first met, I would have laughed and tried the awful-looking stuff, but now I just shook my head and ate the plain well-done steak that I had ordered.

"Cherokee," he pouted, "you're mad at me."

"No," I said, "I'm not angry. But I want to eat what I ordered for myself. And I want to be myself, not somebody's good luck charm."

With his usual bravado, Walt managed to overlook my declaration totally.

That night he lost heavily at the tables, even though I was in the room, holding his hand when he commanded, listening when he whispered, even cheering when he won. I still have no idea of his losses, but I estimate them in the tens of thousands.

He was silent in the taxi back to the hotel, and I would not have spoken for the world. Once in our room, he forced himself on me with a brutality that truly frightened me.

"You took your luck away from me," he muttered through clenched teeth as he thrust himself deeper into me. "I'll show you nobody does that to Walt Denison."

When I opened my eyes to look at the horror that was facing me, I saw cruel hardness, none of the laughing charm that had courted me. Quickly I closed my eyes again and willed my soul to some safe place. There are times when fighting an outlaw horse will get you nothing but worse trouble, and I knew better than to fight this time.

At last, he rolled over and began to snore. I lay for a long time gathering my strength together. My plans for leaving Walt had been vague, unformed, sometime in the future. Now, having seen a cruelty that went beyond what I expected, I knew that I had to leave right away. I couldn't wait for Texas. I don't think he'd have killed me, but he could have hurt me badly—and he could have destroyed my soul.

Finally, I edged carefully out of the bed. But my caution was needless—Walt snored in an alcohol-induced coma that would last several hours. With slow deliberation, I cleaned myself, dressed in street clothes, and packed my few personal belongings. I left behind all the fancy clothes that Walt had bought me, all those slinky satin dresses that made me look like his kept whore.

When I walked out of the hotel at four o'clock in the morning, the doorman asked carefully, "Everything all right, Mrs. Denison?"

"Not quite," I lied. "I've had a call that my aunt is sick, and I need to go to her. Would you call me a cab?"

Inside the cab, I waited to give the address until we were well away from the doorman, lest he hear and later collapse under Walt's angry questioning. Then I directed the cab to Mrs. O'Riley's boardinghouse in Brooklyn, where I'd stayed all those years before, the first time I'd come to New York with the colonel's show. She was, I figured, close enough to qualify as an aunt.

She welcomed me with open arms and no questions. "Tommy Jo! You're a sight for sore eyes. Come into this house!"

Settled into one of her beds, covered by a down comforter, I slept the clock around. Mrs. O'Riley, bless her, never asked a question when I finally appeared at her table.

"Checked in on you a time or two, I did," she said, "just to be sure you were still alive. Lord, you needed your sleep, child!"

"Yes," I said, "I did. And I thank you. Now I've got to wire a friend for money so I can pay you and get back to Oklahoma." It was a great comfort to realize that Walt Denison had no way of finding me.

Mrs. O'Riley sent me off to a nearby office of the Western Union Company, and with still a twinge of reluctance, I sent a wire to Louise asking for money to return home. I gave no explanation, knowing she would demand none until I was once again seated at her kitchen table. That chore done, I returned to Mrs. O'Riley's and reveled in the comfort of her kitchen, the ordinariness of the conversation around her boardinghouse table. I would, I decided, much rather talk to drummers about the sad life of a man whose livelihood depended on sales than talk about the erratic successes of a man whose identity depended upon the gambling table.

"Tommy Jo, you've got a wire," Mrs. O'Riley said, knocking on my door the third morning that I was in her boardinghouse.

I was instantly at the door, though still dressed in my robe. "Thank you," I said. "I'll be able to pay you today, and I'll be on my way home."

She must have seen hundreds of people come through her boardinghouse, most of them much less fortunate than I, and yet that good woman reached out her arms toward me. "I'm glad it worked out for you, love. You're special, among all the boarders I've had." She had never pried into the particulars of what had brought me back to her house this time, but she sensed the nature of the trouble.

I remembered how stern I thought she was when I first stayed there, and I realized how much I'd learned since then. With her praise singing in my ears and money in my pocket, I made arrangements to return to Oklahoma.

Bo met the train in Oklahoma City.

"Bo! What're you doing here?" My delight and surprise were tinged with caution. I guess Walt Denison had taught me to trust no one.

"Came to pick you up," he drawled. "Louise sent me."

Suddenly I convulsed with laughter. When she had her mind set on a notion, Louise sometimes forgot about subtlety. Bo looked right put out with me as I laughed, so I struggled to get enough control to say, "I'm really glad she did, Bo. Thank you."

"Don't know what's the matter with you," he muttered, half to himself, as he loaded my bags into his wagon. "Goin' halfway across the country, getting married to some no-count. Ought to be horsewhipped, you should."

"Yes, sir," I said meekly, climbing into the wagon. "I probably should be."

"Your pa's not happy, either," Bo continued, almost oblivious of my reaction. "Says he knew that Denison fellow was no good for you."

At that I bit back a sharp retort. Papa had been all for my marriage to Walt, and he knew it, but Bo didn't.

Once he finished chastising me, Bo had little to say, and I was shamed into silence, so we rode most of the way to Guthrie without speaking, except for occasional small talk.

"Horses are fine."

"Pardon me?"

"Your horses—Governor, Guthrie, Sam—they're doin' fine."

Walt had argued with me when I said I wanted the horses sent to Guthrie while we were in New York. "I have grooms, you know," he said haughtily. "They're better able to take care of your precious horses than that cowboy in Guthrie." But I had won out, and the horses had been ridden—not shipped on a train—back to Bo.

"Oh. I—I guess I knew they would be. Thanks."

"Need riding, though."

"I'm sure they do. I'll start in the morning."

When we were almost to Louise's house, he ventured, "You back to stay this time, Tommy Jo?"

I thought for a long minute. It was a question I hadn't really faced yet. But at length, when I answered, I could only say what was the truth at that moment. "I don't know, Bo. I think I am. I really think I am. But I can't say. I think—no, I hope, I'm through with show business." I'd made too many decisions in my life that I hadn't lived with. This time I wasn't making any promises to anyone, not even myself.

"That's good," he said with a slight grin.

Louise greeted me with a hug, a mug of hot chocolate, and a calmness that, like Bo's attitude, demanded no answers. I could, I knew, tell my story when I felt like it. Until then, I was home.

We sat at the kitchen table, and I fingered the scars in the wood. Bo and Louise talked about the weather and the lack of rain and whether or not the owner of the print company would be elected mayor, while my thoughts drifted back . . . to the Wild West show, Buck, my dreams of glory and fame and, yes, riches, my days with Walt. All of it seemed hazy compared with the reality of a kitchen table and a mug of hot chocolate. I had been truthful when I told Bo I hoped I was home to stay—it was just taking me a while to realize it. Maybe Guthrie was reality and all the rest was a dream I'd chased too long. Maybe in Guthrie I'd find the real Tommy Jo Burns.

And Bo? I didn't even want to think about him. I could have started things up with Bo again in a flash—I sensed that immediately, but I didn't think that was fair to him, at least not until, if and when, I decided that I was home to stay, that Bo and life in Guthrie were really what I wanted. Bo deserved better than someone who was trying to find her way. Even someone who finally thought she was headed in the right direction.

"Got to be goin'," Bo said, rising lazily from the table. "Start work at six in the morning." He looked pointedly at me.

"I'll be there, Bo," I said. It was a good way to start.

Author's Note

Cherokee Rose is fiction inspired by the life of Lucille Mulhall, the woman for whom President Theodore Roosevelt coined the term *cowgirl*. It should in no way be read as biography. Lucille had an exciting life, the stuff of fiction, and I have woven several parts of her life into this narrative. But more than telling Lucille Mulhall's life, I wanted to tell the story of all the women who rode and roped in the Wild West shows in the first decades of the twentieth century. For the sake of storytelling, I have given personality to people about whom I could find little record and sent Cherokee, my fictional cowgirl, on adventures that are, in truth, borrowed from the experiences of Ruth Roach, Mildred Chrisman, Bertha Blancett, Florence LaDue, and a host of Lucille's contemporaries. Little is recorded of Lucille's two marriages beyond their approximate date and duration, and there, too, I have taken the liberties of the novelist. The character of those two marriages—and other relationships in these pages—is purely a product of my imagination and should not be attributed to the real Lucille Mulhall or anyone associated with her.

But the 101 Ranch show, and that king of them all, the Buffalo Bill Wild West, were very real, and the story of the Wild West cowgirl could not be told without including them undisguised. Even there, though, I have taken liberties—the character of Colonel Zack Miller, for instance, should in no way be confused with the real Zack or Joe Miller of the 101—Colonel Zack's personality grew and took on a character of its own as this story progressed.

I am indebted to several sources for information about Lucille and the 101. Most important among them are *The 101 Ranch* by Ellsworth Collings and Alma Miller England (Norman: University of Oklahoma Press, 1937) and *Lucille Mulhall: Wild West Cowgirl* by Kathryn B. Stansbury (Mulhall, Okla.: Homestead Heirlooms Publishing Company, Box 34, Mulhall, OK 73063). Also of help was *The Cowgirls* by Joyce Gibson Roach (Houston: Cordovan Corporation, 1977; Denton: University of North Texas Press, 1990).

I am even more in Joyce Roach's debt for her lengthy and painstaking explanations of the art of roping and her careful reading of those portions of the manuscript. And I thank Bobbie Simms for acting as first reader and managing to temper her wholehearted enthusiasm with valuable insight and suggestions.

About the Author

JUDY ALTER is the author of over one hundred books, fiction and nonfiction, for both adults and young adults. Her awards include the 2005 Owen Wister Award for Lifetime Achievement, Spur Awards from Western Writers of America for the novel *Mattie* and the short story, "Sue Ellen Learns to Dance," Western Heritage (Wrangler) Awards for "Sue Ellen Learns to Dance" and "Fool Girl," and a Best Juvenile of the Year Award from the Texas Institute of Letters for *Luke and the Van Zandt County War.* She was named one of the Outstanding Women of Fort Worth by Mayor's Commission on the Status of Women in 1989 and was listed by *Dallas Morning News* (March 10, 1999) as one of one hundred women, past and present, who made their mark on Texas. She has been inducted into the Western Writers of America Hall of Fame and the Texas Literary Hall of Fame. A native of Chicago, Alter has lived in Texas for over fifty years and is retired as the director of TCU Press.